GW00470101

Praise for
The Filigree Master's Ap|

Jeannine Johnson Maia sets an adventurous young carpenter's search for a better life against the exciting backdrop of Porto's industrialization in the late 19th century. Her deftly researched narrative is certain to intrigue readers interested in Portuguese history and, in particular, the Douro wine region and its considerable influence on the fortunes of the merchants and artisans of Porto.

-Richard Zimler, bestselling author of *The Last Kabbalist of Lisbon* and *The Incandescent Threads*

∂ ∂ ∂ ∂ ∂

A beautiful novel that transports us to Porto in the second half of the 19th century. Henrique's adventures take us into the world of the jewelers of the Rua das Flores, but also to industrial Porto, a city of material achievements, as embodied by the magnificent Maria Pia Bridge. In a story woven through with personalities such as Gustave Eiffel, Carolina Michaelis, and Telles Ferreira, we enter Porto's *ilhas,* experiencing their sordid poverty, and witness the political contestation against a decadent monarchy. A novel not to be missed.

-Cesar Santos Silva, author and researcher

∂ ∂ ∂ ∂ ∂

The exciting story of Henrique, a young man who leaves his native village in the Alto Douro for Porto and a better life at a time of great social, political, and economic transformations. It's also the story of many of those who triumphed in commerce, industry, and politics in Porto in the 19th and early 20th centuries.

-Manuel de Sousa, historian and author of '*Porto Desaparecido*'
(https://www.facebook.com/PortoDesaparecido)

∂ ∂ ∂ ∂ ∂

I was struck by how much Jeannine Johnson Maia's novel about a filigree apprentice in 1877 reminds me of the beginning of my apprenticeship in the noble art of filigree in the workshop of my father, master filigree-maker Joachim.

-Antonio Cardoso, master filigree-maker of Gondomar

THE FILIGREE MASTER'S APPRENTICE

THE FILIGREE MASTER'S APPRENTICE

Jeannine Johnson Maia

ISBN: 978-989-35275-0-4

To Joy,
who molds clay – and life – into things of beauty

To Teresa,
who constantly inspires me

To Daniel,
where my heart lies

CHAPTER 1

Mesão Frio, Douro Valley, Portugal
October 1877

THE BABY'S CRYING again. Always crying. I shove my few belongings into a canvas bag I can carry on my back. A birth, a death, and a departure. A trinity. My laugh comes out short and bitter. What I did today was nothing holy.

Beside the bed, the oil lamp sputters in the chill wind coming through chinks in the stone walls. It almost goes out, then steadies. In its flickering light, I keep packing. Many have left the Douro Valley before me, headed for a new life in Porto. Some, dreaming of riches, go on to Brazil. It's expected. Accepted. Seventeen is a good age to be going. I put my shaving blade, a comb, a pair of trousers, and two new shirts my mother made into the bag. My leaving would've been like all the others, if only I'd controlled my anger. Today was supposed to be the beginning of an adventure, me striking out on my own. Now it feels like I'm running away.

I push my new shoes – the first I've owned except for wooden *socos* – into the bag on top of a thin blanket, pull the drawstring, and gaze around the room one last time. A packed dirt floor, two narrow beds pushed together for the three of us boys, and hooks on the wall for our clothes. Nothing that says I, Francisco Henrique, lived here.

In the main room, the wind pushes smoke from the fireplace back down the chimney. Mother, the baby still fussing in her arms, coughs.

Father, a man who drinks harder than he loves, is nowhere to be seen. If he decides to miss this goodbye, I won't mind. My brothers, aged nineteen and thirteen, and sisters, fifteen and eight, are here though, waiting.

Luísa, the fifteen-year-old, gives me that funny look she makes when she wants to ask something without saying a word. As if I'm supposed to read her mind. Even if she's the person I confide in the most, that pretty much never works. She's a girl. Our minds work differently. But today – unfortunately – I can. She wants to know how I'm taking the news she dumped on me. I give her a brief, angry glance. She knows how much it bothers me. But if I can help it, she'll never find out what I did. Unless someone happened by chance upon that empty stretch of road a few hours ago and saw me.

"Here's your coat, son," Mother says. She bundles me into it with the hand that's not holding the baby, then reaches up and runs her fingers through my hair. I'm not a boy anymore, but she wants to, so I let her. "They say the damp in Porto can eat into your bones."

"So I've heard."

She pushes a small, cloth-wrapped bundle of food into my hand. "Make us proud, Francisco Henrique." Her arm comes around my waist. I hug her back, hard, breathing in her scent of sweat, soap, and newborn.

"You'll send word?" she asks.

"Whenever I can." I shake my brothers' hands and wrap my arms around my sisters. When it's her turn, Luísa doesn't let me go.

"Don't do anything," she murmurs, her head close to mine. "It was nothing. I promise."

I give her another glare, then whisper into her hair, "Never again. Don't you dare."

The smile she gives me isn't a happy one.

"He's waiting outside." Mother points with her chin toward the door.

I nod and pick up my bag. Then, not knowing what else to do, I put on my hat, feeling awkward, and go to find Father. He's at the edge of the clearing in front of our house, where the land drops, becoming terrace after terrace of vineyards descending to the Douro River, out of sight far below. In the weak light of the half-moon, I can't see that kind of detail, but I know this terrain better than I know my own soul.

"You missed a half-day of work." Father's hands are deep in his pockets. A good sign, since he needs them for beatings. "Can't stand a man who shirks. Bet that goldsmith in Porto won't put up with it either."

I tighten my fist around the rope holding my bag. We just finished the harvest. For weeks, I hauled grapes down the mountains from dawn to dusk, then spent half the night crushing them by foot in vats in the winery.

"I don't shirk, and you know it." Father would mock if I told him I'd gone to say goodbye to the land. Porto's an unfamiliar city, far bigger than any I've been to. It won't look like the Douro.

"Watch your mouth, boy." Father's hands are out of his pockets now. I step backward.

"I have to go." It's stupid of me to expect Father to unbend, to show emotion. But he arranged work for me in Porto with a goldsmith in the Rua das Flores. The Street of Flowers. For that I owe him thanks, if nothing more.

"Doesn't take all night to get to Régua," Father says. "The *barco rabelo* won't leave until dawn."

"Don't want to risk it."

"Risk?" Father scoffs. "It's all downhill from here."

We've already asked for a favor, that I be taken on board one of the boats that carry barrels of Port wine downstream to Porto. I'm not taking the chance it might leave before I get there. And on the way, I have a detour to make. One that's between me and my conscience. It's none of Father's business.

The wind gusts again, so hard it shifts the sack on my back. From the *quinta,* the big wine estate near the top of the hill, come whinnies and the sound of hooves. On a blustery night like this, the horses are uneasy.

I stick out my hand, holding it there until Father shakes it with the strong grip of a carpenter. He squeezes harder than is warranted, making the handshake a reminder of all he blames me for. I stare over his shoulder until he's done, then turn toward the dirt path that leads down the mountain. My eyes have accustomed to the dark and I pick out familiar landmarks easily. The enclosure with chickens beside our house, quiet now, and the garden in front, with the potatoes and turnips and cabbages that save us from going hungry. Farther down, the intersection of two paths is marked by a big chestnut tree. As a little boy I climbed it, not caring if I scraped my knees and palms, and surveyed my domain like a prince. Other times, it was a good place to hide.

Now I'm among the vineyards, on a path below one of the walls of red-brown and gray schist that support the terraces where the vines grow. Swinging my foot forward, I ram my bare toe into a half-buried stone. I curse and catch myself with a hand against the wall. It faces south but now, hours after sundown, holds no hint of the day's warmth. I wave my foot in the air, letting the pain recede.

After a few moments, I limp down the mountainside, terraces all around me. I have one last place to visit. At the spot, a wide dirt path still marked by hooves, I see no one. No sign that I – or anyone else – was there earlier today. I let out a long, relieved breath, then find the path that heads steadily downhill. Only the wind and the occasional call of a night bird keep me company.

The vines rustle as I pass. They're partially denuded, their leaves torn off by pickers so they could reach the grape bunches more easily. It wasn't a good harvest, but at least in Mesão Frio – located at the western limit of the demarcated region where Port wine grapes are allowed to be grown – we'd had one. The vines here haven't yet been attacked by phylloxera, the tiny insects that are destroying the vineyards of the Douro. Everyone says it's just a matter of time.

Here and there on the hillsides, our neighbors' houses are low, dark rectangles. Work comes early of a morning, and at this hour everyone's sleeping. I've said my goodbyes. My friends slapped me on the back, wished me luck, and told me not to forget them when I get rich. I laughed and made no promises. But the thought of Porto and its many possibilities buoyed me, lifting me above the exhaustion of the harvest. A strange sensation, but a good one. As if I were proud, before it even happened, of what I would accomplish.

Right now, though, I'm feeling more than a little ashamed of myself. I shouldn't have thrown that stone. Maybe knowing that I'm leaving made me rash. More reckless than usual. Worse, it did nothing to help Luísa. In Porto, I'll be out of reach of the *quinta*, far from any consequences. But that doesn't mean she is.

As I descend, the wind scrubs the sky clean, revealing more stars than anyone can count. I round a hill. Below me is the Douro River, glinting silver in the moonlight. It's rained – too much and too late for the grapes – and someone said the water's running high and fast. I stop to listen to it rush. People die on that river, and I don't swim. I shake myself and get moving again. I don't care. The chance to start anew in Porto is worth it.

Soon the path drops, becoming a steep incline. It ends at a rutted wagon track that runs along the river. I step onto it, feeling dirt and broken rock under my feet. The horizon isn't lightening yet. Despite the detour, I've made good time, but Peso da Régua is still a long walk to the east. Porto's in the opposite direction, far downstream, where the Douro meets the ocean. Now, after weeks of waiting and years of dreaming, it's two, maybe three days away. Senhor Manuel always told me I'd make it, but I still can't believe it.

Down by the river, the wind isn't blowing. Sweat trickles down my spine. I add my coat to the clothes in my bag and set off again, dust from the road coating my feet. They'll need a good cleaning before I put my shoes on and present myself to Goldsmith Bento. I owe the opportunity to work for him as much to Senhor Manuel as I do to Father. It's a debt I'll never pay. Senhor Manuel knew everything. Or seemed to. He sent for *O Comércio do Porto* once a week, then read the newspaper page by page, his finger moving down the columns. He was the bearer of news, the only reason I know something of the world beyond Mesão Frio.

For years, Father took me into town with him for supplies, then left me with Senhor Manuel while he drank and played cards. Children of the *quintas* have tutors, but there's no schooling for someone like me. Except when it came to counting. Father wanted his family – even the girls – to be shrewd when they went to the shop, or in case they got coins rather than barter for the woodworking we do. Senhor Manuel made my little-boy fascination with the black marks on the paper into a game. Father thought it a time-waste, but I learned to read. So when Goldsmith Bento Gomes – who stopped in Mesão Frio for a day to visit a relative who was the cousin of a cousin of one of our neighbors, or some such – said that was a requirement to work for him, I stepped forward and said I knew how. Senhor Manuel will never know. He died two months ago of a cough that shook his body apart. No one in Mesão Frio sends for *O Comércio do Porto* now.

Somewhere on the hillside, a rooster crows. Morning is coming and animals are being roused and fed. I speed up. Ahead, I hear wheels on the road, the screech-whine of wood against wood. I catch up with a pair of oxen pulling a two-wheeled cart with an enormous barrel on it. Beside them walks a man carrying a thin rod. The animals plod along, looking like they don't need much in the way of guiding.

"Going to Régua?" I ask.

"Yep."

"How much farther?"

"Not far."

The man taps one of the oxen with his rod and we walk on together, the cart and harness creaking loudly in the quiet night. I yawn, so wide my jaw makes a cracking sound in the vicinity of my ears, and eye the barrel. It's one of the big ones, holding hundreds of liters of wine. If I lay spread-eagled, I could sleep on it without falling off. What does *not far* mean?

After what seems ages, the river curves and the shops and warehouses and churches of Régua appear. They're a bright band in the pre-dawn light, hugging the right bank. Four *barcos rabelos*, the Port wine boats, are a dark mass in the water, waiting. Waiting for me.

"Give me a hand?" The man I'm with guides the oxen behind half a dozen other carts waiting their turn to unload.

I nod and follow him down a cobblestone incline until we're at water level. He unhitches the beasts to let them drink and we untie the ropes holding the barrel steady. I position myself behind the cart.

"Ready?" the man asks, and tips the cart backwards. The barrel slides off, landing with a dull, gritty thud. Then it begins to roll. I hold out my hands to stop it, but only succeed in changing its direction. It keeps rolling, massive and heavy as a bull, straight toward the river.

I sprint after it, get around in front, and brace myself. The impact sends me skidding backwards, scrabbling for a foothold on the wet stones. Just before the barrel goes into the water, I bring it to a stop. Around me, everyone is laughing. I scowl. I saved it, didn't I? No one said I had to look pretty doing it.

When it's our turn, we roll the barrel to the base of two sturdy wooden poles that run parallel from the bank to the boat. There the sailors take over and push it up onto the *rabelo*. They're still making fun of me, pretending to let the barrel get loose. I shrug, too busy admiring the way they balance on the poles with such ease. Then our barrel is on board and the crew turns to the cart behind us.

"*Obrigado*," the man with the oxen says, thanking me. He hitches them up and heads back the way we came. I wonder how many times he's traveled this road, and how many more times he will today.

Backing away from the center of activity, I unwrap the bundle

Mother gave me. In it is a hunk of *broa,* our heavy, dark cornbread, and a thick slice of cheese. I weigh it in my hand. It's more than my fair share of our family's rations. I'm hungry enough to eat it all in one go, but can't. It needs to last until I get to Porto. I break off a piece and chew, studying the *rabelo.*

It's a flat-bottomed wooden river boat, maybe the length of ten men and the width of two, with a square white sail. Toward the back, a long rudder – the *espadela* – slopes to the water from a high wooden platform – called the *apegadas* – that's reached by ladderlike structures on both sides. To me, the boat already seems low in the water, and the crew is still loading barrels. Not long ago, I remember, a *rabelo* was so overloaded that it split in half in the middle of the river. Its crew got a dunking, but they lived. They were lucky.

"You, lazybones." One of the sailors calls me. "Gonna be useful or not?"

I pack my food away. Another man positions his cart near the poles and unties the barrel. This time I don't let it escape.

"I'm looking for Senhor Jorge," I tell the sailor who called me lazy. Senhor Jorge, the owner of a *barco rabelo* who owes Father a favor, and agreed to take me to Porto. "You know him?"

The man shakes his head disbelievingly. "Two of you? On one trip? That's just trouble."

I have no idea what he's talking about.

"Over there." The sailor points to a boat farther along the bank. "The *Maria das Graças.*"

Six men are loading the *Maria das Graças.* Actually, four are. Two are standing on barrels, arguing.

"Jorge, who's the kid?" The man asking is tall, with blue eyes and powerful arms. The sun has bleached his hair and turned his skin a deep brown. I've never seen such an odd contrast.

"Our new ship's boy. *Moço* Miguel." The man called Jorge – he must be the Senhor Jorge I'm supposed to find – is wiry, dark, as slight in stature as I am, and missing two fingers. The blond man could probably toss him overboard with one hand.

"Well, *moço* Miguel has no idea what he's doing."

"It's one trip."

"Have you looked at him? He's too scrawny to help with the oars."

At that moment, the boy they're talking about – who looks about twelve – is struggling for balance on the poles. His arms windmill and he slips into the water up to his knees.

"He needs to get to Porto in a hurry," Senhor Jorge says. "He'll do what he's told."

"Where's Ricardo?"

"Not coming."

"But he's our best oarsman."

I interrupt them. "Senhor Jorge? I'm Francisco Henrique."

Senhor Jorge barely moves his head, but I know he's taking me in, head to toe. "Ever worked on a *barco rabelo* before?"

"No, sir." So Father didn't call in a favor. I'll be working for my passage, just like Miguel.

Senhor Jorge gives a disgusted snort. "Yet you've lived in the Douro your entire life." It isn't a question, but I answer anyway.

"Yes, sir."

The blond man's been listening to our conversation. "You want us to take two boys with no experience?" he snaps. "Without Ricardo? With the river running this high?"

"Shut up, Cassiano." Senhor Jorge is almost a head shorter than the blond man, but it's clear who owns the boat. He turns to me. "You, go stow your bag in the *coqueiro*." At my confused look, he adds impatiently, "The covered area in the stern. Tomás will tell you what to do." He nods at a sailor maneuvering a barrel into place near the bow.

Carefully, placing my feet on both poles for stability, I climb onto the boat as Senhor Jorge says to Cassiano, quietly, "Get us to Porto like you always do. You'll get your share."

I'm concentrating too hard on my feet to hear what Cassiano growls back.

Three more carts are waiting with barrels to be loaded.

"Hurry up, men," Senhor Jorge orders. "Sun's a rising."

In the *coqueiro* is a mound of bags and blankets I assume belong to the other men. I toss mine on top and join the rest of the crew. With a minimal amount of talk, we roll the remaining barrels onto the boat and position them so they make a pyramid, pulling ropes tight over them. Now I'm really sweating. When the last one is tied into place, I stretch and examine my hands. The ropes have bitten into them, leaving a network of small cuts among my callouses. I flex my fingers, and wince. Cassiano's nearby, his look daring me to complain. I don't. At least mine aren't bleeding, like Miguel's are.

"Where's Ricardo?" Tomás asks Senhor Jorge.

Senhor Jorge shrugs. "I had enough men for this trip."

Tomás and Cassiano exchange disgusted looks.

"We can't …" Tomás begins.

"What?" Senhor Jorge cuts him off. "You don't have what it takes to handle the boat? If that's the problem, I better find myself another crew."

I hear more grumbling. But Senhor Jorge has won.

"Cast off," he calls.

Cassiano scales the ladder to the platform effortlessly and frees the rudder. So he's the *mestre,* the man who controls the rudder. Best not to get on his bad side either. Senhor Jorge goes to stand in the bow, while Tomás and the other men untie the lines fore and aft. Using boat hooks, they push the *rabelo* away from the shore. I lean against a barrel, staying out of the way, Miguel beside me. He's so close I feel him trembling. Neither of us know if we're supposed to be doing something. The boat, its sail still furled, arcs toward the middle of the river where the current runs strong. The others leap across the barrels, as sure-footed as the goats on the mountains around Mesão Frio, and slide long oars into place. There are four of them, two near the front and two others behind the tall platform.

"Get over here," Tomás barks at us. He's near the bow, swinging his oar over the water.

I clamber over the barrels on all fours, followed by Miguel. Tomás shakes his head. Cassiano, up on the platform, is probably doing the same, but I don't care. The damn boat's rocking and I'm less steady than a toddler. I don't feel like getting mocked for going down, or worse, taking a bath in the river.

"Miguel, you're with me." Tomás points to his oar, then gestures me to the other side of the boat, beside a man who – as far as I can tell – hasn't said a word since I've been on board. I close my fingers around the wood, feeling the oar's heft, its weight. We start rowing as the current catches us. It doesn't take long to get into a rhythm. Oar in the water, push. Oar up and out, pull. Repeat, repeat, repeat.

I look back. Régua is already around a bend, out of sight. We're gliding among the *quintas,* their green-brown terraces cutting across the hillsides on both sides like a comb through wet hair. Push pull, push pull. The Douro here is wide, calm. Tomás says it won't stay that way.

After a few minutes, Senhor Jorge leaves the bow and joins

Cassiano up on the platform. Cassiano doesn't look happy about it. The rest of us keep rowing. My back, shoulders, and legs already feel the unaccustomed movement. The man beside me has thick arms and broad, muscled shoulders. I sense their power in every stroke.

"What do you call yourself?" he asks.

I don't hesitate. "Henrique." Francisco – the name of a saint – is staying behind with my old life on the mountainside. The Henriques of Portugal were kings and explorers. Men who'd made names for themselves. "You?"

"Pedro."

I wait, but that seems to be the extent of Pedro's conversation. "I heard the river's running high," I say. "Here it doesn't seem bad."

Pedro pushes, pulls, not breaking his rhythm. "Bad water's nothing to wish for. Especially when we're down a man."

My muscles tell me I'm pulling my weight, but Pedro apparently thinks otherwise. I decide not to argue.

"I'm not wishing for anything," I say. Although I would've liked to travel to Porto on a horse or – even better – on one of those new trains Senhor Manuel told me about. To arrive in style like a landowner or a merchant rather than a sweaty boy off the land, stained dark by sun and soil. It's a dream, I know. Especially since there's no train from Régua to Porto.

We're passing the area I went by on foot just a few hours ago. Most of the villages in the Douro are higher up, where it's cooler in summer and there's no risk of flooding. Here along the river, I see more oxen pulling carts, a girl tending vegetables, a boy fishing from a rock.

Where exactly my mountain path dead-ended at the river road, I can't say. It's probably behind me now. I inhale, relief filling my chest. I got out. Got away, my destination a place where I can discard the unwanted parts of my life like a worn-out pair of *socos*. With no need to feel guilty. In the Douro, the first son takes over the farm or craft. The second and third go into trade or join the priesthood. That works for me. Anything's better than spending my life in the shadow of that damned *quinta*.

The problem, now, is that my departure leaves Luísa unprotected. My relief evaporates. She should've known better than to let herself be seduced. Especially by Rafael. Granted, he always charmed pretty much everyone. Including me, back when we were young enough to be wearing short pants. He was from the *quinta* and I wasn't, but we were friends – or so I believed. Together, we explored the hills, played hide and seek among the vineyards, and spooked the horses with wild howls we were certain sounded just like wolves. With Rafael, I snuck into the manor house, marveling at the big rooms with their dark, heavy furniture, each one with its own fireplace. In Rafael's bedroom, a rug covered the floor and his thick blankets became fortresses we defended with sticks against the Moors and all other enemies. The only person who could conquer us was Rafael's nursemaid, who would scold and herd us back outside.

"Hard on the right." Cassiano's yell brings me to the present. On the platform, he and Senhor Jorge lean into the rudder, angling the boat toward the left bank. Pedro and I dig in, our oar going deeper, our strokes longer. Across from us, Tomás and Miguel hold theirs steady in the water, its drag helping us turn. Only when we're alongside do I notice the mounds and eddies in the water that signal submerged boulders. I shiver, imagining the boat splintering, the cold wet plunge, barrels forcing me under.

"Do they float?" I ask Pedro. "The barrels?"

"Yes. Unless someone's stupid enough to fill them completely."

Cassiano's head is in constant motion, scanning the river. He yells, "Hard on the left," and we row the boat into a safe channel only he can see.

At this point, olive trees line the right bank. I went that far once, jolting along behind Rafael on his sturdy pony, clutching the back of the saddle to keep from sliding off. Both of us ventured farther that day than we were allowed to, and had welts on our hides to prove it afterwards. Until today, it's the closest to the setting sun I've been.

We pass two girls in the water up to their knees, scrubbing clothes. There are plenty like them in Mesão Frio. So why, two days ago, did Rafael choose my young, innocent sister? Nobles once had rights to a girl before her marriage, I'd heard, but that was long ago. Luísa surely can't be blamed. In his tailored clothes, reining in his horse so it lifts its hooves high, Rafael cuts a fine figure. Out with his father or his university friends from Coimbra, he's aloof. When he rides out on his own, though, every girl in Mesão Frio thinks his smile is for her. Even Luísa, apparently. I thought she had more sense. And I never dreamed she'd forget what he did to us. To me.

I hadn't even realized Rafael was back from university. I never saw them together. So Luísa's confession was a punch in the stomach. A second betrayal, on top of the one that destroyed our friendship – and my future. I was still rigid with anger when, a few hours later, I saw Rafael on that path below me. It was as if I'd summoned him, my rage a hook yanking him within reach. He was oblivious to my fury. I could tell by the way he was riding. Relaxed, reins loose, one hand on his thigh. Raised with privilege. Raised, it seemed, without a conscience.

I crouched down at the end of a row of grape vines, my knee on a rock with a jagged edge. It was in my hand before I realized it. A fist-sized chunk of schist, the stone that nourishes the vines that make the *quinta's* fortune. I stood up and aimed. At his back, his head. At the body I imagined covering my sister's. I closed my eyes, hating the image. I could kill him if I wanted to. He was in range, and I rarely miss.

I pulled my arm back and threw the rock at the horse's hindquarters. It squealed, then bucked. Too late, Rafael hauled on the reins, fighting for control. The horse bolted, plunging downhill and disappearing around a bend. When I last saw him, Rafael was off-balance, sliding, swearing.

I ran in the other direction, clawing my way uphill, my head below the vines. The thud I heard was in my imagination, I'm sure of it. His father put Rafael on a horse before he could walk. He wouldn't go down. If he did, he's fallen a thousand times. He doesn't get hurt. I kept running until I was far, far away.

Later, when my anger ebbed, I knew I couldn't leave without being sure. Circling back to that desolate hillside added a good hour to last night's journey, but at least I was sure there was no fallen rider, no injured horse. It meant I could put what happened out of my head.

Beside me on the river, Pedro straightens up, suddenly alert. I'm left pulling the oar by myself.

Cassiano yells, "Eyes ahead," and I stop too.

In the space of a few minutes, the river has narrowed. Cliffs rise up on both sides, blocking the sun and turning the water an impenetrable grey-green. The boulders at their base are cracked and broken, as if smashed by a giant's fist. Ahead, the river curves. Even if I can't see it, I know something big is ahead. The sound of churning water echoes off the canyon walls.

CHAPTER 2

O ARS OUT OF the water," Pedro orders. We pull ours until it lies flat across both gunwales. Tomás and Miguel do the same.

"Whatever you do, don't let it move," Pedro says. "And be sure we don't hit Dona Mafalda's bridge."

"Wait. What?" I don't see any bridge. How am I supposed to stop us from hitting it or anything else?

Pedro doesn't hear me. He's leaping from barrel to barrel, heading for the platform. Once there, he positions himself facing Cassiano and Senhor Jorge, the long rudder between them. Tomás shoots a doubtful look at Miguel and joins them. All four are still, looking ahead. The roaring gets louder.

We round the curve. Before us, the river is a sheet of white. I can't see where the rapids end. Without warning, we plunge. I brace my legs against a barrel as water sprays across the bow, blinding me. I gasp and fold my body over the oar, holding it with my weight as I grasp desperately for anything that'll keep me from going over the side. If this wild water catches me or the oar, we're gone. Around me, the world roars and crashes, white with foam and studded with slick, treacherous boulders. I shake the water out of my eyes and start to pray.

On the other side of the boat, Miguel – who's half my size and sliding all over the place – throws me a panicked look. I can't help him. They had no business leaving the two of us alone. A rock, taller than our boat, looms straight ahead.

Senhor Jorge shouts something I can't make out. The four men on the platform lean into the rudder, straining to make the *rabelo* turn. We dive into another trough, still heading for the rock. We're going to hit it. I stare at its dark mass, too paralyzed to move. All of a sudden, the current shifts and our boat shoots to starboard. Off-balance, I tip sideways. The oar slides with me. Frantically, I pull it back. We're beside – then beyond – the rock in seconds, but all I see ahead are more drops, more boulders, more frothing water. Senhor Jorge is yelling again. I don't know what he wants. There's nothing I can do to make this go better.

"You all right?" I yell at Miguel.

He stares at me, eyes wild. His jaw is clenched so tight I don't think he can speak.

Our boat hits another trough. Sloshing water soaks my feet and ankles. On the platform, Senhor Jorge and the others force the rudder left, then right, somehow taking us in one unbroken piece through the next rapid. I can't tell how they know where to go. We drop down one step, the frenzy filling my ears, then another and another. After what seems like hours, we glide into calmer water.

Behind us, the roar recedes. I clutch my oar and try to breathe. The men on the platform are looking left, searching for something. High up on the cliff face is a niche with a statue of the Madonna. The sailors take off their hats and cross themselves, muttering thanks to Nossa Senhora da Boa Viagem for taking us safely through the rapids. So do I.

Pedro and Tomás climb down from the platform. I take that as a good sign. We start rowing again.

"That was Barqueiros," Pedro says when I ask. "One of the bad stretches."

"There are worse?"

"There's always worse."

I don't want to know if he's talking about upstream or downstream. "I didn't see a bridge."

"Pillars."

"Didn't see pillars either."

"They're underwater."

Oh.

Pedro smirks. "I take it you haven't heard the story?"

I shake my head. Miguel is listening too.

"Dona Matilda, the first queen of Portugal, was told her child would die in water. To change the prophesy, she ordered a bridge built over this dangerous stretch of the Douro. But her first son drowned anyway, in a pool churned up by oxen. The bridge was never finished."

"So the pillars must be down there somewhere," says Tomás. "Since – as you've seen – there aren't enough hazards on the river already."

We laugh and I feel their disapproval lessen a fraction. Maybe being inexperienced isn't a mortal sin after all. We stop rowing and let the current carry us.

"Two hundred and ten," says Tomás.

"Two hundred and ten what?" I ask.

"*Pontos*. Obstacles in the river that can cause trouble. Rocks. Waterfalls. Rapids. Shallows."

"You counted them?" asks Miguel.

"Not me," Tomás scoffs. "Baron Forrester. Heard of him?"

I have, thanks to Senhor Manuel. Miguel looks down at his feet.

"You couldn't have grown up in the Douro," Tomás says unbelievingly.

"I did," Miguel says defensively. "Near Quinta do Tedo."

"And you don't know…?" Tomás lets out an exasperated breath, then gives up. "Englishman. Wine trader. Painter. He made a map that shows every dangerous point on the Douro."

"Didn't help though, did it?" Pedro says. "The river got him in the end."

"As it might any of us." Tomás makes the sign of the cross again.

Miguel opens his eyes wide. "What happened?"

"His boat capsized in the Cachão da Valeira," Tomás says. "Nasty stretch of water, that one. Forrester's money belt dragged him to the bottom, people say. He never surfaced. No one found his gold pieces either."

"Or if they did," Pedro says, "they were smart enough not to say anything."

"He was with Dona Antónia, traveling to Régua," Tomás adds. "She survived, *graças a Deus*."

Miguel looks uncertain again. I feel almost sorry for him. How can he not know of Dona Antónia Adelaide Ferreira? The richest woman in the Douro, who is almost considered a saint because of the way she takes care of the people who work on her *quintas*.

15

"You must've heard of her," I tell Miguel. "The *Ferreirinha?*"

"Oh." His face relaxes. "Her. Yes."

"The ladies were luckier than the Baron," Tomás goes on. "They floated to shore, their skirts full of air."

"Enough tales," Senhor Jorge snaps from the platform. "Make us breakfast, will you?"

Pedro and Tomás look at Miguel, then at me. I give them a blank stare in return. Pedro groans.

"Watch and learn," he tells Miguel. He's soon got sardines grilling over a metal grate. We eat them with *broa* and a ration of wine. I notice it doesn't come from the Port wine barrels.

When he's finished handing out the food, Miguel takes his bowl and sits beside me.

"Why are you going to Porto?" I ask him.

"My sister lives there, in the Rua do Bonjardim. I'm staying with her until I leave for Brazil."

"You're going to Brazil?" I blink. "Alone?"

"Yes," he says defensively. "To work as a cobbler."

The boy can't be older than my little brother. I'm not sure whether to admire his pluck or think him a fool.

"You make shoes, huh?" Tomás joins the conversation.

"Beautiful ones." Miguel puffs up like a proud chick. "I've apprenticed with my father for three years already."

"So now you're off to fame and fortune in Brazil?" Pedro teases him. Miguel doesn't seem to realize it.

"Father said I'll learn a lot. Then when I come back, I'll take over his workshop."

"Got your life all planned then." The expression on Pedro's face says *don't count on it.*

"When do you sail?" I ask.

"Two days after we get to Porto."

Not long after, we rinse our bowls in the river. I take my place on the oar again, wincing as the raw blisters on my hands make contact with the wood. But the wind is against us and the current is slow, so we row. Pedro begins singing.

Fui ao Douro à vindima. His voice is strong and unwavering. *I went to the Douro for the harvest.* The words echo off the hills and disappear in the fog spilling out of the valleys, song after song about love and loss and missing home. I've heard some before, but the sailors know them by heart. Occasionally they sing along – not as well as Pedro – and we row to the rhythm. On both banks, wine grape vines and trees are tinged with yellow, red, and orange. Autumn hasn't turned their colors bright yet. I wonder if I'll miss the slopes and colors and clouds.

Maybe.

Right now I'm glad to get away.

Every now and then, Cassiano tells us to check for shallows. We stab the boat hooks into the bottom of the riverbed, testing its depth. But the water is running high and we don't get stuck. There are more rapids, but none that require four men on the rudder. We row and row. My shoulders ache and it's not long before I'm hungry again. The sun arcs overhead, moving west, showing the way to our destination even when our bow, following the river, points elsewhere.

At the bottom of a short, intense stretch of choppy water, another *rabelo* waits. Its square sail is open and catching the wind, but it's going nowhere against the current. The *mestre* is on the platform, but most of the sailors are on the rocky bank, a rope over their shoulders, waiting for us to pass. Senhor Jorge orders us to hold the oars steady, slowing the boat.

"How's it upstream?" the other boat's *mestre* calls.

Cassiano opens his mouth, but Senhor Jorge cuts him off. "Worse than last week. You'll need oxen."

The men on the rocks look resigned. Asking a farmer to use his oxen to pull a boat costs money. They'll be the ones hauling the *rabelo* up the rapids if it's humanly possible. Senhor Jorge tells us to start rowing again. I look back. The other boat's sailors are already leaning their weight into the rope, their bare feet fighting for purchase on the rocks. Meter by painful meter, they advance upstream. I'm glad I'm on a one-way trip. Getting to Porto from Régua takes two or three days, and I'm already impatient. Going upriver can take ten, and it's a damn sight harder on the crew.

Pedro puts me and Miguel on the same oar and joins Tomás on his. "Think Cassiano's ready to throw Jorge overboard yet?" he asks Tomás. His voice is so low I barely hear him.

"Wouldn't blame him," Tomás says. "He's the *mestre*. He's supposed to be in charge. Then Jorge shows up and starts giving orders. Why's he along anyway?"

"One less man to pay, for starters."

"Stingy bastard." Tomás shakes his head. "We're already running on a skeleton crew, with those two." He shoots his eyes our way and sees that I'm listening. "No offense. But you're both pretty useless."

"Maybe we should stop rowing then," I say, and hold the oar out of the water.

"Go ahead," Tomás says. "If you want Jorge to boot you off. He's done it before."

I don't believe him. But Miguel shrills, "no, no," and forces our oar back into the water. "I have to get to Porto."

I give in and let him row. Pedro and Tomás go back to talking quietly.

"Jorge has his own personal shipment coming aboard too," Tomás says. "Near Avintes."

"Again?"

"Yeah."

"*Raios.*" Pedro spits out the word. "That's the real reason he came. One day he's going to gamble and lose."

"Better not be on this trip. I need the money."

Tomás and Pedro fall silent.

We come to more gorges, more rapids. With Cassiano and Senhor Jorge on the rudder, we run them easily. Senhor Jorge's missing fingers don't hinder him at all.

When the sun is high overhead, Cassiano tells Miguel to get a sturdy cauldron from the *coqueiro*. "You're in charge of the *caldo de carne*. Think you can handle it?"

Briefly, Miguel looks mutinous. I try not to grin. Maybe he's not as meek as he seems.

"Cooking's the *moço's* job," Cassiano tells him shortly. "On this trip, that's you."

Soon our new ship's boy is following orders and chunks of pork and beans are cooking in the pot. The result isn't half bad. I'm so hungry I'd swallow tree bark if I had to. I slurp it down so fast I scald my tongue.

The river narrows and widens and narrows again, winding its way west until the sun disappears behind the mountains and the water goes dark. The air is damp, the breeze giving me goosebumps even though I'm sweating. As dusk falls, Cassiano steers us to the bank. Senhor Jorge mutters something about pushing on farther. Cassiano ignores him.

We rinse our faces and arms in the river, then eat more sardines with *broa* and wine. Tomás pulls out a harmonica and begins to play. I don't know how long I listen before I nod off. Soon after, we drape a rectangle of cloth over the boat and pull out whatever bedding we've brought. I wrap myself in the thin blanket Mother gave me and find a place on the deck, cheek to toe with the others. Miguel wriggles into the space between me and the curved side of the *rabelo* and we lie back-to-back, sharing the warmth. It's hard and crowded, loud with snores and burps and farts. My shipmates smell. So do I.

But I fall asleep and wake at dawn, when the others start stirring. I'm so stiff it hurts to stand. Handling the oar is torture.

On the morning of that second day, it happens. At first, I hear the sound, like leaves in a strong wind. Miguel and I are on our oars again with Pedro and Tomás. They abandon us and bound toward the platform. Senhor Jorge and Cassiano are already up there, still and watchful. They've been snarling at each other the whole morning – something about customs inspectors – and everyone's grumpy. Miguel and I are trained by now. We pull in our oars and lay them flat across the gunwales.

Pedro said this stretch is studded with rapids that will toss a *rabelo* around like a twig in a waterfall. I tighten my grip on the oar as Cassiano and Senhor Jorge argue about the best route to take. All I see are boulders that poke up like black, broken teeth. A line of them is in front of us, getting closer. Too close. Cassiano bellows and the men on the platform force the rudder to the right. A trough opens before us and we shoot forward, rocks flashing by on either side. Water splashes everywhere. I'm drenched in a second, trying desperately to keep my hold on the oar as the boat bucks. On the platform, the men strain and yell.

Ahead, I see a dark mass under the green water. A huge boulder, with a permanent wave flowing up and over it. Cassiano yells again, telling the men on the platform to *turn, turn!* We veer, but it's too late. The boat takes the wave, one side rising high, wood groaning. Then we're yawing sideways, tilting. Miguel loses his balance and falls to his knees. Beneath him, his oar slides, one end jutting far over the water. A rising wave catches it, rips it away. He cries out and lunges for it. Just before he goes overboard, I grab him by the back of his shirt.

We all hear the oar crack as it hits a rock. Senhor Jorge lets out a string of curses. The oar shoots down the rapids ahead of us. At my side, Miguel collapses into the water in the bottom of the boat and covers his face with his hands.

"I couldn't help it," he moans. "It wasn't my fault."

I hold tight to my oar, knowing there's nothing I can do. Somehow, Cassiano gets us through the rest of the rapids in one piece. Ahead, the oar bobs in the water. I pull it toward us with a boat hook. The flat part is gone. Miguel fingers the jagged edge.

"Fool!" Senhor Jorge is rigid with fury. "Careless fool!"

"I couldn't help it," Miguel moans again. "I couldn't stop it."

"Doesn't matter. You owe me for an oar."

"Wait," I say. "You can't expect…"

Senhor Jorge rounds on me before I finish. "Shut up. Or you'll pay me for not preventing it."

"How could…?" At his furious look, I clamp my mouth shut.

The other men busy themselves bailing out the boat and checking the lines. No one wants to bear the brunt of Senhor Jorge's wrath.

"I can't," Miguel protests. "I don't have money."

"I don't believe you," Senhor Jorge says harshly. "You're bound for the Americas. You have money."

"My sister has it. It's for Brazil."

"Not any more it's not."

"Please!"

Senhor Jorge talks over him. "When we get to Porto, we'll find this sister of yours. Now, you go and take an oar from the stern. And if something happens to that one…" He leaves the threat unsaid and climbs back onto the platform.

Silently, tears streaking down his face, Miguel brings the oar forward. We start rowing again. I glance at him sideways, not knowing what to say. Brazil is going to rip this kid to pieces. If Senhor Jorge doesn't do it first.

"You saw what happened." His voice is choked. "You know I couldn't stop it."

"I couldn't have either." I want to tell him it'll all work out. But what power does he have, compared to the anger of the *rabelo* owner? "Your sister …?"

"Will kill me if I can't go to Brazil. And if I have to go home because I don't have money for the passage, my father will kill me again. I'll never have another chance to leave." His shoulders heave with sobs.

"You know it wasn't his fault," I say to Tomás and Pedro. "Senhor

Jorge can't say it was."

Pedro snorts. "He can say whatever he wants."

"Come on," I say. "Miguel's a child. He can't defend himself on his own."

"Our word doesn't count for anything," Tomás says. "Not when it's Jorge. Believe me."

"So what can he do?" I don't know why I'm pressing the point. I'll never see the boy again after we get off the *rabelo*.

There's a pause, then Pedro says quietly, "Call his bluff. And when we get to land, run for it."

"What?" Miguel blurts out.

"Shhh." Pedro checks to make sure Senhor Jorge is still on the platform. "Keep saying it's not your fault and you won't pay. He can't force it out of you if you don't have it."

I stare at him. It's a crazy plan. "Is that something *you* would do?"

"No, but I work for him. Miguel doesn't. He can disappear."

The boy's eyes are wide and scared. "I … I don't think I'd dare."

"Your choice." Pedro falls silent. No one else seems to have a better idea.

Soon afterwards, Senhor Jorge orders Miguel to start cooking. "It better be good," he growls.

Head down, the boy scrambles to obey.

For the rest of the day and the next, there's no banter, Pedro doesn't sing, and Cassiano is snippier than ever. I can tell their irritation at Senhor Jorge has turned into outright resentment. And no one's happy that we're navigating with three oars rather than four.

After Entre-os-Rios, where the Tâmega and Douro rivers meet, we hit calmer water. Pedro says Baron Forrester found only one *ponto* from there to Porto. It's unlikely we'll be losing or breaking anything more. I want to relax, but can't. It's impossible not to see Miguel's slumped, miserable form every time I turn around.

I wonder if he's destroyed the future he dreamed of. As Luísa may have done hers. Different forms of weakness, same result. I row unseeingly. In the Douro, the eldest daughter keeps house, helps with the children when they're young, and takes care of her parents when they're old. Asking for anything else isn't done. But Luísa grew up with me telling her Senhor Manuel's stories, and she wants more. Or did, until a couple of days ago. I realize I'm clasping the oar as if I want to strangle it. My blisters stick to the wood as I loosen my grip, and I hiss.

Pedro glances my way. I shake my head, telling him *it's nothing,* and turn back to the river.

The first time she said she wanted to join me in Porto, I laughed. She kept at it until I said that one day, when I was settled, I'd send for her. Father will say *no,* but Luísa always finds a way. She's determined. But if she adds another mouth to the family, she'll never leave. What was she thinking? She knows the sons of wealthy landowners play with local girls. They don't marry them. So help me, if Rafael takes her spark, I'll do more than throw a rock at him.

By now, the terraced vineyards on either side of the river have long disappeared. There are still mountains, but their slopes are forests of multicolored trees now, with houses and villages scattered here and there. Before we come to a town Tomás calls Avintes, Senhor Jorge orders us over to the left bank, where the trees come down to the river. I see no place to dock. Without being asked, the sailors run the poles between the *rabelo* and the bank and Senhor Jorge disappears down a barely visible trail. I raise my eyebrows at Tomás.

"Business to attend to," he says.

For a second, I think it's some physical need that can't wait until the end of the day. That happens. But Tomás's tone says otherwise. We wait.

CHAPTER 3

B Y NOW, JORGE *could've navigated the path in the pitch black. And he would if he had to. He hated being that desperate. Hated that he needed money so badly.*

Once among the trees, he dropped the bold front he put on for the men and broke into a jog. His toothless old acquaintance better be ready with the barrels this time. A second delay, and Jorge wouldn't have enough to pay his men. And he always paid his crew.

He'd seen it happen to other rabelo *owners. Fail once, and the news travels faster than water through the Valeira rapids. In a snap of a finger, your reputation and your crew, present and future, gone. Never had he taken that risk. Until that cursed card game with Captain Duarte and the drink he'd had too much of.*

Jorge scowled. He was the one who hadn't been able to pull back in the face of their old, bitter rivalry. He'd played and lost, and the Captain had no mercy when calling in his winnings. If the glass had spilled the other way, Jorge would've done the same.

There was wind in the treetops, but at ground level the air was still. Jorge slowed to a walk, not wanting to arrive out of breath. To appear worried. It was sheer bad luck that those two traveling lads were along on this particular trip. His own crew knew what was coming on board. They also knew not to talk. Henrique and Miguel didn't. But then again, they had no experience. No reason to know that this stop, this new cargo, was anything out of the ordinary.

Ahead, the trees thinned, opening onto a clearing. In front of a ramshackle shack sat a two-wheeled cart that could be pulled by a man. On it were four wooden casks that, when upright, stood just higher than his knee. Jorge released his breath in relief. He was saved.

CHAPTER 4

SENHOR JORGE COMES back, followed by a man who's missing three of his front teeth and is pulling a cart loaded with small casks. Tomás and Pedro bring them on board and stash them under our bags and bedding in the *coqueiro*. Senhor Jorge takes his place beside Cassiano and we push away from the shore as the man with the missing teeth disappears into the trees. Not a word has been uttered.

"What...?" I start to ask when the sound of water covers our voices.

Tomás interrupts me. "You don't need to know."

"It's just water." Pedro doesn't even try to hide his sarcasm. "That happens to taste like elderberry juice."

"Shut up, will you?" Tomás mutters. "Henrique and Miguel are in enough trouble as it is."

I don't need to ask more. Everyone knows it's not unusual, in some places, to add the dark purple juice from elderberries to poor-quality wine to give it color, and then to pass it off as Port. I'm guessing that's what Senhor Jorge's barrels are for. My opinion of him plummets to a new low.

Judging by the sun, we've been heading more north than toward the sea. Then, as the river makes a wide curve to the west, I see something so amazing that I stop rowing. High in the air, where the Douro narrows, two immense iron arches jut out from the cliffs, reaching for each other, but not yet touching. Atop them is a bridge. It, too, is unfinished, with a big gap in the middle. Incredibly, there are no pillars in the river holding any of this up. I stare, mouth open, wondering

24

what keeps the two sides from falling toward each other. The weight of the metal is beyond my comprehension. But the bridge itself, more air than beams, seems light, delicate, like pieces of stiff black lace stretching to the sky. Even Miguel has lifted his eyes off his feet and is gaping.

"The Don Fernando bridge." Tomás is enjoying our reactions.

On the bridge, men swarm like insects, lowering iron beams from the flat span to the arch, then maneuvering them into place. I crane my neck to watch as we row closer. Imagining being that high, without firm land beneath my feet, makes me dizzy. Below the bridge, the water is clogged with boats.

"It's a train bridge," Tomás says. "Travelers from Lisbon to the north won't have to get off in Gaia and take a carriage across the Douro anymore."

I have to look almost straight up to see the top of the bridge now. Our oars are idle, even before Cassiano orders us to use them to slow the *rabelo*. He's looking at the right bank, waiting for a signal that it's safe to pass. There'd be nothing left of our little boat if one of those beams fell.

"When will it be finished?" I ask.

"In a few weeks," Tomás says.

"About time," Pedro mutters. "It's taken two years."

"They couldn't work for months because of the rains last winter, remember?" Tomás says. "And they have to get it right. No one wants it to collapse with the king and queen on it."

"What?" I ask. "King Luís and Queen Maria Pia are coming to Porto?"

Tomás nods.

"And the princes too. They'll all be on the first train to cross the bridge," Pedro says.

I can't help grinning. I might get to see the royal family? Luísa would be so jealous. My eyes are drawn up again to the X's formed by the crossed girders. From where I am, they look as slim and delicate as thread. Even on a stormy day, the wind won't have much to blow against.

When Senhor Manuel said that someday the train would come to Régua, I imagined something solid and heavy. Earthbound. But crossing this bridge would be as close as a body could come to flying. What a grand future lies before Portugal, if we can create marvels like this. My eyes trace its length from one end to the other. Someday I want to be up there, riding on one of the trains.

Cassiano yells at us to start rowing again and we glide under the bridge. I peer ahead, squinting against the sun, eager for my first glimpse of Porto. On the right bank is a steep hill with houses spilling down it. Behind the buildings rises a tall, defensive stone wall with a watch tower, the kind people built to protect cities hundreds of years ago. Below it is a *Ponte Pênsil*, a suspension bridge held up by thick iron cords attached to tall pillars on both sides of the river.

My first reaction is disappointment. Porto isn't that big after all. Then I notice buildings and a tower poking up from beyond the medieval wall. The main city must be behind it, out of sight. It's as if Porto's hiding, keeping its secrets as long as possible from those who don't belong to it.

The river twists again. On the left bank, right above the water, is a chapel under construction. Above it, atop the cliff, is a much larger, round church that shows signs of heavy damage.

"That's the Serra do Pilar monastery," Tomás offers. "The monks ran away during the siege of Porto. It got bombarded pretty badly."

I scrunch up my eyes and make a mental calculation. The siege of Porto, a war between two brothers over who should rule Portugal, was more than forty years ago. I never imagined that its destruction would remain. I turn my attention forward again. All I want now is to see the city. But the tide is against us. We advance slowly, slowly.

Finally we pass under the suspension bridge, and Porto unfolds along the right bank like one of Rafael's mother's silk fans. Dozens of boats, from big, masted ships to tiny rowboats, are moored in the river or docked alongside a wide stone quay crowded with people and crates, oxen and carts. Little ferries dart in and out, tying up wherever they find an opening. One cuts in front of us, earning a shout from Cassiano. Its cargo is a group of women balancing wide, shallow baskets on their heads. In them are loaves of bread for sale, so fresh I can smell them.

Along the quay, the medieval wall is pierced by arched openings that I assume lead to storerooms, shops, or alleyways. On top of the wall are tall, narrow houses with red-tile roofs and iron balconies. Behind them, rows upon rows of houses and churches and other buildings climb the hills, going farther than I can see. I can't even begin to imagine how many people live here. In a big square that Pedro calls

Praça da Ribeira, women's voices, rough and shrill, call attention to whatever they brought to town to sell today. Above us, seagulls wheel and cry.

Cassiano steers us to Gaia, on the south side of the river. We slide into a pack of other *rabelos* waiting to unload. The wide, stone-paved docking area is already covered with casks and boxes. Wood grates against stone as men push heavy barrels up the ramp, away from the river and toward the wine cellars.

"Untie the barrels," Senhor Jorge orders.

Miguel and I work side by side, struggling to loosen knots that the trip has pulled tight.

"I'm going to do it," he whispers. "When we dock in Porto, I'm running away." He's rigid with trepidation.

"You're sure?" I hope the boy is part jackrabbit.

"What choice do I have?"

I check that none of the crew are near us.

"Get out of his sight, then hide," I advise quietly. "He'll catch you if you try to outrun him."

He nods, pale under the grime of the last few days.

Brave little lad.

We finish unloading – everything except Senhor Jorge's small barrels, which are under the rectangle of cloth we drape over the boat at night – then row across the river. It's still afternoon. Darkness won't be Miguel's ally. As we approach the quay, he fetches the bundle that holds his tools and other possessions and hoists it onto his back. I wince. The bulkier he is, the easier he'll be to grab. I collect my bag too, hoping that'll make it less obvious what he's planning. We wait near the side of the boat as Tomás and Pedro tie up the *rabelo*.

Miguel is bouncing on his toes, ready to bolt.

"Hold still," I whisper, lining up behind him. If I'm in Senhor Jorge's way, it'll give Miguel a few extra seconds.

"What do you think you're doing, *moço* Miguel?"

The boy freezes, then very slowly turns. Senhor Jorge is close enough I can smell his rank breath.

"Going somewhere?" The hand with three fingers holds a document I don't recognize. He flaps it in Miguel's face. "You wouldn't jump ship without this, would you?"

"You took my passport?" The boy reaches for it. Senhor Jorge lifts it above his head.

"Your father gave it to me for safekeeping. Probably figured I'd be less likely to go overboard than you were."

Miguel braces himself. "Well, I didn't. May I have it back now?"

Glancing around, I notice that from the deck of the two-masted steamer tied up beside us, a lean man with the darkest skin I've ever seen is watching the exchange.

"You didn't, but the oar did." Senhor Jorge dangles the passport over the water. "You need this if you want to go to Brazil. So I propose we talk to that sister of yours. I get my money and you get your passport." He tucks it into his shirt and gestures for the boy to get off the *rabelo*. "Move."

From the deck of the steamer, the dark-skinned man calls, "So, Jorge. Found someone new to bully?"

I stare at him in amazement as Senhor Jorge's face twists in fury.

"Bootlicker," Senhor Jorge growls. He doesn't take his eyes off Miguel. The exchange ends there, in a loaded silence, as Senhor Jorge gives Miguel a shove. Those two men hate each other, but I have no idea why.

Miguel moves forward with the eerie calm of a trapped animal.

I nod a stiff goodbye to Pedro and Tomás and the others, then jump onto the quay and slip into my *socos*. I should go to the Rua das Flores and find Goldsmith Bento. Instead, I fall into step beside Miguel.

Senhor Jorge gives me an unfriendly look. "You're not needed. Be off."

I pretend not to understand he's trying to get rid of me. Miguel's not my responsibility, but I don't want him to come to harm. And I sure don't expect Senhor Jorge to play fair.

"I'm going to the Rua do Bonjardim," I lie, hoping I've remembered the name of the street where his sister lives. "Miguel said he'd show me the way."

The boy shoots me a puzzled look. Thankfully, Senhor Jorge is too busy yelling orders at the sailors to notice. With a final glance over my shoulder at the dark-skinned man, who is still watching us, we're off.

We pass a two-wheeled crane taking crates off a ship and skirt a line of patient oxen, their carts overflowing with goods for outgoing vessels. Praça da Ribeira teems with passengers coming off the rowboat ferries, men bent under heavy sacks, and water carriers filling their containers at the fountain. Not far from clusters of men in fine jackets and dark trousers – merchants, perhaps, or bankers – peasant women from the countryside pack up whatever produce remains at the end of their market day. I don't know where to look first.

Beneath my feet is stone, most of it covered in a layer of muck. Dirt and mud, certainly, with a generous dose of shit, judging by the stench. Not too different from home, but a lot more concentrated. Looking up, I notice that the buildings look like they were built in different centuries. On the right side of the square they're small and rundown, their upper stories over-hanging the lower ones. On the left side stand newer buildings, five and six stories high, with graceful arcades at street level. Under the arches are shops, banks, and trading offices with people scurrying in and out of them.

Miguel ignores the bustle and leads us into a steep lane he calls Rua dos Mercadores. Merchants' Street. We climb, and soon cross an avenue with large, elegant buildings on either side. More men in fine suits are grouped outside one of them, talking in a language I don't understand.

"You sure this is the right way?" Senhor Jorge grumbles as we trudge up the winding street. The buildings on each side block whatever light is left in the sky, and the damp makes goosebumps rise on my arms. It's so narrow there's no room for us and a cart grinding its way downhill. I back against a wall to keep my feet from under its wheels.

"I memorized the directions," Miguel says.

Senhor Jorge just grunts.

We reach a cross street that's not much wider than the one we were on. To our right, above the houses, rise two granite towers.

"The cathedral." Miguel looks relieved. "I was told to look for it."

We go in the opposite direction, heading downhill until we reach another square. To our left is a broad street still under construction, full of cut stone and dust. I hear but don't see water, as if they're covering up a small river. I get a whiff and my eyes water. A river that's become a sewer. Beyond it, a horse and fine carriage are leaving another street with more tall houses and elegant mansions. I gaze down at it longingly. I hope Goldsmith Bento will give me time to explore.

To our right are the tall walls of another convent. Or perhaps what used to be one. The religious orders in Portugal were abolished decades ago, after the war between Dom Pedro and his dastardly brother, Dom Miguel.

I remember well the times I sat by Senhor Manuel's knee in Mesão

Frio as he recounted how Dom Pedro abdicated the Portuguese throne to become Emperor of Brazil, leaving his young daughter Maria, the future queen, under Dom Miguel's tutelage. But when Dom Miguel ripped up the constitutional charter and made himself a king with absolute powers, Dom Pedro sailed back to Portugal from Brazil, determined to retake the crown.

By this point in the story, Senhor Manuel was always on his feet, marching and gesturing as he described how Dom Pedro's small army entered Porto in 1832 without a shot being fired. But it was a trap, for Dom Miguel then surrounded the city with a much bigger force and laid siege to it. For an entire year, Dom Pedro and the brave people of Porto resisted, until finally Dom Miguel's army withdrew. After his victory, Dom Pedro accused the religious orders of favoring his brother. The monks were kicked out onto the streets right away, Senhor Manuel said, but the nuns were allowed to stay in their convents until the last one died.

There's activity at the door, so maybe some old nuns still live in this convent. I don't know. But I do know I'm happy to live in a city that calls itself *Invicta*. Unconquered. I grin, then glance at Miguel, plodding along with his head down a step ahead of me. Unconquered is not what he's feeling right now.

Everywhere I look, there's so much to see. We pass another square paved in black and white stones whose design looks like waves, surrounded by grand white buildings, with the statue of a soldier on horseback at its center. It's late afternoon and everywhere there are people. Women in long skirts admire gloves and fans in a seamstress's display window as servant girls with aprons tied around their waists head home from market, toting heavy baskets. Outside a shop that sells newspapers and tobacco, men smoke and argue.

I'm not paying attention to my feet, and one of my *socos* skids. I catch my balance and look down. At my feet are two parallel rails set into the ground. Coming along them are two horses pulling a long carriage with at least a dozen passengers in it. I jump out of their way, then hurry to catch up with Miguel and Senhor Jorge.

We continue to climb. Miguel asks directions once. Finally he stops, hunches his shoulders around his ears, and says, "This is it."

I step back to take in the two-story house. It's well-kept and painted light blue. Miguel's sister must be doing well. Maybe the boy is worrying for nothing. On the ground floor there's a door, a window, and a dark, covered passageway that looks like it leads to the back of the building. At the end of the passageway, there's a bend. I can't see what's beyond.

"An *ilha*," Senhor Jorge says in disgust. "I should have known. She better have your money."

It takes me a second to understand. Miguel's sister doesn't live in the big house, but in a cramped row of dwellings behind it. They're not for people who earn a decent living. I've heard nothing good about the *ilhas* of Porto.

Senhor Jorge pushes Miguel toward the passageway. Its walls are covered in black mold. When I follow, Senhor Jorge whirls to face me. He's going to tell me to beat it. And there's no reason I shouldn't. Except that whatever story Senhor Jorge is going to tell Miguel's sister might be a little more truthful if I'm here.

I stand my ground.

Before he can say anything, someone plows into me from behind.

"What's your business here?" asks a short, stout woman as I right myself. Even with a basket of laundry balanced on her head, she looks tough. I'd bet she could beat a man in a fight if she put her mind to it. I back out of her way as Miguel pokes his head from behind Senhor Jorge.

"My sister lives here. Ana Maria."

"Aha. She's been waiting for you." The woman eyes me and Senhor Jorge suspiciously. Then she smiles at the boy and some of her toughness melts away. "Go on then. She'll be glad to see you." She herds all of us down the passageway. I catch up with Miguel and squeeze his shoulder. He looks even more nervous than before.

At the end, the passageway opens into a packed-dirt alley that's barely wider than my arms can reach. It runs between two rows of one-story houses whose whitewash has gone gray. Every few feet are a door and a window. Each one, I gather, is a separate dwelling. Back home, our chickens live in a space that size. Here, the hens have invaded the alley. The air is heavy with the smell of boiled vegetables, damp, and waste.

"Keep going." The washerwoman pushes us forward again, then hollers, "Ana Maria! Company!"

The woman who emerges from a door on the left has the gauntness of one who doesn't eat very well. She hasn't used Miguel's Brazil money for food, that's for sure. Unless she's sick. I can't tell. I can't even see her expression because the scarf holding back her long brown hair has come undone and she's got her arms around her head, retying it. When it's out of her face, she lets out a glad cry and rushes forward.

"Miguel!" She pulls him into her arms as other women from the *ilha* appear in the doorways. "I expected you days ago. What happened?"

"We had shoes to finish." He clings to her. "I couldn't come earlier."

"Well, I'm glad you got here. Your ship leaves the day after tomorrow."

"I know."

Loudly, Senhor Jorge clears his throat. Miguel stiffens, then shifts so he and his sister are side by side, facing the *rabelo* owner. Creating a united front. Ana Maria catches Miguel's unease and eyes us warily.

"I've a matter to discuss with you, *menina*," Senhor Jorge says.

Ana Maria stiffens. It's not unusual to call women of any age *menina* – little girl – but it's clear she doesn't like his tone. Her neighbors gather around.

"Go on," she says cautiously.

"In your…" Senhor Jorge points to the door she just exited.

She shakes her head firmly and doesn't move. "What is it?"

Senhor Jorge gives me an irritated glance. He's not happy I'm still present.

"I brought Miguel to Porto on my *barco rabelo*."

Senhor Jorge has thrown his shoulders back and he's speaking to somewhere above her head. Trying to appear bigger than he is, I reckon. Or to intimidate. Probably both.

"To help the boy in his future endeavors, I asked his father for no payment," he says. "But he broke an oar, and *that* must be paid for. He gave me to understand that you have his money."

"A broken oar?" Ana Maria takes Miguel's shoulders and turns him to her. Her grip looks strong for someone who appears so frail. "Is this true?"

"You doubt my word?" Senhor Jorge draws himself up even further.

Ana Maria gives both of us – me and Senhor Jorge, as if she thinks I'm here to back him up – a hard look, and holds up a finger. "I know my brother. He's honest. I need to hear this from him."

Senhor Jorge grumbles under his breath.

"The oars weigh more than a mule." Miguel rushes his words out.

"They left me alone with one. In rapids. There's no way I could hold it. And now Senhor Jorge won't give me my passport."

Ana Maria bites her lip. "The passport belongs to Miguel. He needs it."

"And you must understand, *menina,* I need my oar." Senhor Jorge scratches the back of his head impatiently. "He goes nowhere until this matter is resolved."

Ana Maria bites her lip again. She must know an oar could cost weeks of a family's earnings, depending on the price Senhor Jorge decides to ask for it.

Slowly, she straightens, making herself as tall as he is. "What I understand is that with no preparation whatsoever, you expected this child" – she rests a hand on Miguel's shoulder – "to handle an oar that weighs more than he does, in waters that have killed many a grown man. Is that correct?"

Her boldness surprises me, and Senhor Jorge too. By now her neighbors – only woman and children, as far as I can see – have formed a tight, airless circle around us. The stout, tough-looking one is right behind Senhor Jorge, breathing on his neck. To a woman, they'll take her side against a stranger. I'm sure of that. Senhor Jorge glances around uncomfortably. I swallow a smile. There might be hope for Miguel after all.

"All he had to do was keep it from moving." Senhor Jorge leans into Ana Maria's face, his voice cold. "One simple task. He failed."

Senhor Jorge knows – as do Miguel and I – that it was nowhere near that easy. But he's trying to frighten her. I open my mouth. Both Senhor Jorge and the sister give me withering glances. She's put me in the same box as Senhor Jorge, and I don't like it.

I catch Miguel's eye and give him a quick nod. He knows I'm on his side. But I hate feeling that I can't do anything to help. Like with Luísa.

"Portugal abolished slavery years ago. So if you were working him, he's owed wages." Ana Maria meets Senhor Jorge's eyes without flinching, challenging him. She knows what's at stake. "Consider them payment for the oar."

I raise an eyebrow. This woman is more willing to stand up to Senhor Jorge than his own sailors. Around us, her neighbors murmur their support. Senhor Jorge can argue that the boy's wages won't cover the cost of a new oar, but at least with me here he can't claim that *moço* Miguel didn't do his fair share of the work.

It's then that I realize something. I'm in Porto. I don't depend on Senhor Jorge for anything now. And what Ana Maria said gives me an idea.

"You can have my wages too. They should cover the oar," I say, then add, "And our silence."

Around us, the women's murmurs still, then pick up again excitedly. Senhor Jorge curls his lip like a dog about to bite. I've stuck my neck out. More than I should've, especially with those last words. We both know he wasn't planning on paying me. But he won't admit that. Not here and now. We've both seen the calculating looks on the faces around us. He doesn't want to be known as someone who won't pay his men. Especially by a gaggle of women who, if they think he's cheating one of theirs, will spread the word more quickly than the Douro floods after a hard rain.

Ana Maria catches Miguel's grateful expression. She gives me a brief, surprised stare and adjusts her stance ever so slightly. Her animosity is directed entirely at Senhor Jorge now. She holds out her hand. "The passport, please."

For a moment, I think Senhor Jorge isn't going to bend. Then he reaches inside his shirt and pulls it out. But as Ana Maria reaches for it, he grasps the passport in both hands and rips it in two. Around us, women gasp. Miguel lets out a moan. Senhor Jorge tears it in half twice more, then opens his fingers and lets the pieces flutter to the ground. With his heel, he grinds them into the dirt. Before he can destroy them completely, Ana Maria drops to her knees and gathers them to her. He stops, not daring to step on her hands. The expression on his face says he wants to.

"That passport's as useful now as my oar," he growls down at her. "And you!" He spits the words at me. "You'll regret this. I swear you will." He shoves his way through the crowd of women and disappears down the passageway.

Around us, the chattering reaches a new level. The *ilha's* got fodder for days of gossip and speculation. I feel like I've put a price on my own head. Then I see Miguel's stricken face. Ana Maria hugs him to her, her hands grasping the shredded document. Over his head, she mouths *obrigada*, but her eyes are worried.

I nod. At least he has proof he had a passport. I have no idea how he'll get a new one, but maybe having the pieces will make it easier. Miguel looks up when I touch his shoulder.

"You didn't lose the money for your passage. That's what counts."
He wipes tears away on his sleeve. I pretend not to notice.

"You'll soon be on your way to Rio. It just might not be on a ship
that leaves two days from now."

"Maybe," he says tonelessly.

Above us, the sky has darkened into night. The neighbors scatter
now that the show is over. It's past time for me to seek out Goldsmith
Bento's shop in the Rua das Flores.

"I wish you a safe voyage," I tell him. "May you prosper."

"*Se Deus quiser*," Ana Maria says. God willing.

"You too," Miguel says. As I step away, he catches my arm. "What
you said," he whispers. "To Senhor Jorge. Be careful."

"I will." Miguel doesn't have to know I regretted the words the
moment I uttered them. "And you. Don't give up."

I shake his hand and shoulder my bag. A few remaining women,
including Ana Maria's tough friend, close around them. I'm glad to be
leaving the suffocating, smelly *ilha*. Rua das Flores has to be better than
this.

At the end of the passageway, I check the street in both directions.
Provoking Senhor Jorge was stupid, but what's done is done. I'll have
to keep an eye out. At least he'll be gone soon, back up the river on his
rabelo.

A somber man with a mustache that ends in two fine points
navigates around me. I stop him and ask how to get to the Rua das
Flores. It seems I have to retrace my steps, at least partway. The
temperature has dropped with the sun. I pull my coat out of my bag
and step out eagerly, following the mustached man's directions to the
Rua de Santo António. A lamplighter is trudging up the street's steep
incline, a ladder under his arm. A lone rider passes me, the horse's
bridle jingling. It's quieter than when we came by earlier and many of
the shops are closed and dark. From every direction, bells ring out the
seventh hour. Here and there, I see glimmers of light in windows on
the floors above. It's dinnertime for many.

I pick up my pace, my stomach growling. It's not a good time to be
knocking on the door of someone I don't know. I pass the convent I
saw earlier. Thanks to the man who gave me directions, it now has a
name – Ave Maria de São Bento. Below it, the wide street where I saw
the fine carriages earlier curves downhill. This, the mustached man
said, is the Rua das Flores. No lights shine in the shops on this street

either. From a kitchen somewhere, the smell of roasting meat wafts toward me. My stomach twists again.

I search the signs – the goldsmiths seem to be mostly on the north side of the street – until I find one that says *Gomes & Filho, Ourives.* The shop of Goldsmith Gomes & Son. Its deep green shutters are tightly closed. Upstairs, a feeble light shines between two curtains. Goldsmith Bento might live above the shop, but I can't be sure. I know better than to disturb a family in their private quarters, especially at this time of the evening.

Standing alone in the dark, I almost regret going with Miguel. If I hadn't, I might've gotten to Goldsmith Bento's in time for a hot meal and a bed inside where it's warmer. I pull out the last scrap of Mother's *broa.* The bread's hard and stale, but I gnaw on it anyway. I have to find somewhere to spend the night.

As I back away from the shop, feeling suddenly lonely, my *soco* slips in the mud – or something worse – and I look down at myself. My clothes haven't been changed in three days and I reek of sweat and travel. I can't meet Goldsmith Bento like this.

I go down the street quickly, barely taking in the noble houses – some with large granite coats of arms above their doors – and a church whose elaborately sculpted stone façade stretches to the sky. At the bottom, I find a fountain. It's built into one side of a square, under a big arch. Even the water carriers have finished their day's work now and no one's using it. I rinse off my *socos*, then give my face, neck, and feet a scrub. I'll change into clean clothes at dawn. I rub my hands together to warm them, feeling more than a little sorry for myself. This isn't the welcome to Porto I'd dreamed of.

I start downhill again. Right now, the river is more familiar to me than anywhere else. I'll look for a protected nook where I can rest until dawn. To my right, I see an enormous building with *Commercial Association of Porto* above the entrance. Building materials are piled in front of it. Chapels, roads, bridges – the whole city seems to be under construction. As my life is. A surge of excitement replaces my loneliness. I'm ready for this adventure.

When I reach the wide road where, earlier, I heard men speaking in an unfamiliar language, I turn downstream, in the direction of the sea. Porto is near the ocean, isn't it? There's no one nearby to ask. I hear yells – a fight near Praça da Ribeira, maybe – but have no desire to go investigate. For all I know, Senhor Jorge might be down there with the crew of the *Maria das Graças*. I'd rather spend the night by the ocean, gazing out over the same expanses as Vasco da Gama and the other Portuguese explorers Senhor Manuel told me about. With a quick step, I set out, passing ship after ship creaking on their anchors. The wind strengthens, chilling my face. I pull my jacket closer and keep walking. The ocean is farther than I thought.

I'm sure I've left the city by the time I come alongside a long white building with *Massarelos Crockery Factory* painted on the façade. Three tall smokestacks stick out of its roof. I imagine the kilns, still warm from the day's firing, and wish I could curl up against one. I stop myself. Thinking of their heat only makes the wind feel worse. I need shelter.

Beyond a church with its back to the Douro, a street doubles back and climbs, paralleling the river road. Beside the three-story house at N.° 110 is a lane that runs downhill to the crockery factory. The houses block most of the wind, but it still whistles up the factory lane, rattling the metal gate that closes it off. It's cold and I'm too tired to go on. I find a patch of hard ground behind a couple of trees, wrap myself in Mother's blanket, and close my eyes.

In my dreams, I'm warm. I wake to shouting and women screaming, and immediately understand why.

CHAPTER 5

BEHIND N.° 110, the crockery factory is burning. I blink, bewildered, at the wild orange glow that silhouettes the houses, dancing as demons must do in hell. On a narrow balcony on the second floor, two women – one of them stooped and old – are calling for help and waving frantically at someone down below. I run to the gate, but can't see whose attention they're trying to get.

From the factory come sounds of popping and crashing and more yelling. There must be men down there, fighting the fire, but they're out of sight. And they must not have noticed the flames licking at the back wall of N.° 110.

On the balcony, the younger woman tries to pull the old lady inside, but she grips the wrought-iron railing with both hands and holds on. From somewhere nearby, a bell tolls. It's a cry for help, the number of rings telling the firemen which part of the city is in danger.

I put my fingers in my mouth and whistle, getting the women's attention. "Get out! Now!"

"Dona Leonor won't leave," the younger woman cries desperately.

"Open the door. I'll help you."

She tries again to pull her mistress inside, but Dona Leonor keeps her hands locked around the railing. The younger woman whirls around, her hair whipping across her face, and disappears. Then…nothing. I run to the front door and give it a shove, wondering what trouble I'll get in if I break it down. Moments later, it opens. The young woman is there, flanked by an even younger maidservant in her sleeping cap, trying to look fierce.

"My mistress doesn't want you to come in." The young woman rubs her hands together nervously.

"I'll do you no harm." I'm already pushing past them. "Where is she?"

The young woman leads me at a run up the stairs, along a hallway, and into a bedchamber. I try not to notice the unmade bed or think how improper it is for me to be here.

"No!" Dona Leonor cries when she sees me. She grips the balcony railing even harder.

I slow my movements, not wanting to frighten her more. From her window, I see smoke billowing from the factory's roof. Even on the balcony, the air is choking.

"Dona Leonor." I cover my mouth with my sleeve to cough, then step forward with my palms facing up – the same way I approached the *quinta's* skittish horses – hoping she'll see the gesture as a sign of goodwill. "We…"

"Beatriz, how dare you let a stranger into my house?" she snaps at the younger woman, then at me. "Who are you?"

"My name's Henrique." I keep my voice low and steady. "It's not safe for you to stay here. I'll get you out."

"My son owns that factory. I want his assistance, not yours."

I exchange glances with Beatriz. That assistance might come too late. "If you'll let me help you out of the house, I'll go find him. I promise."

"But my precious things." She flings out an arm, her gesture encompassing the entire house. "We have to get them out."

My gaze takes in the dour-looking portraits in gilded frames on the walls, the thick rugs around the bed, and a clump of jewelry sitting atop a marble-topped vanity. The room is getting hazier by the second. I can't tell if it's coming from the open window or the hallway.

"You need to get out first." I extend my hand. She rears back. "Please. It's for your own safety." I'm starting to think I'll have to carry her out over my shoulder.

To my relief, Beatriz bustles up with a shawl and places it over Dona Leonor's shoulders. "Come now. Let's go." She takes the old lady's arm reassuringly.

Dona Leonor yanks her arm away and hobbles to the vanity, where she starts gathering up her jewelry. From the ground floor, the little maid with the sleeping cap screams. I rush out to the landing. She's at the top of a narrow stairway that descends into darkness, batting at smoke.

I race back and grab Dona Leonor's arm, not caring if she doesn't want me to touch her.

"Let me go!" She slings a necklace of pearls at my head.

I block it. Then, half-carrying her as she struggles, I get her down the stairs, out the door, and to the far side of the street. Beatriz and the servant girl huddle around her as I try to catch my breath. For a moment, we all stare at the house, its outline a stark black against the red glow.

Dona Leonor moans. "My clothes. My beautiful clock. Our family portraits. The silverware. What will become of it?"

She pauses in her lament and turns to me. "Don't stand there, boy. Fetch my things!"

I open my mouth, then close it, too shocked to react.

"Are you deaf? Or just lazy? Go!"

With that, my control shatters completely. "I got you out, Dona Leonor. But I'll be damned if I risk myself for your possessions."

All three of them gasp at my language. For a second, I feel ashamed. I never curse in front of ladies. But it's clear that to this woman of privilege, whose entrance hall is filling with smoke as we speak, my life is worth less than a clock. Just like at the *quinta*.

"You uncouth boy! I've never heard the like."

The shame evaporates and I roll my eyes at Beatriz. "Shall I go?" I'm sorely tempted to abandon them to their fate.

"Wait." Beatriz regards me pleadingly. "Will you go find Senhor António? Her son? Tell him she needs him?"

I nod and turn away. I expect no thanks from Dona Leonor, and get none.

The gate to the factory lane is still closed, but it's not much taller than I am. I scramble over it and run toward the popping fire, wondering what the hell I'm doing. In the open area in front of the burning building, men have formed a line and are passing buckets of water hand-to-hand from the river. The smoke turns dark grey when the water hits the flames, but otherwise it makes no difference.

The man closest to me on the bucket line has inky black skin that's shiny with sweat. With a shock of recognition, I realize that he's the one from the steamer who called Jorge a bully.

"Dona Leonor's son," I yell. "Where is he?"

He looks at me blankly, not slowing his rhythm. So do the other men. I run along the line, asking again and again. Pedro, Tomás, and Cassiano are here, with buckets from the *Maria das Graças,* but they can't help me. There's no sign of Senhor Jorge. Finally a man points through the entrance into the burning building. Inside, flames are devouring one of the walls.

"That's Senhor António, at the front."

I stop just outside the entrance. The air is crackling, embers flying everywhere. Dona Leonor's son is yelling, ordering the others to work faster, to bring more water.

"Senhor António!"

He doesn't hear me.

I take a few steps into the inferno. "Senhor António!" Smoke fills my lungs. I double over, coughing.

"*Patrão!*" one of the men on the bucket line hollers.

Senhor António turns a soot-stained face in my direction but doesn't stop swinging the buckets. He's got a nasty-looking burn on his hand. "Why aren't you helping?" he croaks.

"Dona Leonor sent me. Her house is on fire." I'm still coughing.

He comes to an abrupt stop, looking more wild-eyed than before. "*Raios!* Where is she?"

"I got her out. Her servants are with her. She's all right."

"Thank God." He tosses me his empty pail. "Keep working." And then he's gone, running up the factory lane.

"Get a move on," someone yells, and I see the contents of another bucket fly toward the flames. The exposed skin on my hands and face prickles from the heat. A few dozen men pissing will never tame this monster. I run with the pail to the river, then join the end of the bucket line.

"Where are the firemen?" The man who takes his place behind me rubs his face, leaving a smear of grime across it. "They should have been here by now."

"I heard bells," I say. "Ages ago."

I'm nearing the front of the line when there's a mighty crack. The few men still inside the factory flee as the roof caves in with a great *whoomph.* With it comes a wave of air, so scorching that I close my eyes and back away. When I open them, they're full of stinging grit. I blink frantically. Everyone around me is doing the same.

"More water!" someone yells, and we come back to life. I race with the others to the river, but it's pointless. The blaze is so big now that we can't get anywhere close. I join the crew of the *Maria das Graças* and we watch the flames devour what's left of the roof.

Then, from the direction of Porto, horns blare. Horses, snorting and lathered, dash up, pulling two wagons mounted with hand pumps, hoses, ladders, and axes.

"The firemen from São João Novo," the man with the smear on his face says. "*Meu Deus.* What took them so long?"

Sprinting back and forth, the firemen attach two hoses to each of the pumps. One they plunge into the river. The other they haul toward the factory.

"Get over here." One of the firemen puts me, the dark-skinned man, and two others to work at the pump. "If you stop, the water stops. Remember that."

We pump until our lungs heave and we're slowing down from sheer exhaustion. On my hands, blisters break and reform. A fireman runs over, sees us soaked in sweat, and finds men to replace us. The dark-skinned man and I move to stand by the wall farthest from the smoke. We lean against it, hacking, hands braced on our knees.

When we're breathing almost normally, I ask, "Do you work here?" I can't think of any other reason he'd be at the crockery factory. "I thought I saw you on a ship."

He straightens. "You probably did. I'm a sailor."

His accent sounds strange to my ears.

He sticks out a hand. "Sálvio, from the *São Pedro.*"

I introduce myself, then ask, "Why are you here?"

"Because my captain – Captain Duarte – is a member of the Brotherhood of the Almas do Corpo Santo de Massarelos."

"The what?"

"You know the church at the bottom of this street?" From where we're standing, houses block it from sight, but I remember passing the big church with its back to the river. I nod.

"Hundreds of years ago, they say, a ship traveling from London to Porto got caught in a terrible storm off the Spanish coast. They lost one of their masts, their sails, and their rudder. For three days and nights, the wind and waves tossed them." Sálvio's shudder turns into a cough. "The ship was taking in water on every side, and the crew knew they were doomed. Until they begged Saint Telmo for help."

"The patron saint of sailors?"

Sálvio nods. "He appeared at the top of their remaining mast and calmed the seas, then led them safely to shore. Then and there, they vowed to build a church in his honor. They did, and the Brotherhood was created to take care of it. When Captain Duarte saw the fire, he ordered us to do whatever we could to stop the flames from spreading to the church. He's here too, somewhere." He coughs again. "And you? Why are you helping?"

"I … was just here." I don't have a reason that makes nearly as much sense as his.

"In the middle of the night?"

"I got to Porto this afternoon." I don't mention who I came with. "I didn't have anywhere to stay tonight, so …" I trail off and watch the firemen.

A man whose face is coated in soot runs by. He sees us and stops. "You two," he orders. "Come with me. We need help at the house."

Sálvio takes a tired breath and pushes away from the wall. "For Captain Duarte," he mutters, then asks, "Coming?"

I shake my head. "I have someone I need to find."

I have no intention of putting myself in Dona Leonor's way again. And I want to talk to Pedro and Tomás before they leave.

More wagons and pumps have arrived and the firemen seem to be getting things under control. Probably because there's not much left to burn. They aim their hoses at the surrounding buildings, soaking the roofs and dousing the embers. Some people stay to watch. Neighbors perhaps, still worried about their houses. But the sailors are peeling away, going back to their ships.

"Take care of yourself," I say.

"I will." He races after the sooty-faced man.

I haven't had much time to think about what happened with Miguel in the *ilha*. But if Tomás, Pedro, and Cassiano are still in Porto, everyone else from the *Maria das Graças* must be too. I soon see them heading down the river road, Pedro with a bucket hanging from his hand, and run to catch up.

"Where's Senhor Jorge?" I ask.

Tomás shrugs. "He keeps his own company – often of the female kind – when we're in Porto. Got a real gift for picking them, he has."

"Yeah," Pedro scoffs. "The ones that are beautiful after you down a barrel of wine."

My laugh becomes a cough. "I bet they say the same about him.

How'd you get here without the boat?"

"Other *rabelos* saw the fire," Cassiano says. "We came on one of them."

"How did Senhor Jorge act?" I have to ask. "When he came back from Miguel's?"

Pedro grimaces. "Before or after he started cursing you? Oh, I forgot. There was no *before*. What the hell did you do?"

I tell them how Senhor Jorge destroyed Miguel's passport.

Cassiano grimaces. "He'll still have to buy a new oar. No wonder he's fuming."

"He's mad at Henrique too," Pedro points out. "Why?"

"I was there. He had to stick more or less to the truth, I guess."

"That's all?"

"Seems so." I'm not telling them that I used the casks of elderberry juice as a threat. They might not be happy on the *Maria das Graças*, but the work puts bread on their tables. It wouldn't do to have them think I'm jeopardizing their livelihoods.

Slowly, the sky lightens.

"When do you go back to Régua?" I ask.

"We were supposed to leave this morning," Tomás says. "Now I don't know."

I want them gone as soon as possible, but don't say it. I don't think Senhor Jorge would know to come looking for me on the Rua das Flores, and it doesn't sound like his ladies are the kind he'd give jewelry to. It's unlikely we'll cross paths again. But I can't count on it.

I wish them good travels and return to the factory. In front of it, on a ramp sloping down to the water, the volunteers who fought the fire are rinsing off hands and arms and heads. A couple jump in, giving themselves a fully clothed bath. I look down. My trousers are plastered to my legs, as sweaty and grimy as the rest of me. They're singed in at least two places. Damn.

A couple of men move aside, making room for me. I peel off my shirt and clean myself as best I can. The water's chill, along with sheer exhaustion, have me shivering. I slip back into my dirty shirt and comb my hair with my fingers. It's time to retrieve my bag, change my clothes, and make my way to my new life in Rua das Flores.

CHAPTER 6

THE BOTEQUIM WAS dark and filthy, but Jorge didn't care. It was where he always drank and did business. He'd gotten his four small casks off the rabelo without anyone asking questions and the money was safe in his purse. It would cover the pay for his men, but not his gaming losses.

That meant he'd have to keep skulking around like a lowlife whenever Duarte's ship was docked in Ribeira. And now he had the extra cost of the oar. And the threat from that bastard Henrique, who knew more than he should about a cargo Jorge had wanted to keep secret. Tomás and Pedro must've told him. Jorge cursed into his wine. Henrique had humiliated him in front of the entire ilha. He'd pay for that. Jorge just didn't know how yet.

The door of the botequim opened, letting in a cold draft, and a friend Jorge had helped many a time stepped inside. He'd just started working for one of the big wine producers in the Douro. Jorge's black mood lifted. Getting a couple of those favors returned — now, that was a good idea.

CHAPTER 7

I T'S PAST DAWN when I get back to Porto. Shops and offices are already opening their doors. I ask a man in a coat and hat the shortest way to the Rua das Flores. He mutters something I can't make out and hurries on. A farm girl with a wagon full of sleepy chickens points me up a narrow street.

"That way," she says. "At the end, look for the fountain and Araujo's paper shop. On the Largo de São Domingos. Rua das Flores goes uphill from there."

"Obrigado."

She nods and continues on toward Ribeira, her wooden clogs clacking on the paving stones.

At the Largo de São Domingos, I recognize the fountain. It's where I rinsed off my *socos* last night. Before the fire. The familiarity, slight as it is, feels good. I'm already getting my bearings, the first step to making Porto mine. The first step to having it claim me as one of its own. Despite my mussed appearance, I try to stride confidently, as if I already belong.

This morning, the dark green shutters of Goldsmith Bento's shop are folded back, exposing two display windows on either side of the entrance. A pug-nosed boy, maybe ten or eleven years old, is out front, grumbling and sweeping the street where a horse just emptied its gut. When I stop, he eyes me. Haughtily, as if he's saying I don't meet his standards and should move along. I'm tempted to laugh, given that he's the one shoveling shit.

Inside, behind a counter housing a glittering selection of gold necklaces, pendants, and crucifixes, the man I met so briefly in Mesão Frio is wrapping a package for a woman in a deep blue dress. Around her neck are as many gold necklaces as Raphael's mother wears on the *dias da festa,* for special occasions. Along the walls are glass-fronted cases full of intricate earrings and pins and brooches.

Goldsmith Bento ushers the woman outside, carefully steering her away from the smelly pile by the boy's feet, and helps her into a waiting carriage. With a little bow, he hands her the package, then clasps his hands behind his back and waits for the horse and driver to carry her away. As he turns, his eyes fall on me. I see the moment he registers the contrast between my appearance and his fine coat and pressed shirt, shiny shoes, and immaculate fingernails. His thick eyebrows come down and he makes a *be off* gesture.

"Go. There's nothing for you here."

He doesn't recognize me. I step forward, my face reddening. "Goldsmith Bento, it's me. Francisco Henrique. From Mesão Frio."

He examines me from head to toe without a smile.

"Pardon my ..."

He interrupts me before I can say *appearance.*

"I expected you weeks ago. I assumed you decided not to come." His expression tells me he wouldn't have minded in the least.

I stand as straight as I can. "I'm sorry if there was a misunderstanding, sir. I thought it was clear that I couldn't come before the harvest. But I'm here now and ready to work."

"Not like that you aren't."

I'm wearing my new shirt, shoes, and trousers, and my hair is neatly combed. I can tell it's not nearly enough. He's not even going to let me cross the threshold. Behind him, the boy with the broom smirks.

"Did you hear about the fire last night, sir? In Massarelos?" I can't let him change his mind about employing me. "I helped fight it. That's why ..."

Goldsmith Bento silences me with a wave of his hand. "Excuses. They don't make you any more presentable." He inspects me again, then seems to make up his mind. "Hugo, take him to the back so he can clean up," he orders the boy with the broom, then turns again to me. "I'll speak with you after that."

"Thank you, sir." I try not to show my huge relief. Hugo doesn't go through the shop entrance, but instead leads me through a second door in the façade that's painted the same dark green. Inside, a staircase leads to the upper floors. Bypassing it, he follows the narrow hallway to the end. Beyond a second door is a walled-in back yard of scraggly grass and dirt. One corner holds a pile of kindling. In another, sad-looking autumn vegetables poke through the earth. A privy is at the back, as far from the house as possible. Through three big windows in the back wall of the building, I see a hefty, bearded man bent over a table. That must be the goldsmith's workshop.

"Hey. You." Hugo points to a well in the middle of the yard. "Wash there."

There's no point in telling him I already did. I drop my bag on the ground, pull up the bucket, and sniff the water. It doesn't smell fetid.

"You can drink it," Hugo says. So I do.

Then I go to work scrubbing my face and neck and hands. No matter how hard I try, I can't get rid of the black that's ground into the lines of my hands and around my nails. Mesão Frio won't let me go that easily. By the time I'm done, Hugo has long disappeared. I wipe my hands dry on my trousers and rap on one of the big windows. The man inside beckons. I go in through the narrow hallway and introduce myself.

"Vitor Teixeira." He gestures at the delicate metal shapes on his workbench. "*Mestre filigraneiro.*"

So he's the master filigree-maker. The one who makes the pendants and earrings in the displays. I can't wait to see how he does it.

Business first though.

Beyond him is a closed door. "Is that the way to the shop?"

He leans back with a sigh and stretches his arms in front, rotating his wrists. "It is. But you can't go in."

"I need to speak with Goldsmith Bento."

"If you enter the shop looking like that, you'll never get the chance to."

I shake my head, exasperated. I won't be able to buy whatever they consider fitting until I get my first wages – or second or third. But I won't get those unless they let me work.

"Could you tell him I'm ready?" I ask. "Please?"

"He'll come when he has time. You'll have to wait."

He bends over his work again without asking me to sit down. That's fine with me. I leave my bag in an empty spot under one of the tables and circle the workshop, taking everything in. Along the walls hang tools and coils of gold wire of differing thicknesses. There's a big cylinder, mounted horizontally on four legs, with grooves running around it and a hand crank to make it turn. A sturdy, blackened pot sits on a counter beside the fireplace. Inside it is a smaller pot crusted with what looks like melted gold. I hold my hand over it, checking the temperature. It's cold. I run a finger over the gold sheen.

"No touching," Mestre Vitor says.

I jerk my hand away. "Sorry." I approach his workbench.

He waves me to one side impatiently. "You're blocking the light."

With quick movements and no wasted motion, he bends the thinnest wire I've ever seen around a metal plate shaped like a heart. Then he cuts shorter lengths of wire and uses them to make veins that curve, like those of a leaf, inside the heart. He sets it aside and begins another one.

"You're not finishing it?" Tiny filigree curlicues usually fill this kind of heart.

"Women's work." He sniffs as if it's something even a child would know. "The *enchedeiras* do that."

"*Claro.*" I keep the sarcastic remark I want to make inside my head. I can't get on his bad side if we're going to work together.

"You're the new apprentice?" He sounds irritated. I don't know why. "Number three?"

"I'm to work in the shop," I say.

He lifts his head, as if seeing me for the first time. "Are you now?"

"I thought you'd be expecting me."

"A shop assistant? No."

"I don't understand. I thought …"

He shakes his head. "Whatever you do, don't plan on staying long. No one does."

"Why not?"

He purses his lips and leans over his metal heart. When it becomes clear he's not going to answer, I go back to wandering around the workshop, examining the strange machines and tools with my hands jammed into my pockets. Finally I sit on a stool on the other side of Mestre Vitor's workbench and watch him. He sighs again, but doesn't tell me I can't. He's moved on to crucifixes now.

What seems like ages later, Goldsmith Bento opens the door from the shop. I jump up to greet him, but he addresses Mestre Vitor instead.

"I've locked up," he says. "You'll be dining with us today?"

The *filigraneiro* nods, not taking his hands off the crucifix. "I'm almost finished. I'll be up in a moment."

Goldsmith Bento turns to me. "How old are you?"

"I just turned seventeen."

"I thought you were younger." He frowns. "That's far too late to begin as an apprentice."

In my chest, my heart stomps ferociously. "You said you needed someone who can read and write and do figures. I came to be… I thought you needed a shop boy. A clerk."

"I expect everyone who works for me to be educated. You misunderstood. Vitor and I are enough for the shop. What is needed is a good apprentice."

Blood, as loud as the rapids of the Douro, roars in my ears. I can't hear what else he's saying. The job I came to Porto for can't vanish into nothing. I won't let it.

Goldsmith Bento looks me over again. I see him wince. "A certain style – finesse – is required to work at Gomes & Filho. In that, you are clearly lacking."

I stiffen. He's judging me after five minutes? Mestre Vitor's *good luck* makes more sense now. But I have to convince him I should stay. Even as a lowly apprentice. I'll prove my worth – I know I will – and I'll advance. Make good.

In the city, a person can do that. Unlike in Mesão Frio, where I knew what I'd be doing for the rest of my life. Every day the same people, the same gossip, the same limits. Only the seasons changing, then coming back around again. I don't want *same*. I take a deep breath.

"Goldsmith Bento, I've made furniture with my father for years. For fine houses in town, for the …"

"That's not …"

I interrupt him. "I know it's not jewelry-making. But I learned to be precise and patient. To make pieces fit together perfectly. I'm good with my hands. And I learn quickly."

Goldsmith Bento glances around the workshop. I can't tell if he's listening. I follow his gaze, noticing how many unfinished pieces litter the worktables.

"Give me a chance to prove myself, sir. You won't be sorry."

Goldsmith Bento looks at Mestre Vitor, who shakes his head.

"Do you have a younger brother?" Goldsmith Bento asks.

Tiago's thirteen. Closer to the age they want. I take a second to answer.

"No." I'm the one who took the risk to come here and Mother needs a sturdy boy at home. Besides, Tiago never talked about wanting to leave the land.

Goldsmith Bento makes a frustrated sound and flicks something off his coat. "You'll get food and a place to sleep. And clean clothes, which you sorely need. You're not to put one foot in the shop until you're properly dressed. Understood?"

I nod, glad Mother can't hear what he thinks about the new clothes she made me.

"You have one month to show that you can make yourself useful."

A month? I nod again.

"Mestre Vitor, you'll teach him what he needs to know about the machines."

"Absolutely not!" The *filigraneiro* rises up so abruptly that his stool falls over. "I'm too far behind on my orders as it is. I don't have time to teach a boy fresh out of the fields. Especially a know-it-all his age. He won't listen to a word I say."

"I ..." I begin.

They talk over me.

"I'd advise you to make the time," Goldsmith Bento says. "Until we find someone more suitable, he's what we have to work with."

Mestre Vitor rights his stool, glaring at both of us, and storms outside. There, he yanks the bucket's rope and pours water over his hands, scrubbing them angrily as if he's trying to remove an unwelcome stain.

"My wages?" I ask Goldsmith Bento.

"Apprentices don't earn wages."

"But ..."

Mestre Vitor comes in from the yard, banging the door behind him. "I've changed my mind," he tells Goldsmith Bento. "I won't be dining with you." He disappears into the hallway. The front door slams.

"If his filigree wasn't of such high quality ..." Goldsmith Bento turns a stony gaze on me and doesn't finish the sentence. "You'll eat here. I'll have Inês bring food down."

"Thank you, sir." The door to the hallway is still open, letting in odors of cooked fish and onions. My last meal was on the *rabelo*. I'm ravenous.

"We open again when the church bells ring three. Mestre Vitor will show you what you'll be doing then."

"Yes, sir."

He shuts the door of a wooden lockbox, pockets the key, and climbs the stairs to the house above. I'd been right last night – his family does live above the shop. In the silence, I explore the workshop again, this time touching – carefully – whatever I want to. I lift the rounds of gold wire, noting their different weights and thicknesses. Their cool hard brightness is foreign to me. Gently, I pick up one of the hearts Mestre Vitor was working on and lay it on my palm. It's got a delicacy the man himself doesn't. Looking at it, I wonder what drew him into the trade. Maybe he's a firstborn son, given no choice but to follow his father. I count myself lucky to have escaped that.

Light, quick steps sound on the stairs. I lay the golden heart back on the workbench and step away. The girl who enters with a tray is about my age, with dark curly hair, a merry smile, and cheeks that are flushed from the heat of the stove. I don't know what's making her happy but I grin back, glad to see a face that seems welcoming.

"I've brought you dinner," she says. "Clear off a place, will you?"

"Here."

She waits until I move a small saw and hammer out of the way, then sets the tray on a worktable.

"*Obrigado.*"

She gives me another broad smile and runs back up the stairs, leaving me with a bowl of vegetable soup, a piece of bread, and cod cooked with rice and onions. I sit and drain the soup in seconds, then dig into the fish with rice. Goldsmith Bento has a good cook. I don't even try to slow down. No one's here to criticize my manners. I wipe my mouth with the back of my hand and lean back, feeling as lethargic as a snake that's eaten its fill.

After a while, the girl comes back for the tray.

"You're Inês?" I ask.

"I am indeed. And you?"

"Henrique."

"You're going to work here?"

"Looks like it." I pause, then ask, "Do they eat like that every day?"

She eyes me curiously. "Well, on Sundays there's meat."

"Oh. Right." I can't stop another grin from splitting my face. They eat like kings. "In that case, I'll definitely stay."

She's laughing merrily when a woman calls her name. She grabs the tray, says *see you later* and bounds upstairs again, all the energy in the room going with her. I look at the door she disappeared through, hoping she has reasons to come down often.

Thumps, a pot clanging, and voices filter down the stairs from above, but the sounds are muffled. The fire's down to red embers, so I add a log. In the workshop, it's peaceful. They've given me nothing to do and last night was a short one. I sit down on a stool, rest my head on my arms, and close my eyes.

"Boy, stop your snoring." Mestre Vitor cuffs me on the shoulder. I jerk upright.

"I'm ready." I rub my eyes. "Ready to work."

"So I see." He positions himself at his workbench and picks up a small gold bar and a file.

"What can I do?" I might not be the eager young apprentice he wanted, but I'll show him I'm worth teaching. While avoiding doing anything he can criticize me for.

He heaves a sigh – he's a great sigher, this one – to make sure I know I'm bothering him. "Wait until I'm done. Then we'll see."

I sit across from him as before and watch as Mestre Vitor files the bar of gold, making a fine powder. Then he takes a gold heart already filled with tiny curlicues out of a bowl of water and sprinkles the powder over it. The powder fills the holes, hiding the delicate design.

"What are you doing?"

"Trying not to let your presence ruin my concentration."

"I want ..."

"Quiet," he orders. He sounds like he's talking to a child who needs to be slapped down for bad behavior. I almost forget my resolution and snap back at him. Instead, I grip the edges of my stool and swallow until anger is no longer clawing up my throat. I know I'm not exactly what he wants, but I'm willing to work, and free labor to boot. He should be grateful.

Mestre Vitor lights a candle with a twig from the fire. Then, through a metal tube, he blows the flame in the direction of the heart. As he moves it up and down and from side to side, the gold powder melts away and the design reappears. But now the heart is discolored, as if someone buried it in the dirt.

"Why ..." I start to say, then stop. Maybe I'll have to learn more from watching than asking. Like with Father. Too many questions earned us a smack with whatever he was holding at the time. It's the way things were done, but it's not an experience I feel like repeating.

After a few seconds, Mestre Vitor picks up the heart. "When the *enchedeira* is done filling it, nothing holds the design in the frame except pressure. Each wire pushes against the others. I just soldered the heart so it won't fall apart." He places it in a shallow dip on his worktable and taps it with a hammer until the heart takes on the same gentle curve as the wood. He repeats the process with a second heart, making one mirror the other, then solders them into a single piece. He holds it up for inspection. "Now I clean it and it's done."

"May I touch it?"

He hands it to me. It's already cool. I cup it, feeling its solidity and weight, then run my fingers over the design, pressing lightly.

"If you'd done that earlier, all of those spirals would have popped out," he tells me. "Hours of an *enchedeira's* work, gone to waste."

I'm tremendously glad I didn't choose this heart to pick up earlier. I might've ended up paying those *enchedeira* hours myself, out of my non-existent wages. Or, more likely, I'd have been tossed onto the street, butt over heels. This isn't Father's carpentry shop where – except on rare occasions – a piece of wood falling to the floor isn't a tragedy.

Now that Mestre Vitor has started talking, I decide to try again.

"What do you want me to do?" There's nothing worse than idle hands.

"You know absolutely nothing of jewelry-making, do you?" He knows the answer is *no*.

I shake my head anyway.

"Then we'll start at the beginning." With a key from his vest pocket, he opens the lockbox. It's in the corner of the workshop, far away from the fireplace. From it he takes a small chest of polished wood. He unlocks it and lifts the top. His body blocks most of my view but I can see it's filled with gold balls, each one about the size of a ladybug. There are hundreds of them.

"If I ever see you near this chest, you'll have exactly one minute to leave this shop. And you'll never come back."

Mestre Vitor stares me in the eyes, and for a frightened moment I wonder what he's heard. Except for oranges and lemons from the *quinta*, I never took anything in my life. But that's not the story evil tongues in Mesão Frio insist on retelling. I'm glad they're too far away for their tales to reach Porto.

In any case, I understand Mestre Vitor's caution. That chest contains unimaginable wealth. After I nod, he scoops out some of the balls and weighs them on the scale. Thirty grams.

"We melt these to make bars, then stretch the bars into wire with those." He points to the grooved cylinder and to another machine that's mounted with a metal plate containing a line of holes, each one smaller than the next. "Watch now."

He's still talking to me as if to a youngster, but I'm grateful. After his anger earlier, I was afraid he'd brush me aside, then tell Goldsmith Bento I was incapable.

He pours the balls into the pot with the gold sheen, hangs it over the fire, and hands me a wooden stick. "Stir."

"Sim, mestre." At least I can't get this wrong.

He goes back to his workbench and picks up a crucifix. It's hot standing over the fire but I keep stirring, occasionally leaning forward to peer inside. The balls melt slowly at first, then collapse into a gleaming liquid.

I stir it one last time. "I think it's ready."

He checks for himself, then says, "Patience."

A short while later, using tongs, he lifts the pot off the fire and pours the gold into a thin channel cut into a metal block.

"Tell me when it's cool," he says, and goes back to work on the crosses.

I don't let myself grumble, even under my breath. So much depends on changing his first impression of me. "All of the filigree in the shop is yours?"

"Yes," he grunts, and lapses back into silent concentration.

When I tell him the gold bar is at room temperature, he knocks the block against the table to break it out of its mold, then threads it into the grooved cylinder.

"Turn the crank."

I do, and rub my blisters raw again. I try not to flinch. Each time the bar comes out the other side, ready to be wound around and threaded into a narrower groove, it's longer and thinner.

"Keep going," he urges. "Don't break the rhythm."

We keep working as the wire lengthens to one meter, then two, then many more. I feel the strain from the constant bending and turning in my arms and back. Finally the wire passes through the narrowest groove and we're done. It's thin and much longer than I would have imagined. I straighten, stretching my shoulders, and watch him coil the wire into a circle. He hangs it on the wall behind his workbench, unlocks his box again, and pulls out another gold bar.

"Next one," he says.

Now I'm the one sighing. The work is mindless, but I can see why he needs an apprentice. Two people are required for this job. We keep going, doing a second bar, then a third. He's threading the fourth when Inês reappears at the door.

"I'm to take your measurements," she tells me. "Come here. Near the windows."

No one has ever measured me for clothes except for Mother and my sisters. I glance at Mestre Vitor, who's waiting for me to crank the machine. He shrugs and waves me in her direction.

"Of course we can take a break so *monsieur* can get fitted," he says. "Shall we bring in the shoemaker next?"

I stammer an apology, but he's already turned away. I hold out my arms so Inês can wrap a length of string around my chest, waist, and neck. She extends it along my arm, then kneels in front of me to run it up the inside of my leg. I shift my weight, cheeks burning, and look at anything but her. Not at all bothered, she weighs my foot down with her hand.

"Hold still."

Her movements are quick and efficient. If I'm the third apprentice they've had recently, she's had a lot of practice. She's so close that I'm sure I feel the heat of her body. I close my eyes and rein in my imagination. When she leaves, I'm relieved.

Later, with daylight almost gone, Mestre Vitor arranges his worktable neatly and goes to the lockbox. But instead of putting the new pieces in it, he pulls out a cloth bundle.

"What time do we start tomorrow?" I ask.

"On a Sunday? You'll be at Mass and so will I." He pulls the top layer of cloth aside. Below it are pieces of filigree, their frames ready to be filled by the *enchedeiras*. Carefully, he places today's work between other layers. The whole bundle goes into a box with hard sides that's much wider than it is deep. He slides the box into a well-worn leather pouch that he closes with three buckles.

"Oh. *Claro.*" I'd lost track of the days. "I'll see you at Mass then."

"Not unless you plan to be in Gondomar." He secures the lockbox and slides his arms into his coat. "That's where I spend my Sundays."

"You have family there?" I remember Tomás mentioning Gondomar. A town far upstream, well before we got to Porto.

He nods. "My wife and daughter. Both *enchedeiras*." He settles the strap of the pouch across his body. "I'm sure you'll enjoy your time with the Gomes family." His smile seems off balance, and I wonder what's in store for me tomorrow. "See you Monday."

"*Se Deus quiser,*" I say as he goes to take his leave of Goldsmith Bento. God willing. How bad can tomorrow be? Mass, then – I hope – free time to explore the city. And to see how Miguel's doing, if I can find the *ilha* again.

Mestre Vitor leaves the door to the shop ajar. He and Goldsmith Bento look my way but I can't hear if what they're saying is good or bad. I did all that was asked of me today. I go to the privy to relieve myself, shivering. With nightfall, the temperature has dropped. Even the air feels damp.

When I return, Goldsmith Bento is still in the shop. I remember Mestre Vitor's warning and don't go in. He's with customers, a young couple from farther north. The Minho, judging by the girl's dangling earrings and colorful blouse. Goldsmith Bento lays three long necklaces out on black cloth. In the dancing light from the oil lamps on both ends of the counter, the gold shimmers. Between the dark outside and the soft light within, the whole shop glows like the hoard of a dragon from one of Senhor Manuel's stories. In the silent moment before the girl reaches out to caress one of the necklaces, it feels like a place where magic is worked.

Then she says, "That one," in a nasal, whiny voice, and the spell is broken.

I sense movement behind me and turn. Inês is back with another tray whose contents I can smell from across the workshop. Beans and onions, cooked in rice. There's not as much food as at midday, but it's still a feast. Especially for me. I've done no physical work to merit it. She's taken the empty tray away by the time Goldsmith Bento pulls keys out of his pocket, closes the shutters, and locks up the shop.

He enters the workshop holding an oil lamp and what looks like the money box where Father stores his coins. He places it in the lockbox and checks it – twice – to make sure it's secure. Only then does he turn to me.

"You've eaten?"

"Yes. Thank you."

"Good." He pokes the embers in the fireplace, spreading them thin so the fire will go out, and gestures me through the door that leads into the hallway. I pick up my bag and go. He locks that door too.

"We leave for Mass tomorrow morning when the bells ring 10 hours 30." He looks me up and down again, not even trying to hide his displeasure. "You truly have no other clothes?"

"I have another shirt."

"Like the one you're wearing?"

"Yes."

"If it's clean, wear it." He locks and bolts the front door. "I'll ask Inês to bring you something to shine your shoes. Wash up as best you can." He leans toward me and sniffs in the general direction of my head. "Rumpled is one thing. Smelly is another."

I jerk away. "I beg your pardon?"

"Wash your hair." He seems to have no idea he's gone way beyond the bounds of common respect. "You stink of smoke."

I nod, afraid of what I'll say if I speak.

We stop at the bottom of the staircase and I wait to follow him up. He frowns.

"Where do you think you're going?"

"I thought I was to accompany you." We're standing in a drafty hallway full of locked doors. Where does he expect me to go?

He scowls. "Didn't Inês show you your sleeping arrangements?"

"No."

He strides back down the hallway and pulls back a curtain hiding a niche under the staircase. The lamp he's carrying casts light into the dark, narrow space. I see a pallet on the floor with blankets on it. Nothing else.

"You sleep here," he says. "If you hear any disturbance in the shop during the night, you're to bang on the door at the top of the stairs. All right?"

I'm to sleep on the floor and guard the shop? I understand why Inês didn't show me. There's not even a chamber pot.

Goldsmith Bento seems to read my mind. "Unlatch the back door if you need the privy. There's a washing cloth on the bed." With that he's gone, taking the lamp with him.

I grope my way to the pallet and sit down. Even after my eyes adjust, I can see very little in the feeble light that comes through the glass of the back door. The goldsmith promised me food, a bed, and washed clothes. At least the food is good. I stretch out, feeling the slats through the thin straw mattress. My feet hang off the end. More evidence that they expected someone younger. In Mesão Frio, I wasn't locked in and I had my brothers to keep me warm. I was stupid to have imagined a real bed here, maybe even in the house upstairs. I tug off my shoes, pull the blankets over me, and try to sleep.

CHAPTER 8

LAST-MINUTE NEWS: FIRE

At 1 a.m. today, a fire broke out in the crockery factory of Sá Lima & Brother in Massarelos. By the time the towers gave the signal, the fire was raging with such intensity that it was impossible to stop its progress.

The fire started in the part of the factory that served as a depository for firewood, leaving only the walls, and then spread to the house at n.° 110 Rua da Restauração, where widow Lima, the mother of the owners of the factory, lives.

Most of the furniture was saved, albeit with much damage; but that which was in the part of the building reached by the fire was devoured by the flames. [...]

Among the people who first came to the rescue, it is worth mentioning a black man, a sailor on one of the boats anchored in the Douro, who rendered relevant services, working with extraordinary ardor to save the furniture and provide water. On seeing him stressed, full of anxious fatigue, one would have said that he was working to save his own possessions. [...]

According to what we can ascertain at this time, the first fire wagons to arrive at the site were those from the Crystal Palace, coming from the Rua da Restauração side, and from São João Novo (4th station) which came along the coastal road that leads to Foz.

O Comércio do Porto *newspaper*
6 October 1877

CHAPTER 9

I OPEN MY eyes, not sure what awakened me. Perhaps simply the ingrained habit of rising early. Where the curtain enclosing my niche ends, I see gray light. Dawn is near. I stretch, groaning, and get to my feet. The blankets are thicker than I first thought – probably Inês's doing, not the goldsmith's – and my stiff muscles tell me I slept without moving all night. There's no sound from upstairs. Good. Last night I was too exhausted to strip down by the well and wash. Now I wish I had. It was darker then and more private.

I pull my singed trousers back on, take off my nightshirt, and go outside. As far as I can see, no one's peering out an upstairs window. The water in the bucket is shivery cold. I bend over and pour it over my head, gasping and scrubbing, trying to get rid of the remaining stench from the fire.

I pull up another bucket and use it to wash my chest and under my arms. My nether parts are going to have to wait until night falls again. By now there's a puddle around my feet. A vigorous rub with the cloth and I'm finished. Inside, I feel around in my bag until I find my second new shirt and trousers. They're clean and odorless. I dress and run my comb through my hair, then sit on the pallet. I hope all my nights and mornings aren't going to be waiting like this.

Finally, there's movement upstairs. One set of footsteps, then several. A door opening, and voices. Someone coming down.

"Henrique? May I come back?" Inês has stopped – for modesty's sake, I suppose – near the front door.

"Of course." I stand to greet her. On the tray this morning are bread and cheese. And a thick brush.

"For your shoes," she explains.

I smile my thanks, wanting to ask her about herself, but she flits back upstairs before I get a chance. Taking my food, I go outside to eat, then set to work on my shoes. There's not a speck of dirt or mud on them when I'm done, but they'll never shine like Goldsmith Bento's.

When the goldsmith calls me inside, a small crowd is assembled on the threshold. An elegant woman pulling on long gloves is about his age. She's wearing jewelry as fine as anything I saw in the shop. A pale girl who stands a hand taller than Inês is adjusting a hat over her blond hair and complaining about new shoes that pinch. Goldsmith Bento's wife and daughter, I presume. An older woman, her face wrinkled and her hands red and knotted like Mother's, hangs her apron on a peg in the entryway. It seems Goldsmith Bento takes his whole household to Mass together.

I've gone every Sunday, all my life, and don't mind. As little boys, we got to play afterwards, racing and throwing rocks while the adults gossiped. Later, we flirted with the girls. The *quinta* has its own chapel, so Rafael wasn't there. His family only appeared at Christmas and Easter, and even then, he had to stay with his parents. I remember one time – we must've been no more than waist high and weren't friends yet – when he spent the entire morning tugging at his mother's hand, trying to break free so he could play. He never did.

Maybe here in Porto it's different and we all mingle. What better way to have my first taste of society than stepping out with the family of a goldsmith? I move eagerly toward the front door.

"Henrique." Goldsmith Bento stops me before I reach it. "Turn out your pockets."

I'm not sure I hear him correctly. "Pardon?"

"I want to see what's in your pockets. Coat and trousers."

He thinks I've taken something. My face goes hot, and I have to bite my tongue to avoid saying something I'll regret. Very deliberately, I do as I'm told. I've nothing in my money pouch except the few *tostões* I brought from Mesão Frio.

"Open your mouth." Grasping my chin between finger and thumb, he tips my face back and forth, examining every crevice.

I stare stonily over his head towards the open doorway. His daughter gives us a brief glance, then goes on talking to her mother as if what he's doing is nothing out of the ordinary.

Goldsmith Bento releases my chin. "Come along then. We don't want to be late."

No apology. No excuses. Inside, I seethe.

As I step over the threshold, his daughter meets my eyes. I'm the one who looks away. She'll surely treat me as her father does. The goldsmith doesn't even introduce us. I wonder if it's because he thinks my stay with them will be too brief, or because I'm not good enough.

Goldsmith Bento tucks his wife's hand into the crook of his arm. We join the crowd making its way up the Rua das Flores, pausing repeatedly for the family to receive handshakes and *how are you todays*. No wonder Goldsmith Bento was worried they might be late. I watch these people, dressed in their Sunday best, and wonder if they treat their workers the same way he does.

Inês falls into step beside me. I tense, then relax. She didn't witness my humiliation. Nor would she have reason to think her station is above mine.

"Where are we going?" Porto has churches and chapels everywhere.

"Congregados. At the top of this street."

Not far then.

"Where are you from?" I ask her.

"Póvoa de Varzim."

"Where's that?"

"North of here. Along the coast. My father's a fisherman."

"Have you been in Porto for long?"

"This'll be my second winter."

"You came by yourself?"

"So many questions." Inês tosses her head. "We were too many sisters in a too-small house. I miss the laughter. But my father needed boys to fish and I wasn't that." She gives me a twisty smile. "I help by being one less mouth to feed and with the wages I send home every month." The look she shoots me is sly. "Well, *most* of my wages. And I'm learning skills. To keep a big house and to cook. I'm a very good cook."

She's also surprisingly chatty, especially with someone she hardly knows. I'm happy to listen.

"Dona Ilda's teaching me. Mistress Alcina and Lisete already compliment me on my *doce de ovos*." Inês has sparkling brown eyes and a dimple in her cheek when she smiles, which she does often. The names she rattles off are unfamiliar but aren't hard to work out. "Dona Ilda's getting old," she continues. "When she can't work anymore, I'll be ready to take her place."

"She knows you want her to leave?" I ask.

"Don't be silly. I'm talking about *someday*." She laughs merrily, then changes the subject. "Did you sleep well?"

"What do you think?"

She gives me a knowing grimace.

"Where do you stay?" I ask. "Since you aren't sleeping under the stairs?"

She lifts an eyebrow. "With you? Now that wouldn't be appropriate, would it?"

I widen my eyes, more than a little shocked. "I ..."

She laughs again, clearly not as embarrassed as I am. "Dona Ilda and I share a room in the attic. She monitors my behavior as closely as Mistress Alcina does Lisete's." Her lips turn downward. "Sometimes I wonder if she's my mother in disguise. You're lucky you don't have to deal with that."

I'm trying to define *lucky* when she switches the questions back to me. She, a fisherman's daughter, is teasing me about my trip down the Douro – *"surely you weren't afraid of capsizing, with the banks so near?"* – when Dona Ilda shushes us. The church is straight ahead. Inês immediately clasps her hands together and adopts a worshipful expression. She's like a different person altogether. I sober too, following her example. Then, playfully, when Dona Ilda can't see, she crinkles her eyes at me.

Inside, the tall stone walls have kept their chill. I'm glad for my coat. Goldsmith Bento and his family, nodding left and right at fellow churchgoers in silk and ribbons, walk down the center aisle to a pew in front of one of the ornate, gilded chapels near the altar. Dona Ilda, Inês, and I find space toward the back. Inês wiggles her fingers at two girls sitting behind us. With Dona Ilda sitting stiffly beside her, though, she doesn't speak.

The priest appears and I stand, sit, kneel, and recite along with everyone else. *The Lord is my shepherd. I shall not want.* Well, I do want. Especially after the last twenty-four hours. I want respect. Trust. Not to bear the brunt of unfounded suspicion or to be lorded over because I wasn't born of people who have it all. I had enough of that in Mesão Frio. Talking to Inês on the street, I forgot my resentment. Here in the church, where we should all be equal before God but clearly are not, it's back, stronger than ever. Thanks to the goldsmith's behavior this morning, the memory of when Rafael first betrayed me – and the price I paid – has me in its teeth, and it won't let go.

It was years ago, but I can still feel the weight of the ceramic horse in my hands. Still see the way its eyes glistened when I turned it in the light. It was shiny and black, with a red saddle rimmed in gold, and no taller than my nine-year-old foot was long. Half of a matching, rearing pair that Rafael snuck out of his father's library. I didn't know they came from the Far East and were a gift from a distant relative who was a count. I don't think Rafael did either. It wouldn't have mattered. They were our secret treasures, our brave mounts.

The first day we galloped them over and under Rafael's bed, along his shelves, and up his walls. The next day, we took them riding among the vineyards atop his pony. As I slid off near my family's house, happy and exhausted after a day of fighting dragons and flying to mythical lands, he told me to keep mine.

"Then I'll have a horse and so will you," he said.

I was young and didn't think twice, just hugged it tightly. That night I slept with it at the head of our bed, to the great envy of my brothers.

I didn't go back to the *quinta* the next day. I don't remember why. Maybe Father had chores for me. That evening, the *quinta*'s overseer erupted into our house like thunder and sent me stumbling to the bedroom to retrieve the horse. Then, with a grip on my ear that I thought would tear it off, he dragged me to the manor house. Father followed behind, cursing all the way.

In the courtyard, the overseer pushed me to my knees at the foot of the wide staircase that led to the manor's front entrance, where Rafael's father was standing. He called me a no-good, a disgrace to my family. Rafael, the coward, was nowhere to be seen. Twice I opened my mouth to explain. Both times the overseer cuffed my head so hard I couldn't see. Rafael's father shouted that we'd never again play together, and ordered me to stay away from their house. Tears were already blurring my eyes before the overseer started caning me.

Afterwards, Father took me home and beat me again. I limped for weeks. Once, I saw Rafael's nanny on the road and hoped she'd have a message from him, but she turned her head away. Rafael never sent word, or returned to any of our hiding places, or guided his pony past my house. Never once did he stand up for me or try to clear my name.

Later, I learned his father sent him away to a boarding school in Porto, then to university in Coimbra. For years, I only saw him in the distance or in a crowd of people. By then, I avoided him more than he did me. In Mesão Frio, there were always some who wouldn't let the story die. Especially since, to this day, the *quinta* won't spend its coin on anything that comes out of my father's carpentry shop. For that, Father will blame me forever. Nor am I allowed to work the harvest on their lands. I didn't think it could be worse, until Rafael put his hands on my sister.

"Henrique." Inês pokes me with an elbow. "What is it?"

I come back to the present and realize I'm breathing noisily, my hands clenched. Around us, people are kneeling for a prayer. I didn't hear a word the priest said. Dona Ilda frowns at me. I get on my knees and bow my head, praying the ghosts and rumors will stay where I left them.

Finally we rise to leave. Inês trades a few words with friends, but Dona Ilda quickly herds us toward the Rua das Flores. I drag my feet.

"We have to go directly back?" I can't spend Sunday cooped up in that hallway.

Inês senses my dismay. "Dona Ilda lets me go out after Goldsmith Bento's lecture," she whispers. "Maybe he'll allow you out too."

"Lecture? We just spent the morning in church."

I get another of her twisty smiles. "You'll see."

At the house, I head down the hallway toward the back yard – to do nothing, again – as everyone else troops upstairs. Dona Ilda stops me.

"Bring up some wood, will you, Henrique?"

"Yes, ma'am." From the pile near the back door, I gather as many logs into my arms as I can. At the top of the stairs, the door to a dark foyer is cracked open, but I see no one. "Dona Ilda? Hello?"

"In here," she calls. I follow her voice into a large, welcoming kitchen. "Stack it there. She indicates an empty space beside a black iron stove. "And get the fire burning stronger, will you?"

Inês is stirring the contents of two big pots that are already on the stove. She scoots over so I can toss in branches of gorse for kindling. When the embers spark to life, I add logs. The kitchen smells of seared meat and coriander. Inês and Dona Ilda must have made the midday meal before going to Mass. I take my time with the fire, not wanting to leave their company.

When I get to my feet and move toward the door, Dona Ilda says unexpectedly, "You don't need to go." She points at the long table in the middle of the room. "When you're not working, you'll have your meals with me and Inês."

I sit down on the bench and breathe the *thanks* that I neglected to say during Mass. Eating alone is for the sick and bedridden. I run my hand along the table, feeling its history in my fingers. Nicks from knives, hollows where meat is pounded. Edges that tell of generations of people leaning against it, rubbing it smooth with hands and shirts. Across from me, Inês takes down one of the gleaming pots hanging from a hook above the table and starts beating eggs and sugar. Along a wall, dried herbs are suspended from shelves full of preserves. The kitchen is clean and well-cared-for, the domain of women who love what they're doing.

"Have you worked for Senhor Bento a long time?" I ask Dona Ida.

She pours rice into one of the pots, stirs, and covers it. "My mother worked for Senhor Bento's father. Back when Senhor Bento was the *filho* in Gomes & Filho."

"He has no sons?"

Dona Ilda shakes her head. "Just Lisete. It worries him greatly, having no one to take over his trade one day."

"What about Mestre Vitor?" I suggest.

She snorts, but not unkindly. "I'm not saying he wouldn't be interested. But he's not family. He's married. Goldsmith Bento needs to find a son-in-law who is a goldsmith."

"One Lisete will accept," Inês adds.

"Humph." Dona Ilda uncovers the rice pot and stirs it again. "She'll do what's best for the family, I'm sure."

From across the table, Inês throws me a glance that says *no, she won't*. It makes me wonder if the two girls are close. In age, certainly. But if confidences were exchanged, it was probably without the goldsmith's knowledge or consent. It's clear he wouldn't want his daughter mixing with the servants.

Soon, Dona Ilda sends Inês to set the table and call the family into the dining room. I wait in the kitchen while the two women bustle in and out carrying white serving dishes that look too fragile to touch. Soup, then a steaming plate of *arroz a portuguesa*, rice with choriço and chunks of beef, carrots, onions, and cabbage. Its aroma takes me back to one of our rare days of plenty in Mesão Frio. Inês takes in a carafe of dark red wine. I'm starving again and almost sneak a spoonful of the rice while the women are gone. I resist.

When the family finishes, Dona Ilda and Inês bring everything back to the kitchen and carefully wash and put away the fancy dishes. Only when they're done do they set out earthenware plates the color of brick for us. I eat fast, too fast, and then apologize. Mother would be appalled. Dona Inês smiles and takes it as a compliment.

"Why didn't the other apprentices stay?" I ask when we're starting on Inês's egg custard.

"Who told you that?" Dona Ilda shoots Inês a disapproving glance.

"Mestre Vitor."

"Isn't he just the one, to worry you before you even get settled?"

"Well …?" I prompt when it looks like she won't continue. "There were three?" I imagine them marching into the shop, doing an about-face, and trooping right back out. It's not reassuring. Inês looks sideways at me, sideways at Dona Ilda, then ducks her head and concentrates on her food.

"Since January," Dona Ilda says.

"What?" That's even worse. Apprentices should stay for years, not a few months.

"I'm not one to carry tales," Dona Ilda says primly.

"Oh goodness," Inês exclaims impatiently. "It's not a secret. The youngest one kept running away, back to his family. His father brought him back in tears three times, until Goldsmith Bento said that was enough."

That seems reasonable. "And the others?"

"The second refused to study. He said he'd had four years of school and that was enough. He even said no when Goldsmith Bento arranged an hour for him with the tutor who comes for Lisete."

"Ungrateful wretch." Dona Ilda's disapproving look was back. "He was soon out on his ear. Goldsmith Bento likes an educated household."

"So I understand. And the third?"

Dona Ilda lowers her voice. "He stole. From the workshop."

I go still.

"It was quite the scandal."

"We aren't sure of that," Inês says.

"Hugo said he saw him, and Mestre Vitor discovered an earring was missing," Dona Ilda says. "He's not one to accuse someone lightly."

"No, but …" Inês lets her voice trail off.

My humiliation at Goldsmith Bento's hands before Mass makes some sense now. Still, I'm worried. Mother says rumors have wings. All I can hope is that she's wrong, and that those about me won't be strong enough to fly over the Serra do Marão mountains to Porto.

Goldsmith Bento calls us as Inês and Dona Ilda are washing the last of the dishes. We gather with his family in a room whose windows would overlook the Rua das Flores if they didn't have long curtains in front of them. It's dark and formal. A crucifix hangs on the wall above the sofa where Mistress Alcina and Lisete sit. Dona Ilda, Inês, and I settle onto chairs across from them. Goldsmith Bento faces the fireplace, a candle burning on the small round table beside his armchair. He puts on spectacles and flips through a worn, leather-covered Bible that's probably been in his family for generations. We have one like it in Mesão Frio, with weddings and births and deaths written inside the front cover.

"For God will bring every act to judgment, everything which is hidden, whether it is good or evil," Goldsmith Bento reads. He closes the Bible but keeps his hand resting on it as he begins to talk, slowly and monotonously, about duty, honesty, weakness, and obedience. I try to listen but am more conscious of the chair swaying under my weight, its legs in need of tightening, than of the goldsmith's words. We've been sitting all day, and where I am, close to the fire, it's smoky and too warm. Even with the edge of the chair digging into the back of my knees, my eyes droop. I shake myself and breathe out, louder than I mean to. Dona Ilda looks at me warningly.

Across from me, Lisete sits primly, her gaze on her hands in her lap. Whether she's listening or in her own thoughts, I can't tell. Then she tilts her head sideways so her father can't see and rolls her eyes. It's so unexpected that I laugh, then disguise it with a cough, my hand in front of my mouth. Over his spectacles, Goldsmith Bento frowns. Lisete hides a smile.

"My apologies," I say. Maybe the goldsmith's daughter is more spirited than the spoiled girl I took her for. I bet we'd both rather be out walking – or doing anything but this – right now. She's examining her hands again, her thoughts back in a world I can't imagine. I laugh at myself. We won't go out walking together, that's for sure. We haven't even been properly introduced. And I'm most surely not the person Goldsmith Bento is searching for in a son-in-law.

I nod off again, jerking fully awake only when Goldsmith Bento stands and says, "You're free until nightfall, Henrique. If you're not back in time for dinner, you won't get any."

Behind him, Inês gives me a wink. I'm pretty sure she'll feed me.

"Yes, sir." I jump to my feet and make my escape.

CHAPTER 10

L UÍSA HADN'T NOTICED *that her knuckles were bleeding. Now there were red streaks on the bedding. She stopped singing along with the other women and made an irritated sound. Bending over the washboard, she scrubbed the fabric again, then rinsed it in the cold water of the tank.*

The stains gone, she heaved the sheets into her basket – careful to keep her knuckles from grazing them – and examined her hands. They were chapped and red from the soap and the roughness of the fabric. Her nails were ragged but momentarily clean, until she worked the soil again.

She lifted her basket and asked one of the washerwomen, a girl about her age, to help balance it on her head. The others, still scrubbing vigorously, said goodbye and picked up their singing where they'd left off.

Luísa hummed along until she couldn't hear them anymore. The walk through the vineyards was long, but she didn't mind. Especially the leaving home part. Not because her basket was lighter then, the laundry still dry. It was the all-too-brief sensation of getting away that she loved. Washing was a chore like any other, but on days like this, it tasted like freedom. A few precious hours away from her parents' demands and the unending needs of her siblings. A chance to catch up on the chatter with no one looking over her shoulder, scolding her about wasting time. And a chance to think.

It wasn't a surprise that she hadn't seen Rafael. She was secretly glad. Kissing the heir to the quinta *had been heart-stoppingly exciting and as foolish as the day was long. She wished now that she hadn't told Francisco Henrique. She'd wanted to show him she was capable of rising above their lot, as he was, by his move to Porto. That she could attract to herself a life that was more than mere drudgery.*

Her brother saw only a man who couldn't be trusted and the risk of a soiled reputation. He was right. Even she knew that in Mesão Frio, dreams of being allowed to climb the ladder were only illusions. Especially for a woman. If she remained, doing what was expected of her, there was no rung that wouldn't splinter the moment she placed her weight on it.

CHAPTER 11

OUTSIDE, I LIFT my face to the sky and fill my lungs. Free, with an entire city to explore. But first I want to find Miguel. I'm on Senhor Jorge's blacklist because of him and his passport. I want to know it was worth it.

The streets are full of people enjoying – as I am – the sunny autumn afternoon. Unlike me, most are parading their Sunday finery, the women sidestepping animal droppings with lifted skirts, pretending to ignore the muck at their feet. As I cross the busy square with the statue in it – which Inês called Praça Nova, or New Square – hooves sound behind me and a horseman on a prancing mare almost runs me down. For a second, from the back, I think it's Rafael. Then he shortens the reins and digs in his heels. Showing off, the fool. The mare bucks and the horseman almost goes over her head. Rafael would never ride like that. Although even he might be unseated if his horse bolted unexpectedly. I shake off a twinge of guilt. He touched my sister. Across the street, the horseman's friends double over, hooting with laughter.

I find the *ilha* easily and follow squawking chickens into the narrow corridor behind the main house. Two women scrubbing laundry in tubs stare at me, their hands momentarily stilling. I feel like I've entered a space where strangers aren't welcome.

"I'm looking for Ana Maria," I say quickly. "And Miguel."

"They're with Senhor Joaquim." One of the women hooks a thumb over her shoulder. "Sixth house on the right."

Walking along the alley, I pass a cat with torn ears that's perched on a windowsill, its eyes trained on the chickens pecking the ground below. Through the sixth door on the right is a cramped space I could cover in three big strides. It looks like a living area, kitchen corner and bedroom alcove all in one. Inside but out of sight, a man is talking.

I knock on the wall. "Miguel? Hello?"

"Henrique?" The boy comes around the door. He looks pleased to see me, but worried too. "Is something the matter?"

"I wanted to know how you were. That's all."

He gives me a relieved smile as Ana Maria comes to stand beside him. She places her hand on his shoulder.

"It's kind of you to stop by," she says formally.

I shrug. "Not at all. Have you found out how to get a new passport?"

"Not yet," Ana Maria says. "Our father arranged for the first one. I'm not even sure where to go."

"I told you I'll help," the man inside says crossly.

I lean forward to see around the door. The somber man with the pointed mustache who gave me directions as I was leaving the *ilha* the day before yesterday is seated at a small table, tapping the end of his pen as if he's been interrupted while doing something of great importance.

"Good afternoon," I say.

He nods in return, then asks Ana Maria, "Shall we continue?"

"Senhor Joaquim is writing to my father," Miguel explains. "Telling him I can't leave Porto right away." The boy shuffles his feet uncomfortably. I don't blame him for not wanting to transmit the bad news.

"Shouldn't you wait until after you ask? You don't know for sure."

"We only have money for Miguel's passage. It's not enough for a new passport and stamp," Ana Maria says. "He'll have to work to earn that."

"Your father can't send more?" I already know the answer. Father allowed me to take a few of the *tostões* I earned during harvest time, and even that was a sacrifice for the family. Miguel's a mere slip of a lad. But he, like me, is expected to make his own way now that he's left home.

Ana Maria shakes her head. "They already did more than was possible."

Miguel looks up defiantly. "I can do it," he says. "Without asking

74

for anything more."

"Of course you can." Realistic or not, I admire the boy's courage.
"I …"

Senhor Joaquim interrupts us. "I'm expected at the Aguia d'Ouro shortly. If you'd like to continue your conversation outside …?"

"No. Wait." Ana Maria puts out a hand to keep him from rising, then says to me, "We really must finish this letter."

"Of course." I step back from the door, wondering what the Aguia d'Ouro is. For someone who lives in an *ilha*, Senhor Joaquim dresses well. His jacket and vest were once probably as fine as the goldsmith's. Now they look a little worn. And he certainly is self-important, although he's probably only a few years older than I am.

"I'll check on you in a few days," I tell Miguel. He shakes my hand like a man as I leave. I hope his father is proud of him.

The bells of a nearby church ring four o'clock. I have time. From the Rua do Bonjardim, I wander through the city. It goes on and on, too many houses and shops and squares for me to keep track of. At length, I come out on a cliff high above the river. On the other side is the Serra do Pilar, the damaged, circular church I noticed when I first arrived, with the Port wine cellars and *rabelos* below it. To my right, a cobblestone street descends in a straight line to the Douro. Upriver, the majestic metal bridge is at eye level from where I'm standing. It's almost complete, the arch and span missing only a few meters in the middle. I hold up two fingers to cover the gap and imagine it whole.

Today, with no one working, the scene looks frozen. I try to memorize every detail. It's all so much bigger than I am. Not just in size, but because of what it represents. Knowledge. Skill. The ability to build structures that no one has imagined before. The majestic terraces of the Douro were once like that, before powdery mildew and phylloxera and other plagues and crises turned so much of the region into a mortuary of dreams and lives. I shake my shoulders, not liking the direction of my thoughts, and focus again on the bridge. On something that symbolizes the future. Hope.

Finally, I turn and descend the cobblestone street to the river, thankful to be going down rather than up. From the bottom, I walk to Ribeira in no time. *Rabelos* and ships of all sizes are moored along the quays and in the river. There's some traffic across the suspension bridge, but it's the Lord's Day, so probably less than usual. From this distance, I can't see the *Maria das Graças*, Senhor Jorge, or anyone else

I recognize. I hope they're on their way to Régua, or Pinhão, or wherever they're going. Any place that isn't Porto.

Dotted along the quay are barrels and crates of various sizes, waiting to be loaded onto the big sailing ships and steamers. I spot Sálvio on one of the crates, elbows on his knees, gazing at the fast-flowing water. Last I saw, he was running up the hill to Dona Leonor's house. I'm glad to see he survived both the fire and that woman's sharp tongue.

"Afternoon," I say. "You're still here?"

He brings his thoughts back from wherever they were and gives me a nod of recognition. "We sail tomorrow. After we load these" – he thumps the crate he's sitting on – "and the passengers."

"You carry passengers?"

"Always. People and goods."

"To Brazil?" Maybe Miguel …

"Never." He says it so forcefully I'm surprised. "We do the Lisbon-Porto route. Never America."

"But … aren't you from Brazil?" That would explain his accent.

"I am. But I'll never go back."

"Why not?"

He shrugs and doesn't answer. I lean against one of the crates, wondering why I don't feel more awkward asking him. Sálvio's a complete stranger. Maybe it's because his life – and appearance – are so far outside my normal experience that there are no expectations.

"Slavery is allowed in Brazil," he says finally. "I'll never go back to that." He says it so quietly, so calmly, that I'm not sure I catch his meaning.

"You worked as a slave?"

"You don't work as a slave. You are one."

I settle on a crate beside him, waiting for him to go on. When he doesn't, I ask, "Where?"

"On one of the coffee plantations. In São Paulo. Where we collapsed and died and were replaced without a thought, because our lives had no worth." He shakes his shoulders as if he's stretching old scars.

"One day, we decided to fight back. We gathered hoes, shovels, whatever we had on the plantation. We didn't have a chance, but we couldn't live like that anymore." Sálvio keeps his eyes on the river. "It didn't matter, in the end. They found out and came for us. My wife begged me to run. Said they'd kill me. So I did." He wraps his arms around his chest. "Leaving her nearly killed me. I shouldn't have done it."

"She's still in São Paulo?"

He shrugs unhappily. "A man here in Porto writes letters for me. I don't know if she gets them. I can't tell her where I am." For the first time, his voice trembles. "I'm sure they punished her for what I did. And I wasn't there to protect her."

His pain hits too close to home. For both of us. I search for a different subject.

"How did you get to Portugal?"

"I stowed away on a ship. The captain only does European routes now though."

"He knows you were a slave? It doesn't bother him?"

"When I stowed away, he's the one who helped me."

I blink. "What?"

Sálvio nods. "I trust him."

My thoughts veer back to Miguel. "Do you …" I stop, then start over. "Would your captain help another stowaway? Someone who needs to get to Brazil?"

"You're not thinking to go and get rich, are you?" Sálvio sounds almost disappointed in me. "Only a very few, very lucky men do. The rest come back sick. Or poor. Or not at all."

"It's not for me. A boy I know was supposed to travel in a few days. But he, well … He lost his passport."

"He's better off getting a new one."

"That could take ages."

"Brazil's not going anywhere." He locks eyes with me. "I wouldn't encourage anyone to stow away on an ocean-going ship. No one. You shouldn't either."

"You did it."

"Listen to me. Have you ever been on a ship?"

I shake my head.

"On our last trip to Porto, we had high seas. Imagine, if you will, this ship" – he gestures at the *São Pedro* – "covered bow to stern in vomit."

I grimace as he continues.

"Believe me, an ocean voyage is much, much worse. Even passengers who have paid are jammed below deck, where it's dark and dirty and stinks. There are never enough bunks to go around. The floor's always pitching. Everyone eating from the same *tina da comida*. When one gets ill, they all do. Measles. Dysentery. Last year it was yellow fever."

"People still go."

He raises a hand. "I'm warning you. Don't put your boy on a ship without knowing what you're getting him into."

"I'm not. I just want to help him find a way to Brazil."

"Well, that's the wrong way. What I described are conditions for paying passengers. If he stows away, he'll likely die."

I check the sun. It's lowering behind the hills. But I can't leave before hearing the rest of his story. "How did you survive?"

"I barely did." He moves a hand to his stomach. "The food I brought lasted four days. Our voyage took forty-two. It didn't rain, and it was hard to sneak into the area where they kept fresh water. One day, when I so weak I couldn't climb the ladder to hide, the ship's boy found me. Told the captain. I don't know why, but Captain Duarte hates slave owners. Instead of flogging me, he ordered me to work for my passage. Afterwards, I stayed with him on the Lisbon-Porto route." Sálvio pauses, then asks, "How old is your boy?"

"Twelve or so?" I pause, then add, "Remember the other day? When you called Jorge a bully?" I'd been surprised then that Sálvio had the courage to stand up to him. I wasn't anymore. "That's the boy. His passport is gone because Jorge ripped it up." I've decided to drop the *senhor*. The owner of the *rabelo* doesn't deserve the respect.

"Meu Deus." Sálvio whistles softly between his teeth. "He's one I'd never sail with. Your young man was unlucky once. Don't make it twice. Not if you care for him at all."

"He's not ..." I start to say *family*, then realize it doesn't matter. "I just thought it might be a good idea."

"It's not."

In front of us, the masted steamer has become a gently rocking black mass in the gathering dusk.

"Where's the rest of the crew?" I ask.

"Eating. At a *botequim*. Last night on shore, you know."

"Not you?"

"I'd rather eat on board."

He doesn't say more, but I wonder if people stare at the color of his skin – as I first did – when he goes into shops or taverns. Whether he gets along with his crewmates, and if they'd defend him in case of

78

trouble.

Church bells ring, and I realize how late it's getting. I don't want to miss the evening meal.

I stand and hold out my hand. "Until we meet again."

Sálvio shakes it. "God willing."

I walk back to Gomes & Filho slowly. I've got whole new worlds to think about, thanks to Sálvio. It's only when I raise my hand to knock do I realize that I still don't know why he dislikes Jorge so much.

CHAPTER 12

LISETE'S DOOR WAS ajar, but Inês still rapped before entering. In her hands was a pitcher of water Henrique had brought from the well. She put it on the washstand near a blue and white ceramic basin.

"Do you want me to brush your hair tonight?" Lisete usually did, but Inês knew her place and never assumed. The goldsmith's daughter, nine months older than she was, had her moods, and sometimes Inês didn't feel like it either.

"Yes. Thank you."

Inês smiled knowingly. Lisete had gotten her first good look at the new apprentice today. There were things to be said.

"Put on your warm dressing gown then, and sit down." Inês closed the door. Confidences were, after all, confidential.

Obediently, Lisete took a seat at her vanity and folded her hands in her lap. On the table lay the simple gold chain and earrings she had just taken off, a crystal perfume bottle, and a brush and handheld mirror with silver backs. Inês had heard Lisete lament, more times than she could count, that it was the only mirror in the room.

"If vanity is a sin, as Mother says, it surely can't be an important one," she'd sigh as Inês took her own mirror, no bigger than her palm, out of a pocket so Lisete could get a glimpse of the honey-blond hair cascading down her back.

Tonight, Inês brushed with especially long, gentle strokes — not yanking or pulling as Mistress Alcina was wont to do — and waited for Lisete to relax. Then, almost always, she'd talk.

"He's rather old, don't you think, for an apprentice?" Lisete finally said. "I'm surprised Papa agreed to take him."

"After all the bad experiences with younger ones, maybe he thought Henrique *would work out better."*

"Maybe," Lisete said doubtfully. "This morning, Papa treated him exactly the same way he used to do the others."

Inês kept brushing. "What do you think of him?" she asked cautiously. With her sisters she'd have said, without hesitation, that he was just shy of cocky in a way that made her breath quicken, with good strong hands that weren't too roughened by toil. He was clearly uncomfortable in his new position. Maybe she could help him. Inês bit her lips to suppress a smile. It wouldn't do for such thoughts to show on her face. Nor could she say any of this to Lisete. Certainly not before Lisete signaled what attitude she would be taking with him.

"Why should I think anything?" Lisete asked indifferently, but Inês could see the corners of her lips turn upward.

"You do, though." Inês laughed. "Tell me."

Lisete sniffed. "I'm sure he'll be presentable once he's properly dressed. But I won't have him as my husband. Even if he becomes the best goldsmith in Porto."

Inês laughed harder. Partly, she admitted to herself, in relief. "My goodness. Whoever is asking you to?" She gave Lisete's hair a playful tug. "But that doesn't mean it won't change things, having a young man our age in the house."

"For you, maybe. I never see anyone, except Mother's tedious friends. I'm not even free to go to the market alone, as you are." Lisete shifted irritably on her bench. "I don't know how I'll ever meet the man of my dreams. I won't marry just anyone my parents choose!"

"Of course you won't," Inês said soothingly. She wondered what recent and obviously interesting conversations between mother and daughter she had missed overhearing. "Now sit still. I'm not finished." She lifted the hair off Lisete's neck and began brushing it from underneath. "So ... the man of your dreams, eh? You have someone in mind?"

"Perhaps," Lisete said, so quietly Inês hardly heard her.

"Really?" When had this happened? "Who?"

"Nobody, really." Lisete ducked her head, pink staining her cheeks. "Just my imaginings."

With that, she shut her mouth. To Inês's intense frustration, she couldn't get another word out of her.

CHAPTER 13

I N THE MORNING, after breakfast in the kitchen, Goldsmith Bento comes downstairs to open the workshop. The praying and lecturing of yesterday don't seem to have put him in a better mood than before.

"Is there anything you're capable of doing on your own?"

I've worked for him for one day. He knows the answer.

"I'll start the fire."

He nods and begins opening the shop. I arrange thin branches of gorse amidst logs in the fireplace, then fetch embers from the kitchen stove. The fire's crackling and dancing in no time, taking the edge off the day-old chill. Goldsmith Bento goes back and forth, carrying pieces of jewelry from the lockbox into the shop. When he's done, he opens the shutters and unlocks the front door.

Outside, a thin, determined-looking woman with damp patches under her arms is waiting for him. She talks, waving her arms dramatically, as if she's trying to convince him of something. The goldsmith shakes his head glumly. She shakes hers right back. Up and down the street, church bells ring a robust seven-thirty. Her arms keep time with them. I wonder if the drama here always starts so early.

From my spot by the workshop door, I see Mestre Vitor join them. He must've gotten up hours before the sun to get here from Gondomar at this hour. The woman drops her arms and leaves abruptly. The two men step inside.

"… let him go," Goldsmith Bento is telling Mestre Vitor. "It's the fourth time in as many weeks. That boy is utterly irresponsible."

"She says he's sick," Mestre Vitor says.

Goldsmith Bento snorts. "Sick of working, perhaps."

"You of all people should understand."

I back out of the way so they can enter the workshop.

"This has nothing to do with me," Goldsmith Bento says haughtily. "You know I've gone out of my way to help that unfortunate family."

"You're not the only one who's frustrated. I have errands for him too. But people living in hovels like that catch all kinds of illnesses." Mestre Vitor gives himself a small shake, as if dislodging any whiff of sickness that might've jumped from the woman to him. "I'm just saying it might be genuine."

"Hugo's lazy. That's my verdict. I think any doctor would agree," Goldsmith Bento says, and stalks back into the shop.

Mestre Vitor sets his pouch on the worktable with a sigh and looks at me. "We still need an errand boy. Today, that's you."

I bite back the angry words that threaten to spill out and say, as evenly as I can, "Good morning, Mestre Vitor." From shop boy to apprentice, and now they're pushing me even farther down the ladder. Moving my dreams even farther away. There's so much to learn, and I need to show them how quickly I can catch on. How good I can be with my hands. I glance down at them. I have slim, strong fingers. Today, covered with blisters that have barely healed, they seem too big and clumsy for the delicate work of filigree. But messenger boys don't even get the chance to learn a trade. When he's not running errands, Hugo sweeps.

Mestre Vitor is waiting for my reaction.

I take a breath. "I'm here to do whatever you need."

Something changes in his eyes, and I know he's aware of the internal battle I just won.

"Thank you." He opens the pouch and takes out the wooden box. Lifting off layer after layer of protective cloth, he reveals hearts, crosses, flowers, and other shapes. All of their interiors have been filled by the tiny, elegant curlicues of the *enchedeiras*.

I lean closer but keep my hands by my sides. These pieces haven't been soldered yet. I point to a variety of teardrops, circles, and rectangles. "What are those for?"

"I'll show you later." With great care, Mestre Vitor transfers them one by one to the worktable. "The errands won't take all day."

"Good." I say it with more force than I intend.

Mestre Vitor gives me a brief smile. "I need you to …"

Goldsmith Bento interrupts him. "Henrique, you're to deliver this to Monsieur Gustave Eiffel." He holds up an envelope with *G & F* stamped into the red wax that seals it. "Give it to no one but him." He says the name as if he expects me to know who it is.

I take the envelope, noticing Mestre Vitor's resigned expression. I'll figure this out as I go along. "Where will I find Monsieur Eif …?" I stumble over the name.

"Eiffel. His office is in the Commercial Association. If he's not there, ask. He might be at the bridge."

"Bridge? The new one?"

"What other? Just find him. There are only a few weeks before the inauguration ceremony. I need his approval today."

"Yes, sir." I can't help grinning. I'm going to meet someone who's working on the most magnificent structure I've ever seen.

"Off with you now."

"Yes, sir." I pull on my jacket and bolt, not giving him time to demand to see the inside of my pockets or my mouth. I turn around once. Goldsmith Bento is watching me from the doorway.

At least the Commercial Association building is one I don't need to ask directions to. On a Monday morning, there's a stream of men going up and down the two-sided staircase that leads to its main entrance. Inside, the doorman directs me left, down a hallway that skirts a large atrium with a grand, sculpted staircase on the far side. It gives the impression of money and power. Probably exactly what the merchants of Porto want. On the floor above, I find Eiffel's office.

At my knock, a young man opens the door. "Yes?"

"I have an envelope for Monsieur Eiffel." I crane my neck, trying to see if anyone else is in the office.

The clerk holds out his hand. "I'll take it."

"I have to give it to him."

"He's busy."

"I'll wait."

An irritated look passes over the clerk's face. "He doesn't have time…"

"I was told to put it in his hands and wait for an answer. And that it's important." Maybe it's not important for Monsieur Eiffel, but it is for me. This is the first task they've given to me to do on my own. I'm not getting it wrong.

"Qui est-ce?" comes a gruff voice from within the office.

The clerk moves aside so I can see two men. One is standing. The other, seated at a desk, peers at me. His round face makes him look young, but his hair, short beard, and mustache are going gray. In front of him, covering the entire surface of the desk, is a detailed plan of the metal bridge. The words at the top are upside down for me, but I can read them. Dom Fernando Bridge. On a separate, smaller sheet of paper on top of the plan are line after line of calculations.

The clerk answers the man in the same language. I don't understand a word.

The clerk turns back to me. "Monsieur Eiffel wants to know who sent you."

"Gomes & Filho. The goldsmith." I hold up the envelope. Monsieur Eiffel isn't just someone who works on the bridge. He's in charge. And I get to meet him.

Monsieur Eiffel pushes his chair away from the table and stands. As he does, the man beside the desk pulls a watch out of his pocket and turns it to face him.

"Je sais," Monsieur Eiffel tells him. He taps a forefinger on the page with the calculations. *" Émile, regardez ce chiffre. Il y a quelque chose qui cloche."*

Monsieur Eiffel must have pointed out a problem with the calculations because the other man adjusts his spectacles, picks up a pencil, and goes to work.

Inside the envelope I brought are two pieces of paper. Monsieur Eiffel regards one briefly and sets it aside. The other he studies more carefully, frowning. *"Ce n'est pas correct."* He crooks his finger at me. Now that I'm closer, I notice the deep circles under his eyes.

On the paper are drawings of two ovals. In one are three letters – AEG – whose shapes are modified to follow the curve of the oval. In the other is an image of the bridge over the Douro. That's the one he's displeased with. He says something else I don't understand, then draws a vertical line on it.

"Your design only has six pillars," the clerk translates for me.

I approach the desk. He's right – the plan of the bridge shows four pillars on the south side. Goldsmith Bento's oval only has three.

Monsieur Eiffel scribbles *NON!* on the paper, gives it back to me, and turns back to talk to his colleague about the calculations.

"Tell your master to fix his design." The clerk waves me out the door. "Then bring it back. This is not approved."

"I understand." Didn't Goldsmith Bento go see the bridge himself before making the design? No one wants a dissatisfied customer, especially someone with the prestige of Monsieur Eiffel. Reluctantly, I make my way back to the Rua das Flores. I hope the goldsmith isn't the sort to punish the messenger.

He's busy with someone in the shop when I arrive. I sneak into the workshop through the hallway, glad he doesn't see me.

Mestre Vitor looks up. "Well?"

"It's not approved."

He drops the heart he's working on. "What?"

"Look." I show him Monsieur Eiffel's revision. "That can't be too hard to change, can it?"

He shakes his head, his eyes going uneasily to the shop door. "It's a matter of time. And disposition."

"What does that mean?"

"They need to be ready for the inauguration of the bridge. Cufflinks in themselves aren't that difficult, but making the stamp with the design takes hours of work."

"Cufflinks?"

Mestre Vitor pinches the end of his shirt sleeve together with his fingers, and I understand. Monsieur Eiffel ordered fancy buttons, connected by a chain link, that rich men use to decorate their shirt cuffs for special occasions. Like the inauguration of the metal bridge.

"He doesn't always … take things well." Mestre Vitor looks genuinely worried. "And he already started on this. I hope it's not too late." He stands up from his stool. "I should be the one to tell him." He opens the door to the shop and says, "Bento, when you have a moment …"

A few minutes later, the goldsmith appears. His eyes go from me to Mestre Vitor, immediately wary. "What is it?"

"Nothing," Mestre Vitor says quickly. "Almost nothing."

"He didn't like them?" Goldsmith Bento sags against the wall, his face drained of color, as if a mask has dropped. I'm amazed at the transformation.

"On the contrary, Monsieur Eiffel was happy with them." Mestre Vitor doesn't look at me. "Very happy. He just requested one small change."

"If we don't get that order, it'll be a catastrophe."

"We'll get the order. Don't worry. As soon as Henrique takes back your new design." Mestre Vitor shows him Monsieur Eiffel's modification. "You can do this."

The goldsmith doesn't respond.

"You can do this," Mestre Vitor repeats forcefully, holding out the paper.

Finally Goldsmith Bento takes it. "I'll work on it right away. Can you stay in the shop?"

He's talking to Mestre Vitor, not me. Of course. I don't even have my new clothes yet, much less any knowledge of what they're selling.

"I can for a while. While Henrique runs an errand for me. This afternoon I'll need to work too."

"But ... who will watch the shop? We can't close." Goldsmith Bento looks panicky again.

"We'll leave the door open and Henrique can tell us if someone comes in. It'll be fine," Mestre Vitor says reassuringly. "Get your drawing tools and sit down. I'll bring paper." He's talking like a parent to a frightened child.

I have no idea what's going on, except that I'm being sent on another errand. Mestre Vitor holds up a finger – *wait* – and gets the goldsmith settled on a stool. "We'll leave you in peace so you can work," he says, then gestures me into the shop and shuts the door.

"What's ...? Why did he react like that?"

"We'll talk about it later. Right now I need you to go to the Royal Palace."

"Palace?" The king's court is in Lisbon.

"Yes. In Rua do Triunfo. The Carrancas Palace. It's the royal residence in Porto." He sees I still have no idea what he's talking about. Quickly, he sketches a map and writes a name at the top. "Ask for the chief butler." He taps the name and hands me a metal disc with *V. Teixeira, Mestre Filigraneiro* etched onto it. "Show them this. It proves you're there on my behalf. Then come straight back with what he gives you."

"Yes, *Mestre*," I say, and out I go again, feeling a bit like I'm floating. My feet will be touching the ground where the king and queen of Portugal have stood! No one at home will believe this.

I head in the opposite direction this time, along the Rua dos Caldeireiros, a narrow street that winds uphill from the Rua das Flores. Clothes flap on lines one or two stories above my head, drying in a breeze I can't feel at all here on the ground. I pass the door of a *botequim* and get a noseful of fried fish and garlic, then make my way around a knot of men outside a barbershop. The air is smoky, and from every side comes the banging and clanging of metal. The blacksmiths' street is a world away from the delicate tap-tapping of the *filigraneiro's* mallet.

At almost every door, pots and scissors and tools and fishhooks and horseshoes and ladles hang from nails pounded into the frames. In the dark spaces inside, fires burn and the hammers of blacksmiths and coppersmiths rise and fall. Outside several of the doorways, artisans sit on the street giving copper pots and plates decorative bumps and hollows and keeping an eye on their merchandise. They nod as I pass.

At the end of the street, I stop to study Mestre Vitor's drawing. I see an open space – a market, maybe? – and beyond it a long granite building with columns. That must be the Misericordia hospital. The Royal Palace is somewhere behind it, not far at all now. I grin and speed up.

When I find it, though, I'm disappointed. It's only two stories tall – stone on the ground floor and painted the color of rust above – and isn't nearly as grand as I expected. Maybe because the king and queen don't spend much time here. To one side, I find a courtyard with a service entrance. I get there just as a driver pulls up with his horse and wagon. Two servants come outside to help him unload bags of potatoes and baskets of carrots, apples, and more. I wait my turn. One of the servants hefts a bag of potatoes onto his shoulder and heads back inside. The other, much younger, leans against a wheel, flexing his foot as if his ankle hurts, then swings his head over to contemplate the contents of the wagon. He's just picked up a bundle of cabbages when he sees me.

"What do you want?"

"I need to see the chief butler."

"He's busy."

Everyone in this city is busy, it seems. Or they want people to think they are. I remind myself to remain well-mannered and hold up the token. "I have this for him."

The servant turns it over in his fingers as if trying to determine whether it's real.

"The chief butler is expecting it," I say. "This morning." If everybody else can claim busyness, then I can certainly claim urgency.

"Yeah?"

"Yeah."

He looks doubtful. "It's your hide, not mine." He offloads the mass of cabbage into my arms. "You unload, and I'll find the chief butler."

"What?"

But he's already gone, scampering gleefully into the Palace, sore ankle forgotten. With my arms full of cabbage, I follow him into a storeroom full of other provisions.

The older servant eyes me wearily. "Gotten someone else to do his work again, has he?"

I shrug, put the cabbages down where he tells me to, and go back to the wagon. I'm lifting two baskets of eggs packed in straw when the servant reappears. With him is a man wearing a monocle on a chain around his neck.

"Teixeira?" he says loudly.

The servant points him my way.

The chief butler looks scandalized. "What in the name of God are you doing?"

"Unloading."

Judging from his expression, that's a bad answer.

"Take those eggs," he orders the young servant, who jumps to relieve me of the baskets.

The chief butler returns the token and hands me an envelope the color of the butter Mother makes. It's twice as large as the one I took to Monsieur Eiffel and is closed with a wax seal bearing the king's crown and coat of arms. I run my fingers over it, savoring the moment. This is probably the closest I'll ever be to royalty.

"The cross must be delivered well before the royal family arrives, so we can have it blessed." The chief butler does a mental calculation. "I want it by the 26th of October. At the latest. I cannot emphasize this strongly enough."

I nod. "I'll tell him."

"Mestre Vitor knows it must be his best work ever. Queen Maria Pia will wear it when she and the king inaugurate that new bridge. They'll be the first people ever to ride across." He shudders and makes the sign of the cross. "May God preserve them."

I nod again. Making something that's supposed to keep the queen safe is a heavy burden for a filigree maker. No matter how good he is.

"I'll tell him, sir." I bid the chief butler good day and tuck the envelope inside my shirt. I'm tempted to carry it in my hand, the seal turned outward for all to see – *I'm carrying a missive from the Royal Palace* – but I don't. The streets of Porto don't seem dangerous during the daytime, but even I know better than to tempt fate.

Mestre Vitor is manning the shop when I get back. I deliver the envelope and the message. He scans its contents with a relieved smile.

"Now I really have to get to work," he says.

"May I see?"

He turns the drawing toward me. It's an intricate filigree cross as big as my hand, filled with what must be thousands of whirls and curlicues. I whistle softly. Across the top is scrawled the word *Approved*. There's a signature below that, but I can't make it out.

"How can I help?"

Mestre Vitor glances in the direction of the workshop, then at my clothes. "You'll have to stand in the doorway. Tell us as customers arrive, so we can greet them properly. That way Goldsmith Bento and I can both keep working."

"Nothing else?" The euphoria I felt during the errand to the Royal Palace evaporates.

"I don't have time to show you anything."

"I can practice on my own." I don't care if I sound a little desperate. "Make a heart, maybe?"

He huffs impatiently.

"I want to learn. What good am I to you if I'm idle?" Those words – Father's, not mine – are out before I can stop them. He regards me thoughtfully and I immediately regret putting the thought inside his head. "Please?"

"Come with me." He goes into the workshop and tells Goldsmith Bento all is well with the queen's cross. From a drawer below his bench, he takes out one of the heart-shaped metal plates that serve as the pattern, along with pincers and a tiny pair of scissors. He places them on the small table beside the door leading in the shop, then cuts a length of gold wire as long as my forearm.

"Practice with that," he says. "But you still have to keep an eye out for customers."

"I will. Thank you." My voice comes out rough with gratitude, and I clear my throat. He's giving me a chance.

"The bad ones go here." Mestre Vitor plunks a shallow plate beside my tools. "To be melted down and reused."

He goes back to his workbench and sets out the materials he'll need for the cross. I sit too, and examine the tools in front of me. On Saturday, I watched him do this for hours, over and over, effortlessly. Snip, press, bend, twist. From those movements, a perfect heart emerges. How hard can it be?

I soon find out. I try to mimic what I saw him do and end up with something that isn't a heart or anything even vaguely recognizable. I poke and prod, trying to fix it. Now it looks like something a dog chewed. I set it on the plate and snip another length of wire.

By the end of the afternoon, Goldsmith Bento has cursed his way through two attempts to redraw the design for the cufflinks. He finally sighs and sits up, holding one he's satisfied with. I, on the other hand, am humbled. My efforts are beginning to look heart-shaped, but there's not a single one Mestre Vitor – or I – would want to keep. I grit my teeth, ask for more wire, and try again. The workshop is getting dark when he tells me to stop. He stands up and stretches, then sifts through my pile of rejects.

"Not as easy as you thought, eh?"

I think he's mocking me. "I. Will. Master. This."

He gives my shoulder a squeeze. "A *filigraneiro* isn't made in a day."

"It's just that I thought ..." I trail off. I don't know what I thought. That it would come more easily? That I'd show more skill? I have only to look at the pile of mangled wire to see I was fooling myself.

He grins shrewdly. "Remind me tomorrow to show you a better technique," he says, and I realize my fiasco today was a lesson. I nod, doing my best to accept it with good grace. He's promised me a lesson tomorrow. I can't ask for more.

"I will," I say, and rise to look at the queen's cross. The outline in gold wire is already there, the vertical axis longer than the horizontal, all four ends flaring gracefully. The drawing he's working from shows a flower shape where the body of Christ usually hangs, circle after circle of filigree petals surrounding a gold center that's fitted with a large red jewel. Maybe they don't want the queen to be wearing a symbol of pain and sacrifice when she'll be high in the air on that narrow train track.

I lie on my pallet that night, thinking. I started the morning bemoaning my lot for being relegated to errand boy. How mistaken I was. I met the man building the Douro bridge and got a glimpse into the Royal Palace. Now I'm to learn the art of filigree from someone whose skill is recognized by the queen herself. Tonight the world doesn't seem so dark.

CHAPTER 14

"*C*APTAIN, LOOK." THE São Pedro's *first mate, recently arrived from Brazil, leaned against the ship's rail, a telescope to his eye. He extended it to Captain Duarte, completely ignoring Sálvio between them. "Whales."*

Duarte pushed the scope away. As long as the beasts weren't close enough to damage his ship, he didn't care. He did care, however, about the lump at the first mate's waistline that the man's short coat failed to hide. He frowned.

"You're not carrying a weapon, are you?"

The first mate's hand went protectively to the bulge. "Always do. Helps keep the crew in line, I've found."

Duarte's lips thinned. What kind of captain had this fellow been working for? "Guns on this ship are locked away. All of them."

The first mate opened his mouth as if to argue, then saw Duarte's unyielding glare and changed his mind. "Aye, Captain. I'll take care of it." He stepped away from the railing.

"Give it to Sálvio."

"What?" The first mate shook his head vehemently. "I'll take it to my quarters."

"Give the pistol to Sálvio. He'll lock it in the weapons cabinet."

The first mate halted, his face a map of unease. "A slave has access to your weapons?" he blurted out.

Duarte's gaze turned even colder. The first mate would never know he'd had a son who might've been much like Sálvio if he'd lived to adulthood. Nor, for that matter, did Sálvio.

"You question my orders?" He kept his voice quiet enough so the crew couldn't *hear, but the menace was crystal clear.*

The first mate flinched and plowed on anyway.

He was a fool.

"No, sir. I was thinking of our safety, sir. Since ..."

"You're not in Brazil anymore," Duarte grated. "You will treat every member of this crew with respect, or you won't be with us long. Is that understood?" They were only hours out from Porto, with Lisbon still days away. How had this fellow come so highly recommended?

"Aye, Captain." The first mate's tone was deference itself. But the eyes he slit at Sálvio as he handed over his pistol were anything but kind.

CHAPTER 15

HUGO IS BACK in the morning, looking sulky and sneezing but otherwise none the worse for wear. Goldsmith Bento orders him to sweep the shop and then carefully folds his new design for Monsieur Eiffel's cufflinks into an envelope.

"Don't come back without his approval," Goldsmith Bento tells me. He could be joking – I've no control over what the bridge-builder likes – but it doesn't sound like it. He's as worried as he was yesterday. Maybe more so. He paces the room as I set aside the heart I'm making and run to get my jacket.

Broom in hand, Hugo glowers at me. I wonder if he's being punished or if the goldsmith thinks I'm more dependable. Not that it matters. This is an errand I'm more than happy to run.

At the Commercial Association, Monsieur Eiffel's office is closed and locked. I ask the doorman, but he says he hasn't seen him today. Back outside, I hesitate. I still don't know why Goldsmith Bento reacted the way he did yesterday, but I do know he'll worry when I don't return straight away. There's nothing I can do to change that. I turn toward Ribeira, my steps light. I'm outside in the unusually warm autumn sunshine and not at all displeased at the prospect of seeing the metal bridge up close. If Monsieur Eiffel isn't there, I'll keep searching until I find him.

Down by the quay, Sálvio's ship is gone and another is tied in its place. A breeze comes upriver from the ocean, freshening the air and momentarily sweeping away the reek of waste and rotting fish. I inhale with pleasure. Everywhere I look, wagons and carts crisscross Praça da

Ribeira, their wheels crunching the grit underfoot. Some stop in front of the ships to load or unload cargo. From the back of others, parked on the square, women from the country hawk fruits and vegetables. Fish are in baskets on the ground, their silvery forms still twitching.

"Fresh fresh fresh!" the fishwives holler. "Get them now!"

I navigate through them, enjoying the bustle. It's then that I see him. On the far side of the square, leaving an office. Rafael. This time I know I'm not mistaken. The false friend who thinks he has the right to my sister is in Porto. Anger balloons, filling my chest. The rock I threw didn't do nearly enough damage. I want to jump on him. Pummel him. But he's with two other men on a crowded square. I'm here to start a new life that the *quinta* is no part of. I turn away abruptly, as I have for years, and my feet tangle in a basket. Fish spill in every direction.

"Ay la! Got no eyes in your head, boy?" the fishwife scolds.

I crouch down to help her gather them, my back to Rafael. That she wasn't selling eggs is a small mercy. When I straighten again, he's gone. In Mesão Frio, I spent years going out of my way to avoid him and his family. Here, I won't do that. Porto will be mine, not his. I take the path along the river toward the new bridge, scowling. Next time – if there is a next time – I won't be the one turning away.

I pass the bottom of the steep cobblestone street I descended yesterday. Women in black are laboring up it, bent double under immense bundles of spiky gorse – the stuff I've been using as kindling to start the goldsmith's fires – that's being offloaded from skiffs in the river. The prickly branches, tied together with rope, are bigger than the women are and probably about as heavy. They climb in zigzags, the slope too steep for them to go straight up.

I don't need to close my eyes to feel the burning muscles in their legs, the lungs that strain for air. It's not unlike carrying grapes up and down the mountains during the harvest. But these – my eyes follow the street all the way to the top – these are all women. Halfway up the incline, one slips, falls. Others, still laboring under their burdens, make their way to her, gathering around until she's hidden from view. I send up a quick prayer for her good health and continue on.

The metal bridge is a kilometer from Ribeira, if not more. But as I approach on the path that runs between the river and a tall cliff, I see more and more people. All traffic on the water is stopped and the valley echoes with hammering. High in the air, workmen are attaching long metal girders to the ends of the unfinished arch. The two sections of the arch are almost touching now, held apart only by cables that are fastened to the span above.

Back at Gomes & Filho, the goldsmith is probably pacing in circles, awaiting my return. I push through the crowd to get closer, telling myself I have to, for my errand.

"What a marvelous feat of engineering!" a man near me exclaims.

I don't know what *engineering* means, but a feat it is indeed. I follow its curves with my eyes, feeling almost weightless. As if I could soar with it.

A loud whistle sounds. Everyone falls silent and looks upward. Standing on the span, not far from the place where there's still a gap, are five men. One has his arms above his head, making a 'V'. He brings them down and together in front of his chest. For a moment, nothing happens. Then the cables holding the sides of the arch are loosened and the whole bridge groans. Ever so slowly, the two segments come together with a screech of metal. The man who gave the signal advances to the joint, workmen scramble to the center of the arch, and they yell back and forth. I can't make out what they're saying.

The man on the span makes a 'V' with his arms again. The whistle sounds a second time. There's a whine of engines and the cables tighten, pulling the two sides of the arch apart. From around me come murmurs of disappointment.

The five men make their way off the span, then descend a staircase cut into the cliff. As they get closer, I recognize Monsieur Eiffel. The tension I didn't know I was feeling leaves my body. I found him. Getting to him is another matter. They reach the ground and I lose sight of him in the crowd. I push forward, urgently. With so many people around, I could miss him altogether if he leaves.

Then I see the men again, entering a low building that stands alone between the cliff and the pillar. An office, perhaps. The door shuts. The onlookers who haven't drifted off follow them. So do I. As we stop in front of the building, the chatter intensifies.

"Something went wrong."

"They should've hired my cousin. He's the best builder in Porto."

"A Frenchman's in charge. You'd think he'd get it right."

"If God wanted us to go that high, he'd have given us wings." A tiny, wrinkled woman makes the sign of the cross. "It's unnatural."

Impatient, I blow out a breath. These people might have time to gossip, but I'm here for a reason. I push to the front of the crowd and stride to the door, feeling a hundred pairs of eyes on my back.

I rap twice. The crowd waits silently, hoping for information. Or for my humiliation. No one answers. I try again. This time, the door practically flies open under my hand.

"What do you want?" The face isn't one I've seen before.

Before I can say anything, a man behind me yells, "What's wrong with the bridge?"

The man in the doorway waves the question away. "Nothing's wrong. Go about your business."

"When are you …?" The clamor of voices resumes as the man starts to close the door.

"Wait." I lean forward. "I need to see Monsieur Eiffel."

"Not today you don't." The man slams the door shut.

I reel back, barely avoiding a smashed nose. My face goes hot. I turn and slink back into the crowd, avoiding everyone's eyes. I don't want to see them smirking at my embarrassment. There are still dozens of people milling around, staring up at the bridge and talking about what should have been done. Bit by bit the numbers dwindle. I don't dare leave. I can't imagine Goldsmith Bento's reaction if I tell him I found Monsieur Eiffel but didn't get an answer. I'll stay here until he comes out, that's all.

I follow the path a short way upstream to see the bridge from a different angle, always keeping the building in sight. After a while, I return and knock again. The man's *no* is even more annoyed this time.

Along the riverbank, I find a patch of grass and lie down almost directly underneath the bridge. It arches above me, grander than any church. Clouds drift behind it, giving the impression that it's moving.

Falling.

On me.

I look away, then back, repeating the strange sensation. Even here, looking straight at it, I can't comprehend how massive it is. How heavy. How can they know that the ground is solid enough to hold it, and that the weight of the train won't make it collapse? That the wind won't blow it over? They must, or they wouldn't let the king and queen cross it.

I hear what sounds like a door and sit up, afraid to miss Monsieur Eiffel, but there's no movement around the office. I lie down again, my stomach hollowing out below my ribs. If I'd known the errand would take so long, I'd have asked Inês for bread and cheese. There's not even a *botequim* where I can eat while keeping an eye on the office. I watch the bridge, falling endlessly, and try to think about something else. Inês. If I could offer that merry girl a trip across this high bridge, would she dare? Would she love the thrill? I bet her answer would be *yes*.

Time passes, and still, no one leaves the office. I try to count how many X's are made by crossed girders on the bridge, but there are too many. I doze off, waking with a fearful start. The sun has moved west and the breeze is cold. I wish I had something warmer than my jacket.

Suddenly, there's movement. A gathering of people along the top of the cliff, the crowd massing on the ground. I join them, watching as workers scramble again toward the center of the arch. The group of men I saw earlier make their way from the office to the stairs.

"This time it'll work," a woman tells a small boy whose hand she's holding.

A tall man looks down at her. "How on earth would you know?"

"My sister's husband is up there." She points at the men high on the arch. "He said the pieces didn't fit right the first time."

"Didn't fit? Why not?"

"He said heat made the metal swell. It had to cool down."

"Metal swelling? That's crazy talk, woman."

She shrugs. "That's what he said."

Far above, the five men walk onto the span again. On the ground, we're still. There's another whistle. One of the men makes the 'V' and brings his hands together. As before, the machinery grinds into motion, loosening the cables. There's a tremor under my feet, as if the earth is shifting as the bridge does. I hold my breath. Slowly, the sides of the arch inch toward each other, then clang together. No one moves. We're waiting to see if all is right this time.

On the arch, workers climb to the center and examine the joint. Again, there's yelling back and forth between the span and the arch. The man on the span raises an arm, and everyone around me breathes *oh, no*. But this time, it's a fist raised in victory. The sound of hammers on metal fills the air. I cheer with everyone else as the men on the span shake hands and clap each other on the back.

"You were right." The skeptical man still can't believe it.

"Always," responds the woman with the boy, smugly.

"What a glorious day," someone else sighs.

"Work o' the devil," says the tiny, wrinkled woman.

The smiling, excited people pay her no attention.

The five men descend the cliff again. Surely now I can get Monsieur Eiffel's attention. I go to meet them, but the same man blocks my way.

"I need to see Monsieur Eiffel."

"Now's not the time."

"When is the time then?" My frustration threatens to explode. "I've been waiting all day."

"Maybe tomorrow."

"That's not …" The group has almost reached the office. I break off to yell, "Monsieur Eiffel! Monsieur Eiffel!" But he's talking and doesn't hear me. Once again, the door closes.

"Damn." I pull the envelope out of my shirt. "He asked for this. He wants it."

The guard is unperturbed. "He asked for no interruptions. You'd do well to respect his wishes."

He waits until I walk away. Insisting will only aggravate him, and probably Monsieur Eiffel too. But I can't give up now.

Little by little, as darkness approaches, the activity on the bridge slows and the workers climb down. There's coming and going from the office, but Monsieur Eiffel doesn't appear. Inside, they've lit oil lamps. Every time I approach, the guard waves me away. I bounce on my toes to keep warm, hands in my armpits. I'm going to starve to death.

It seems an eternity later when the light in the office shifts, as if lamps are being blown out. A line of men files out the door and moves away in a clump, still talking.

"Monsieur Eiffel," I yell desperately. "I have the design from Gomes & Filho." I realize too late that he probably doesn't understand what I'm saying. "Monsieur Eiffel. Gomes & Filho." I wave the envelope frantically, praying he'll recognize the name.

He looks my way, then leans toward the clerk I met yesterday. They break away from the group and approach, the clerk holding up a lamp so they can see my face. This time, the guard doesn't interfere.

"Sir, I have your design." I give him the envelope. "I've been waiting all day to give it to you."

"As you can see, he's been busy," the clerk says as Monsieur Eiffel examines the new drawings. I hear it as a reproach.

"Of course. Please give him my congratulations. "The bridge is …"

What word is big enough? "Magnificent." Who am I to praise him? But saying it can't hurt.

The clerk nods. "I will."

"J'ai compris." With a tired smile, Monsieur Eiffel looks up from the drawing. I think he's seeing me for the first time. *"Merci."*

"He says thank you," the clerk translates.

"De nada." I mean it with all my heart.

Monsieur Eiffel pulls a pencil from a pocket, writes something, then signs it. The tip of the pencil goes through the paper, making a little hole.

"It's approved," the clerk says.

"Thank you. Thank you so much," I say as I tuck the envelope back into my shirt. I'm shaking with cold, hunger, and relief.

Monsieur Eiffel nods. He and the clerk rejoin the men waiting for them and I head back into Porto.

CHAPTER 16

I

T'S WELL AFTER dark. The path along the river is quiet enough now that all I hear, here and there, is water splashing down from somewhere high on the cliff. Even Ribeira is almost deserted. Most people are home, finishing their evening meal. I'm certain I missed mine. How strict is the goldsmith's curfew?

As I walk along below the old city wall, the smell of sizzling meat fills my nostrils. I check my money pouch. My *tostões* from the harvest are still there. I'd rather not spend them, but my stomach is yowling like a famished wolf. I'm not taking the chance I won't eat today. At this point, a few minutes more won't matter.

Voices come from above my head. There must be *botequins* up there, along the Rua de Cima do Muro, the narrow street that runs atop the wall. I find stairs and climb them, each step giving me a better view of the entire length of the quay. At the first establishment that has noise and light spilling from it, I stop. It's a tavern, raucous and dirty. The men in it are smoking and hollering across the room at each other. Locals and sailors, most likely. They give me a look-over and go back to their bellowing. Inside, there's no wind and one table free. I sink onto the bench thankfully, rubbing my hands to warm them.

Tonight they're serving beef with potatoes. I ask for wine and bread, right away. The girl plonks *broa* and an earthenware mug on top of a reddish-brown stain in the middle of the table. I decide I don't want to know what it is. The bread is hard enough to break a grinder tooth. I practically inhale it anyway, then force myself to make the wine last. The beef comes out leathery and crispy around the edges, and it's more potatoes than meat, but it's been cooked with garlic and oil and smells like heaven. I shovel it in. The animal in my stomach grumbles happily.

I'm giving a coin to the girl when the ruckus begins outside. More yelling, but this time in anger. Or fear.

"Back off!"

The others hear it too. The tavern empties as they crowd through the door. Whatever it is, I'm not interested. But I have to get through the pack to leave. I tread hard on a few feet, opening a path.

"What's happening?" one of the men still inside the tavern yells.

"One of those dandies, looks like," someone calls from outside.

"In this part of town? Alone?"

"At night?"

With a final shove of shoulders and elbows, I'm outside. Clouds cover the moon. On the street that runs atop the wall, maybe fifty meters away, I make out three figures. They struggle, then one breaks free and runs. The others lunge and get hold of the back of his coat. The running man twists. One of the others punches him in the head, and he drops to his knees. The men from the tavern watch silently.

"It's not a fair fight," I blurt out.

"Not our business," says the fellow beside me.

"Maybe he had it coming to him," offers another.

Neither of them takes their eyes off the fight.

It's even less my business than theirs, and I don't dare risk the precious cargo under my shirt. The man in the coat gets to his feet, one hand against the waist-high wall that protects the street from the long drop to the quay. The other two promptly lift him up and drape him over it. Below his head, there's nothing but air. His hands scrabble against the stones, seeking a grip. The attackers are pushing his head down, raising his legs skyward.

They're going to throw him over the wall.

"For God's sake!" I'm disgusted with the men from the tavern, with the attackers, and with myself for not leaving well enough alone. With a yell, I run at them. The attackers swing to face me, but it's too late. I barrel into one, knocking him hard into the other. They both go down, cursing. I jump away, beyond their reach.

"Filthy dogs!" I yell. "Get out of here!"

From the corner of my eye, I see the man with the coat find his feet and push away from the wall. Half-crouching, he backs toward me until we're almost side by side. Behind us, pressing closer, I sense the dark mass of men from the tavern. The attackers must see them too.

"Son of a bitch!" They turn and run, still cursing.

I rub the shoulder that took the brunt of my rash action and watch them go. I'm putting off looking at the man in the coat. As soon as he scraped himself off that wall, I knew who it was.

Rafael.

If I'd known, would I have come to his aid? Standing there, flexing my shoulder and avoiding his gaze, I can honestly say I don't know.

"Henrique."

Much as I'd like to, I can't walk away. I close my eyes, then open them to face him. He's dusting off his trousers and adjusting his coat. Then, gingerly, he probes his temple with his fingers.

"Obrigado."

Now that the excitement is over, the men from the tavern file back inside. We're alone.

"It's nothing." Angry as I am, I won't provoke him into a second fight. Not tonight.

"They wanted my purse. For some reason they took offense when I told them to get screwed. Can you imagine?"

He's recovered enough to joke about it. That means my assistance is no longer needed.

"If you're all right, I'll take my leave," I say stiffly. "Good night."

"Wait." He puts out a hand. I step out of reach.

"What is it?"

"We need to talk."

"You haven't needed to talk to me for years. And when you should have spoken up, you didn't." The accusation draws from a well of bitterness I sometimes thought would drown me. "I need to go." I spin away from him, trying to turn my mind to the reception I'll get at Gomes & Filho. Hoping it'll be a good one, given the news I bring. Through my shirt, I touch the envelope. A little crumpled, maybe, but intact.

"I'll come with you," Rafael says.

"No." I'm already moving away, careful to go in the opposite direction his attackers did.

He keeps pace beside me. "You're talking about the horse, aren't you?"

For a frozen second, I think he found out about the rock I threw.

Then I realize. Of course he means the ceramic horse. I trudge on, not looking at him. If he doesn't leave me alone, I might change my mind about that second fight.

"I told the truth," he says. "I swear I did."

"You told them I took it home. That was your truth."

"I got a beating too. For taking them out of the library in the first place. It just wasn't as public as yours."

"So you think I deserved one too? That's why you didn't stop them?" He doesn't know I got whipped twice, by the overseer and then by Father. It doesn't matter.

"Come on, Henrique. I was nine. Do you think they listened to me?" He laughs without mirth. "They locked me in my room for two days, then shipped me off to a boarding school here in Porto."

"Your reputation wasn't ruined." I feel like a dog that wants to bare its teeth and snarl. "Everyone thought me untrustworthy. Some still do. Even now, your father hasn't relented enough to let me work the harvest at the *quinta*." The shame was etched into every bone and muscle in my body. I'd hoped to escape it by coming to Porto. I hadn't.

"That's what you believe?" He looks thoughtful. "I thought you were avoiding us. Me. You always went the other way."

"I'm sure." At least I was, at the beginning. I haven't tried to work their harvest in years, but instead went directly to other *quintas*. "You're a grown man. Your father will surely listen to you now."

He grimaces. "I'd rather not bring it up. Especially since he's probably forgotten all about it. What purpose would it serve?"

"For one thing, he might start buying from our carpentry shop again," I snap. Father's blamed me for that for eight years. "My family needs the income. Unlike yours."

"Whoa there. The *quintas* are going through hard times too."

We've reached the Largo de São Domingos. I stop by the fountain. He and whatever he's brought from my past are already too close to my new home.

"Forget it," I say. "It's better if our families stay far apart. Especially you and Luísa."

Even in the dark, I see his gaze turn wary. "She told you?"

"You preyed on my innocent sister." I knot my hands into fists. "What are you going to do about it?"

"About what? It was just a few kisses."

"Kisses that could ruin her." I'm almost shouting.

He frowns. "I told no one. If she's telling people, then whatever happens is her own fault."

As a man, I get that. But his harsh words are for my little sister. I bristle.

"I wouldn't spread it about. You know me, Henrique."

"I do *not* know you. Not anymore."

"I promise you I did not dishonor your sister."

His story and Luísa's were almost the same. It was small comfort. His kisses had Luísa's cheeks flaming and her hands twisting in her apron. Rafael knew better and had still taken advantage of her. Until I talk to her, I'll have no idea whether rumors about them are flying or not.

"Do you believe me?" he asks.

"A kiss from you is dishonor enough."

For a second, he looks shocked. Then he grins. "Come on, Henrique. I'm sure you've kissed a girl without ruining her."

"Not a girl. My sister." He doesn't know how close I am to slugging him. "I have to go."

"Wait," he says. "Tomorrow evening. I'll still be in town. I'll take you for a drink."

"No."

"To thank you for getting me out of the hands of those ruffians. I insist."

"You owe me nothing." I don't want his company.

"I insist," he repeats.

I shake my head. "I wish you luck with your business in Porto." I distance myself with the formality of my words. "And I bid you good night."

I nod but don't extend my hand, then head up the Rua das Flores. This time, he doesn't follow me.

Gomes & Filho is closed and dark, as I knew it would be. I lift the knocker and let it fall. No one comes to let me in. Goldsmith Bento surely isn't serious about leaving me on the street if I return later than he wants. Especially not tonight, when I bear important news.

I bring the knocker down again. Still no answer. It's too early for them to be in bed. Backing away, I see a dim light between slats of the shutters upstairs. This time, I bang the door so loudly that it echoes around the street.

A window across the way opens.

"Off with you, boy," barks a man's voice. "This is no time to be disturbing decent folk."

I growl at him, then turn back to the door. I am decent folk, and I need to get inside.

Bang, bang.

More shutters are thrown back, but not the ones I want. At this point, I don't give a damn if I make a scene. I am not spending the night outside.

Bang, bang, bang.

From the window above me, Dona Ilda hisses, "Henrique, have you gone crazy? You know the rules."

"And they are *stupid!*" I yell at her. "Especially after I spent the entire day waiting for the answer Goldsmith Bento asked for. Now you're telling me he doesn't want it?"

"Shhh." Dona Ilda takes in the neighbors' open windows and cringes. "Calm down. Please. Just wait a minute."

"Fine."

"No more banging?"

I step away from the door, plant my hands on my hips, and glare up at her.

"I'll be right back." Her head disappears.

I turn in a full circle, glowering at every window on the street that has a head sticking out of it. With calm restored, some shut. Not all.

From inside the house, a lock turns and a bolt slides. Then Inês is in the doorway, pulling me into the hallway.

"My, don't you make a right fuss." Her smile is brief and worried. I'm in no mood to return it.

"He's got no business making an example of me. I was doing his bidding."

"You've got to understand," she whispers, leading me upstairs. "He's not well. When you didn't come back, he ... He's been locked in his bedroom for hours. Mistress Alcina is beside herself. She and Lisete have been taking turns sitting outside his door."

I frown. This is not normal behavior. "Where's Mestre Vitor?"

"He stayed on a while after closing the shop, then left. He was pretty upset too."

What in the world did they think I'd done? Stolen the plans and run away?

"Why didn't they come looking for me? They knew I'd be where

Monsieur Eiffel was."

"They sent Hugo. He said he couldn't find you."

"Then he didn't look very hard." Useless child. I'm not taking the blame for whatever state Goldsmith Bento has gotten himself into. But I can't let it cost me this job. "Monsieur Eiffel was at the metal bridge all day. I waited for hours until I could see him." I'm so angry I'm tearing the heads off my words. "If Hugo had come there, he would have found me."

Inês leads me through the entry hall into the sitting room. Mistress Alcina is there, brushing away Dona Ilda's attempts to comfort her. She regards me with such rage that for a moment I think she's going to slap me.

"Where have you been?" she shrills. "Do you realize what you've done?" She inhales, about to say more. I cut her off.

"I did exactly what he ordered me to. He told me I wasn't to return until I had Monsieur Eiffel's response. Here it is." I thrust the envelope at her. "He said yes. The design is approved."

Mistress Alcina snatches it, gathers her skirt in her hand, and dashes up the stairs to the bedrooms. The sitting room falls – mercifully – into silence. Dona Ilda waves her hands at me, as if she's shooing a chicken.

"It's better if you go downstairs now," she says.

I don't move. "I want to explain. He needs to understand why it took so long."

Dona Ilda waggles a finger back and forth, a clear *no*. "I doubt that either of them wants to see or hear any more from you tonight."

"He needs to know. This is not my fault."

"Tomorrow. If he gets up, you can tell him."

"*If* he gets up?"

"God willing, what you brought will give him a good night's sleep. We'll see if he's better disposed in the morning."

"I don't understand. What's wrong with him?"

Inês starts to speak, but Dona Ilda puts her finger to the girl's lips.

"No," she says. "This is the family's affair. We'll not be talking about it."

"But …"

Dona Ilda eyes me sternly. I know I'll get nothing more.

"I'm sorry if my absence caused you or the family distress." I escape into formality for the second time tonight. "It was not my intention. Nor was it within my control."

They both notice my tone. Dona Ilda opens her mouth, then closes it, visibly struggling.

"This isn't the first time and it won't be the last," she says as I make my way downstairs. "We'll see what tomorrow brings."

The words bring me absolutely no comfort.

CHAPTER 17

"WHAT'S YOUR PLEASURE?" *asked the barman at the Aguia d'Ouro.*

Whatever's strongest, Joaquim wanted to say. A barrelful of it. So he could get drunk and drown himself at the same time.

"Whiskey," he answered instead, not even raising his eyes to meet the barman's. In an envelope on the table in front of him were papers from Aveiro that showed with appalling clarity the ruin his finances were in. His visit to the bank that morning had confirmed it once again. Yet another refusal of a loan that could get him back on his feet.

The barman plunked the whiskey down on his table.

"Another," Joaquim said before the barman turned away. One wouldn't be nearly enough. The second glass arrived before he'd even touched the first. He stared at them morosely. The last time he'd truly enjoyed a drink was months ago, back in Aveiro. When his father was still alive and running the pharmacy, with Joaquim as his apprentice, preparing for his pharmaceutical exams at the University of Coimbra. Before his father's self-made disaster.

Joaquim knew it wasn't entirely his father's fault. But the man was a pharmacist, not a merchant. He should never have invested their savings – without a word to his son – in cotton from the Americas that could so easily disappear under the waves.

Joaquim swallowed the first whiskey in a single gulp, its contents burning his throat. His father had gone to the banks, tried to get credit, and was beaten back every time. Joaquim had noticed his sunken eyes, his drinking, but didn't ask. That regret would stay with him forever. By the end of that horrible day four months ago, the day his father admitted what he had done, he was dead, poisoned by his own

109

hand. In those strange, disturbing moments between waking and sleeping, Joaquim still saw him prone on the floor, surrounded by substances that were supposed to heal, not kill.

Hands came down on the back of the empty chair across from him. "May I take this?"

Joaquim nodded, and a fellow from the Academia Politécnica whisked it away to an increasingly raucous table of his friends. No one would ask to sit at his table now. All the better. The idea of joining the inevitable conversations that the afternoon would bring wearied him. He had no patience today for men whose passionate examination of a subject from every possible, minute angle never resulted in calls to action of any kind.

He chugged back his second drink and signaled for another, his thoughts still tangled in the past. He had no qualifications, no pharmacy, and too little money to continue his studies. To be honest, he hadn't enjoyed them that much anyway. In Coimbra, he'd shown much more aptitude for pranks and protests with his friends against the social wrongs of the day. He was glad he'd never disappointed his father by telling him. He'd hoped to find like-minded people in a bigger city, like Porto. Make a new start. So far, though, that wasn't working out particularly well.

It was partly the financial crisis rocking Portugal. Banks were slamming their doors in many a face, or closing down completely. People blamed Brazil and the ongoing political crises in Lisbon. Why they didn't place the blame squarely on the monarchy, Joaquim didn't know. He did. He massaged the finger wearing his father's gold band, one of the few possessions he'd managed to keep, then fiddled with the empty whiskey glass.

The royal family's lavish voyages, the queen's penchant for clothes and jewels whose value would keep the country fed for years, the king's expensive infidelities – these were driving the country to ruin on the back of banks that financed the follies of the royal house instead of people who truly needed it. Like his father and himself. Joaquim peered at the whiskey glass and realized that if he squeezed much harder, it would break. He pushed it to the far side of the table. Even those who had the courage to criticize the monarchy did so much too politely. They'd never dare act. When he was with them, Joaquim kept the full extent of his fury hidden.

The Águia d'Ouro was filling up with smoke and noise. Joaquim knocked back his third drink, wishing the numbing effects worked more quickly, and stood to leave. What did he expect? Portugal's population was passive and illiterate. They'd never fight for the change that was needed.

CHAPTER 18

MESTRE VITOR ARRIVES to open the shop as the bells ring half past seven. Inês tells me Goldsmith Bento didn't come down for the morning meal. I'm grumpy from lack of sleep and her news doesn't improve my mood. I tossed all night, the straw in my mattress rustling beneath me, reliving the hours at the bridge, the shock of meeting Rafael, the humiliation of being kept outside when I arrived with good tidings. Looming above it all is Goldsmith Bento's strange behavior and my fear that he might tell me my services are not needed. No wonder I slept poorly.

Now Mestre Vitor eyes me severely as he transfers sparkling pieces of jewelry from the lockbox to the display cases. "What happened yesterday?"

I open the shutters, letting in the early morning light, and recount the events of the day to the point where I got Monsieur Eiffel's approval. What occurred with Rafael is my business.

"I know it took longer than expected," I say. "Even so, Goldsmith Bento's reaction doesn't make sense."

To my frustration, Mestre Vitor offers no information. "You should've sent word."

"I didn't think to," I say honestly. Maybe there had been boys at the bridge who could have taken a message, but I'd been too focused on what I needed to do to notice.

"You should have. Today would be a lot easier."

"But why is he in such a state?" I can't hide my bafflement.

"You've seen how many goldsmiths there are in Porto. We need that order." His tone tells me that's all he plans to say.

I swallow the question that begs to be asked. *If it's so important, why isn't he down here working on it right now?*

Mestre Vitor finishes putting the jewelry in the display cases, then takes the queen's cross from the lockbox and returns to his worktable. In the last day, he's added veins throughout, sectioning off various shapes that'll be filled by the *enchedeiras*. I can already imagine how ornate it'll be when it's completed. How heavy it will feel in my hand. How many *reis* it'll earn for the shop. Goldsmith Bento might not be pulling his weight right now, but Mestre Vitor certainly is.

I start a fire, then go back to my stool by the door leading to the shop. I still haven't made a single heart worth keeping. Hugo is here today, stacking firewood that a driver and wagon just delivered, hauling water from the well, and emptying chamber pots into the privy. Each time he gets near my worktable, he sniggers at my efforts. I want to smack him.

"I returned with the news Goldsmith Bento wanted," I say when I know Hugo is out of earshot. "That must count for something." I desperately want Mestre Vitor to say my place here isn't at risk. But when I look over my shoulder, he's hunched over the cross, his nose practically touching it. If he hears me, he gives no sign. I go back to my hearts, stopping only to alert him to customers. Except for the occasional pop and crackle of the fire, the workshop is a place of calm and concentration. I wish it could always be like this.

Sometime after our midday meal, I finish a heart that might be up to Mestre Vitor's standards. As I turn to tell him, Inês enters, her arms draped with clothes.

"These are for you." She holds up, in turn, two white shirts, two pairs of dark gray trousers, a sleeveless vest, and a matching jacket. I touch the fabric. I've never had anything this fine.

"*Obrigado.*" I'm grateful, and too surprised to say anything more.

Inês looks at me expectantly. "Try them on."

I widen my eyes at her. She expects me to strip in her presence? She gives me a devilish grin and turns around.

"Better?" she asks over her shoulder.

I see Mestre Vitor's mouth working. He's trying not to laugh.

"No. It's not." With all the dignity I can muster, I gather up the clothes and stalk into the hallway, shutting the door firmly. I hear her giggle.

I shake my head, chuckling too. She pushes me off-balance, yet I want more. Behind the relative privacy of my curtain, I pull one of the new shirts over my head, button up my trousers, put on the vest, and slide my arms into the coat. I lift my arms, flex my shoulders. Everything fits.

When I present myself to them, Inês runs a critical eye up and down my body. I hold still, hoping neither she nor Mestre Vitor notice my reddening face. She stoops to tug on the bottom of one trouser leg, then rises and fastens a button on my shirt that I missed. She's so close I can hear her breathe. I realize I'm staring at the part of her anatomy that moves with her breath, and reluctantly drag my eyes away.

"You dress up fine." She steps back, nodding approvingly. "Now that you're presentable, Goldsmith Bento wants to see you."

Her switch from playful to serious is abrupt. My less-than-gentlemanly thoughts vanish.

"Now?"

"Yes." She tilts her head in a *come with me* gesture. "Now."

I mouth *sorry* to Mestre Vitor as I abandon my post by the door once again. He shrugs and waves me off. Goldsmith Bento wants to see me alone. What does he have to tell me that Mestre Vitor can't hear?

I fidget with my new clothes as I follow Inês. He wouldn't give them to me if he wasn't keeping me on, would he? That's a notion I don't want to test. I can't antagonize him again. I repeat that over and over to myself as we climb the stairs.

I hear Dona Ilda humming in the kitchen as we pass. Outside the sitting room, Inês knocks and waits until Goldsmith Bento says, "Enter." She nods me in and shuts the door behind me.

As before, the curtains cover the window and the air is smoky and stuffy. This is the third time I've been in this room. By now, I've come to dislike it intensely. Goldsmith Bento is in the same armchair as before, watching the fire. Its light dances unevenly over his form, making him look stooped and tired.

"Come here."

Standing before him, I see it's not the light playing tricks. His eyes are sunken and his skin is pallid despite the glow of the flames. For the first time, it occurs to me that he could be not angry, but truly ill. Even with the fire at my back, I feel a chill. He contemplates me – not asking me to sit down – for what seems a long while, as if he can hardly muster the energy to speak. Finally he inhales deeply.

"Your actions yesterday were utterly out of line.' His voice is stronger than his appearance led me to expect. There's no doubt he's furious.

Life in the shadow of the *quinta* taught me to be humble. Or to pretend to be. I lash my resentment down, tying it tighter than a barrel onto a *barco rabelo*.

"I apologize if my actions caused you anxiety." Almost the same words I said to Dona Ilda and Inês. Last night, though, they were entirely sincere. "I came back with Monsieur Eiffel's approval. I did exactly what you asked."

"It took you hours!"

"They finished the arch of the metal bridge yesterday." In the drama that followed, I'd almost forgotten the excitement of that moment. "Monsieur Eiffel could not be disturbed."

"I need to know you're honest."

"I was at the bridge all day. I didn't leave, or eat, or do anything else until I spoke to him." My voice trails off. I can't prove any of this. Besides, the goldsmith seems to be referring to something else. Something bigger than yesterday's mix-up. "My loyalties lie with you, sir, and no one else."

"Is that so?" He gives a short, harsh laugh. "I'll expect you to prove it."

"Yes, sir." I swallow, not daring to say more. Questions ram into each other in my head. Why did he turn the conversation to honesty? Because of the thieving apprentice? Or is it something to do with his designs and the threat from other goldsmiths that Mestre Vitor referred to? With Rafael in Porto, my claim to honesty has someone who – if ever he wished me ill – could contest it. His word would certainly carry more weight than mine.

Goldsmith Bento regards me again. "I see my tailor worked quickly and competently. I expect you to earn those clothes."

"I will, sir."

"May you not bring disgrace upon this house." Now he sounds, in words and tone, like Father, except that Father always added the word *again*. What makes Goldsmith Bento think I would?

I shake my head. "I won't."

"You may be dismissed."

I nod and let myself out. Inês and Dona Ilda are chattering in the kitchen, but I step softly and get to the stairs unnoticed. With a quiet click, the door closes behind me. In the semi-darkness, I sink onto a step and rest my forehead on my palms. Whatever went on before my arrival is not my fault. I'll be fine. Everything will be fine. I force myself to breathe, then get to my feet and return to the shop.

At my workbench, the good heart I made is missing. I look under and around the table. Nothing. Hugo's in the back yard, his face turned to an upstairs window. Probably taking instructions from Dona Ilda. I glare at him, then seek out the bucket where he deposits everything that's swept off the floor or retrieved from the workspaces. At the end of each week, Mestre Vitor told me, they sift through its contents so that every bit of gold, even the specks of dust, is recovered, melted down, and reused.

The bucket, when I find it, holds a few snips of wire but nothing more. Gritting my teeth, I dump out my plate of rejects. And find the heart. I stare at it. I know I didn't put it there. I'm back at work when Hugo passes by my table. I stick out my leg to block his passage.

"Paws off my work," I growl, low enough so that Mestre Vitor and the customer he's with won't hear me.

He widens his eyes. "Don't know what you're talking about."

I have younger brothers and sisters. I know pretend innocence when I see it. "I'm warning you."

"You think I'm scared?" He lifts his legs high to get over mine but lets the broom trail behind, leaving a swath of dust and dirt across my new trousers. I brush it off, cursing.

"Is there a problem?" Mestre Vitor asks from the doorway.

This is between me and Hugo. I keep my focus on the hearts. "Not at all."

Goldsmith Bento comes down soon afterwards. He acknowledges our presence without speaking, then gets comfortable on his stool and begins examining his designs. When customers arrive, Mestre Vitor attends to them. The *mestre filigraneiro* doesn't show his impatience at having to break his concentration over and over again, but I can imagine it.

As the afternoon wears on, I make several hearts I think are acceptable. I push the three best ones to the left of my table, where Mestre Vitor can see them as he goes to and from the shop. Finally he stops.

"Not bad." He picks up the one in the middle.

I can't tell why that one is better than the others, but I'm grateful for the praise.

"I'll show you how to solder this. Then you can practice on the others." He takes the heart to his worktable. In actions that are becoming familiar, he lights an oil lamp, sprinkles a pinch of metal dust onto the open joint at the bottom of the heart, then uses a tube to blow the flame at it. The dust melts, sealing the joint. In seconds, it's cool enough to handle.

"Ready to try?" he asks.

"Yes," I say decisively. He chuckles at my enthusiasm. Quietly, so as not to disturb Goldsmith Bento.

At first, I use too much dust and end up with metal blobs. Then I sprinkle too little and the joint doesn't hold. I count the hearts as I solder them. Out of twenty-three, five seem, to my eyes, to be passably done. I show them to Mestre Vitor. He pokes through all of the hearts with a finger. The expression on his face says *needs improvement.*

"Not too bad. For a first time." Without ceremony, he dumps all twenty-three of them into the melting pot, then shrugs at my expression. "What did you expect?"

"N ... nothing," I stammer. "May I try again?"

"Right now I need more wire. I want you to make the bars. We'll pull them into wire tomorrow." He measures out a weight of gold balls and pours them into the pot with my discarded hearts. "Start with this."

The fireplace is directly in front of Goldsmith Bento's worktable. He can't help but see me moving about. Every time something I touch clunks or bumps, he huffs impatiently. Mestre Vitor gestures at me to continue. I try even harder to be quiet, but my hand slips and one of the metal blocks we make the bars in thunks onto the counter.

"For God's sake!" Goldsmith Bento throws down his tools and glares at me. "How do you expect me to have steady hands with all this commotion?" He stands up and storms out of the workshop. I send a desperate look in Mestre Vitor's direction.

He sighs heavily. "It'll pass. Go back to work."

I unfreeze and do his bidding. But now I'm the one whose hands are shaking. I pour too much of the melted gold and it overflows the mold.

"Damn." When it cools, I'll have to knock it out and start over again. I fill another two molds, being extra careful. Why does

Goldsmith Bento take everything I do the wrong way? I want to ask Mestre Vitor, but fear disturbing him too. I jam my hands in my pockets and wait for the bars to cool.

While I do, I study Goldsmith Bento's abandoned drawings. There are five or six of them. Except for one, where his hand clearly slipped, I don't see any difference between them. He's scaled the image of the bridge down to its final size, an oval little bigger than my thumbnail. It's so detailed I can see the tiny X's along the arch and span.

"Henrique." Mestre Vitor looks pointedly at the pot I left on the counter.

"Sorry." I return the pot to the hook over the fire and give its contents a stir. The remaining gold hasn't hardened. After I finish six bars, Mestre Vitor says we'll stop for the day. I'm organizing the workspace around the fireplace when I hear the shop door open.

"After this customer, come help me close," Mestre Vitor says.

"All right."

I'm scraping the half-hardened gold from the inside of the pot when Mestre Vitor calls, "Henrique. In here, please."

"Coming." I must've missed hearing the customer leave. I shake my sleeves over the waste bucket to dislodge any specks of gold that might cling to them and hurry into the shop.

I notice Rafael at the same time Mestre Vitor says, "This gentleman is asking for you."

Something jagged lodges in my throat. I swallow. He must've heard the commotion I made last night and knew how to find me that way. I want to push him out of Gomes & Filho, far away from this new life I'm building. Instead, I give him a hard look. Mestre Vitor takes in the fine cut of Rafael's clothes and the top hat in his hand, then looks at me with a raised eyebrow. He's expecting an introduction.

"This is Rafael, from Mesão Frio." I don't give his full name. "Rafael, may I introduce you to Vitor Teixeira, *Mestre Filigraneiro*."

"Pleased to meet you." Rafael grins. He knows he's put me in a position where I can't speak my mind. "I promised to take Henrique for a drink when I came to town. So here I am."

"I don't know if that's a good …" I begin.

"I'm only here one more day," Rafael interrupts. "Mestre Vitor, is it too much to ask for the pleasure of his company for a few hours?"

I attempt to catch Mestre Vitor's eye, to signal that he should refuse. A pleasure is decidedly not what I'd call a forced evening with Rafael.

I can't figure out why he's insisting, as if my *no* last night meant nothing. He and Mestre Vitor are chatting cordially, and I can't toss him out onto the street. Arousing suspicion by appearing ill-behaved is the last thing I want to do.

"Shall we go?" Rafael asks.

"Mestre Vitor, don't you need help with …?"

He interrupts me. "Give me a hand closing the shop, then you can be off."

I wish he hadn't chosen now to be so obliging.

"I'll inform them" – he jerks a thumb toward the ceiling – "that you'll be coming back late. To avoid another scene."

"But Goldsmith Bento. He'll not …"

"I'm giving you permission. That's sufficient."

"Yes, Mestre."

Rafael loiters on the street while we load the jewelry into the lockbox, close the shutters, and lock the front door.

I try once more. "I don't have to go if …"

"What is wrong with you? A boy your age, and new to town?" To my astonishment, Mestre Vitor presses two coins into my hand. "Go. Take advantage of the opportunity."

"Thank you." I give in to the inevitable. "I'll see you tomorrow then."

CHAPTER 19

THE WALK TO the São Bento convent with Rafael is a silent one. Beyond it, he points to the Rua de Santo António and says *that way*. We climb, passing the Baquet Theatre and the shops of seamstresses, shoemakers, tailors, and hatmakers. I adjust my jacket. Maybe my new clothes were made on this street. In any case, I'm glad to be wearing them. Rafael was born to his fine suit and wears it with assurance. I wasn't, but at least now the contrast between us isn't as striking.

"Rafael, why did you come?"

"My father wants to sell grapes to Dona Antónia."

That isn't what I meant, but I let myself be sidetracked. "She's the biggest wine producer in the Douro. Why would she need your grapes?"

"Phylloxera. A lot of her vineyards have been hard hit. Around Mesão Frio, we've mostly been spared. So far. It could be good for both of us."

"You're in Porto to meet Dona Antónia?" The *Ferreirinha* is mythical, like someone in a story you want to believe exists, but aren't sure. Despite myself, I'm impressed.

He shakes his head. "The administrator of her estate has his office here. I'm to meet him tomorrow."

"Oh." That isn't nearly as interesting. I return to my original question. "Why did you come to Gomes & Filho?" He won the first skirmish – getting me out when I said I didn't want to see him – and I need to know what terrain I'm fighting on. "What do you want?"

119

"Look, Henrique." He's still walking, not looking at me. "We're adults. Our families and their feuds are far away. Do we have to carry them with us our whole lives?"

I scoff. Him wanting to call an end to hostilities in Porto doesn't mean he'd treat me differently than he always has in Mesão Frio. He's surely not suggesting that we be friends. Inside my new jacket, I fidget.

Ahead of us, a group of young men are laughing and trying to shove each other into the lumps of manure scattered up and down the street. I'm uncomfortable, yes. But it's the first time I'm going out at night in Porto, with permission, and with no obligation other than to myself. With the added benefit of knowing that I'll be spending Rafael's *tostões*, not my own. Wasting this opportunity would be a sin.

He's watching me, waiting for an answer.

"All right." My laugh comes out bitter and short. "We'll call a truce. For tonight."

"That's not ..." He decides not to argue the point and holds out a hand. "Deal."

I clasp it and meet his eyes, wondering if he can read the challenge in mine: *You will not betray me again.*

I release his hand. "Where do you suggest we go?" I could definitely use a drink. Or several.

"To a café in Praça da Batalha. We're almost there."

At the top of Rua de Santo António, I look back the way we came. The city swoops down to Praça Nova, then rises up on the other side to the Clérigos church and its monumental tower. Porto is a city of hills. Rising and falling, like in the Douro. Maybe that's one reason it feels like home.

We follow the group of young men to a three-story building with a sign at the roofline that reads *Aguia d'Ouro*. The Golden Eagle. Inside, it's humid, smoky, dark, and noisy. The floor is sticky under my feet and in places it crunches. It's in a better neighborhood than the *botequim* last night, but I wonder why Rafael chose it. We weave among the tables and snag one against the wall as two men stand to leave. Every other chair in the place is occupied and everyone – except for us – seems to know each other. In the enclosed room, the noise is deafening. Especially after the quiet of the goldsmith's shop.

Rafael orders a bottle of red Douro wine. When it arrives, I salute him with my glass and then sit back and drink, watching as men move from table to table, conversations forming and reforming. Everyone is dressed as well as Rafael is. I glance down at my new clothes and grin. As we are. No common workers or sailors here.

A newcomer claps Rafael on the back. He twists to say good evening, then rises to follow the man to another table, where he's greeted with much familiarity. I was wrong – of course people know him. He went to boarding school here. And as the representative of a *quinta,* he's certainly met the city's merchants and bankers. It's not my world – not yet – but I savor this taste of it.

Rafael's left his wine. I suppose that means he'll come back. Honestly, I'd rather sit alone. Random words and phrases swirl around me. One table is talking about floods, harvests, wine, and the English factory. Someone chimes in with a bit of good news.

"Did you hear? The *Casa de Paços* in Barcelos won an award. At the International Exhibition in the United States, no less. And ..."

At another table, a man is saying, "*Oi,* Ricardo Jorge. That can't be true. The unsanitary conditions in this city ..."

"Think about it," someone else is arguing right behind me. "In *Good Sense and Good Taste,* Antero wrote ..."

"Fontes will come back to lead the government," insists a loud voice across the room. "Mark my words. But what he'll do about the public debt ..."

I have no idea who or what they're talking about. That's fine, as long as no one asks for my opinion. But I realize how much I'll have to learn if ever I want to fit in.

A gentleman with a full, dark mustache passes my table.

"Freitinhas!" Three men at a table in the middle of the room stand to greet him. "We thought you weren't going to make it."

Across from me, Rafael slides back into his seat. "The best things on the menu are the pork chops. Are you hungry?"

"Always."

He signals to the bartender to bring two plates. I pour more of the deep red wine and discover why the house specialty has such a good reputation. I've just taken my second bite of meat when the man called Freitinhas and a bunch of others push several tables close together. It must be a signal because the noise drops a level and a line of men come to stand behind those sitting at the tables. There's an expectant hush that's broken by the bartender.

"Out of my way, man. Move." He's holding a bottle and three glasses high, going in circles searching for the people who ordered them. On his way back to the bar, he bellows, "Anybody who wants something can come to me to get it. I'm not serving you lot if you move all over the place."

His complaint is greeted by gales of laughter. The group Rafael and I followed in toast his health loudly and wish him more stamina in bed than he's showing tonight. The bartender shoots them a sour look, but I have the feeling it's a game he and the customers have played many times before. The multitude of conversations resumes.

Then a deep voice from a red-haired man says, "Liberty, equality, fraternity. It's a utopian dream. We'll never achieve it in Portugal."

"You've already given up hope? When we've hardly even started?"

From across the table, Rafael grins at me. "Here we go. You can always count on at least one good debate a night."

"Who are they?" I know he'll know.

"Professors from the Academia Politécnica." He gestures at his rowdy friends across the room. "And their irreverent students. At least that's what they call us in Coimbra." He scans the room again. "Doctors. A lawyer. And that" – he nods toward the man the others called Freitinhas – "is José Joaquim Rodrigues de Freitas. A journalist with *O Comércio do Porto*. He was a member of Parliament in Lisbon a few years ago. So he's worth listening to, unlike most of these rabble-rousers."

Rafael seems content to follow the conversation, and I'm glad. It's easier than making the effort to keep a civil tongue in my head.

"How can there be equality?" the red-haired man continues. "When no one's educated except for a few elites in Lisbon?"

"What about us?" one of Rafael's friends intervenes.

Rafael laughs and lifts his glass to him.

The red-haired man keeps talking. "Eight out of ten people in Portugal are illiterate or can write no more than their name. We'll never catch up with the rest of Europe."

"That's why we need a better system of education." Freitinhas speaks for the first time. "Open it to workers. Country folk. Maybe even to women, someday."

His proposal is greeted with jeers.

"We can't expect people to know how to vote if we don't give them the tools," Freitinhas says.

"It'll never happen," says an angry voice. "Not as long as we have a corrupt, incompetent monarchy that oppresses the people." The speaker is standing to one side, partially hidden from my view. I lean forward and realize it's Senhor Joaquim. He's well-spoken and well-dressed and fits in better here than he does in Miguel's *ilha*. I catch his eye and nod. I don't think he recognizes me.

"That's why parliament has to be stronger," Freitinhas says. "So it can act as an independent force, not a servant of the king."

"But what can you do?" someone calls out. "You and your new Republican Party aren't even represented in Parliament."

"Patience," says Freitinhas. "Elections aren't until next year."

"Even if you are elected, I'd be amazed if they let you take your seat." With his fingers, Senhor Joaquim twirls the end of his mustache into the finest of points. "Why would the king allow a party whose objective – and an excellent one it is, in my opinion – is to overthrow him?"

"Change takes time, Joaquim," Freitinhas says. "We need to create the right conditions for a republic. Portugal isn't ready yet."

"A Republican who doesn't want a republic. Is that what I'm hearing?" one of the students jeers. With that, the noise level in the room rises as conversations splinter again.

Looking disgruntled, Senhor Joaquim drains his glass and goes to order another one. As he passes our table on the way back, he regards me quizzically. "We've met, have we not?"

I stand and shake his hand. "With Miguel and Ana Maria."

"Your first time here?"

I nod.

"Well, I hope you're armed with patience. These debates are interminable."

"They're ... um ... interesting." I don't know how else to describe them.

"Interesting. Bah! If we want change, we need to act." He rejoins the conversation in the center of the room.

"Who was that?" Rafael asks.

It pleases me that I know someone he doesn't.

"A gentleman I met. Conducting business for a friend." That's all the detail he's getting. "What do you think he means by *need to act?*"

Rafael shrugs. "Probably nothing. Blowing off steam, I'd say. You might want to cultivate a less discontented set of acquaintances though."

I frown. It hasn't escaped me that he didn't offer to introduce me to his friends. The next time I visit Miguel, I won't hesitate to wish Senhor Joaquim good day.

"My acquaintances are none of your concern," I say shortly.

"Must you be so hostile?"

I answer his question with a glare.

He exhales noisily. "Didn't we work this out? Decide bygones should remain bygones?"

"You ..." I can't believe it. Can he truly think that a few words would change everything? "I lived for years with blame I didn't deserve because you didn't defend me. I faced a future with no prospects, with a father who will forever resent me for ruining his relationship with the *quinta*." My words pour out. I can't stop them any more than I could a landslide. "Why do you think I so wanted to leave Mesão Frio? And then I learn that you kissed my sister and you think it's all right. It isn't. It never will be."

I see a range of emotions flicker across Rafael's face. Surprise, sadness, irritation, resignation, and others I can't identify. I plow on.

"I'll always treat you with the respect that's due the *quinta*. It's more than you did for me. But I'll never again be the ignorant child who believes there's a world in which we could be friends." I push back my chair and stand.

Rafael opens his mouth, then closes it and gives me a curt nod instead.

"I thank you for the meal." I hope he understands that this is goodbye.

Senhor Joaquim regards me – approvingly, I think – as I leave. He must have overheard us. I meant every word, and can't believe I finally said them out loud. My steps feel almost light with relief and pride. I've taken the bit for far too long. No more.

Outside on the dark square, though, realization hits me. What if all I achieved was to make Rafael angry? I'm free of the *quinta*. My family isn't.

CHAPTER 20

*L*ISETE SAW HIM *almost every day. She looked forward to those moments with great girlish anticipation, always taking care to arrange her curls and bright bows most artfully and to choose the color of her dresses according to the message she wanted to send. He, in his tailored jacket and shiny black boots, would see her and bow, as a gentleman should. She would nod serenely, giving him a secret smile after checking to make sure no one was spying on them. It was all very thrilling – except that they had never exchanged a single word.*

He was always on the street, face tilted upwards, while she was eternally perched at the sitting room window, three heights of a man above his head. Worse, every time he strolled by, he was in plain view of the shop and her father, who highly disapproved of the notion that someone might court her without his permission. They had to make do with long, longing glances, the hasty retrieval of a glove or handkerchief she – oh so carelessly – might let fall, and minute, fluttery hand waves that a stray glance would mistake for something else entirely.

She'd never actually seen anyone swoon, but she'd read about it. It was wonderfully romantic and must be, she thought, very close to the light-headed feeling she got when he blew her a kiss from behind his fingers. In bed at night, she imagined receiving letters studded with tender phrases. "My dearest love," he would say, "I yearn to kneel at your feet." Such missives, unfortunately, had not been forthcoming. Until today, when Inês slipped a small square of paper into her palm. Lisete fled to her room, away from the maid's inquisitive gaze, and read it with flaming cheeks.

How I would love to see the city's most beautiful bird take wing and fly, he wrote. *Perhaps to alight in the gardens of the Crystal Palace, where the music is, on Sunday afternoon? Could you? Would you?*

With my utmost affection, I am your
Ernesto

CHAPTER 21

I N THE MORNING, Goldsmith Bento opens the shop and Mestre Vitor and Hugo arrive as expected. We're all present, accounted for, and apparently calm. I send up a quick prayer that the day will pass without incident, but the tension doesn't leave my shoulders. In the workshop, Goldsmith Bento bends over his design for Monsieur Eiffel. Mestre Vitor sets the queen's cross on his table and regards it thoughtfully, then runs his eyes along the rounds of gold wire hanging on the wall. He grimaces.

"Bento, we're going to have to pull some wire this morning. It's going to be noisy. I'm sorry."

I hold my breath, fearing the fragile balance of the last few minutes is already being shattered. Even Hugo stops sweeping and ducks his head. I don't want Goldsmith Bento to storm out of the workshop again. I can't see his face, but his fingers clench around his pencil. Very deliberately, he flattens his hands on the worktable and rises to his feet.

"Do what you need to. I'll run the shop this morning." His stare goes from Mestre Vitor to me to Hugo. "But this workshop will be as silent as a graveyard this afternoon. Is that clear?"

"That's fine," Mestre Vitor says. "It's enough time." From the lockbox, he fetches the gold bars I made yesterday, then hustles over to the cylinder with the grooves of different sizes. "Come on, boys," he says. "Henrique, if I get it going, you can thread the wire, can't you? Like we did the other day?"

"Yes."

"Hugo, turn the crank." Mestre Vitor waits until the boy gets into position. "Go ahead."

Hugo leans his weight into the crank and the drum with grooves begins to turn. Mestre Vitor pushes the bar into the widest one. When it comes out on the other side, he catches it and puts it into the second widest groove, then into the third and the fourth. Each time it comes out longer and thinner. When it's long enough to wrap around the drum, he asks me, "Ready?"

I nod and he stands aside. "Watch your fingers."

At first, I'm not quick enough. The end slides out of the groove before I can grab it and thread it into a narrower one. It hits the floor and the rest of the wire follows.

"Hugo, stop." Mestre Vitor shows me again where to stand, where to put my hands. "Try again," he says. "Hugo, go more slowly."

I focus on the machine, not caring that Hugo is sneering. This time, I manage to catch the wire, bring it under the drum, and insert it into the next smaller groove. As I do it again and again, we pick up speed.

"Good," says Mestre Vitor. "Keep going like that." He leaves us for the shop.

Hugo maintains the rhythm for a moment, then slows way down. I feel it in the way the wire slides through my hands, in the loss of tension.

"Don't mess around," I say. "Go faster."

Without answering, he throws all of his weight onto the crank. The wire slices across my fingers, burning like a whip. I yank my hand away, blood blooming red across my thumb and two fingers. "Son of a bitch! Why did you do that?" I grab a rag and wrap it around my hand.

"You told me to speed up," he says.

"I ..." This is pure malice. "What is wrong with you?"

He reaches for the crank again. "Ready to work when you are."

I don't move. He's not my little brother. It's not my place to beat him. But this can't continue. "You've been angry since the moment I arrived. Why?"

He slits his eyes at me. "I should be the new apprentice, that's why. Not you."

I make a sarcastic sound in my throat. His eyes and mouth draw together in a look of pure fury.

"My mother arranged it with Goldsmith Bento. Then you showed up and he took you on. Even though you're way too old." His voice rises higher. "It's not fair. It's never fair."

He releases the crank and stamps outside to the privy. Before going in, he makes a disgusted face and pinches his noise shut. It stinks horrifically, but Dona Ilda had his hide the last time he pissed against the garden wall.

Mestre Vitor chooses that moment to check in on us. He frowns when he sees Hugo is missing and I'm at a standstill.

"Everything all right?"

"Nature called," I say.

"Right." He returns to the shop.

I peel away the rag. The bleeding has slowed – the cuts aren't deep – but I can't continue working the wire with bare skin. I fold the rag to get a clean spot, then tie it tightly around my hand. I have no idea what the goldsmith told Hugo's mother or what false hopes she may have put in his head. He probably feels like the world has come to an end. If he were my brother or Miguel – someone I liked – it would be easier to sympathize. To be kind after what he just did … I clench my hand, hoping it'll stop the stinging. That's a lot to ask.

In the end, I don't even have to try. Mestre Vitor and Hugo return to the workshop at almost the same time. From then on, my conversation with the boy is limited to essential instructions. He follows them with ill humor but correctly. Each time we finish, Mestre Vitor takes the wire we've made and, using pliers, pulls it through tinier and tinier holes pierced in a metal plate attached to a machine he calls a *fieira*, drawing it out until it's as thin as a hair. After a couple of hours, I bet we've made enough to go up and down the Rua das Flores more than once. Then we take two wires, twist them tightly together, and flatten them so they're ready to use.

Finally, Mestre Vitor calls a halt. "That's enough for now. We need to let Bento in here. Good job, boys." He thanks us equally. Hugo is still sulking and doesn't respond.

When the shop closes for the midday meal, I wash and rebind my cuts before sitting down to eat with Dona Ilda and Inês. They're back to their teasing, humming, doing-a-thousand-things-at-once selves. Below their good humor, though, anxiety lingers.

"I have to go to the market," Inês tells me as she and Dona Ilda clean up. "Come with me? If your injury permits, of course." She taps my rag bandage.

Once again, I'm taken aback by her forward manner. And inordinately pleased. But I have no idea how to respond. Especially with Dona Ilda here, regarding Inês disapprovingly.

"What?" Inês widens her eyes. She's clearly skilled at playing the innocent angel. "There's lots to buy and you said you're too busy. His arms would come in handy."

"I don't think I can. The shop will open soon. I'm expected to be there." It's not what I want to say. Knowingly or not, Inês is offering us time alone. The thought sends a shudder of anticipation up my spine.

"It won't take long. Dona Ilda will tell them you're on an errand for her. Won't you? Please?"

Chuckling, Dona Ilda gives Inês an affectionate pat on the cheek. "You do know how to brighten my day, don't you, dear? That's just as well, since you complicate it beyond measure."

"*Obrigada.*" Inês didn't get a firm *yes* but unties her apron anyway, fetches two wicker baskets, and pushes me out the door.

I go willingly.

"We'll be back in no time," Inês tells Dona Ilda.

From an upstairs window, Lisete waves to us wistfully. She looks like she'd love to get out of the house too. The air has that foggy dampness that says rain is on the way. Inês takes in the grey sky and hastens her step.

"We'll have to make this a quicker trip than I planned."

Is she disappointed, or is it my imagination? Me wanting her to want to spend time with me? If she does, it's mutual. Until now, I've seen little about her that I don't like. But there are always other people around, with their eyes and their demands, getting in the way.

"That is a pity." I emphasize *is* and watch to see how she'll interpret it.

She lifts an eyebrow. "Eh la. You're flirting with me."

Her response is so unexpected that I choke on my own spit. I end up half-laughing, half-coughing. She's utterly unlike the girls who giggle behind their hands with their friends if a man walks by. And now she's laughing at me.

"Are you never, ever embarrassed?" I ask when I finish coughing.

"Nope." Her face glows with merriment.

"Right." I'm tempted to ask her how she likes to be wooed. But she'll laugh at me again. I'm not ready for such directness. Besides, there are other pressing matters to discuss, now that Dona Ilda isn't here to stop us. "Inês, what's wrong with Goldsmith Bento?"

She transfers her baskets from one arm to another, then back again. I know I've put her in a delicate position.

"I won't tell anyone. I just need to know. So I'm not always doing things that make him mad."

"It's not you. Or not just you." She scrapes a bit of dirt off a basket with her fingernail, then meets my eyes. "He's been like that since I came to work here. It comes and goes. Nothing for months, then something happens and he stays in his room and refuses to eat. Once he didn't come out for four days. We didn't know where to turn."

"What makes him act like that?"

"Dona Ilda says it's melancholy," she says as we turn onto the Rua do Bonjardim.

"And the doctor?" I ask.

"The last time Mistress Alcina called the doctor, he prescribed milk and rum before getting out of bed" – Inês gags – "Port with tea mid-morning, sherry with the midday meal, more Port with dinner, and ale with morphia before bedtime. Mistress Alcina said it made everything worse. She hasn't called the doctor since."

"It's melancholy that makes him so angry?" That sounds contradictory.

"It's mostly low spirits. He doesn't work, and that makes him even more upset because then everyone worries about money. And he becomes suspicious of everything and everyone."

Inês takes a right off Rua do Bonjardim long before we get to the *ilha* where Miguel is staying. Ahead, I hear the loud voices of vendors calling out their wares. The market isn't far. A block farther on, Inês stops before a long, open square surrounded by a black iron railing. At the far end, beyond rows of wooden stalls, water from a stone fountain spews into a big tank.

"Welcome to Bolhão."

Now it's the smells that hit me. Apples and onions. Smoke and sausages and roasting chestnuts. Fried fish and grilled fish, and fish that's been sitting out too long.

Inês slides her baskets onto my arms, then tallies the items we need on her fingers. We plunge into the bustling crowd. She bargains hard, but it's surely her gaiety that gets her extras at the stalls. An additional egg here, a bigger cabbage there. I don't want to take my eyes off her.

"For you, *menina*." A knife-wielding butcher twice her size weighs her order, then adds an extra soup bone.

I chew my lips to keep a sober face, then hold out the baskets so she can load her purchases into them. They're considerably heavier now than when we started. I can see why Dona Ilda sends her to do the shopping. A few raindrops spatter on my hands and head. They damp down the dust, but the market stays busy. Inês is efficient and we're soon on our way home.

"About Goldsmith Bento," I start.

"Again?" Her face scrunches unhappily.

"Please." I'd much rather ask her about herself, but can't let this opportunity pass. "You said melancholy makes him suspicious."

"Yes."

"Is that what happened to the third apprentice? The one who was accused of stealing?"

"Maybe. It's just not something I think he would have done. They searched everything he owned, but didn't find anything."

"He could have sold it."

"It doesn't seem like him."

Momentarily, I feel jealousy nip. Has she been as friendly to all the apprentices as she's being to me? I rein in the thought, realizing how stupid I'm being. The other apprentice was years younger than both of us.

"He was enthusiastic. A good learner. We all thought Goldsmith Bento was getting quite fond of him." She makes a long face. "Can we talk about something else?"

"Certainly." I understand more now, but it doesn't make my position any less precarious. At every step, I'll have to be careful. Attentive that everything I touch is accounted for afterwards.

"You there. Serious man." Inês nudges me with an elbow and points to the baskets. "They're not too much for you?"

"I think I can manage." Especially since by now we're barely a stone's throw from Gomes & Filho.

"Good." She rubs her upper arms contentedly. "I feel quite the proper lady, arriving home with someone else carrying my purchases. We should do it more often."

"You want me as your servant?" I draw my brows down and pretend to be offended. "I think not."

She crinkles her eyes at me. "That is a pity."

I realize she's teasing, throwing my words from earlier back at me. It's too late to respond in kind. We're already in front of the shop, and

Lisete is looking down at us from the upstairs window. Inês waves at her, then holds her arms out for the baskets.

"Hand them over."

On impulse, I blurt out, "Would you like to go walking with me? On Sunday afternoon?"

She taps her cheek with a finger, as if the question requires much thought.

"Maybe," she says. Her smile leaves me hanging. The rain starts to come down in earnest. She grabs the baskets and we duck inside.

Back in the workshop, silence rules. Mestre Vitor is bent over the queen's cross, making whorls and petals that will be filled by the *enchedeiras*. Goldsmith Bento's put the drawing for the cufflinks flat on the table in front of him, along with small hammers and a set of tools that taper to pointed tips and thin edges. He's pushing on the metal oval with one of them, using a technique completely unlike filigree to press and bend the metal. I try to find a spot where I can watch without bothering him, but Mestre Vitor shakes his head warningly. I return to my table. No distance is safe today. Mestre Vitor sets me shapes other than hearts to practice. To the sound of rain thrumming on the windows, I go to work.

By the end of the afternoon, Goldsmith Bento seems satisfied enough with his progress to let me approach. He straightens up, shaking out his hands, then detaches the cufflink from a pad made of pine resin that was holding it in place. I lean in to examine it, my fingers laced behind my back. The outline of the bridge is already clear, but the structure looks much lighter and more fragile than the real one.

"See how the bridge on the front is raised?" he asks.

I nod solemnly, hiding my surprise. It's the first time he's explained anything to me.

"I hammered it from the back to make the relief." He rolls a couple of tools with rounded ends back and forth under his hand. "With these. That's called repoussé. Adding detail to the front is chasing. That requires tools with sharper edges and shapes." He holds up two tools with a line of miniscule XXXX's on their ends. "I'll use these for the arch and pillars."

"To look like the crossed girders," I say softly. I can't believe the detail he's planning to put into such a small object.

"Exactly." He seems pleased with my interest and proud of his skill. As he should be. The design he's creating couldn't be more delicate or precise.

"It's already beautiful," I say.

He beams. "It's far from finished. This is a good start though." His contentment is a welcome contrast to his grumpiness this morning.

"Vitor, I'm done for now," he says. "You'll close up?"

"Of course."

Before leaving, Goldsmith Bento wraps the cufflink in a soft, clean cloth, puts it in a wooden box that's smaller and flatter than the ones we use to store the jewelry from the shop, and deposits it and his drawings in the lockbox. Mestre Vitor and I close the shop soon after.

I'm still in the kitchen after the evening meal when we hear a man's voice calling from the dark street below.

"Há estrume p'ra bender?" Manure, he's calling. Who has manure to sell?

Inês stops wiping the table and twists her mouth in disgust. "You're not going to like this," she warns me.

"Not like what?"

"It has to be done though." Dona Ilda ties a kerchief over her nose and mouth. "We've let it go too long as it is."

Downstairs, I hear her open the front door and call out. Wagon wheels grind to a stop.

"It's a farmer. Come to empty the privy." Inês shuts the kitchen window with a thunk. "Stay here. And be prepared to hold your nose."

On the street, an ox bellows. Then feet tramp down the hallway, past my sleeping spot and the door to the workshop. From the kitchen window, I see a man and a boy carrying two buckets cross the back yard to the privy. In the man's arms is a large rectangular container. Hanging from his trousers is something that looks like a funnel. Even through the closed window, the stink of human and animal waste clinging to them makes me gag. From the sitting room, I hear Goldsmith Bento curse once, then again, even louder. I pray he doesn't order me to help them.

Inês ties a cloth over her nose and mouth too. For once she's not smiling. Nor is Dona Ilda when she rejoins us, looking rather green in the face.

I watch through the closed window as the boy drops the bucket into the privy hole, allows it to fill with excrement and urine, then pulls it up with a rope. He passes it to the man, who pours most of the contents down the funnel into the container as the boy fills the second bucket. Whatever misses the funnel spills onto the ground. They make no effort not to step in it. When the container is full, the man plugs the hole with straw and together they carry it across the yard, along the hallway, and outside onto the street. They empty it into the wagon and return to repeat the procedure, dripping filth every step of the way. My stomach roils. They're passing half an arm's length from my sleeping pallet. If that. I swallow repeatedly, willing my half-digested meal not to rise into my throat and choke me.

"We'll clean up when they're done." Inês has read my mind. "But it'll be days before the smell is gone."

I grimace. Even if I ask to sleep with the back door open, the air coming in from the yard will be foul. Back home, we dig a hole, use it until it's full, then cover it and dig another. The waste is there if a farmer needs it, but he would never traipse though our house with the stuff. I find it hard to believe that this is how civilized society in Porto deals with the problem.

Church bells tell me that it takes them more than two hours to finish their task. Finally, the farmer calls Dona Ilda from the bottom of the stairs.

"Inês, Henrique," she says. "Come with me." Downstairs, the farmer drops a few coins into Dona Ilda's hand and takes his leave. Inês is already pulling me toward the back yard.

"Watch your step," she warns. Unnecessarily. Where I'm putting my feet is the only thing I'm looking at. The filth is spattered the entire length of the hallway. Streaks along the wall show where buckets or the container bumped against it. Big globs of the stuff are seeping into the bottom of the curtain around my sleeping space. The air is thick with the stench, like something solid I have to push my way through. The yard is little better.

"Give me a minute." There's no way I'm touching any of this in my new clothes. I duck behind the curtain, change hastily into my old shirt, trousers, and wooden clogs, then join her at the well. I heave bucket after bucket of water onto the floor of the hallway so Inês can sweep the muck out into the Rua das Flores. Dona Ilda busies herself cleaning the wall. After we've rinsed and scrubbed the hallway three times and can see every bit of the floor, Dona Ilda calls a halt and tells us to clean ourselves as best we can.

"That's all we can do tonight," she says. "We'll go over it again in the morning when the light is better. Hugo can dig what's outside into the plant beds."

Inês does as she says, then plods tiredly up the stairs. I regard my curtain. The bottom is less soiled than before, but it's completely soaked. I lift it to my nose.

"*Porra!*" My eyes water and I thrust it away. I can't bed down near this.

"Unhook it and put it outside on the woodpile," Dona Ilda says tiredly. "We'll wash it in the morning. Your clothes too."

Looking down, I see I'm spotted with the filth. These clothes are staying outside with the curtain tonight. I'll have no privacy, but I doubt anyone will come down. It'll be just me, wishing I could be somewhere else. Like Goldsmith Bento and his family, who stayed cloistered upstairs during all of this. I'd never expect them to help. But, remembering how quickly the stench invaded the kitchen, I can't stop myself from hoping it did the same in the bedrooms on the floor above. If I can't escape this dreadfulness, why should they?

CHAPTER 22

R AFAEL TOSSED THE *horse's reins to the stable boy and bounded up the stairs.*

"*Where's Father?*"

The young girl washing the floor of the entry hall ducked her head timidly. "In the study, sir."

Rafael shoved open the double doors an instant later, not even thinking to knock. The pen his father was holding skidded across the quinta's *ledger, marring its neat line of figures.*

"*What the hell, son?*" *Rafael's father threw down his pen in disgust. "Look what you ..." He took in Rafael's wide grin and his ire disappeared as fast as it had come. "Welcome home. I take it you have good news."*

"*I do.*" *Rafael wanted to savor the moment. This had been his first journey alone to Porto for the* quinta *and he was sure he'd done well.*

"*Do tell.*"

"*Nothing is signed, of course,*" *Rafael cautioned, taking a seat on one of the settees. His father joined him. "But they agreed to send someone to see if our wine from this year's harvest is up to their standards. If it is, they'll buy it, for shipment to Gaia in the new year."*

"*Well done, son.*" *His father beamed with satisfaction. "Our grapes are good and Dona Antónia will give us a fair price."*

His father's praise didn't come often. Rafael nodded his thanks. Their relationship had changed since he'd gone to university – the first in the family to do so – in ways Rafael was still trying to understand. His father had always been stiff and formal, with little time – or perhaps desire – to talk to a mere boy. Now, though, his words were accorded more respect. His suggestions were pondered, if not necessarily followed.

"God knows we need a good year," his father continued. "With those cursed insects coming closer all the time, I don't know how many more abundant harvests we'll have. It's a miracle anyone manages to stay afloat."

"Especially when it's not just phylloxera," Rafael said indignantly. "There are too many people selling wine they call Port that's never seen the deck of a barco rabelo."

"There's always been fraud, I'm afraid."

"Not like now. If it doesn't change, we may as well throw the wine overboard ourselves and save the shipping costs. No foreigner who gets bad wine when he's expecting good Port is going to trust us enough to buy it again. Even if what we're offering is the real thing."

His father gave Rafael's knee an approving pat. "We might not want to go to quite such extremes as that, son." A smile tugged at his lips. "But I'm pleased to see you're thinking about these things. You've matured a lot."

"I care what happens here. With our wine. With the Douro." The statement wasn't a lie. It wasn't the full truth either. His father was finally starting to treat him like a successor, an heir. But Rafael wasn't sure he wanted the position being held out to him. At least not right away. The Douro was his childhood, full of hidebound traditions and practices that made him impatient. Lisbon, on the other hand, sparkled in his imagination like a jewel, full of possibilities.

His father was still beaming at him. Now was not the time for that conversation. But Rafael did want to bring up something else that was preying on his mind.

"Father, I ran into Henrique in Porto."

"Who?"

"The carpenter's son. We played together when I was younger." After what Henrique had told him, Rafael expected to see at least a flash of anger in his father's eyes. There was none.

"Ah. And?"

"He said you don't allow him to work our harvest. That his father's carpentry shop gets no orders from the quinta."

His father frowned.

"Is it true?" Rafael asked. "His beating wasn't enough? For a childish game, so long ago?"

"I never gave orders that he couldn't work the harvest. Maybe the overseer did. Or maybe your friend thought it would be too humiliating to return and went elsewhere." His father shrugged. "That incident was resolved to my satisfaction years ago. I haven't given it a thought since."

"And his father? Not getting any orders from us?"

138

"He's coarse and unpleasant and the quality of his work isn't superior to others. I don't know if he ever did do work for us, frankly."

So it was a misunderstanding? Rafael couldn't think of any reason his father would lie.

"Your friend's in Porto now?"

"Yes. Apprenticing with a goldsmith."

"Then he's probably better off than he was in Mesão Frio."

"Perhaps. But he feels like it ruined his life here. He resents the hell out of us."

His father clearly had no idea how the abrupt end to their friendship had hurt. But Rafael had been able to leave, to move on. Over time, the unpleasant memories had faded. Henrique had stayed in this town of wagging tongues. Rafael hadn't realized until they spoke how much he'd suffered for it. Even if it sounded like the situation was worse in his head than it was in reality.

"Well, by all means set him straight, if you want to," his father said. "I wager everyone but him forgot about it long ago."

CHAPTER 23

"*MEU DEUS!*"

I lurch upright, shaken out of a poisoned half-sleep by Goldsmith Bento's loud lament. He's at the door of the workshop, moving once again like a bent old man. I'm guessing the night wasn't kind to him either.

The hours that passed have done nothing to clear the air. My hair, my lungs, my skin, and each and every stitch of clothing I own have absorbed the stench. I bet if I cut myself again, even my blood would stink.

"Dona Ilda!" the goldsmith bellows. "Get down here and clean this place up! Now!"

Quick footsteps sound on the floor above. I jump up and pull on my clothes in a rush, finishing just as Dona Ilda and Inês appear at the bottom of the stairs. They hover there anxiously as Goldsmith Bento jams his key into the workshop door. He turns it so violently I think he's going to break it. I take a deep breath, already dreading the rest of the day. I'm on my way to the well to wash the cuts Hugo gave me when I hear him roar.

"Henrique!"

I race back inside. "Sir?"

"What did you do with them? Where are they?" Goldsmith Bento is in front of the open lockbox, his face distorted with fury.

"I didn't touch anything, sir. I swear I didn't."

"My cufflinks are gone. So are the designs." He jabs a shaking finger at the lockbox. "I put them right here." The space he's pointing at is filled with the boxes of jewelry that Mestre Vitor and I brought in from the shop last night. His flat one is nowhere in sight.

I move toward him. "Sir, I think it's …"

"Don't you come near this lockbox!" he thunders.

I freeze. Once, on the bank of a stream, I surprised a wolf with her cub. She leaped in front of it, her snarl terrifying. For agonizing moments, I stood stock-still, knowing I was doomed if she attacked. Finally, she decided I wasn't a threat and melted soundlessly into the woods with her cub. Right now, I feel like I'm facing another wild animal, but one even less likely to see sense than the wolf.

Inês and Dona Ilda huddle in the doorway, their faces pale and frightened. There's nothing they can say in my defense. I feel the blood rush to my face, then out again, leaving me dizzy. I want to throw his irrational anger and accusations right back at him.

The silence is broken by the front door opening.

"Caralho!" It's the first time I've heard Mestre Vitor swear. It's quickly followed by an embarrassed *Oh dear* and an apology to Dona Ilda and Inês. They separate so he can enter the workshop.

"What an atrocious stench." He catches sight of me and Goldsmith Bento and halts. We're as still as if in a painting, but the antagonism flowing between us is unmistakable.

"What's going on?" He speaks like a trainer wishing to quiet his animals. It's a calm I can't imagine he feels.

My mouth clamped shut, I back away, giving Mestre Vitor a clear path to the lockbox. Then I wait, more than a little self-righteously, for what's about to happen. Mestre Vitor will show the goldsmith the truth. Then, if he has any decency, he'll apologize.

"The box with the cufflinks." Goldsmith Bento is shuddering with anger. "It's gone. And so are my designs. I put them right here. I want to know what he's done with them."

Nothing! My jaw hurts from wanting to yell the word. I fist my hand around a poker we use to stir the fire and squeeze it so hard the handle digs into my skin, fighting for control. If I close my eyes, I'm on my knees in the *quinta's* courtyard again, but with Goldsmith Bento berating me instead of Rafael's father.

"Look!" The goldsmith's voice pitches higher and higher. "He dares threaten us! With a poker!"

I unclasp it immediately. Threaten them? I give Mestre Vitor a beseeching look.

"Calm down, Bento. Please. I'm sure it's not what you're thinking." Mestre Vitor approaches carefully, as one would a snake that might strike. "May I look?"

Goldsmith Bento moves aside but keeps one hand on the lockbox door. His eyes flick back and forth from Mestre Vitor to me, as if he needs to reassure himself that I'm not coming closer.

"Let's see what we have here." Mestre Vitor keeps his voice low and soothing. There are two stacks of boxes of jewelry from the shop, one behind the other. He lifts them out and places them on the table where I'm usually stationed, then reaches to the far back.

"Here's your box." He holds it out to Goldsmith Bento. "And the designs. We didn't want to pile everything on top of them last night. I didn't realize you had put them in a specific place."

Goldsmith Bento snatches them to his chest, swaying a little. Gently, Mestre Vitor leads him to his workbench and gets him settled on his stool, the box and drawings in front of him. The goldsmith just sits there, head bowed, his arms hanging limply.

Mestre Vitor turns to Inês. "Go get Mistress Alcina, please," he says quietly.

I still haven't dared to move. Mestre Vitor makes sure the goldsmith is steady on his stool, then takes me by the elbow and guides me toward the workshop door, keeping himself between me and Goldsmith Bento. He's got deep furrows between his brows.

"Why don't you go out for a while? Come back this afternoon. We'll talk then." When I start to speak, he holds out a hand. "Later. Please."

I leave, walking blindly. I want nothing more than to ram my fist into something. To never be forced to face Goldsmith Bento again, or to bed down on that smelly pallet. If only I could work with Mestre Vitor and no one else. Then I'd have the chance to learn the trade. Make something of myself. With the goldsmith, I don't think that's possible.

Narrow cobblestone streets wind up and down under my feet, but I pay little attention to where they take me. It's only when the air changes that I look up to see an open expanse. It's a modest park, longer than it is wide, with houses along one side and what appears to be a deep valley on the other. I approach a railing whose black metal bars stand taller than I do. Beyond it is a sheer drop. No one would survive that fall. To my left, the Douro twists and flows out of sight behind another hill. If I could fly like one of the seagulls circling above me, perhaps I could see the ocean. I grip the railing, its bars feeling like a cage, and shake. It doesn't budge.

Goldsmith Bento is clearly ill. His family and Mestre Vitor seem to be used to it. I hate it. I don't know how to react or what will bring his wrath upon me. It happens even when I'm doing exactly as they ask. Each time, I'm left with the sick feeling that he's seeking a reason to dismiss me and that I'm helpless to do anything about it. I give the railing another furious shake. Then I unclench my hands and back away, trying to push aside the unwelcome image of others who, seeing their future careening out of control, might have chosen to leap over this precipice in a desperate effort to take it back.

Right now, my only choice is to trust Mestre Vitor. A man I've known for a week. A week that I began with enough optimism to fill the sky. I hardly recognize that person now. On the street behind me, a carriage passes, pulled by two horses as black as my mood. I dread going back to the goldsmith's shop. I turn my back on the precipice and head across town to see Miguel. Hopefully he's fared better than I thus far.

Outside the *ilha,* a group of dirty, tired men has gathered. They're blocking the entrance, listening to someone. I start to sidle by, then recognize Senhor Joaquim and stop.

"You work sunup to sundown, with hardly time off to go to church," he's saying loudly. "Yet you take home barely enough to keep these miserable roofs over your heads, while the owners of the factories live in luxury. Who among you thinks that's right?"

The men around him shift their weight, cross their arms, and mutter.

"Of course it's not right."

"Not fair. Not fair at all."

"Nothing we can do about it."

"But there is," Senhor Joaquim says. "Demand higher wages. Better conditions. You're not animals."

"And the door will slam behind us before we realize we've been thrown out," someone scoffs. "Men line up for our jobs. The factory owners don't need us."

"That's why you have to organize, as workers do in other countries. Numbers give you the power you need to force a change."

From inside the *ilha,* a woman calls. "Carlos, get in here. Or you won't have time to eat."

The jeering man detaches himself from the group. "I've got a wife and four little ones. I'm not risking my job by speaking out." He disappears down the dark passageway, along with most of the others.

One of the last ones to leave shakes his head and mutters, "Your advice is nothing but trouble. A bad job's better than no job at all."

I don't have his certainty. Not today, at least.

Only one younger man is left, and me. Senhor Joaquim throws his hands in the air. "They'll be sorry they didn't listen," he says to both of us. "It won't get better." He eyes me more closely. "You again? What are you doing here?"

"I've come to see Miguel."

He nods and strides ahead of me into the *ilha*. I wonder again why he's living here. He's nothing like the other residents. Two bent women in black eye me as I carefully step over their chickens. Ana Maria's door is open. I still knock.

"Come in." Her knees are under a table that takes up half the room and she's making stitches in a flowery fabric. A spinning wheel and a cot that I assume is Miguel's take up the rest of the floor space. Behind her is an alcove in the wall that's just wide enough for a narrow mattress. She puts down her sewing.

"Miguel's not here," she says before I can ask. "He's apprenticing for a cobbler in the Rua Bela da Princesa."

"That was fast."

"He was fortunate. The other apprentice had an accident just as they got an important order. The shoemaker needed someone who already had training."

"So he won't go to Brazil?"

"Not yet. Since he's not boarding with them, he'll be paid a small sum each week. And I've taken in extra piecework." She taps the pile of fabric on her table. "When we've saved enough for a new passport, he can go."

"You told your father?"

"We sent him a letter." She picks up her needle again. "I've got to get this done before the end of the afternoon. If you'll excuse me."

CHAPTER 24

Dear Father,

I'm writing to tell you that I arrived safely in Porto. Please tell Mother that the rabelo *trip down the Douro was uneventful – as I am sure my voyage across the ocean will be – and that she mustn't worry about me.*

It turns out that the ship I was to sail on has been delayed, so I have taken work with a cobbler whose apprentice broke his hand. Thus far he seems well pleased with my mastery of our craft. The shop is bigger than ours but smells the same, of tanned hides and wax.

Much of his trade is sensible work shoes, but the commissions he receives! Yesterday, a lady with peacock feathers in her hat told him she wanted shoes that were 'sumptuous.' I didn't know what she meant. But master showed her fancy buttons, leathers in a dozen colors, even tiny stones that glitter like gems, and she left content after hearing what he proposed to make.

Master later told me she was the wife of a Brasileiro, *one of the Portuguese who made his fortune in the Americas, who is proud that his spouse stands out from the others. I am sure I'll do well here while waiting for my passage to Brazil.*

Ana Maria is well and sends her regards to you and Mother.

Your dutiful son,
Miguel

CHAPTER 25

I BID ANA Maria good day and leave her to her work. Miguel has already found a master. I hope his is better than mine. A little demon in my head whispers *why him and not me?* but I unseat it with a shake. Who am I to begrudge Miguel his good fortune? I just wish some of it would rub off on me.

Like most of the doors in the *ilha*, Senhor Joaquim's is open. He's inside, poring over a newspaper. At my knock, he takes off his glasses and looks up wearily.

"Can't find your way out?" He doesn't invite me past the threshold. Understandably. Two grown men would make the small space uncomfortably crowded.

"I was thinking about what you said in the Aguia d'Ouro." My voice trails off. Newspapers cover the unmade bed and are piled on a three-legged stool that's the only other seating in the room. In Mesão Frio, Senhor Manuel got *O Comércio do Porto* once a week. It looks like Senhor Joaquim buys it daily. And keeps it forever. "I didn't mean to interrupt."

Senhor Joaquim shrugs. "A few minutes won't change the perfidy of this government."

"Perfidy?" I don't know the word.

"Treachery, deceit."

He must see the confusion on my face because he continues. "Haven't you noticed? France has become a republic. Even Spain, for a while! The modern age will come for them. Yet in Lisbon, the government won't even debate constitutional reform. If this continues, Portugal will remain poor and backward, a ragged fingernail on the edge of a great continent. Mark my words."

"But why do you call that perfi …?" I've forgotten the word already. "Treachery?"

"Because Portugal's collapsing. We've got an agricultural crisis and our finances are a disaster. Yet what do the wastrels in Lisbon do? They throw money at the king so he can pay off his indiscreet liaisons, and of course the queen mustn't be asked to live without her jeweled bracelets and lavish toilettes." Joaquim's intensity fills the room. "The money comes from the public purse and our useless government doesn't even have the balls to cut their allowance! They're incapable of looking out for the public good. I'm talking about my welfare. Yours. That of a factory worker who writes his name with an X."

"But … do you really expect them to?" I ask. "Lisbon is far away. I doubt anyone there cares about us."

"Members of Parliament are elected from all over the country," Senhor Joaquim snaps. "That includes Porto and the north."

"I know that." I'm not letting him think I'm completely ignorant. "But the president of the council and the ministers serve the king. Not us."

"That's why we need change."

He suddenly reminds me of Senhor Manuel, although they're nothing alike. Senhor Manuel always gave his opinion in a quiet, measured tone. In an argument, I'm sure Senhor Joaquim does his fair share of yelling. But in both of them, knowledge runs – or ran – deep and wide. Senhor Manuel was the first to encourage me, and Senhor Joaquim hasn't yet turned away in disdain over my inexperience. And I like what he says about wanting the concerns of people like me to be recognized and addressed.

"What kind of change?"

"Patient people say education. Constitutional reform. Giving more people the vote," he says derisively.

"What do you say?"

Under his mustache, his mouth sets in a hard line. "Something else might be needed."

I wait, but he doesn't go on.

"Maybe you should run for a seat in Parliament," I suggest. "Change things yourself."

Senhor Joaquim snorts. "There's not a party in Portugal that thinks like I do. That we have to tear it all down to rebuild. But someday …" He pulls out a pocket watch, then stands. "I must be going. Come to

147

the Aguia d'Ouro tonight if you want to continue this conversation. You'll see what I mean."

"Tonight …" I have no idea what'll happen when I return to the goldsmith's, but I doubt going out a few hours later would be looked upon favorably. I certainly can't risk arriving at the shop after Mestre Vitor has left and finding no one will let me in. "I can't."

Senhor Joaquim shrugs. "As you wish." He shuts his door and strides away like he has a purpose.

Everyone, it seems, has something important to do. Except me. Mestre Vitor said to come back later. How long is *later*? Every time I think about Goldsmith Bento's accusations, I want to hit something. I finally slam my fist into a tree in the park of São Lázaro. All it gets me is torn skin on my knuckles and a startled *oh!* from two ladies who scurry away.

Back across town, seated at a worn table in the Porta do Olival café, my back against stones that were once part of Porto's medieval wall, I nurse the bruises along with a large glass of wine that's rough on my tongue. I'm not drinking it for its quality. I'm mustering my courage. And my calm, in case Goldsmith Bento starts yelling again. Lashing out at him would do me more damage than it would him. As the tree had. My head spinning more than a little – and my battered hand sorer than ever – I stand and pay, wishing I'd had enough *tostões* with me to order food too. Maybe Inês saved me some of the midday meal. Reluctantly, I turn my feet in the direction of the Rua das Flores.

At Gomes & Filho, Mestre Vitor is laying a gold necklace out on a rectangle of black velvet for a lady in rich green brocade. With a tilt of his head, he indicates the door to the workshop. I take a deep breath and do what I'm told. The smell of muck from the privy still fills the air, but it's less suffocating. Dona Ilda and Inês must've worked hard this morning.

The workshop, blessedly, is empty. No sign of the goldsmith, and Hugo's at the back of the garden with more shit and a shovel. I start to release the breath I was holding, then eye Goldsmith Bento's workbench apprehensively. To my relief, it's been cleared. There's nothing he can accuse me of stealing, or touching, or even breathing on the wrong way.

I sit at my usual table near the door to the shop, my arms crossed. Awaiting instructions. After a few minutes, Mestre Vitor bids the woman good day and comes to stand over me. He sniffs loudly. Twice.

"You were drinking?" he asks. "On a day like today? When we all, Lord knows, must be on our best behavior?"

"I had a drink," I snap back. "I'm not drunk and it's not a crime."

He opens his mouth to say more but I cut him off. "Where's the goldsmith?"

"Be respectful," Mestre Vitor says curtly. "Goldsmith" – he emphasizes the title – Bento is in his bedroom, resting."

"When will he be down?"

"I don't know."

"Do I still have a job?" My words come out hard and sharp, like an ax chopping wood.

Anger darkens his eyes and he doesn't answer. I chomp down on my tongue. Mestre Vitor isn't the source of my wrath.

"I'm sorry."

He makes me wait, then finally says, "Apology accepted."

"Can you please answer my question?" I hate pleading. "He's not going to dismiss me, is he?"

Mestre Vitor sighs deeply. "He was in no condition to discuss that, as I'm sure you understand. You're doing what is asked of you. We just need to get beyond these constant misunderstandings."

"Good luck," I say bitterly. "I think misunderstanding is his last name."

"When he's better, I'll talk to him."

"When will that be? Tonight? Tomorrow?"

"I'm not a doctor, and that's entirely out of our control. Now, are you capable of working this afternoon? Or do you need to lie down too?"

I'm thinking of a sharp retort when I see his mouth twitch. He's mocking me gently, trying to inject some humor into this worst of days. I appreciate the effort.

"What needs doing?"

Mother always taught us not to be glad of someone else's misfortune. But Goldsmith Bento remains indisposed for the rest of the day and all the next, and I savor the calm. Mestre Vitor and I pair up companionably when a task needs four hands, and the rest of the time he's working on the queen's cross. He sets me to making various filigree forms, with instructions to *practice, practice, practice*, until my fingers can practically make them in my sleep.

After we close Saturday evening, he makes sure Dona Ilda knows he gave me permission to go out. I head straight to the Aguia d'Ouro, where I sit at Senhor Joaquim's table and listen to his never-ending commentary. His exchanges with the men at the table in the center of the café are cutting and sarcastic. I honestly can't tell if they enjoy the arguments or detest each other. Even when I disagree with his most outrageous statements, I leave it to others to contradict him, and I wager he finds me fine company.

At Gomes & Filho, Dona Ilda, Inês, and Hugo have cleaned and cleaned. By Sunday, the stench of privy droppings has faded to an occasional whiff. After my soiled curtain is washed, dried, and rehung, I get a much better night's sleep. When I go upstairs for breakfast, Inês and Dona Ilda are bustling about, clearing the family's dishes and setting out food for us, aprons tied over their Sunday dresses. Inês pours coffee and we take our places around the kitchen table.

"Goldsmith Bento didn't come down," Inês says, before I ask. "Mistress Alcina took him a tray."

"He's hardly eating," Dona Ilda frets. She picks apart a bread roll, then leaves it on her plate. "His trays come down barely touched."

"Come now. It's not that bad. He won't starve," Inês says, then turns to me, her laughter sparkling. "The good news is that there will be no lecture today after the midday meal. We'll have the entire afternoon free." She draws out the word *entire*. "Won't we, Dona Ilda?"

The older woman frowns suspiciously.

I widen my eyes at Inês, trying to signal caution, then study the inside of my coffee mug. I don't want Dona Ilda to think I have anything to do with Inês's remarkably cheerful behavior. In my chest, though, excitement vibrates. It's clear she's looking forward to walking out with me as much as I am with her. I smile secretly into my mug. What man wouldn't be pleased to have Inês's hand on his arm, her steps dancing beside his? To make the color come to her cheeks when she giggles? I like that I make her laugh. I also know she does so easily, and mock myself for feeling jealous that others share that pleasure.

Given the forward way she talks, I suspect she's been kissed. It's not a question I can ask her outright, of course. But if I could bring my lips to hers, I bet I'd know. Maybe she'll let me, when we're alone. I keep my gaze on my hands and the mug they are gripping. These are definitely not thoughts I want either of them to guess.

Dona Ilda purses her mouth primly. "Inês, getting out of hearing the Lord's word should not make you so happy."

"I get quite enough of the Lord's word on Sunday from the priest, thank you."

Dona Ilda looks scandalized.

"Well, it's true," Inês continues. "Wouldn't you agree, Henrique?"

"Oh no." I raise both hands in surrender. "I'm not getting in the middle of this."

I'm saved by the tolling of bells, calling us to the top of the street for Mass. Lisete and her mother sweep into the foyer. It suddenly crosses my mind that I'll be escorting four women, two of marriageable age and pretty, and none of them family. I stand tall and gesture them gallantly down the stairs ahead of me. It's time to show them what a perfect gentleman I can be.

CHAPTER 26

I CLUTCH MY *bedclothes to my nose, elbows pressed against my ribs, my fingers claws, rigid and bent like the rest of my body, every muscle taut to stop my limbs from moving but still I tremble and my wife leans over me, asks if I'm cold but my eyes are fixed unblinking on the wall and I don't answer but then feel the weight of another blanket, they're smothering me, crushing me and I need to push them off but don't have the strength because everyone around me laps up my energy, like mongrels drinking from a puddle, draining it, sloshing it until everything becomes muddied, unfocused, which is what they desire, the other goldsmiths, my neighbors and predators, circling, snarling, wanting my secrets, my commissions, my apprentices, not a one I can trust and now a hand hovers near my face with a spoon while I clamp my lips together and shake my head, the soothing voice must be a trick, they want to poison me, liquid runs down my cheek into my hair and she wipes it off and tries again, massaging my neck to make me choke and swallow, if I die who will take the Eiffel commission and the shame, oh the shame, if I lose everything, and my women are too frivolous, that must be why money always runs low, and who can I depend upon? My head fills with a sound like water rushing, catching on branches and underwater boulders, so turbulent and cloudy that thought becomes impossible. Against my will, my staring eyes close.*

CHAPTER 27

I NSIDE THE CHURCH, I move to escort Mistress Alcina and Lisete to their seats in the front. Mistress Alcina stops me, her expression almost queasy. As if she thinks I intend to sit with them. I keep my face impassive and stand aside to let them pass, then take my place in a row in the back, failing miserably in my attempt to slide in beside Inês. I'm barely seated when Dona Ilda waves for my attention and pats the pew on her other side. I stare straight ahead, pretending not to notice, but the second I start to shift onto my knees in a position of prayer – which she won't interfere with, certainly – her hand snakes out and grasps my wrist.

"Over here," she whispers.

I give up and put Dona Ilda between us. It doesn't make much difference. I'm still more aware of every movement Inês makes than I am of the sermon.

We're on the way home, Lisete and Mistress Alcina a few steps ahead of us, when my plans for the afternoon come crashing down.

"Even if Father can't come with us," Lisete says to her mother, "we should still go out."

"You and me? Alone?" Mistress Alcina places a hand over her heart. "That wouldn't do at all."

"The Crystal Palace is full of people on a Sunday afternoon." Lisete changes her tone, mid-sentence, from impatient to cajoling. It's so noticeable that Inês and I trade glances. Something's up.

"You know that, Mother. It's perfectly safe."

"No. It's not proper."

Lisete protests, but Mistress Alcina cuts her off. "Your father would never agree. Besides, with him in such a state, we need to remain at home."

"I spend my whole life at home, Mother. It's like a prison." She stops and clasps her hands under her chin. "Please don't tell me I can't go out," she says mournfully. "I'll go mad!"

Mistress Alcina grips Lisete's arm and gets her moving again. "Don't overreact so, my dear. You have every freedom a girl of your age and station can expect."

"In other words, none," Inês whispers to me. "She wouldn't know how to use it anyway. That girl knows nothing about the ways of the world."

I'd have thought Lisete more sensible than that, but Inês knows her better than I do. She treats her with a certain tenderness, as if Lisete were the younger of the two, rather than the other way around. Now I'm curious about two things. First, what confidences Lisete has shared to make Inês think she wouldn't behave responsibly. And second, how much Inês, Miss Sure-of-Everything, knows herself about the ways of the world.

"We'll spend a lovely afternoon reading," Mistress Alcina continues. "And you can finish your needlework. That way I'll be near if your father needs me."

Lisete's shoulders slump and she drags her feet, her whole body rejecting her mother's suggestion. Suddenly she straightens, gives me a head-to-toe appraisal, and turns back to Mistress Alcina.

"Uh, oh," Inês mutters.

"If you can't go, then Henrique will walk with me." Her words tumble out over her mother's protest. And over my own. "With Dona Ilda, of course."

Inês frowns and studies her feet. She's no happier with this turn of events than I am.

"There's nothing improper about that, Mother. I so need the fresh air and a view of something besides the street we live on."

"My sister is unwell," Dona Ilda says firmly. "I can't accompany you."

"Oh." Lisete is taken aback, but recovers quickly. "Then Inês will come along. She'll take good care of me. It's not as if I could get lost."

"Oh yes, you could," Inês mutters beside me. "And on purpose."

"What?" This conversation has moved into unfamiliar waters and I don't much like where it's taking us. I have no intention of spending the afternoon escorting the goldsmith's daughter.

"Then it's settled, Mother," Lisete says. "I'll have two very capable chaperones and we won't be gone long enough for you to even miss us." In front of their house, she stops with a determined smile on her face, her body blocking the door.

I give Inês a perplexed look. Surely Lisete's mother will see through her wiles and keep her at home.

To my amazement, Mistress Alcina throws up her hands and gives in. "My dear, you're much more persistent than is proper." The instructions that follow are directed at all three of us. "You'll take a *diligence* there and back. With no one else inside, and no stopping on the way. You're to stay together at all times and speak to no one. Is that clear?" She waits until we nod, then says, "Fine. You may go." Pointedly, she holds the house key up in front of her nose. Lisete scoots out of the way, quietly triumphant. Inês and I are decidedly not.

Why Mistress Alcina said yes, I can't fathom. Pure exhaustion, maybe. But it means I'm tethered to Lisete for the afternoon. I set my mouth grimly as four swishing skirts precede me up the stairs. Although I much prefer Inês's dark beauty, the goldsmith's daughter isn't at all hard on the eyes. If circumstances were different, maybe I'd be allowed to court her after a few years of faithful service in the goldsmith's shop. With the father she has, though, there's no chance of that.

Her father. He'd be more likely to tan my hide than allow such an outing. Lisete knows it, as does her mother. But since it's my hide and not theirs, maybe they don't care. I imagine Goldsmith Bento racing after us, fists shaking and nightshirt flapping. What's worse, Lisete's little game has ruined my afternoon alone with Inês.

"Henrique?" Inês calls, and I realize I'm still at the bottom of the stairway. "Bring up wood, will you?"

By the time Mistress Alcina bundles us into the carriage she had me hail, Lisete has changed into a dress of filmy, pale lavender with fine gold ribbing around her neck and wrists. When she moves, she practically floats.

Inês frowns again when she sees her. Even during the privy clean-up, she was better-humored than she is now.

"Don't be ridiculous," Mistress Alcina scolds as she follows Lisete down the stairs. "You'll catch your death. Go change into sensible clothes."

"It's a beautiful afternoon, Mother." Lisete doesn't slow a bit. "And look. I'll wear my cloak." She drapes a gray woolen cape over her shoulders. "Besides, the *diligence* is here. You always say it's bad manners to keep someone waiting." She halts her rush out the door and reaches out to stroke her mother's cheek. It's a gentle, affectionate gesture. Mistress Alcina covers Lisete's hand with hers and smiles back, her eyes glistening.

"My darling girl," she says.

"Try to rest while we're gone, Mother," Lisete says softly. "Promise?" She waits for a *yes,* then allows the driver to help her into the carriage.

Inês follows. I take a seat across from them and we're off. After a wave to her mother, Lisete sits back, looking thoughtful. It's my first time in a *diligence,* and it fails to impress. The bench is hard, everything creaks, and past occupants have left odors that have me breathing through my mouth. Every rut and hole jostle us from side to side. It doesn't help that I'm facing backwards. We cross Praça Nova and climb toward the Clérigos church, pedestrians skittering out of our way. I try to ignore the unsettled state of my gut so I can enjoy my uncommon position looking down at others.

Lisete's pensive air is no more, and she's saying something silly to make Inês giggle. Inês doesn't respond.

"What's wrong with you?" Lisete finally exclaims. "You must be as glad to get out of the house as I am. And you like the Crystal Palace too, don't you?"

"Yes. Of course," Inês says in a monotone.

Lisete leans forward and puts her hand on Inês's knee, suddenly concerned. "Are you all right? You're not falling ill, like Papa?" Her voice is high, like a frightened child's.

Inês sighs, then shakes her head. "Don't you worry. I'm perfectly well."

"Then don't scare me so!" Lisete's affection for Inês is clear, but she's oblivious to the fact that the girl beside her might have had other, personal plans. It's not my place to blurt that out, but I want to. I look out the window instead. We're on the Rua do Triunfo, passing the Royal Palace. I find myself wondering when Mestre Vitor plans to deliver the queen's cross, and if he'll let me accompany him when he does.

Minutes later, the driver pulls the horses to a stop before a curving gate. Beyond it are extensive gardens teeming with couples, families, and children playing chase. Behind them is the Crystal Palace itself, an immense structure of iron and glass and granite with a grand arched entrance. I stare at it, mouth agape. It's more magnificent by far than the Royal Palace down the street. Inês said it was modeled on an even bigger Crystal Palace in London. She also said I'd never be able to count the number of windows. She's right. I jump out of the carriage and chivalrously help the young ladies down.

"You'll return for us when the bells toll five?" Inês asks the driver. He grunts in assent and slaps the reins across the horses' backs.

"Let's start inside," I suggest.

Inês gives me an *aren't you naïve* look. "The gardens are free," she says. "The Crystal Palace isn't."

"Besides, I want to stay outside." Lisete tosses her head. "Come along."

Being gentlemanly, I offer her my arm. She flounces off alone, leaving me with my elbow sticking out.

Inês snickers. "Isn't your face a fetching shade of red," she says, and hastens after Lisete.

"And aren't you a funny girl." I jog to catch up. I should've known the goldsmith's daughter would always treat me as a servant.

Ahead of me, Lisete's marching toward a wide, gravel-covered avenue lined with linden trees, Inês fluttering around her.

"Shall we go to the lookout over the river?"

"No." Lisete keeps straight on.

"Why don't we go down to the fountain and the grotto? It's so pretty there. And romantic."

"No."

We're on the linden tree avenue now, following it along one side of the Crystal Palace. Ahead, I hear music.

"Do you want to light a candle in the chapel?"

"No."

"Lisete. Stop." Inês slows the other girl with a grip on her sleeve. "What's going on?"

"Nothing. I want to listen to the quartet in the *Concha Acústica*. Hymns are fine, but sometimes I pine to hear other music."

"You do?" Inês gives Lisete, then me, a disbelieving look. "Well, isn't that new."

"No, it's not." Lisete shakes off Inês's restraining hand. "But if you and Henrique aren't interested, go see your romantic fountain or enjoy the river view. I'm perfectly fine on my own."

"I would never!" Inês jams her hands on her hips, elbows out, looking spiky all over. "Mistress Alcina would have my head!"

"Oh goodness." Lisete rolls her eyes and starts off again. "Come along then."

"Leave her alone indeed," Inês huffs. She seizes my wrist and pulls me along behind Lisete. "Last time, she disappeared. When I found her, she said she'd sat down to rest near the fountain and I left her behind. Said it with the face of an angel, she did, every lying word. I almost died of nerves."

So that's why Inês is so upset. Not because our walk was postponed, but because she's worried about Lisete. Trying to hide my disappointment, I search for the source of the music. It's coming from an outdoor stage just off the linden tree avenue, where a small crowd has gathered.

"Did you get into trouble?" I'm amazed that Inês still has her job. "No."

I stare in disbelief.

"You think we were stupid enough to tell anyone? Lisete needed the secret kept as much as I did." Inês pauses. "I made her promise to never do it again. You must help me keep an eye on her."

Given Inês's distress, I know better than to say it out loud, but how hard can that be? We're so close to her that Inês treads on one of Lisete's heels.

"Ouch!" Lisete whirls around.

Inês runs right into her.

"*Desculpe.* I'm so sorry," she stammers.

Lisete pushes her away with a stiff arm. "Stop it. You're worse than my mother."

"But…"

"No buts. I said I wouldn't wander off. I'll keep that promise, but you have to give me some room. And your discretion. Both of you."

Discretion? I shoot Inês a worried glance. She's too focused on Lisete to notice.

"What are you going to do?"

"I told you. I'm going to listen to the music." Lisete trots off once more.

"*Merda merda merda,*" Inês swears.

I regard her in shock.

"I grew up with fishermen," she says without shame. "Come on. Lisete's getting away."

The goldsmith's daughter stops at the edge of the crowd. As Inês and I take up positions on either side of her, she lets out an exaggerated sigh. She sways briefly, as if transported by the notes of the violin, then gets down to business, scanning the area. The turn of her head is slow, nonchalant, but she's alight with hope. Searching for someone.

So is Inês. But her movements are jerky, like an animal sensing an ambush but not knowing which direction it's coming from. Around us, skirts rustle, feet tap, and fingers play along with the music. Lisete nods politely to a busty lady I assume she knows. Everyone claps at the end of one piece, and another begins. Then another. As time passes, Lisete's eyebrows draw together in disappointment. As church bells ring five o'clock, the quartet takes a bow and the crowd disperses.

"Time to go." Inês herds us back the way we came. "The *diligence* will be waiting for us."

We haven't seen anything yet.

"I wanted to …" I begin.

"Yes," Lisete interrupts. "We're leaving. I've had enough." Without waiting for an answer, she marches off. I glare daggers at her selfish back.

Midway down the avenue, a gentleman steps out from behind a tree and tips his hat. Lisete's irritation falls away.

"*Merda,*" Inês whispers.

"Ernesto." Lisete beams at him. "You came."

"How could I not?" the man says as he tucks a pocket watch away. He's young, with the conceited, self-assured bearing of a slightly overweight dandy. His paunch is disguised by clothes that show a certain wealth, like the goldsmith's. "But you were enjoying the music so much, I thought it inappropriate to interrupt."

"How very thoughtful of you." Lisete's tone says she would have preferred him to show up earlier, when she expected him, but it no longer matters. She's glowing.

Inês is not.

"Lisete, we must go. We don't want our driver to take someone else." Inês tries to hook her arm around Lisete's, but the older girl holds her own stiff at her side.

"Certainly," Lisete says smoothly. "Ernesto, will you accompany us to the *diligence?*"

"Of course, little bird."

I hear Inês's sharp intake of breath as Lisete places her fingers lightly on the arm he offers. Then, locking eyes with Inês, Lisete uses the hand Ernesto can't see to point to a spot several steps behind them. Clearly, that's where we're to walk.

Inês shoots me a panicky glance, but what can we do? We can't pull them apart or do anything that might draw attention to Lisete's inappropriate behavior. I place Inês's chilly hand in the crook of my arm and we follow, trying to pretend we're just a couple on an unremarkable stroll. But with Inês tensing every time Ernesto bends to whisper in Lisete's ear, I doubt we're at all convincing.

"If word of this gets back to Goldsmith Bento…" Inês doesn't finish the sentence. We both know who'll be blamed if there's a scandal.

Finally we reach the street and Inês exclaims, "Thank heavens. The *diligence* is here."

She hovers, glowering, as Ernesto gallantly bends over Lisete's hand.

"Goodbye, little bird." He hands her into the carriage, then steps aside so Inês and I can get in. As we depart, he bows deeply. "I live only to see you again. Soon, my bird."

I want to laugh. He sounds so ridiculous. But Lisete is waving and smiling. I roll my eyes.

"Stop it!" Inês grabs Lisete's hands so she can't wave any more. "We're going to be in such trouble! What were you thinking?"

Lisete sinks back in her seat, her face soft and dreamy. "It'll be fine. Don't worry."

"Fine for you, maybe." Inês snaps. I've never seen her so agitated.

"There's no reason Papa and Mama will find out. And if they do, I'll say it was a family friend, being polite." Lisete rests her chin on her hand, her elbow propped against the window-frame, and closes her eyes. "Please be quiet. Don't ruin my glorious day."

Inês clasps her hands together, squeezing so tightly that I think she's going to bruise her skin. I long to reach for them, to comfort her, but I can't. Not with Lisete here. As we bump along, Inês's apprehension invades me. We failed in our task, and I know better than to expect Goldsmith Bento to be indulgent. We return to the Rua das Flores in a troubled silence.

CHAPTER 28

ORGE HADN'T REALIZED that the drunkard in Régua – that mangy pile of rags he usually stepped around – hailed from Mesão Frio, nor that he could spew gossip like a fountain. Tonight, by chance, they'd ended up in the same tavern along the quay.

Jorge listened with one ear as the man rambled on, telling tales of a witch tossed into the river for refusing to find a lost child, a priest who took his church's treasure for his secret love, and a boy who stole a statue that belonged to a count. When he slowed and begged for another drink, Jorge pushed what was left of his own into the man's shaking hands and bade him continue.

The drunkard's memory was fuzzy and which detail belonged in which narrative wasn't clear, but that was unimportant. He'd given Jorge an idea. Why not make up a sordid past for Henrique? One that would cause him problems in Porto, as he'd done for Jorge? Gossip was so very easy to spread.

Suddenly the drunkard's eyes rolled back and his body collapsed gently onto the table.

"Oh no, you don't," said the man tending the bar. He pulled the unconscious figure out of the tavern, heels dragging across the floor, and propped him against the side of the building.

Back inside, the barman took Jorge's coins. "Best not to encourage him," he said. "He's too seldom lucid as it is."

"Never again." Jorge smiled grimly, like an avenging angel. "There's no need."

CHAPTER 29

I'LL HAVE TO kneel in earnest prayer on Sunday, begging forgiveness, for as the days pass, I continue to be thankful that Goldsmith Bento remains indisposed. I can't help it, although I know it worries the women and that Mestre Vitor is struggling. The bars and shapes I make to his satisfaction and my help stocking or putting away display cases isn't the relief he needs. Finally, after he slams down his tools once again to wait on a customer, I make sure Hugo's not around and ask if I can assist in the shop.

"That's not the job of an apprentice," he says.

He didn't say *no*, so I press on. "I can handle the responsibility. You'll see."

"Goldsmith Bento …"

… is the bane of my existence. I don't say it out loud.

"I'll go back to my place when he returns to work. But you need uninterrupted time, don't you? More than you need my filigree hearts?"

"About those hearts …" He grimaces.

"I'll work on them extra hard when Goldsmith Bento is back."

He ponders, then says, "There's immense value in that shop. What you're asking is not to be taken lightly."

"I know." I look him straight in the eye, doing nothing to hide my desire to prove myself.

"I'll think about it."

The next morning, when the first customer steps through the door, Mestre Vitor tells me to come along. For the rest of the day, I shadow him. What he does is almost a ritual. A polite greeting – sometimes by name – as they enter, followed by a small bow, then the careful,

162

unhurried selection of the pieces they want to handle. Never more than two at a time displayed on the soft black velvet. A glowing description follows, then the unveiling of the price – for them, it's always a special price – and then bartering until money finally exchanges hands, the package is wrapped, and he ushers the customer out.

Dusk is falling and I'm lighting the lamps in the shop when Mestre Vitor tells me, "The next one is yours." He smiles at my grateful surprise. "Your job is to make them fall in love with something."

"Thank you, Mestre." Back at my table, I try to shape perfect filigree spirals, like the one Mestre Vitor gave me as a model. But I can't stop glancing at the shop windows, hoping to see someone on their way in. Each time I lose concentration, the spiral in my hands bends rather than curves. After a dozen attempts, I sigh in exasperation. Mestre Vitor looks up from the queen's cross. Damn. I've interrupted him again.

"Relax," he says mildly. "There's always tomorrow. You'll get your chance."

I nod and vow to be as quiet as water in a well. Twenty minutes later, a woman and her gangly, flat-chested daughter push open the door. I'm on my feet and in the shop before they are. They're from Viana do Castelo, up north, the woman says, in town to shop for the girl.

"It's her first filigree necklace," she explains. "For the festival of Our Lady of Agony."

A special occasion then. I smile knowingly. Much of Mestre Vitor's work is on display during celebrations like this one, where the women parade in bright red shawls and headscarves, colorful embroidered aprons, and enough gold jewelry to sink a *barco rabelo*.

I touch one of the long chains that's paired with a substantial heart. "Something like this?"

The woman frowns. "Smaller," she says. "She's still a girl."

I gulp and avoid glancing at Mestre Vitor. I've offended her by suggesting something beyond her means. A smarter move, I realize, would've been to do the opposite – show her a less showy piece and let her demonstrate her wealth and generosity by requesting something bigger. I scramble to make up for it.

"How about one of these beauties?" I unroll the black velvet onto the counter and place two thinner chains of different lengths and with smaller hearts on it. They gleam against the soft, dark background.

The girl fingers the longer one. "May I try this one, Mama?"

She gets a nod. I help her slip it over her head. They both admire the way it falls on the girl's chest, then the mother brings the heart close to her face. The way she examines every detail makes me think she's probably done this many times for herself.

"What are you asking for it?"

From behind me, Mestre Vitor approaches. Whatever else I may learn to do, he'll remain in charge of the money box.

"May I present Vitor Teixeira, *Mestre Filigraneiro*," I say to the woman. "He made this beautiful piece."

I move aside, watching and listening and feeling rather pleased with myself as he compliments her on her choice, bargains a little to make her happy, and concludes the sale.

After he walks them out, I look at him questioningly. "Well?"

"Needs some improvement," he says in the gruff, good-natured way I'm getting to know. "Like those hearts of yours."

I'm still in the shop, putting Mestre Vitor's newest filigree earrings in the display, when a boy wearing trousers with a hole in one knee shows up. He's holding an envelope addressed to Mestre Vitor.

"I'll take it to him."

The messenger backs up a step. "I'm supposed to take an answer back right away."

Yet another interruption.

Mestre Vitor lays down his tools with a sigh. In the shop, he scans the letter and blinks. "He wants a filigree cigarette case by Tuesday?" He's talking more to himself than to either of us. Shaking his head, he goes back into the workshop and rummages around in a box of metal pieces. "Let's see if I have …" He grunts with satisfaction and returns with a message of his own for the messenger. "Take this back and return as quickly as you can with his response."

"Yes, sir." The boy lets the door slam behind him and races off down the street.

I step outside to watch his progress. After his initial show of energy, he slows to a walk, stopping now and again to peer in shop windows.

"I hope you're not in much of a hurry," I say.

"Why?" Mestre Vitor settles himself at his workbench again. "Is he going the wrong way?"

"I don't know. Where's he supposed to go?"

"To Taylor's. One of the big cellars over in Gaia. One of the managers wants to give the case as a gift."

"Not a bad present."

"A last-minute one, apparently." He grins wickedly. "We'll see if they'll accept my price. You pay more, you know, if your order is to take precedence over the queen's."

After dark, I make my way to the Aguia d'Ouro, once again taking full advantage of the permission Mestre Vitor has granted me to go out. I'm almost a regular now. The waiter – who I now know is called Nico – gives me a familiar nod when I enter and brings me a small jug of red wine without asking. Joaquim – who told me irritably to stop calling him *senhor* – missed yesterday but is here tonight, blowing a very red nose and presenting his arguments with none of his usual force. In fact, he's hardly participating in the general discussion at all. I slip into the seat opposite him as he pokes at a piece of sausage.

"Where were you yesterday?" I ask. "The Aguia d'Ouro isn't the same without your … um … eloquence."

"My tirades, you mean. Isn't that the word they use?" He coughs and blows his nose again. "Living in that *ilha* is going to kill me. When it rains outside, it rains inside. The walls are black with damp. I don't know how anyone survives." He prods his food again, hardly paying attention even when the loudest conversation in the room – a group of students with opinions on everything – turns to the poor conditions of factory workers in Porto.

"Did something happen?"

"I hate being sick." He takes a miniscule bite of sausage. "That's all."

There's obviously more, but he's not sharing it. He's staring pensively into his glass when a lanky, sober-looking young man I haven't seen before strides into the room.

"Sebastião!" The noisy table greets him with back thumps, handshakes, and another chair.

"I've got a wager on this, old man," says one of the friends, putting a heavy hand on the newcomer's shoulder. "Please tell me that the king and queen will be drinking your wine when they come to Porto to inaugurate the bridge."

"We're one of the Port houses that has been given that honor, yes," Sebastião says modestly.

"I knew it!" His heavy-handed friend raises both fists triumphantly in the air. "You're aware that no Port can be poured into the royal glasses without us tasting it first, aren't you? To ensure it's of the required quality, of course."

"Of course!"

"'Tis true!"

The students bang their glasses together, sloshing their contents all over the table.

Sebastião crosses his arms. "Dream on."

Joaquim regards them morosely, then pushes his plate away. It's still got half a sausage that smells of the grill, an untouched egg, and cooked cabbage and carrots.

"Have at it," he says. "I'm done." He lights a cigarette.

"Thanks." I pull it toward me. I can always eat.

At the noisy table, Sebastião is saying, "You lot know we only supply the best. I'll take our Port straight from our cellars to the Royal Palace. So, my indiscriminately guzzling friends, I regret to say that we'll have no need of your services."

His friends groan.

"Greedy bastards," grumbles the heavy-handed one.

"Well, then," says another. "We'll need something else to quench our thirst. Nico!"

"Taking it yourself, are you?" the heavy-handed one asks as Nico comes around with a new bottle. "You expect someone to steal it off the streets of Porto?"

"Someone like us!" one volunteers.

"No," says Sebastião. "But we have to protect our reputation. Did you hear …?"

"Your reputation …"

"… as a womanizing …"

"Will you lot please shut up?"

Sebastião's friends sit stiff and straight, like children called to order by a schoolmarm.

"My sincerest apologies."

"You have my attention, young wine king."

They dissolve again into mirth.

By now I'm smiling. Joaquim isn't.

"Watch it," Sebastião warns, "or I'll give you the rubbish that's ruining our reputation in France and England. Inferior grapes mixed with elderberry juice! That'll scorch those irreverent tongues of yours. We'll see who's laughing then!"

Elderberry juice? I pay closer attention.

"Ack. You know we only drink the finest," says his heavy-handed friend. "Personally, I think we should drown the fraudsters in their own swill."

"I second that," says another, raising his hand.

Sebastião laughs humorlessly. "Go right ahead. We're betting on labels."

"Labels?"

"Yeah. The days of handwritten notes tied around the necks of bottles are over. There are too many scoundrels out there. Labels are a guarantee of quality."

"But what good will it do, really?" one of the group asks. "Most wine is sent abroad in barrels, not bottles. No one …"

I turn to Joaquim. "The *barco rabelo* I came on had elderberry juice aboard. I don't know what happened to it once we got to Porto."

Joaquim stops puffing on his cigarette. "You were carrying elderberry juice and barrels for a *quinta* on the same boat?"

"Yes."

"The owner has some kind of stupid courage then. The emphasis, mind you, is on *stupid*. If the *quinta* finds out, he'll be out of business before I can snap my fingers. Or in prison."

A chill of dread goes up my back. I knew elderberry juice was frowned upon, but didn't realize the sanctions were so severe. No wonder Jorge lashed out when I said what I did in front of the women of the *ilha*. I shut my mouth, sorry I said anything to Joaquim. If Jorge ever gets caught, I don't want there to be any way he can blame it on me.

CHAPTER 30

A T THE MARKET, Inês accepted the paper-wrapped parcel and told the butcher thank you. As she turned away from the stall, a woman with graying hair appeared, her basket overflowing with autumn vegetables.

"Inês, may I have a moment?"

Inês nodded, surprised that the woman knew her name. They'd crossed paths before, but Inês had always stood by idly as Dona Ilda and the woman gossiped. She worked in the household of a wealthy couple. Writers and poets, Dona Ilda had said.

"Your presence is requested at the home of my mistress, Carolina Michaëlis de Vasconcelos," the woman continued.

Inês drew back in surprise. "My presence? Why?"

"It's not my place to say." The woman pursed her lips. "I believe it has to do with an employment opportunity."

"A what?"

The woman huffed impatiently. "Cook had a tongue-wag recently with your Dona Ilda, who apparently praised your budding culinary skills. Our kitchen assistant is going off to get married. With Mistress Carolina expecting a baby soon, and her and the Master still entertaining, Cook is in desperate need of help."

Inês took a startled step backwards. "And Mistress Carolina wants…me?"

"She wants to talk to you," the woman corrected.

Even with her eyes wide open, Inês had no trouble envisioning grand tables set with white tablecloths and fine porcelain and silver. Elegant dinner guests woven together by threads of gay conversation. Perhaps even dancing, after dessert was served. A baby. Scenes a world away from the solemn silence that ruled over mealtimes at the goldsmith's home. Although, she reminded herself, it wasn't so dour now that Henrique was there.

"Does Dona Ilda know?" she asked.

"Now that would be putting the feast before the hunt, would it not?" the woman replied briskly.

"Y ... yes," Inês stuttered. "Of course."

"You know the house?"

Inês shook her head.

"159, Rua de Cedofeita. Come a week from Wednesday. In the morning."

Such a possibility, in a fine house! She'd never have dreamt it. Never have dared. Even the thought of being accorded an interview made her feel dizzy. Behind it, though, wafted the faint smell of disloyalty. She owed every skill she had to the kind, patient woman in the kitchen in the Rua das Flores. She'd not say anything. Not just yet. Probably nothing would come of this, after all. But surely it wouldn't hurt to go, just to see?

"Yes, ma'am." A shiver of excitement raced through her as she said it. "I'll be there."

CHAPTER 31

"WE'LL CLOSE AT noon today," Mestre Vitor says on Saturday morning. He's setting out jewelry as I open the shutters.

"Why?" I ask.

"I have to take the cigarette case to my wife and daughter in Gondomar. Normally I give the *enchedeiras* a week to work, but I need this for Monday." He makes a wry face. "I'll have to grovel and buy them new hats, I know it. Especially if they have to work on the Lord's Day."

I can tell he doesn't mind.

We're having to close because I can't man the shop alone and Goldsmith Bento's still not back. Even I'm worried now. Monsieur Eiffel's cufflinks aren't done. Mestre Vitor had to send the messenger who asked about them away with an unsatisfactory *they'll be ready soon*, followed by a robust *dammit!* as soon as the boy was gone. "We can't lose that commission."

Even so, I can't help but rejoice that I'll have Saturday afternoon free. And maybe …

"What are you doing this afternoon?" I ask Inês as we sit down to our midday meal. "I don't have to work."

"Lucky you." She stops ladling thick, steaming vegetable soup into my bowl. "I do. Today's washing day." She holds out a water-wrinkled hand. "Can't you tell?"

"Yeah." So much for that plan. I dip a chunk of bread into my soup and ask hopefully, "What about tomorrow? After Mass?"

"I don't much fancy walking about with you and Lisete," she says snippily.

170

THE FILIGREE MASTER'S APPRENTICE

"I don't much fancy walking with you and Lisete either." I mimic her tone. To my relief, she chuckles. But still doesn't answer.

It's chilly and bright when I leave Gomes & Filho. On the threshold, I thrust my arms in the air, both stretching and embracing this unexpected, marvelous freedom.

By the river, Ribeira's teeming with people and animals, as always, as is the Pênsil bridge. On the river, *barcos rabelos* and rowboats ferrying people and produce thread their way between big sailing ships. Chickens in a cage fight, talons out and feathers flying. A farm woman screeches and whacks them apart with a stick, making more of a racket than the chickens.

Farther along, Sálvio's ship is tied to the quay. He and half-dozen sailors are on its deck and up in the rigging.

I shield my eyes against the sun and hail him. "You're back."

"Every week, like clockwork." He comes down the gangway.

"Good voyage?"

"Rough. There's a storm out there somewhere. The passengers couldn't wait to get off."

"That bad?"

He grimaces. "We had a lot of unpleasant cleaning up to do. And the new first mate isn't …" He hesitates. "He likes to give orders."

"That's his job, isn't it?"

"Depends on the way they're given." Sálvio shrugs. "The captain'll make him toe the line. Or get rid of him. It's happened before." He doesn't say the first mate treats him more harshly that he does the others, but I wonder.

"I've never seen the ocean," I say. "I can't imagine waves high enough to rock a ship as big as yours."

"Really? It's not far. You can get there easily on foot."

"Maybe I will."

"If it's waves you want, today's a good day. We had an awful time entering the mouth of the river, it was churning so much."

From the deck, someone calls Sálvio's name.

"Back to the mop and bucket," he sighs. "See you later." He climbs the gangplank, the water below him speeding toward the sea. I decide to follow it. It's high time for me to see where the river I've lived with all my life ends up.

I walk past the long granite customs building and the narrow houses climbing the hills of Miragaia. In Massarelos, where the ceramic factory echoes with the sound of hammers and saws, the biting wind carries the smells of charred wood and stormy gray clouds. I pull my coat tighter and push on. The farther I go along the dusty road, the fewer houses there are. Across the river, the Port wine warehouses have disappeared, making way for green hills. Porto's behind me now.

The river bends and widens. I pass an old lighthouse watching over a cluster of moored fishing boats. Even here, well inside the mouth of the river, the water rushes and churns, first hiding and then revealing the sharp rocks below the surface. I imagine the riverbed littered with the rotting hulls of those unlucky enough to have run into them.

Finally, beyond an old stone fortress, is land's end. I stop behind a wall that seems too low to protect anything and stare at the heaving gray-green expanse. It's capped in every direction with the white of breaking waves. All my life, the horizon has ended where mountains or rooftops begin. Things I can measure. Distances I can pace. This vast, unfamiliar space without landmarks makes me uneasy.

I gaze at it for a long time, trying to come to grips with its immensity as the cold north wind tosses salt spray in my face and teases the swells to greater heights. Beyond the river's mouth, five ships wallow and buck, apparently unable to reach quieter water inside. I don't envy them or their passengers. They wouldn't make it to land if something happened to their ship. The wind whistles and tries to pull my hair out by the roots. Shivering, I turn back to Porto. This ocean is not for me.

In the Aguia d'Ouro, with the contents of a glass of wine warming my stomach, my fingers thaw enough to turn the pages of Joaquim's newspaper. It's hard to read. Too dark, and I don't read often enough for the words to come easily. Besides, the noise from the big table in the middle keeps distracting me. Joaquim is listening too.

"Twelve years?" exclaims the red-haired man I saw when I first came here with Rafael. "To make a map of Porto? What are you doing? Counting every paving stone?"

His friends guffaw. But the man he addressed, who has the ramrod-straight, commanding bearing of a soldier, answers mildly, "Just about, my friend. We're working to a scale of one to five hundred."

"Whatever does that mean?"

"It means that every five meters in the city get a centimeter on the map. The façade of this café alone will be three centimeters." He demonstrates the distance between his forefinger and thumb. "It's a massive project, with new roads and buildings appearing all the time. Not to mention that city hall has given me a grand total of four untrained workers, two of them boys." He shakes his head in dismay. "So there will be errors to be found and fixed. And fixed, and fixed. Hence, twelve years."

"To your legacy then." The red-haired man lifts his glass. "To the great Telles Ferreira mapmaking project." His friends join in the toast. The mapmaker, too, stops looking so serious and laughs with them.

On the way home, I pace off the distances – across Praça da Batalha, down the Rua de Santo António, along the façade of the São Bento convent. It's already a lot of map centimeters. I try to imagine this vertical city of spires and skylights and squares transferred onto the flat sheets of a map. I hope I'll be here in twelve years to see it.

CHAPTER 32

AFTER MASS AND the midday meal, as I tap my feet impatiently under the table and Inês dries the plates, she tells Dona Ilda that she's going out for the afternoon.

"I'm meeting a friend." She doesn't glance my way.

"Oh? Who?"

"No one you've met."

No one Dona Ilda has met?

Inês shoots me a warning look. "I'll be home in time to start dinner, as usual."

Dona Ilda doesn't raise an eyebrow, so this must not be unusual for a Sunday afternoon. As a servant, Inês is a lot freer than the daughter of the house.

"Well, don't get wet. It's looking stormy out there."

"I'll be fine." Inês turns to me and winks.

I'm glad to see her good mood restored. She's been unusually pensive for the last couple of days.

"Henrique, be a gentleman and escort me out, will you?"

"Oh Inês, don't bother the poor boy," Dona Ilda scolds. "I'm sure he's glad to have some time free as well."

"No. It's fine," I say hastily. "I'm going out too. It'll be my pleasure to take Miss Inês wherever she wants to go."

"In that case," Inês says, "I do believe I'll choose Paris."

"I'll call the *diligence* right away," I say.

We all laugh until Dona Ilda looks guiltily at the ceiling and shushes us. I stay in the kitchen, telling her about the map that'll take twelve years to draw while Inês runs upstairs. She comes down, still in her Sunday dress, with a dusky pink ribbon in her hair. I can't help but notice that it goes very well with the color of her lips.

"Is there anywhere you want to go?" I ask her when we're out on the street. "Because I want to see the Crystal Palace gardens. Properly." It's true. I do. But I'm also remembering her remark to Lisete about how romantic they are. Now that this lovely girl has agreed to go walking alone with me …

I tell my most sensitive bits to calm down and make a silent vow to be a gentleman.

"It's quite a long way," Inês says.

Not compared to my trek to the sea yesterday. "I don't mind. Do you?"

She turns her face to the sky. "Let's hope the rain holds off." She makes a point of putting her hand on my arm, like a lady. That lasts for about one hundred meters. Then she goes back to normal, her hands gesturing, chatting up a storm. I like her much better that way.

We pass Clérigos church and cut through the park beside it.

"This used to be outside Porto's medieval wall," she tells me. "It's where the ropemakers worked long ago. That's why it's called the *cordoaria,* the ropery. I heard that the area in front of the prison" – she points at a heavy, intimidating building – "was once used as a hanging ground." She shudders, delighted with imagined fears. "There must be ghosts here."

"Don't worry. You've got me to protect you."

She rolls her eyes, and I poke her in the ribs to show I was joking. It's easy to say now. This peaceful leafy space, with a pond in the middle and crisscrossed with walks, gives no hint of a turbulent past.

"Their Majesties will be here in two weeks, with the little princes," she says enthusiastically as we pass the Royal Palace. "I do hope they'll go out in their fine carriage so we can see them."

"They'll be riding in the very first train to cross the Dom Fernando bridge," I tell her, passing on what I heard at the Aguia d'Ouro. "We'll all be able to see that." I for one can't wait to see a train for the first time.

"I mean up close."

"Oh." It must be a girl thing. Luísa would love the festivities too. I'm more excited to see how Monsieur Eiffel's bridge holds up. Someone at the Aguia d'Ouro said that to test it, they'd stop eight train cars and two of the heaviest locomotives in Portugal in the middle of the arch, where there are no pillars to support the weight. That it will collapse seems inevitable. I shake off that dreadful thought and focus on the girl beside me.

At the Crystal Palace, she seems to enjoy exploring as much as I do. We circle the huge building itself, taking in its mixture of iron and glass and stone, and the lake and grotto behind it.

When we reach a chapel, she says, "This was named after a king, Carlos Alberto, who wanted to free Italy from the Austrians. He died here, in exile."

I squint at her. "How do you know all this?"

"I listen," Inês says. "And I like learning about what happened before I walked this earth. If girls were allowed to go to university, that's what I'd study."

"You would?" I regard her with surprise and admiration. I'd never considered she might harbor dreams like that beneath her cheerful demeanor. Then again, why not?

"What about you?" she asks. "What would you study?"

"Engineering." I say it with certainty, although I'd never heard the word before coming to Porto. Lots of engineers and soon-to-be engineers from the Academia Politécnica frequent the Aguia d'Ouro. "So I could build things like the metal bridge and the Crystal Palace."

"Maybe someday you'll be able to."

"Yeah," I scoff. "At Gomes & Filho, maybe – someday – I can make a tiny gold replica. If I have the skills. That's about as close as I'll get to building anything. I'm not ungrateful, of course…" I trail off as we climb a staircase that winds up and around a tower overlooking the Douro. We hug the stone wall, not looking at how far down it is until we're safely at the top. But the wind has picked up, blowing Inês's long skirts and cloak, and we descend hurriedly.

"Before we go, let me show you one of the best views I've ever seen." She guides me down moss-covered steps and under a canopy of bare autumn trees to a small garden with a fountain in the middle. To the west and far below, the river flows choppily toward the ocean. Above it, barreling directly toward us, are clouds heavy with raindrops. They start to come down gently, then fall in torrents.

"Uh, oh." I grab Inês's hand and pull her toward a grotto carved into a wall. "Over there. Run."

The grotto is filled with water, but dry boulders line one side. We squeeze together on top of them, the overhang giving us some protection from the downpour.

"You told Dona Ilda she didn't know the person you were walking with today," I tease.

Inês tosses her head. "She doesn't need to know everything. Besides, I don't want to have to sneak about or lie because she gets the wrong idea."

"What kind of wrong idea?" We're close enough that I can feel her shoulder and hip. It's not enough. Gently, I turn her so we're face-to-face. She tips her head up, her breath warming my cheek, and I pull her closer. Her arms come around my waist.

"May I ...?" I'm asking when she lifts herself onto her tiptoes. Her lips brush mine, and I'm on fire. Holding her full against me, I crush her mouth and hear a muffled *oh* of surprise. She's surely less experienced than I am. I gentle the kiss, then deepen it, the sensations so strong I'm sure we're giving off sparks. I thread both hands through her hair, prolonging the kiss, my body aching. My need to touch her astounds me.

Finally, slowly, I pull back. We're both breathing hard, clinging to each other. I wipe a raindrop off her forehead with my thumb. Beyond the edge of the grotto, the rain cascades down, turning mid-afternoon light to dusk.

Inês snuggles into me contentedly. "At least we have Dona Ilda's permission not to hurry back."

"We do?" With Inês's body pressed against mine, I'd gladly remain here forever.

"She said not to get wet, didn't she?"

"I don't think this is what she meant." I run a finger along her jawbone, amazed at what I'm daring and what she's allowing. She trembles. I pull her closer. "Would it be that bad?" It's not as if I'm reaching above my station. But judging by Dona Ilda's reaction when I sat beside Inês in church, I know the answer is *yes*.

"Well, this hasn't exactly happened before. To me, at least." Inês's look dares me to challenge her. "She'd feel obliged to tell Mistress Alcina, who would forbid it and tell Goldsmith Bento, and we'd be kept apart and watched every second, which would be horrible, or they'd make one of us leave, and ..."

"Stop," I say. "I get it. We won't tell." Keeping this from Dona Ilda is going to be complicated. I twist my hands into her hair again, bringing her face close to mine. "Can we not talk about them anymore?"

"I don't think you want to talk at all," Inês murmurs.

I chuckle and kiss her again, hard, wishing there weren't so many layers of clothing between us. Much too soon, the downpour eases, its drumming giving way to drops falling from branches and water snaking in rivulets along the saturated ground.

Inês breaks free of my arms. Instantly, I feel colder.

"We should go," she says. "It's better if no one sees us like this."

She's right, I know. I eye her shoes doubtfully. "Your feet are going to get soaked."

"What? You're not going to carry me?" Now that the serious business of kissing is over, her merry laugh is back.

"And here I thought you wanted to avoid a spectacle. But I can get you across this." I swing her into my arms, cloak and skirt and all, and take a big step across the little stream that's formed in front of the grotto.

She squeals. "Stop! I didn't mean it."

I grin and give her another kiss.

"You're crazy." She swats my shoulder, giggling. "Put me down."

I slide her down very slowly, keeping our bodies close together.

Nearby, someone clears his throat. We jerk apart to see a man with a top hat and walking stick staring at us disapprovingly.

"*Merda merda*," Inês whispers into my coat as he turns away. "Just when we were doing so well."

We burst into laughter, not stopping until our sides hurt.

"At least you weren't still carrying me," she says when she's regained her breath.

"It's hard. You wiggle."

"I wiggle?" She snorts. "Now that doesn't sound ladylike at all. Come on." She laces her fingers in mine and pulls. "We really must go."

I match her determined strides with some discomfort, my trousers chafing in all the wrong places. That she'll haunt my dreams tonight, I have no doubt.

CHAPTER 33

I N RUA DO *Almada, Joaquim found the place he was looking for. A pharmacy that was also a* drogaria, *selling acids and chemicals as well as medicinal preparations. It was sandwiched between a clanging, banging ironmonger and a* botequim. *Inside, tall painted wood cabinets lined three walls, their shelves holding glass bottles, porcelain canisters with all manner of herbs and plant names on them, soaps wrapped in colorful paper, and a multitude of other products.*

He stopped on the threshold, twirling his mustache into a sharper point and breathing in lavender, thyme, and sandalwood, along with a sharper chemical tang. It was the first time he'd entered a pharmacy since he'd been forced to hand over the keys to his father's. How appropriate that he should be in one now, searching for retribution.

The bell over the door brought the pharmacist out of a back room to help him. Joaquim steeled himself and marched to the curved counter, past the Agua da Florida *perfumes, the hair tonics, and the* licores *for toothache that he knew so well.*

"I need muriatic acid," he said. He was going to do this.

"Certainly."

"In some quantity."

"How much?"

"Five liters."

One of the pharmacist's eyebrows went up, making his face look lopsided. "Five?"

"Yes." Joaquim kept his expression neutral. With an ironmonger next door, this request couldn't be that unusual. Muriatic acid got rid of rust. More

importantly, for Joaquim's purposes, it corroded metal.

"Are you sure you need that much? What's it for?"

"I'm sure." The answer to the second question was none of the pharmacist's concern.

"I don't have that quantity on hand. Come back next week."

"You'll have it then?" If not, Joaquim would have to look elsewhere. He didn't have much time. "You're sure?"

"Yes, yes." The pharmacist nodded with certainty. "Not to worry. Come back in a week."

CHAPTER 34

THE FIRST HINT that our reprieve is over comes at breakfast. I'm ripping off a chunk of bread when Inês comes in with an armful of dishes from the dining room.

"Goldsmith Bento is coming downstairs today," she says nervously. "We're to act as if nothing happened. Mistress Alcina's orders."

My entire body tenses. "As if nothing happened?" I put the bread down, my hand shaking. I always knew this past week was too perfect. That Mestre Vitor couldn't run the business forever. And I'm surely several steps closer to hell for wishing Goldsmith Bento would remain bedridden indefinitely. I like helping in the shop and I do it well. Inês let me kiss her and I suspect she will again. I don't want things to go back to the way they were.

Inês deposits the dishes in the sink and joins us at the table. She and Dona Ilda are both watching me.

Inês puts her hand over mine. "It'll be all right, Henrique. You'll see."

"I wish I could believe you." I feel like I've been punched in the stomach. "If he starts yelling at me again for no reason …"

"He won't," Inês says.

"You can't be sure!" I retort, then see her hurt expression. "I'm sorry. I just … I …" I stand. "I hear Mestre Vitor. I need to go." I escape down the stairs, their worry like a weight on my back. I'm trying so hard to make a place for myself, to fit in. And it's working. But only because the goldsmith hasn't been around. I dread his return more than anything.

Mestre Vitor accepts the news with a relieved nod. "Good. He must finish those cufflinks."

"I guess so." I busy myself tightening a screw that's come loose on one of the jewelry displays. Mestre Vitor catches my distinct lack of enthusiasm.

"Henrique."

I straighten up.

"I know this is hard. But if Gomes & Filho is to survive, we need him here, working. You understand that, don't you?"

"Yes. Of course."

"He's not an easy man. But if you can build a relationship with him, you'll learn from the best."

"I've tried. He hasn't."

"Try again."

"I've given him no reason to be suspicious, yet he is. What if he says I can't help you with customers or touch the displays?" I brace my hands on the counter to steady them. "What if he never lets me..."

"Don't worry so much. Usually when he recovers from something like this, he's milder for a while. Calmer."

"For a while," I repeat bleakly. "What about afterwards?"

"I'll talk to him. Tell him how well you've done during his absence. All right?"

"Thank you, Mestre. Truly." Words can't express my gratitude.

"*De nada.*" He shrugs off my thanks. "Come here. I'll show you the cigarette case." With the utmost care, he unfolds a cloth, revealing the case's top, bottom and four sides, all filled with tiny spirals.

"Your *enchedeiras* must've worked night and day."

He smiles wryly. "They did. And as I suspected, I now owe the two women in my life new hats."

"That's not a bad price to pay." Their work is precise and spectacular. And unfinished. The spirals will fall out at the touch of a finger until they're soldered. I keep my hands safely behind my back.

"I'll finish it today," Mestre Vitor says. "You can deliver it tomorrow."

"I'd be honored." He hasn't made a piece like this since I've been here. I'm eager to see it. More than that, by placing it in my care, he'll be showing Goldsmith Bento he trusts me. That's a gift I have no idea how to repay.

It's midmorning and I'm helping a customer when I hear the

goldsmith's voice. A brief glance over my shoulder shows him staring at me from the workshop. I take a steadying breath and keep up the patter that I hope – now more than ever – will lead to a purchase. When the man decides on the ring he wants for his wife, I call Mestre Vitor to handle the money while I package the gift. It all goes flawlessly and I escort the customer out. After another deep breath, I turn around.

"It's good to have you back, Goldsmith Bento." Even if I'm lying through my teeth, I try to sound welcoming. "I hope you're feeling better."

"I am."

He looks gaunt, hollow, as if his energy bled out during his illness, like sap from a tree. Something unhappy – or unkind – smolders in his eyes.

"I'll take over the customers now. You can go back to your place."

It's exactly as I feared. I'm about to say *yes, sir* when Mestre Vitor intervenes.

"The cufflinks, Bento, the cufflinks. That's your priority. Monsieur Eiffel wants them as soon as possible. Henrique and I will manage the shop."

Goldsmith Bento sets his mouth in an irritated line.

"Bento, please. I'll get everything ready for you. Just work your magic."

The goldsmith looks from Mestre Vitor to me and back again. Finally he nods.

"Give him as wide a berth as possible," Mestre Vitor says almost inaudibly as he takes the cufflinks from the lockbox.

For the rest of the day, I'm painfully aware that Goldsmith Bento is judging my every move and word. It's exhausting, like balancing on a high wall and expecting to be shoved off. When I'm not with customers, I make myself as invisible as possible. Thankfully, the hours pass without incident, but also without the joy I felt the other days. Even during my few moments in Inês's presence, I know I'm unusually quiet and moody. She calls me *Senhor Grumpy*, but for once her playfulness does nothing to lift my spirits.

By the end of the day, Mestre Vitor has soldered and assembled and polished the cigarette case. He displays it on his outstretched palm, the gold gleaming in the late-afternoon light.

"It's magnificent," I say as he hands it to me. "And heavy."

"They're getting their money's worth."

Goldsmith Bento stands stiffly and joins us. I have to stop myself from backing away. As he, too, praises the piece, the three of us are united momentarily in admiration of Mestre Vitor's craftsmanship. Then the goldsmith leaves to put the cufflinks in the lockbox, breaking the spell.

"Be extra alert. Even if it's daytime," Mestre Vitor instructs me the next morning.

He's wrapped the cigarette case in thin, crackly paper the same dark green as the shop door, then tied a thick, bland brown paper around it. Nothing indicates that anything of value is inside. I can tuck it under my arm easily. Still, my palms are sweating. I run them along my trousers.

"Yes, Mestre. I will." I remember the attack on Rafael only too well. I shrug into my coat, repeating the address and customer's name back to him one more time. On the stairs this morning, Inês gave me a kiss for luck. I take the package, avoiding the goldsmith's dark gaze. I'm jumpy enough as it is.

This is the first time I've crossed the Pênsil bridge. Mestre Vitor gave me money for the toll – five *reis* each way. I pay before crossing, then join the stream of wagons and carts and carriages and horsemen and barefoot women balancing baskets on their heads. I step carefully, not wanting to get to Taylor's with my shoes coated in muck. Following Mestre Vitor's instructions, I take a road that climbs steeply uphill, fighting a brisk wind all the way.

"What do you want, boy?" asks a man at the gate to the property.

"I have a package for Senhor Alberto. From Gomes & Filho, the goldsmith."

"Ah. You're expected. Come this way."

As soon as we're inside, the scent of fermented grapes transports me home, to evenings knee deep in the day's harvest, crushing the fruit into pulp with weary legs. I haven't missed that one bit. The smell is where the similarity ends, though. Taylor's is all dark wood, blue and white tiles, and rich furnishings. There are no stomping vats here, and the barrels and vats of wine are somewhere out of sight.

I'm taken to a small office, its walls lined by bookshelves holding tall leather-bound ledgers, each one with a year stamped on its spine. The man behind the desk rips open the packaging without a word, then carries the cigarette case to the window to examine it. I wait, idly taking in the office. On the desk is a package from Araujo & Sobrinho, the shop at the bottom of the Rua das Flores. It's open. I tilt my head to read what's on the slips of paper within.

TAYLOR'S

REGISTERED TRADE MARK

1875

VINTAGE PORT

BOTTLED IN OPORTO

TAYLOR FLADGATE & YEATMAN

These must be the labels the men in the Aguia d'Ouro talked about. The ones they said would help ensure that only true Port wine is sold abroad under that name. They look nice, but I wonder how much difference they'll really make.

Senhor Alberto catches me looking. I straighten up quickly.

"Is the cigarette case acceptable, sir?"

"Very much so." On a piece of paper, he writes, *Received, one cigarette case from Vitor Teixeira*, and signs and dates it. "Tell your master I thank him for his fine work."

Mestre Vitor said nothing about receiving payment and it seems none is forthcoming. I'm beyond relieved.

Outside, low clouds scud across the sky, promising more rain. I hasten downhill, past a line of *barcos rabelos* being unloaded, and back across the bridge. It begins to mist, blurring the outlines of buildings and making this city of granite more somber than ever. I turn up my collar at the corner of the Rua Nova dos Ingleses. Ahead, a man is struggling to keep a bulky, three-legged piece of equipment upright against the wind as he tries to cover it. A strong gust rips the cover from his hands and sends it flapping past me.

"Grab it!" he yells.

The cover rolls and twists as if possessed. I leap after it. On my third try, I stomp on a corner with my foot, ending its flight. The leather is dirtied, but at least it wasn't lost. Holding it away from my clothes, I return it to its owner.

"*Obrigado*," he says, and I realize it's the man they called Telles

Ferreira, the mapmaker. He drapes the cover over a tube at the top of the three-legged stand and secures it with a cord. Around us, the rain starts to fall in earnest.

"*Raios!*" he says.

"Can I help?"

Without hesitating, he points to a wooden case at his feet. "Take that." He hoists the three-legged contraption into his arms and takes off up the hill. Soon we're running through Praça Nova and the narrow streets behind it, the heavy box banging against my legs. By now, my hair is plastered to my scalp and my shoes squish with water.

"Here we are." He stops, unlocks a door covered with flaking red paint, and hustles us both into a hallway. It's cold and damp. As soon as I stop moving, I start to shiver.

"Come in. I'll get the fire going."

The room he enters is a workspace crowded with tables, more equipment I don't recognize, and square sheets of paper as long as my arm. On the wall is a blackboard with numbers scrawled on it. I place the box on the floor where it won't drip on anything and go stand by the fire. As the logs begin to burn, the heat comes through my trousers. I move as close as I can without bumping into him.

"Is this where you make your map?"

From his crouched position by the fire, he glances up in surprise.

"I heard you talking about it in the Aguia d'Ouro."

"Ah. I see. Yes, this is where we do the planning and much of the drawing." The flames are dancing now. The mapmaker rises, takes the cover off the stand with the tube, and dries it with a cloth. "When we're done, we'll have hundreds of those." He nods at the pile of paper. "But we just started in August. Most of the work now is outside, taking measurements. And," he mutters grimly, "fixing other people's measurements when they get it wrong."

"What's that tube thing?"

He chuckles, but I sense no mockery.

"That tube thing is a theodolite. It measures horizontal and vertical angles."

"And that?" I point to another instrument.

As we rotate in front of the fire, he tells me about altimeters and alidades and graduated tapes and plane tables. The only tools I recognize, thanks to the woodworking, are levels and rulers. But when he explains how they make some of the calculations, it makes sense.

My coat and trousers are still more wet than damp, but I've stopped dripping. Outside, the wind has swept the deluge farther inland.

"I should go. Thank you for answering my questions." I have a million more, but he's moved away from the fire and is examining one of the big sheets of paper. I can't impose any more on his time. "What you're doing – it's fascinating. I wish I could learn more." It's a wish that'll never come true. This is the work of an engineer. Not a goldsmith.

"It was nothing. Thank you for your help."

I nod and step out into the fog.

CHAPTER 35

"**W**HAT ARE YOU *doing here?*" *Hugo shoved past the neighbor women crowding their one-room home and knelt beside his mother. She lay in bed, her knee bound in a cloth. "Mama, what happened?"*

"It's nothing." She raised a hand to ruffle his hair. "I'll be fine."

"Well, you aren't now," said their next-door neighbor. Her meddling always drove Mama crazy. To Hugo she said, "Your mother fell when she was bringing the gorse up from the river. They had to carry her home."

To Hugo's horror, tears ran down Mama's cheeks and into her stringy hair. She wiped them away angrily. "Don't scare the boy. The knee will heal. It just needs time."

"Mama, how will we manage?" Even with both of them healthy, they were always hungry, always cold. Always on the slippery edge of just getting by.

"You're a strapping lad," said the meddlesome neighbor. "You can do the deliveries for her. If you don't, the others will take them and she'll be left with no customers."

Mama moaned and tried to sit up.

"Stay still." The neighbor pushed her back down.

"But I already work," Hugo protested. The last time he tried to lift one of those gorse bundles, he hadn't gotten it above his knees. The strength in her skinny body was one of many reasons he didn't smart-talk Mama. Seeing her lying in bed like that, though, scared him.

"The gorse gets to Porto early. You can deliver it first, then go to work," said another neighbor. "I'll check on your Mama while you're gone."

These women had decided everything. Furious, Hugo slitted his eyes. But he was

188

less angry at them than at the unfairness of it all. At the slick slope where Mama fell, at Goldsmith Bento. And at stupid, arrogant, too-old apprentice Henrique, who sat around on his butt all day learning a trade, leaving the dirty, unpleasant work – and now the worry – to Hugo.

"Go away. All of you. Leave us alone."

What he really wanted was to lay his head beside his mother's and cry.

CHAPTER 36

DAYS GO BY, and the atmosphere in the workshop lightens as Goldsmith Bento regains his strength but not his bad humor. On the same afternoon, he and Mestre Vitor put the finishing touches on the queen's cross and Monsieur Eiffel's cufflinks. Inês tells me they opened a bottle of vintage Port upstairs later to celebrate.

The next morning, Mestre Vitor tells me I'm to accompany him to the Royal Palace.

"You're my guard," he says.

He's more massive than I am, by far. I laugh.

"It would take a determined thief to get that cross away from you, I think."

"Truly, he'd take his life in his hands." Mestre Vitor pretends, rather fiercely, to throttle someone. "But if ever he succeeded, I'm counting on you to chase him down."

"I consider it my solemn duty, sir."

Our joking keeps worry at bay. I do notice, however, that he ties a rope around the handle of the satchel holding the cross and loops it several times around his wrist. Mestre Vitor's arm, it seems, will go wherever the queen's filigree does. As we step outside, passing Goldsmith Bento, who is back to manning the shop, I feel every muscle go on high alert. Mestre Vitor plods along, looking no more excited than if he were going to buy a newspaper. He's used to this, I guess. I'm not.

Despite my misgivings, we arrive safely. At the Royal Palace, there's a line of carts with potatoes and apples and turnips and leafy produce waiting to be unloaded. They're clearly stocking up ahead of the royal arrival. Another line leads inside to a table where the head butler I met last time is taking notes and issuing instructions. We join it and inch forward.

When it's our turn, Mestre Vitor draws from his satchel a dark, polished wooden box the size of my two open hands put together. Gomes & Filho is painted in ornate gold lettering on the top. He opens it slowly, showing the reverence both the object and the queen deserve. The cross and its thick chain shimmer in their nest of deep green velvet.

There's a moment of silence, the three of us completely still. Then the head butler breathes, "Magnificent. The queen will certainly be pleased."

Mestre Vitor expands with pride. "Thank you for your confidence, sir. It's been an honor."

The head butler signs and hands over an official-looking paper. "Here's a promissory note to give to the bank."

All I glimpse, before Mestre Vitor folds it away, is the first line:

This note entitles the bearer, Vitor Ernesto Maria Teixeira, to

Damn. I'd love to know what he got for it.

"Thank you, sir. I am, as always, at your disposal." Mestre Vitor gives a small bow.

After we take our leave, I say, "That went well."

Mestre Vitor radiates quiet satisfaction, but says simply, "No reason for it not to."

I hope that, over time and under his tutelage, I'll develop skills like his and the self-confidence that comes with them. We stop briefly for a celebratory drink at the Porta do Olival café on the way back, offered by Mestre Vitor. For the first time in weeks, I see him relaxed, almost jolly. It doesn't last.

"Go back to the shop now," he tells me when we reach Praça Nova. "It's best not to leave Goldsmith Bento alone for too long. I need to stop by the bank."

I'd rather not, but keep my mouth firmly shut and do as I'm bid.

As Gomes & Filho comes into sight, far down the street, I see Hugo. The boy has paused in his sweeping and has his face turned up to a slight man who is talking to him. I jolt to a stop, feeling like I'm going to be sick. Jorge? Here?

I rush down the street, dodging people and carts and carriages. By the time I reach the shop, the *rabelo* owner is gone. I have no reason to go after him. Rather the opposite. I want him as far removed from my life as possible. And far away from Goldsmith Bento. I don't even want to imagine what could happen if the two people I like least start talking about why they don't like me either.

Hugo rests on his broom, smirking at me.

"What did he want?" I ask.

"Who?"

"The man you were talking to." I try hard not to yell. "What did he want?"

"Directions."

"Liar."

"Prove it." With a vigorous swipe of his broom, Hugo sends his pile of debris flying toward me. I jump back, dirt flecking my shoes and trousers.

"Son of a bitch!" I'm dying to shake the truth – and the insolence – out of him.

He matches my glare, knowing as well as I do that I won't. And that I have no complaint I can take to the goldsmith.

"Snotty little kid." Exercising a control I didn't think I had, I dust off my trousers, stomp my feet, and enter the shop.

Goldsmith Bento is showing dangly earrings to a customer in a manner much like his normal self. I skirt him and busy myself in the workshop, getting wood and stoking the fire. When Mestre Vitor returns, we've gold bars and wire to make.

During the afternoon, Monsieur Eiffel comes in person to collect his cufflinks. He nods in recognition as I hold the door for him. I'm so grateful that he's departing with those cursed cufflinks, I could dance.

CHAPTER 37

THAT SAME AFTERNOON, a messenger brings me a letter from Luísa. I ask Mestre Vitor for a moment to read it in the privacy of the back yard.

Dearest brother,

I am writing to tell you that our family is well. Father says he hopes you are proving yourself useful to the goldsmith in Porto. (He said more than that, but I cannot put it into a letter.) Mother asks if you're healthy and keeping warm enough. The baby is growing. She drinks Mother dry as a prune, but cries a little less these days.

Our brothers are busy with Father in the carpentry shop. Tiago tells me of some techniques he wants to try, but Father won't hear of them. I honestly think Tiago could be the best carpenter in the family if given the chance. Don't tell anyone I said so.

Father came with surprising news the other day. He got an order for a table from the quinta. *He said it's the first time in years. I shall spare you what else he said. I'm sure it has nothing to do with you being gone. The* quinta *surely doesn't keep track of such things. In any case, he's determined to make a fine object so other commissions will follow. He's riding the boys hard to make it perfect.*

I have started teaching Emilia letters. Our little sister learns so quickly! Mother knows, but we hide our efforts when Father is around. You know how he feels about us wasting time.

I have other news. I am being courted! João arrived soon after you left to take care of the quinta's *horses. I see your hackles rising, but don't worry. Father and our brothers are keeping a close watch on him. Too close. I pray they don't scare him away. You should see how gentle he is with the horses, especially the young ones. I believe he'll be gentle with my heart too.*

Your loving sister,
Luísa

I read the letter once, unbelievingly, then again. Luísa isn't scarred for life. And this time, it seems, the rash words I couldn't contain had done some good. I punch my fists in the air with a jig and a loud *yes!* that brings Inês to an upstairs window. I wave the letter at her and grin.

CHAPTER 38

ISETE! COME HERE right now!" Mistress Alcina climbs the stairs, her voice as piercing as a chisel. I hold my head, wincing. Hugo notices and adds an extra clatter to everything he does.

I celebrated a little too much – to the extent that my limited means would allow – at the Aguia d'Ouro last night. I was fine until Joaquim asked for the source of my good humor. I didn't mention Luísa's letter, but told him we'd delivered two of the shop's most prestigious orders. That's when he called for another bottle of wine and things got blurry.

I made it home and to bed with no problem. Only Inês, who let me in – and pushed me away with a grimace when I tried to kiss her – was the wiser. Today, though, everything between my ears pounds. I don't even feel up to wondering why Mistress Alcina is yelling. I just hope she does the rest of it behind closed doors.

Alas, that's not to be.

Inês appears in the workshop. "Henrique, we're wanted upstairs."

I frown. "We?"

She nods seriously. "Come on."

Lisete is on the sofa in the sitting room, carefully studying her hands. Mistress Alcina is pacing. She whirls to face us when we enter.

"Stop. You stand right there. Both of you."

I flinch at her sharp tone, and not only because of my headache.

"How could you?"

I stare back warily. Wearily. What is it now?

"My apologies, Mistress Alcina," I say. "I don't know what you're referring to." Too late, I see Lisete mouthing silently, *let me talk.*

"You allowed Miss Lisete to be accosted by a strange man at the Crystal Palace! How could you be so irresponsible?"

"Mother, I told you …"

"Don't lie, Lisete. I saw Dona Fernanda this morning. She asked me who that young man with a pocket watch was. The one with you on his arm. I assume, Henrique, that you do not own a pocket watch?"

I shake my head, and instantly regret it. "No, Mistress."

"Mother, I've seen him at Mass," Lisete jumps in. "He offered to walk us to our *diligence*. Hardly any distance at all. From here to across the street, nothing more."

She's a damned good liar.

"You had Inês and Henrique to walk you to the *diligence*, Lisete!"

"Mother, he was simply being polite. No harm was done."

"No harm, you say? When a busybody like Dona Fernanda sees you? The whole town could be talking about it."

"I hardly think so, Mother. I hope you told her it was the young man who is apprenticing with Papa."

"Lisete! One shouldn't tell falsehoods."

"Well then, what did you say?"

"God forgive me, I told her it was Henrique." Mistress Alcina raises her eyes heavenward. "But only because she hadn't yet mentioned the pocket watch, mind you. I didn't think it necessary to disabuse her of the notion afterwards."

"You see?" Lisete claps her hands. "It's not such a problem after all. I promise it won't happen again, if it concerns you so much."

Inês gives me a disbelieving look. We both know it's another promise Lisete will surely find a way around. Mistress Alcina sighs, then turns to Inês and me. She may be defeated by her daughter, but she's not done with us yet.

Inês bites her lips, then says, "Mistress, Henrique and I didn't want to cause a scene. And since it was clear Lisete knew him, we thought perhaps he was a friend of the family."

Meu Deus. It's not only Lisete who is a formidable liar. Mistress Alcina doesn't stand a chance.

"We never left her side, Mistress. I swear we didn't."

"Young ladies don't swear, Inês," Mistress Alcina says primly, and I cough back a laugh. She turns on me. "Henrique, what do you have to say for yourself?"

"Uh …" I flounder. "Uh, it's as they say, Mistress. Nothing

inappropriate was said or done." Frankly, I have no idea what they whispered to each other on the way to the *diligence*. But if the girls are willing to duck the truth to avoid getting into trouble, I damned sure am too.

"Oh goodness. How would you judge that?" Mistress Alcina snaps. "You know nothing of city ways."

"Yes, Mistress. I mean, no, Mistress," I say miserably. There's no right answer. All I want is to go somewhere where no one is talking. "I'm doing my best to learn, Mistress."

"Mother, let's not bother Papa with this misunderstanding. Please? He's been so unwell." Lisete's request is as self-serving as it is sincere, but I can't fault her for it. Her guile is saving all of our hides today.

"My dear, I do hate keeping things from your father." Mistress Alcina's hands smooth her dress in a motion that looks more lost than purposeful. "But I suppose you're right."

Behind her mother's back, Lisete throws us a triumphant glance. Then, with the tone of a martyr, she asks, "So, Mother, what sewing do you have for me today?"

CHAPTER 39

I

T HAPPENS SATURDAY evening, as we're closing. Goldsmith Bento's bringing in jewelry from the display cases while Mestre Vitor and I finish up in the workshop.

"Henrique, didn't you make four gold bars today?" Mestre Vitor asks.

"They're on your table." I hear silence behind me, and turn. He's holding them up and there are only three. "Where's the other one?"

"I don't know," Mestre Vitor says.

Goldsmith Bento stops whatever he's doing in the lockbox and straightens up, staring from me to Mestre Vitor and back again.

Like an animal, I feel the hairs on my neck rise. There is danger here.

"It must've rolled off." In two giant steps, I'm beside Mestre Vitor's workbench. I circle it, but don't find the bar. I widen the search and doublecheck that it isn't in its mold. Still nothing. I retrace my steps from hearth to worktable, eyes searching in every direction. I'm sure I put all four of them on his table. Dropping to my knees, I jab my fingers into the spaces between the wooden slats on the floor, my breath coming in fast, noisy pants. Behind me, Mestre Vitor and the goldsmith are ominously silent. I scramble to my feet.

"It's got to be under there." I pull the worktable to one side and yank up the wooden slats, praying for a glimpse of gold. There's only bare floor. Panic closes my throat. This can't be happening. Not again.

"Are you sure it's not in the lockbox already?" I choke out.

"I'm sure," Mestre Vitor says.

Frantically, I race around the workshop, checking windowsills and toolboxes and the ledge by the fireplace, knowing there's no reason the bar would be anywhere other than where I left it. In the corner, I paw through Hugo's waste pail, but turn up only leftover snips of metal. And the memory of the boy's malevolent scowl.

"Where's Hugo?" I ask desperately. "Did you check him?"

"We always do before he leaves," Mestre Vitor says quietly.

Goldsmith Bento's lips are pulled back so tightly that he looks like he's baring his teeth. Before the glazed, crazy look in his eyes, I cower.

Then he speaks.

One word.

One devastating word.

"Strip."

I flinch like I've been whipped.

"What?"

"You heard me."

"You truly can't think …"

"Now." His quiet voice is a dagger.

With my eyes, I beg Mestre Vitor to say something. But his mouth is set in a hard, angry line and he's glaring at the wall.

Dizzy with humiliation, I do as the goldsmith says. As each item of clothing comes off, Mestre Vitor bunches the fabric in his hands, making sure nothing is hidden in a pocket, a hem, or a fold. When I'm completely naked, Goldsmith Bento orders me to hold out my arms and turn around. I'm shaking so hard I can hardly make my feet move.

When I'm facing them again, hands in front of my privates, Mestre Vitor grates, "Bento, that's enough. I'm sure Henrique didn't …"

The goldsmith ignores him. "Bring me everything that's in your sleeping area."

"May I get dressed first?" I hate how my voice quivers.

"No."

"Bento, stop!" Mestre Vitor's hands flap helplessly at his sides.

The goldsmith doesn't even acknowledge him. "Not unless you want to strip again afterwards," he tells me.

I wouldn't survive it a second time. But what if one of the women comes downstairs and sees me? There would be shrieking, fainting. And if that woman were Inês, my shame would never end. I check that the hallway is free, then dash across it to grab my clothes, my bedding, and the sack I brought from Mesão Frio. With the bundle covering my front, I rush back to the workshop.

Goldsmith Bento orders Mestre Vitor to go through it, piece by piece, then tells him to check around and beneath my sleeping pallet.

"Bento!" Mestre Vitor protests. The goldsmith stares him down. Mestre Vitor stalks away, the muscles in his jaw working. Time creaks to a stop as I wait endlessly, numb and shivering.

Mestre Vitor doesn't find the bar.

Of course he doesn't.

"Get dressed," Goldsmith Bento orders me.

I do, my movements so jerky I can hardly do up my buttons.

"Leave," Goldsmith Bento says. "You're dismissed. Take your things and go, or I'll have you arrested."

"Bento, listen," Mestre Vitor begins. The goldsmith's furious glare silences him.

"Please …" I say at the same time.

"Shut up and get out. You're to keep your distance from all of us." The goldsmith lifts his arm and points at the door. "I don't want to see you near here again. Ever."

"Mestre Vitor," I beg. "Please."

"I'm sorry, Henrique." His jaw is so tight he has trouble saying my name.

He isn't standing up for me.

I leave them and stumble into the night, with everything I own in the bag on my back.

CHAPTER 40

THE FRONT DOOR *closed. Henrique was gone.*
Around Vitor's chest, despair tightened like a band.
"I knew he couldn't be trusted, Vitor. I knew it!" The air in the
workshop vibrated with Bento's rage. "Was there anyone suspicious in the shop
today? Anyone he could have given it to?"

Vitor closed his eyes, trying to summon calm. Instead, he felt a wild desire to
bellow and throw things. Bento was crazy and a fool, and was just getting worse.

"No, there wasn't," he growled. "I'm sure Henrique didn't ..."

"Why, oh why, did I harbor another thief?" Bento lamented. The face he turned
skyward was red and perspiring. "God, why are you punishing me? I try to be an
upright man. Why is this happening?"

Vitor leaned both hands on his worktable, almost too weary and dispirited to
stand. Once again, the goldsmith was spiraling into that place where reason had no
home. It was unmistakable, and impossible to stop. A sharp pain lanced across
Vitor's chest. He sat down and hunched over, sweating. He'd never understand
why Fate had decreed that he would work in Bento's shop rather than the other
way around. As always, he was the one who'd have to deal with the crisis.

He breathed through the pain until it lessened. "Bento, it's not that ..."

"We're on unsteady enough footing as it is! You can't let bars of gold disappear!
It'll be the end of us!"

"Calm down, Bento. I didn't let anything disappear."

"But you did. He took it under your watch. You're failing in your responsibility
to me and to the shop."

With effort, Vitor straightened. "Don't you dare! I carried us when you were
sick. I have a steadier stream of orders than you do." His tone was as accusatory

as the goldsmith's, his words just as harsh and utterly lacking in respect. Vitor didn't care.

"I don't believe for a minute that Henrique stole from us. But if he did, you lost your best chance of finding that bar by sending him away. You realize that, don't you?"

Vitor stopped speaking. Bento was twirling like a dog after his tail, going much too fast to see whatever he might be searching for. The maddening narrative inside his head was the only thing the goldsmith was listening to now.

Halting suddenly, Bento brought his face so close to Vitor's that their noses almost touched. "You insisted we keep him, after the first incident!" he shouted. "This is your fault!"

Another unwarranted, meaningless accusation, after so many others. This time, something in Vitor shattered.

"Enough!" he yelled, spit spraying the goldsmith's face. "I've had enough of your craziness! You'll ruin us if you keep this up!"

Bento rocked back, his mouth slack with shock. "Don't you ever ..."

Vitor pressed a hand against his breastbone. "I can't handle this anymore. I just can't." He snatched up his coat and satchel and tottered away as fast as his unsteady legs would carry him. Behind him, the goldsmith still roared. In his haste to get out, Vitor almost knocked Inês down in the hallway.

"Mestre Vitor, what ...?"

"Bento dismissed Henrique," he choked out. "He's not coming back."

And he, Vitor, had allowed it to happen. He lurched out the door, the pressure in his chest cutting off his air. This unhealthy shop was going to crush him.

CHAPTER 41

FOR A TIME – I have no idea how long or where – I wander. I'm staggering more than anything, my body hitching to one side as if it isn't sure how to remain upright. A man on the street pulls his lady companion aside and places himself between us. It's so unnecessary that I laugh. The result is grotesque, a leer. I'm too numb to care – or to think. It's better this way, for the alternative is to remember. I'd rather place my hands on a searing stovetop.

At some point, I find myself under Monsieur Eiffel's bridge, knee deep in water, screaming upward at the unfairness of it all. At Goldsmith Bento. At Rafael's father. My mind must be troubled, because I see them hovering above the water in front of me, cackling as they merge. I'm a poor, barely educated boy from the Douro. It's clear they think I deserve nothing more.

My voice finally gives out, and the sinister figure evaporates with it. So does my defiance. I slip on a rock and almost go down. There's no sure step for me in any direction.

I shudder, envisioning my welcome if I get on a *barco rabelo* and go back to Mesão Frio. The boy who stole from the *quinta* returns. Not as a prosperous young man, with a trade or riches from Brazil, but as one dismissed for thievery. There's not a soul who would believe my side of the story a second time around. *It's in his character*, they'd say, burning the disgrace into me like a red-hot brand.

Or I could go forward, step by slippery step, until it's too deep to stand. Let the Douro have its way. Then I wouldn't have to think anymore. Would never have to face anyone or try to explain. Of the two choices, this one is by far the more tempting. The current tugs at my legs, cold and insistent.

From behind the clouds, the moon peeks out, bathing the colossus above me in pale light. I tip back my head and regard it listlessly. Marvels such as this bridge are someone else's dream. Accomplishments that couldn't be farther from my small, miserable life. Whatever made me think I could create something beautiful? Something useful? I can't even make myself step deeper into the water, when it should be so easy.

Maybe I'm a coward. Or maybe… I hear a woman's laugh echo from somewhere high above the riverbank. No matter what I decide, I can't go without telling Inês that this is not who I am. Slowly, slipping again and again on the hidden stones beneath my feet, I make my way back to shore. And to the oblivion I know I'll find in the Aguia d'Ouro.

"Henrique, slow down." Joaquim joins me when I'm well into my second jug of wine. "Trying to drown yourself?"

I narrow my eyes and concentrate as I pour him a cup, then upend what's left into mine, hardly sloshing at all.

"I failed even at that today." My feet and legs are soaking and my throat hurts from the yelling, but the wine helps. I don't take my glass from my lips until it's empty.

Joaquim leans back, like a caged animal sensing peril. That quick look of panic, followed by wariness. He doesn't want to hear my woes. He's in luck, because I don't want to tell them either. He stands to shake the hands of a few acquaintances, then gets drawn into a conversation about politics.

I don't listen. I don't care. I do know he keeps glancing my way and wish he wouldn't. My misery really doesn't want company. I wave at Nico. He brings another jug as Joaquim sits down again. I have nowhere to sleep and probably too few *tostões* to pay for a bed, so I may as well spend them here. I'm poorer now than when I arrived in Porto. I pour myself more wine. Joaquim has hardly touched his, so I don't have to share.

I lift my glass in a sloppy toast. "To days that can't end soon enough." I chug it down, then ask bitterly, "How was yours?"

"Right." He sharpens his mustache with his fingers, still wearing that *I don't want to be here* look. "What happened?"

"You're the one who reads the newspapers. You tell me." I snicker wetly at my own cleverness.

"You want to have a normal conversation or act like an ass?"

"Must I choose? I'd rather not." I honestly don't believe I can. Thinking is too hard.

He rolls his eyes, then regards me somberly as I pick up the jug. I tilt it and see bottom.

"Here. You finish it." I hold it out, hoping he'll notice how generous I am. What a good, honest person I am. I lift my hand to hail Nico.

"Stop it." Joaquim pushes my arm down. "Talk to me."

Shaking my head, I refill my glass.

He takes it away. "There'll be plenty of time to drink afterwards. Talk."

"I am no longer a goldsmith's apprentice. He threw me out." I'm biting the words off in anger. "There. I've talked. Are you satisfied?"

I beckon Nico again. This time, Joaquim doesn't stop me. He does ask for details. I sigh into my wine and give him the minimum.

"I don't know where it is. He didn't give me time to search properly," I finish. "It's like he'd already decided I was guilty and nothing I could do would prove otherwise. And Mestre Vitor ..."

I stop. I was nothing but loyal to him. He should've stood up to Goldsmith Bento for me. Or, at the least, asked me about the bar when the goldsmith wasn't listening.

"You can't go back and ...?" Joaquim stops. He won't offer false hope. "I'm sure you'll find another job."

I slump so my nose almost touches my glass and squeeze my eyes shut, willing tears back. He's voiced what I don't want to admit. The dream that brought me to Porto is dead. My stomach heaves. I double over and vomit on the floor. Joaquim swings his legs out of the way with a grunt of disgust.

"*Caralho!*" he swears. "Let's get you out of here." He calls Nico over, apologizes in my stead as he pays, and wrestles me to my feet. "Come on."

The floor is rising and falling in waves, except that it's not water. Even with one arm over Joaquim's shoulder, I have trouble putting one foot in front of the other. My throat burns and my mouth tastes like bile. Outside, I spit and blow my nose. Little chunks from an earlier meal come out. I brace my hands on my knees and retch again. Joaquim props me up, then hands me a handkerchief.

"Let's get you home," he says. "Which way?"

"Uh …" In my head, my future had gone no farther than the Aguia d'Ouro. "Until today, home was the goldsmith's."

"*Raios*," he swears again. "You left with nothing?"

"I have a bag." I peer blurrily around my feet. "Where is it?"

"Did you have it in the Aguia?"

"Yes." I think I did.

"Don't move." He leans me against a lamppost and goes inside. When he reappears, he's holding my soiled bag at arm's length. "It was under the table." His nostrils pinch together. "At least you didn't lose it."

"No," I say dully. It's too much effort to care.

When I wake, I'm lying on my side on a dirt floor, a foul-smelling chamber pot beside my head. Behind it is a wall with a crack from top to bottom. Greenish-black mold has grown up it and along other, small fractures that split off to either side, making a vaguely treelike shape. I regard it in dazed bewilderment, my head pounding. The blanket and wisps of straw I'm lying on are damp and I have no idea where I am.

Carefully, I roll away from the wall. Joaquim's little table, still covered with newspapers, has been pushed against his sleeping alcove to create space for me. Against one wall is a cabinet that's missing a door. Slowly, slowly, I sit up. He's not in his bed, or in the room. The door and window stand open, letting in daylight so bright that I wince. I hear voices and Joaquim's deep cough.

A second later, Miguel pops his head in. "You're awake. Finally."

"Don't talk so loudly."

"Senhor Joaquim said you drank your weight in wine." His gaze travels to the chamber pot with a young boy's glee at everything disgusting. "And that you threw up about as much again."

"Wait 'til it happens to you." My stomach is still churning. "You won't find it funny then." As for me, I really don't want to remember the night. "What time is it?"

"Mid-afternoon."

"What day?"

He cackles, then stifles it when I hold my temples. "Sunday. You didn't sleep that long."

Sunday. The goldsmith's shop is closed. I don't have to worry about being late. Then the memory hits me, as if I've slammed face-first into

Monsieur Eiffel's bridge. There's no job to be late to. No earnings – except the bits of pocket change Mestre Vitor gave me – for three weeks of work. No chance of a recommendation to another goldsmith. And Inês. Goldsmith Bento ordered me to keep away from them all. I drop my head onto my chest and groan.

"You all right?" Miguel asks.

After a few moments, I unfold stiffly and struggle to my feet. "I need a privy."

"There." He points toward the end of the alley. It looks as far away as the moon. I take it a step at a time, keeping a hand on the wall. Protesting, the chickens get out of my way.

"Hey." Joaquim interrupts his conversation with a bent, black-clad neighbor woman. "Take the chamber pot, will you?"

I'm too focused on my destination to answer, much less turn around. That doesn't stop me from noticing the stares as I make my way past all the other little houses. After relieving myself, I return to the blanket and let sleep take me again.

When I open my eyes next, the shutters and door are closed and the cramped space is lit by a single oil lamp. Thankfully, my headache has dulled to a rhythmic throbbing behind my forehead. Joaquim is perched on the edge of his bed, knees under the table, eating out of a bowl.

He glances up from his newspaper when I push myself to a sitting position. "Back to the land of the living?"

"I guess so." I'd sleep for days if that would keep reality away. "Thank you. For last night, I mean. For not leaving me on the street."

"Yes. Well." He coughs, then clears his throat. "I wouldn't do that. But you will have to find other quarters."

"Tonight?" I droop.

He rolls his eyes heavenward. "Of course not tonight. Although I know that floor's not comfortable."

"It's better than the alternative."

"I'll ask around tomorrow. See if anyone in the *ilha* knows of a place."

"I …" My hand flies to my money pouch. It's still there, with the few coins I have left. Enough for a meal or two, maybe, but not a room. "I owe you for last night."

He shrugs. "It wasn't that much."

Maybe not. But if he's living here, he doesn't have a lot either.

He waggles his spoon at a second bowl. "That's for you."

I put a hand to my stomach, calculating what it might be able to hold. It's unsettled, but I can't tell if that's the result of last night or because it's empty. I roll the blanket into a corner and pull his stool up to the table. In the bowl is tomato rice, like Mother and Luísa make. I lean over, breathing in its warm, familiar smell, and my stomach cramps. I take a cautious bite.

"Ana Maria brought it."

"That was generous."

"The women in the *ilha* cook for me. She made extra today."

Another person I now owe. "It was kind of her."

I make my way steadily through the tomato rice. Joaquim is silent too, except for grunts of disapproval as he turns the pages of the newspaper. I know I'm imposing, but can't muster the will to do anything about it. When the food is gone, I remain there, slumped, staring at the dirty bowl and spoon.

Joaquim taps a finger on the table to get my attention. "Tomorrow you need to find a job."

I don't answer. I can't. Thinking about my failure is like having a mountain collapse on me. "I need the privy."

Once again, going and coming, I ignore the curious glances from residents chattering from their doorways. Back inside, I unroll the sleeping blanket.

"You can't avoid it, Henrique."

"For a few hours, I can."

A rooster crows as morning comes, but I don't rise with it. Instead, I curl into a ball. I don't think I slept. Or if I did, my waking and sleeping nightmares were the same. Me in the workshop, shivering and defenseless, my worth stripped away with my clothes. Anger came in the river, too late to be of service. Even now, howling and scratching in my chest, it provides no armor I can use to fight back.

Joaquim moves around, opens the door. For a brief moment, I smell cigarette smoke rather than mold. I'm hoping he'll leave, do whatever he does all day. I have no idea what that is. From somewhere in the *ilha*, a dry, rhythmic *clack clack* begins. A weaver, beginning his day at the loom.

"Henrique, get up." Joaquim says from outside. "Ana Maria

brought us coffee."

"Wait!" I grab my trousers and pull them on under my long nightshirt. I'm thrusting my arms into a rumpled shirt when Joaquim comes in with a blackened metal pot.

"Relax. It's just me." He pours us each a cup.

"Oh." I wrap my hands around mine, grateful for the warmth.

"What are your plans?" he asks.

I give him the answer he expects. "I'll look for work."

He nods. "Do you have money? If I find you somewhere to stay?"

"Not until I start working."

He grimaces. "That's going to make it hard."

"I'm sorry. To inconvenience you, I mean."

He gives a one-shouldered shrug. "It won't be for long."

Message received, loud and clear.

The men from the *ilha* have already left, off to factories in the neighborhoods of Bonfim and Paranhos. Joaquim gives me directions. I skulk away resentfully, wishing he were the one going out so I could stay curled up on the floor.

I know I've reached my destination when the overpowering stench – from tanneries, tobacco, soap lime, and cloth dyes – makes my nose burn and my eyes tear.

Outside the long white façade of the *Companhia de Fiação Portuense*, I start toward the entrance, stop, back up, take two strides forward, and stop again. I must look like a halfwit, going back and forth in front of the factory, muttering to myself. But despite all the arguments in favor of walking through that door and joining the ranks of spinners and weavers, I can't make myself do it. Going to work in a factory – any factory – means admitting that I failed. That I'm destined to never learn a valuable trade, or use my mind or hands to do anything out of the ordinary. That the life I dreamed of will never be mine. I can't do it.

I spend the rest of the day walking. In the early evening, as it starts to drizzle, I go back to Joaquim's, empty-handed and ashamed.

"No, I didn't find anything," I say, my eyes on my shoes. "Not yet." He's not my father, able to impose his will. But he is housing and feeding me, so he has the right to ask.

He puts down his newspaper. "The fellow two doors down said his factory needs workers. You can go with him tomo …"

"I don't understand you!" I snap. Embarrassment fuels my anger.

"For someone who's always going on about how horrible the factories are, you're trying awfully hard to get me into one."

"Ah." His voice is suddenly cool. "I thought you were someone who might appreciate a hand getting back on his feet. Forgive my mistake. Please, do it your way, since it's working so well." Pointedly, he goes back to the article he was reading.

"Wait. It's not ... I ..." Damn. I take a long breath. "I apologize for my tone. But it's true. You act like factories are pure evil. Yet now you're telling me to go work in one?"

He waits a few beats, long enough that I fear he's decided not to talk anymore. "They are. And that won't change as long as our government and his oh-so-Royal Majesty care nothing about the misery of the people." He waves his hand indignantly around the room. "They have no idea how we live or what we need."

Nor, I'm sure, do people who are much, much closer. Like Goldsmith Bento and the other inhabitants of the Rua das Flores. But I'm in no mood now for one of Joaquim's tirades about the monarchy. Thankfully, he switches direction.

"If those who govern us won't change anything, then it's up to the people to fight for better conditions. If you had a factory job, you could lead the battle from within. I heard you stand up to that young man in the Aguia d'Ouro. You could do it." He raises an eyebrow. "What do you think?"

I think he's crazy. Who am I to make a difference? A glance around the *ilha* – which I know is one of many, and they're all equally miserable – makes it clear change is needed. With that I agree. But I don't see how my joining the masses filing in and out of a factory each day would help.

"If it's such a good opportunity, why don't you jump on it?" I'm sure what he really wants is for me to earn money so I'm able to find another place to live.

"Because I'm more useful on the outside," Joaquim says smoothly.

"Ah." I nod, not liking him at all right now. "I think I am too."

"Well then. What skills do you have?"

"Woodworking," I say without enthusiasm. "Farming. Harvesting."

"Those last two won't do you much good in Porto. You'll have to find a carpenter who needs help."

"Maybe." If I do that, I may as well have stayed in Mesão Frio. I notice the table is still pushed against his bed, leaving room for my sleeping blanket.

"No one else can take me in?" I'm as irritated at his company as he seems to be at mine.

He shakes his head. "Families live here. Sometimes seven, even ten people in a house. They pile chairs on the table at night so the children can sleep under it. And those with fewer souls – like Ana Maria and the widow next door – are understandably reluctant to have a young man who isn't family bedding down with them."

"Of course." Damn. "As you said, it won't be for long."

In the morning, I start my search with some seriousness but no more enthusiasm. I crisscross the city, carpenter after carpenter saying *no, I don't need anyone*. Many give me the names of others I can try, but I've no luck with them either.

With each refusal, my rage builds. What is Goldsmith Bento saying about me, now that I'm not there to defend myself? I can only pray Inês doesn't believe it. Twice, I take a detour to the Rua das Flores, going close enough to see the façade of Gomes & Filho but staying far enough away that no one inside will spot me. And there I wait, my heart aching to stay and my mind warning me to leave, hoping an errand will bring Inês outside. I have to see her. I have to justify myself.

In the end, it doesn't matter. She never appears.

CHAPTER 42

FOOTSORE AND IN low spirits, I return to the *ilha* in the evening. As usual, Joaquim is muttering angrily as he pores over the newspaper.

"What's the matter now?" I ask.

He jabs at it with a scowl. "The extravagant inauguration of the Dom Fernando bridge, that's what. With our cherished royal family in attendance, and all the ridiculous pomp and circumstance that accompanies them."

Here he goes again. I try to distract him. "Remember when I told you I went to the Royal Palace? We were delivering a filigree cross that Mestre Vitor made. Queen Maria Pia will wear it during the ceremony."

"Seeking heavenly protection for that first bridge crossing, is she?" Joaquim's voice is full of spite. When he's at the Aguia d'Ouro, the indignation he aims at the monarchy makes him ironic and sarcastic. Here, with no one around but me, he's granite-eyed with anger.

"Why do you despise them so?" Instinctively, I lower my voice and check that the door is closed. Even though he lashes out at them all the time, it still feels wrong. Disloyal.

"Because all of the money in this country is funneled to the royal house or goes for things like roads and that stupid bridge," Joaquim snarls. He sounds like he'd like to leap at someone's throat. "The banks have no credit for the rest of us. People who work hard and deserve it, like my father." He tells me about the shipwreck, the pharmacy, the studies he abandoned. "We'd be better off if the royal family disappeared from the face of the earth."

"Whoa." I hold up my hands. "Threatening the king can get you into trouble."

His regard is defiant. "Within these four walls, I say what I want. Unless you're planning to turn me in."

"What?" For shooting off his mouth? "Of course not. Anyway, you're not serious, are you?"

"Of course not." The way he repeats my words, eyes glinting in the lamplight, makes me uneasy. I break the awkward silence.

"You don't really think railroads and bridges are bad, do you?" In the Aguia d'Ouro, I heard that a carriage needs seven days to get from Lisbon to Gaia, while people who come on the train take only eight hours. With the new bridge, there'll be a direct line across the river to Porto and on to the Minho. "Everyone says Portugal will never become a modern country without them."

I'm not sure I followed his logic when he drew a direct line from the king to his father's suicide, and I know I can't hold my own in a debate on the merits of transportation. But every time I think of that bridge soaring over the Douro, it gives me hope. Its's worth defending.

He regards me sourly. "Look around you. How many people in this *ilha* benefit from those trains? You can't wear them or eat them or sleep on them. The money would be better spent going to those who produce, who labor." He stands and yanks his coat off a hook on the wall. "I need to walk." He slams the door behind him. If he's going to the Aguia d'Ouro tonight, I'm clearly not invited.

In the morning, a still ill-tempered Joaquim rousts me out of my blanket. He's got five glass jars with water in them in the cabinet that's missing a door, but when I reach for one, he snaps at me to leave it alone and to get my own from a fountain. I do, and start my job search with renewed vigor. First, I try the Massarelos crockery factory. They'll surely need a carpenter as they rebuild after the fire.

When I explain why I've come, the foreman shakes his head. "We're almost done," he says. "We don't need anyone now."

I force out a polite *Thank you for your time* and trudge back along the river. As the visit of the royal family nears, the city is being transformed. Plants in big pots line the streets and multicolored pennants flutter in the breeze. They make the city look like it's dancing. I bet Joaquim would rip down every single one if he could.

At the bottom of the Rua das Flores, I stop and marvel.

Everywhere, autumn flowers and leaves climb poles and trellises and are being laid out to make designs on the street itself. More flowers made of colored paper or fabric adorn shop displays and are draped over the carved stone crests on the façades of some of the grander houses. For the royal family, the Street of Flowers will live up to its name.

There's so much activity, so many people wandering about, that they certainly won't notice in Gomes & Filho if I walk by. It's not wise, but I can't let day after day pass without seeing Inês. I stay on the far side of the street, keeping a gaggle of women carrying their market baskets between me and the shop. If only Inês would come out. My little group continues on, me moving with them, and she doesn't. I want to yell in frustration.

When I'm far enough to safely pull away from the market women, I check over my shoulder one last time, and the miracle happens. Inês is letting herself out the door, and she's alone. I stop so abruptly that a man behind me steps on my heels.

"Move along there, lad!"

"Sorry." I don't take my eyes off Inês, afraid she'll disappear if I do.

She comes closer, her mouth set with determination. The light-hearted bounce that's usually in her step is missing. I can't help wondering if my absence has anything to do with it. She's only meters away when she shifts her basket from one arm to another and glances my way. Instead of the smile I so hoped for, worry flashes across her face.

"Henrique, you can't be here." Now it's her turn to look over her shoulder. She pulls me into a side street. "Goldsmith Bento still curses your name. If he sees you…"

My mind registers her warning. But all that matters, this very second, is making sure that his accusations haven't turned her against me.

"They didn't find it?"

"No."

I draw her to a stop and look her full in the face. "I didn't take it. You must believe me."

"I know."

Two simple words that change everything.

I grab her hands and kiss them noisily. Then – remembering her reputation – I drop them and step back.

"So does Dona Ilda. And Lisete too, although she can't say it out loud." We start walking again, going in the general direction of the market.

"And Mestre Vitor?" I ask.

"He hasn't come in this week."

"Why not?"

"He sent word that he was ill and had gone home to Gondomar to recover. It's put Goldsmith Bento in an even fouler humor."

"You think he's really sick?"

"I don't know. I haven't seen him since the night you ..." She stops speaking.

I'm not sure what to think. "Is Hugo still around?"

"Unfortunately." Inês grimaces. "He has the midday meal with us now. Something about him not getting enough to eat at home. I hate seeing him in your place. He truly seems to think he'll be made apprentice."

I clench my jaw, fighting my desire to suggest they feed him something that doesn't agree with him.

"He glories in calling you a thief," Inês goes on. "He doesn't even use your name anymore. But what's most curious is that he says he already knew you were one. That he'd heard it from someone you knew from back home."

The image comes back so clearly that I almost miss a step. Jorge and Hugo in front of the shop, their faces close together. Jorge said he'd make me pay. Did he somehow hear the story about the ceramic horse and decide this was the way to do it? But in that case, why didn't he take his tale directly to Goldsmith Bento? Probably because he has nothing but hearsay. He'd have no idea that such a story, however unfounded, would hit me at my weakest spot. Or that it would be the very thing Goldsmith Bento would latch onto. Had Jorge instructed Hugo to warn the goldsmith about me? Or...

"I think Hugo took it." The boy detested me for taking the apprenticeship he thought should be his. If he learned I'd been accused of being a thief elsewhere, his little mind could easily figure out how to make the same thing happen here. What setting could be more perfect than a jewelry shop? Perhaps Jorge had even told him to steal something. "There's no other way that bar could disappear. I just can't prove it."

"I wondered that too," Inês says thoughtfully. "Especially since something similar happened to another apprentice. But Goldsmith Bento makes him turn out his pockets before he goes home each day. And wouldn't he have enough to eat at home if he'd gotten his little paws on a bar of gold?"

"They don't check him every time he sweeps the street in front of the shop."

"Or maybe it fell off the table and rolled to a place where it'll be found one day."

I regard her doubtfully. "I still think it was Hugo."

After a few moments of silence, she says quietly, "I was afraid you'd left Porto."

I tell her about my job search, about Joaquim and the *ilha*. "I miss your cooking," I say.

Inês arches one eyebrow, looking suddenly more like her old self. "Is that all?"

"You know it's not." I want to thread my fingers in hers. To hold her. But I can't. Not in public. I wish we were back at the grotto in the gardens of the Crystal Palace.

She gives me a secret smile and bumps her shoulder against mine, somehow making it appear like it wasn't intentional. "I have news too." Her whole face lights up.

"You do? What?"

"Another house – a fine one – needs a cook's assistant. I've been invited to present myself." She hugs herself, ashiver with nerves and anticipation. "Today."

"Today?" I repeat stupidly. I catch myself and try to match her enthusiasm. "You want this, right?"

She nods like a child receiving a present.

"Then you'll get it."

"They might be interviewing others too." For a moment, her face falls.

"Come now. I can't believe they wouldn't want to snap up the best egg custard maker in the city."

It works. She swats my arm, chuckling. "Silly."

I'd so missed her. Her laugh. Her presence. Knowing that she's in the same house as I am, sometimes only an arms-length away. Even when I couldn't touch her.

"Is Dona Ilda happy for you?"

"I haven't told her." She lifts her chin defensively. "If it doesn't work out, I don't want anyone to know." She pauses. "Dona Ilda has been so kind. I'd hate to abandon her. But I don't want to waste this chance either. It's been so miserable at the house."

"Because I'm gone?" I tease, trying to lighten the mood again. I couldn't be more serious about the answer I want.

She cuts her eyes at me. "Aren't you conceited? Because of the way Goldsmith Bento's acting, of course." She waits until I glance away in disappointment, then laughs at me. "Of course, because of you. Goldsmith Bento is around and you're not."

I've seen Inês in all sorts of moods, but never with the tender look she gives me now. It makes my whole body warm, as if the sun is pulsing under my skin. I stop myself from reaching out to her, from saying something impetuous. Inês might have a grand new place of employment after today. I have nothing. Why would she be tempted to tie her horse to mine? Suggesting it would show a monumental lack of respect.

I smile tightly, not wanting my rush of emotion to make her pull back. "If all goes well, you won't be there for much longer either."

She's guided us through Praça Nova and into some of the narrow, uphill streets behind it. This isn't the way to Bolhão market.

"Where are we going?"

"To the house of Carolina Michaëlis de Vasconcelos in the Rua de Cedofeita. I've decided you're walking me there."

"With pleasure." That she wants my company at this important moment means everything.

"I'm nervous." She holds out her hands, exaggerating their trembling. "About getting the job, but also what my life will be like if I don't. Is that crazy?"

I shake my head. "You'll be changing the direction of everything you know." When I left Mesão Frio, I felt the same. And I was thrilled, because the change was of my own choosing. As this would be for her. "Think of it as excitement rather than nerves."

"I'll try," she says dubiously.

Soon afterwards, she stops and points at a three-story house a few doors away. "That's it." She takes a shaky breath. "Wish me luck."

"You know I will. You'll do fine." I keep my distance, even though I'm dying to encourage her with a hug. God forbid that her possible future employer should suspect her of impropriety. But as she turns away, I stop her with a touch on her wrist. "Wait. When will I see you again?"

"I don't know when I'll have another excuse to go out."

Inspiration hits me. "Sunday. For the inauguration of the bridge. Say you'll come with me. Please."

Her smile crinkles her eyes. "I'd love to. Now I really must go."

"I can't wait to hear your good news."

"Shhh!" She gives me a mock glare. "Don't jinx it."

Grinning, I wave her away, then watch until she's admitted inside.

CHAPTER 43

T HE LETTER WAS *from his father's bookkeeper in Aveiro. Joaquim slit it open with his pocketknife and scanned its contents. Then, swearing, he crushed the letter into a ball and threw it as hard as he could across the room.*

CHAPTER 44

INÊS WILL GET the position. I believe it because I'm determined to. And if that merry slip of a girl can change her situation, so can I. If I want to be worthy of her, stay in Porto, and live with myself, I must.

After she's inside, I trek across town to yet another carpenter's address that I was given. In the warren of streets behind Praça Nova, a sudden thought stops me in my tracks. It's not realistic, but still …

I slow, get my bearings. Just ahead, on the right, is a door with flaking red paint. The mapmaker's office. Do I dare? I have few qualifications that would make me a mapmaker's choice, but I do have enthusiasm in abundance. I lift my hand and knock. No one answers. I try twice more before giving up. He must be out in the city, measuring and calculating.

In the neighborhood of Fontainhas, I find the carpenter closing up his workshop. Like the others I've met, he has no need for an assistant but suggests there might be work with the barrel-makers in Gaia. I thank him and turn to leave, unable to suppress a frustrated sigh. A surprising number of people are passing by, going in the same direction.

"Coming?" the carpenter asks.

"Where?"

"They're running trains across the new bridge. Testing it. We all want to see if it's still standing when it's over."

"Wouldn't miss it." My excitement comes rushing back. I hadn't realized that the tests begin today. Joaquim probably read about it in his newspapers. But with his distinct lack of love for the bridge and all it represents, he didn't bother telling me.

I recognize where I am when the road we're on dead ends at a cliff high above the Douro. To my right is the steep cobblestone street down to the river that the gorse carriers climb. In the other direction, the bridge's arch and its reflection in the water almost form a circle. Already, a crowd has gathered on the *alameda*, a long open area protected from the cliff's sharp drop by a low wall. Here, too, they've hung colorful garlands and other decorations.

There's no sign of a train. People have settled in for a lengthy wait, spreading blankets and bringing chairs and baskets of food. Off to one side, beyond where they're building some kind of pavilion, smoke from a grill billows into the air. I smell sausages and finger my money pouch. The carpenter finds friends and peels away.

Out on the span of the bridge are tiny figures of men who stop, bend down, then continue on. Perhaps Monsieur Eiffel is among them. A spot on the low wall opens up beside a man who's sitting with a pigtailed girl and a serious boy who look about six years old. I swing my legs over. Below my feet is a long, sheer drop, but the view to the bridge couldn't be better. I push away the memory of the last time I was near it, swaying and shocked and up to my knees in cold water. Today is a celebration.

Ignoring the chatter around me, I imagine myself on the span, the metal vibrating under my feet, a few bands of iron keeping me suspended in space. Would I shuffle, not daring to separate my feet from the platform, or stride boldly across? Monsieur Eiffel walks confidently, I'm sure. So, I'd wager, would the mapmaker. Men who make their own future stride. But how can I, if I don't know where I'm heading?

The men leave the bridge eventually, and for a while nothing happens. Then, with a screech of metal, a steam engine pulls four freight cars onto the bridge. It's followed closely by a second one. The little girl and boy squeal and clap. They aren't the only ones. The trains advance until they cover the bridge, then stop.

"Would you look at that?" The man with the children whistles in admiration. "They're using Sharps. Those are the heaviest locomotives we have in Portugal," he tells the children. "Sixty tons each. And I bet those cars are heavily laden too."

We wait, but the trains just sit there.

"What happened, Uncle?" asks the pigtailed girl. "Did they break?"

"No, my dear." Her uncle laughs. "They need to make sure the bridge is strong enough to hold the train. They're testing it."

Sure enough, after a while the locomotives pull the cars off the track. Then a steam engine with four cars appears from the Porto side. It stops in the middle, with the locomotive squarely on top of the arch. After a wait, it backs off and the same happens from the south side. All the while, Uncle provides a commentary about how the wheels stay on the track, why the wind won't blow the whole contraption over, and why it's steam, not smoke, that's coming out of the locomotive's chimney. I eavesdrop without shame. It's too bad Miguel isn't here. I bet he'd like it.

Finally, from each side of the river, the two locomotives steam toward each other along the single track at the same time, pulling four cars each.

"They're going to run into each other!" The serious little boy bounces, both horrified and fascinated at the prospect of witnessing the smash-up. His uncle grabs the back of the child's shirt, preventing him from pitching forward off the wall.

"Not today, I don't think."

As the steam engines grind to a stop a couple of meters apart, their uncle tells them about brakes. The children slump, clearly disappointed. While we wait for whatever is to happen next, their uncle makes the boy and girl lock hands, their arms out straight. Then he presses down, his hands the train and their arms the bridge, testing how much weight they can hold. They giggle as their span gives way and Uncle's hand plummets down, down, down.

On the real bridge, the trains aren't moving. My gaze wanders, taking in the gossiping, drinking spectators. Off to the side, at the top of a few steps, is Joaquim. He's completely still, reflecting none of the anticipation around him. I leave my perch.

"You've got the glare of a jilted lover," I say when I reach him.

He lets out a short laugh. "No love lost here."

"Why come then?"

"Morbid curiosity, I suppose." He runs a probing gaze from the base of the pillars to the top of the arch, along the span, then down the pillars on the far side of the river.

"Your hating it won't make it go away, you know. It'll be here long after we're gone."

"We'll see."

I roll my eyes. For me, it's a marvel. He calls it morbid. We'll never change each other's minds. There's a groan of metal from the bridge and the two trains back away from each other, leaving the span empty.

Joaquim departs soon afterwards. I'm glad to see him go. But when it seems clear that nothing more will happen today, I leave the *alameda* too. Until tomorrow. I'll be back then to watch the speed tests. Preferably without Joaquim around to dampen the fun. He'll never understand how I yearn to be part of something so majestic.

CHAPTER 45

HUGO MADE SURE *that both hands were in plain view and clutching his broom when Goldsmith Bento glanced into the workshop. Whenever the goldsmith was around, Hugo did the same with the pail, shovel, firewood, or whatever else he might be carrying. No holding his hands behind his back, no touching anything of value except under the goldsmith's direct supervision, and no eye-rolling when he was told to turn out his pockets at the end of the day. Nothing that would make suspicion fall on him, as it had on the apprentices. He made sure of that.*

He couldn't get passed over again. Not after being everyone's drudge for the past year. That had to count for something. But every time he offered to do something other than sweep, Goldsmith Bento brushed him aside, never giving a reason why. What if he couldn't read or do sums? He'd learn, if someone would teach him. After he no longer had to deliver the gorse for his mother every morning, he'd learn. He wouldn't be falling asleep on his feet, as he was now. Would be able to concentrate.

With a jerk, he opened his eyes and swept vigorously, thankful that Goldsmith Bento was occupied with a customer. Even if apprentices weren't paid, he'd get meals and a few tostões for spending money, as Henrique had. Enough to take the burden off his mother. Hugo's sweeping slowed again. As time passed, he'd grow into the man she expected him to be, with money and the status that came with a job in a prestigious goldsmith's shop. One who treated others however he felt like it, rather than being the dog who always had to wag his tail.

By then, Lisete would certainly be a haughty old maid. But if she and her father begged enough, maybe he'd let them persuade him to ask for her hand. He wiped the smile from his face before Goldsmith Bento wondered why it was there and began wielding his broom with industry around the table where Henrique used to sit. Good riddance, that one.

True to its name, the lockbox was locked. Pointedly, Hugo showed no interest in it. All that mattered was that far back in the narrow, dark gap between the lockbox and the wall lay a gold bar that would remain hidden until the day he found it. Then he'd be hailed a hero.

CHAPTER 46

THE NEXT DAY, I'm back at the *alameda* with another excited crowd to see the speed trials. I don't tell Joaquim where I'm going and am relieved when he doesn't show up. Today, two locomotives, hitched to each other, clatter across the bridge, pulling a freight train that never seems to end. I count seventeen cars. After that, a single steam engine with a shorter train thunders onto the bridge going – according to the uncle yesterday – a magnificent thirty-one kilometers an hour. It's across in a few blinks of an eye. Around me, everyone chatters happily.

When the day's trials are over, I head back to the mapmaker's office with determined steps, willing him to be there. To my delight, he is, frowning at two pages of figures.

"Henrique, isn't it?" he asks.

"Yes, sir."

He puts down his pen and massages the ink-stained fingers of one hand with the other. "What can I do for you?"

Off to the side, an assistant busily wipes equipment off with a rag. I turn my back to him.

"I'm looking for work, sir."

"Weren't you working for a goldsmith?"

"Not now." I don't want to go into why I'm not.

"I don't know that you have …" the mapmaker begins.

"I can do sums," I say, remembering his complaints in the Aguia d'Ouro about the quality of the assistants he'd been given. With one of them right behind me, I can't say much. "I'm very careful," I add.

"And precise."

"Why are you coming to me?"

At least he didn't immediately say *no*.

"I ... I want to do something that matters." I stumble over my words and slow down. "Something that will make a difference. Like your map."

One side of his mouth quirks up in a smile. "And how do you think my map will make a difference, young man?"

I'm not sure if he's mocking or testing me.

It's more a feeling than anything else. For a moment I flounder. "Well ..."

He waits, clearly expecting a sensible answer.

"I think that if you can see the city spread out on a map, you can understand where it's going," I say slowly. "Where it needs to go. How it should develop." That I can put my feeling into words surprises me, but they're sincere. "It'll be one of the tools Porto needs – like the Douro bridge – if it's to become a modern city."

My answer isn't eloquent, but it earns me a nod.

"It will be, indeed," he says thoughtfully. "I'm glad I'm not the only one who sees it that way." Then, turning businesslike, he picks up his pen. "Come back on Monday. I'll have an answer for you then."

"Yes, sir!" I say with more force than either of us are expecting.

He chuckles. "You'd be available to start anytime, I take it?"

"Whenever you want."

He nods again. "We'll talk on Monday."

"Thank you, sir."

On the street again, I have to stop my feet from dancing. From flying. I know it's too early. There's a good chance he'll say he doesn't want me. But at least I have a chance. A chance at a future. Maybe even one I can offer Inês. I can't ask for more than that.

As I walk away, I sober. If the mapmaker asks for references, I have none. I certainly don't want him talking to Goldsmith Bento. And Joaquim seems angrier every day. He won't be pleased – any more than I am – when he learns that he's stuck with me until Monday, and probably beyond.

I tell him about my appointment the next morning. Joaquim is less than impressed.

"A mapmaker?" he says flatly. "If you're serious about wanting a job – which I'm starting to doubt – you'd do better by focusing on your strengths." His tone is cutting. I have no desire to admit to him that he's right.

"How would you know what my strengths are?" I snap, then remember that I listed them for him the other day.

"Whatever they are, you'd better find use for them soon." His eyes are as hard as his voice. "You can't expect me to prop you up indefinitely."

My irritation collapses. He's right, and I'm ashamed. As far as I can tell, he doesn't have an income now either. "I know. I'm sorry. I'll pay you back – for lodging and food – as soon as I have a job. I've gone to see almost every carpenter in Porto. I'll try the coopers and shipbuilders next. I promise I'll keep looking."

His only answer is a growl in the back of his throat as he goes back to his newspaper.

I leave the *ilha* under the watchful gaze of the ragged-eared cat on the windowsill. Even in its slow-blinking gaze, I read disappointment. Porto was supposed to be a new start, a shedding of old shames and blames. But they must've ridden downstream with me on the *barco rabelo,* hugging me like an invisible cloak.

Throughout the city, more decorations are going up. Entire streets, strung with colorful garlands and banners, appear to ripple in the breeze, the excitement flowing into the people below. My feet, as so often these days, have followed my heart to the Rua das Flores. Even though I know the chances of seeing Inês are slim and the danger great, I go.

This time I pass too close and am unlucky. Hugo is outside, lips curled in distaste as he cleans the muck that a horse dropped squarely in front of the shop door. A malicious grin spreads over his face when he sees me. I see his mouth open and flee, dodging people and wagons and horsemen, expecting any second to hear him yell *thief* and run to fetch the goldsmith. Only when I'm at the fountain in the Largo de São Domingos, well out of sight, do I slow, my blood throbbing in anger and frustration. How can it be that I command no respect even from a spiteful child cleaning shit off a street?

Disconsolately, I wend my way downhill toward Ribeira and the quay, wishing I had somewhere to curl up and nurse my wounded pride. But the city is swarming with people and I don't yet know where its secret, safe places are.

On my way, a man carrying a suitcase stops me and asks where he can find a room. "Everywhere I've gone is full. Can you help me?" I shake my head. I can't even help myself.

It's Friday, and as usual, one of the masted steamer ships tied to the dock is Sálvio's. He's not on deck – nor am I in the mood for company – so I move on. I've only covered a few paces before he calls my name. I sigh and turn as he jogs down the gangway to greet me.

"You've arrived just in time for the royal visit," I say as we shake hands. "You don't get enough of the king and queen in Lisbon?" Inwardly I grimace, thinking how that comment would sound to someone passing by. As if Joaquim's distaste for the monarchy is rubbing off on me.

"I noticed the finery." He nods at the rainbows of banners adorning every balcony and the gay crowds admiring them. "That's about as close as I'll ever get to royalty."

"Me too." I shrug. "At least it gives everyone an excuse to make merry."

Sálvio eyes my solemn face. "You don't look particularly happy about it."

"I'm excited about the new bridge." I try to draw on my enthusiasm from yesterday, but it falls flat. I need to be alone. "I've got to go," I'm saying when someone calls, "Sálvio, get up here."

Sálvio's expression darkens. "Bastard of a first mate will not leave me alone," he mutters. He erases his frown before turning.

"Hurry up," the first mate says. "I have an errand for you."

"No, you don't." The captain has come up behind the first mate. "I need him here."

Sálvio's expression turns a tad self-righteous until the captain continues, "… not loitering about on the quay."

Sálvio gulps. "See you later, Henrique."

"Captain Duarte, it won't take long." The first mate hasn't given up. "Surely you can spare him."

"No, I can't. Find someone who's not on my crew for your personal business. Or do it yourself."

The first mate narrows his eyes. He's standing so Sálvio has to push past him to get on board. His gaze falls on me. "You there. Sálvio's friend."

I stiffen at the contempt in his voice and pretend I don't hear him. He says, more loudly this time, "Boy! I have a job for you. You'll be paid."

Paid. That word brings me to a halt. He strides down the gangplank, bulky and pompous and half a head taller than I am.

"You're to fetch a parcel."

He's issuing commands and I haven't even said *yes*. I stare him in the eyes, refusing to admit that we're not equals. He doesn't even notice. I see Sálvio on deck, shaking his head.

"Go to the place where the river bends. Beyond the new bridge. A man will be waiting for you."

"My payment?"

The sum he names won't make a dent in what I owe Joaquim.

"It's a long way to go." I stick my hands in my pockets and feign disinterest.

"Come now," he barks. "You'll be there and back in less than an hour."

I wait, pretending to admire the decorations waving from the riggings of the dozens of boats anchored in the river.

He huffs, then adds a few *tostões* to the number.

"I want half now."

He smiles tightly. "You'll get it when you bring the parcel. Or not at all."

I wouldn't have paid me ahead of time either, but it was worth a try.

"You know your figures?"

"I do." I don't add that I can read too.

He nods in approval. "Before you accept the parcel, make him open it so you can see that the papers inside it are printed with 1-8-7-5. Don't take it unless they are. Understand?"

"Yes. But who am I to look for? In these crowds?" With every passing hour, more people are pouring into Porto, filling the streets and shops with noise and laughter.

"It's out of town. Not a busy place. Fellow's about your height. Answers to Afonso. You tell him you're picking it up for Ricardo."

"Is that all?"

"Yes." The first mate waves me away. "Go now."

Sálvio has disappeared. His head shake makes me more uneasy than I want to admit. I hope he wasn't trying to tell me that the first mate doesn't pay what he promises.

The clouds lowered while we were talking and now shroud the tops of the hills on both sides of the river. The chill is damp on my skin, but it's not yet raining. I weave between clumps of people strolling, greeting, and gossiping about the royal visit. I'm eager to get this errand over with. I leave Ribeira and see that the first mate was right. Beyond the Pênsil bridge, the crowds thin. By the time I get to Monsieur Eiffel's bridge, there's little activity either below or on it. No hammering, no men, no trains. Just grey fog that hides one section and then another as the bridge awaits its day of glory. Church bells, faint in the distance, ring three times.

The river bends. Behind me, I can no longer see the city. I pass a couple of wagons coming the other way and spot a man pissing against the cliff, but no one seems to be waiting for me. I slow, wondering if I should go farther or return to the metal bridge. Done relieving himself, the man buttons up and retrieves a package that's lying on the ground.

He's familiar. Too familiar. The chill I was feeling is replaced by anger, hot and quick.

"You?" Jorge snarls as I approach. He's reached the same conclusion I have.

"Looks like it. *Afonso,*" I can't help adding, sarcastically. "That's for Ricardo?" I nod at the brick-sized package. It's wrapped in brown paper and tied with a string. I watch him, cursing my bad luck. Jorge holds the package and the power. He won't let that go easily.

"Where's my money?"

"What money?" For a second, I think he's talking about the oar.

He holds up the package. "For this."

I spread my hands wide. "I was told you'll get it in the usual fashion, whatever that is." If the first mate wasn't going to pay me ahead of time, he certainly wasn't going to trust me with money for Jorge. "Open it. I need to see what's inside."

He unties the knot with his good hand, pulls the string away, and spreads the flaps to reveal two piles of paper with a crown and the number 1875 printed on them. Along with the words Porto and Vargellas. My eyes widen. These are Port wine labels, similar to those I saw at Taylor's. The ones that are supposed to prove that the wine in the bottles is of legitimate origin. Yet here they are, trading hands on the banks of the Douro in the most suspect of ways.

I stare down at them, not wanting Jorge to know what I've realized. This isn't the kind of activity I want to be involved in. What if I'm caught with them? What if Jorge turns me in? There will never be a doubt in anyone's mind that I'm a thief. Then again, Jorge expects to be paid for this too. He wouldn't ruin his little business to spite me, would he? Reluctantly, I reach for the package. I'll carry it this one time, and get my money. Then I'll never go near that first mate – or Jorge – again.

"You better make sure it gets to Ricardo," Jorge says before releasing it. "I'll be following you."

"You could've just delivered it yourself then, couldn't you?"

His mouth twists nastily. There's a story there that he has no intention of telling me.

"I want to get paid too," I say.

"I bet you do. Now that you've lost your job at that fancy jewelry shop."

"What would you know about that?" Bastard. If he wants a confrontation, I'll give him one. The years have hardened him, but he's no bigger than I am.

He leans forward, right into my face, and smirks.

"I saw you talking to Hugo," I spit out. "What did you say to him?"

"The shop boy?" Jorge pretends to look surprised. "Such a young, impressionable lad, isn't he? And he doesn't like you at all. Funny how you manage to get on everyone's bad side. Even the goldsmith's, apparently. He was so quick to dismiss you."

"What did you say to Hugo?" I repeat.

"Me?" Jorge grins maliciously. "You know children. They'll make up any manner of tale. Especially for a coin."

Clutching the parcel, I step toward him. "You paid him to carry tales about me to the goldsmith?"

He moves backwards, not letting me get within punching distance.

"Or you paid him to steal and blame it on me?" I step forward again.

Jorge is wearing the self-satisfied sneer of someone who got exactly what he wanted. Then something occurs to me.

"Then you should be swimming in money. Yet here you are, a lowly delivery boy just like me. What went wrong?"

He flashes me a murderous look.

"Hugo didn't give you what he took, did he?"

Jorge wouldn't be on this misty riverbank if he had a bar of gold to sell. Now it's my turn to mock. And to hope. If Hugo's so needy he's eating with Inês and Dona Ilda, he hasn't sold it. That means he probably still has it. I still have a chance to clear my name.

I look down at the package in my hands, one thing becoming clear. This isn't the person I want to be. I'm not helping anyone who's going to discredit Port wine for their own gain. I back away from Jorge and heft the parcel to shoulder height.

"I don't want this job as much as I thought. And you need to stop destroying people's lives." Pulling my arm back, I lob the package as far as I can over the water.

"Son of a bitch!" Jorge leaps toward me, too late. I dodge out of reach as the package hits the water and breaks open. Jorge lets out an agonized cry, changes direction mid-lunge, and plunges into the river. The labels float downstream in little clumps. Jorge goes after them, his legs kicking hard. It's clear he's not going to drown. Not that I could help him anyway. On shore, I keep pace with him.

One by one, the labels sink. The current carries any that stay afloat toward the metal bridge, out of his reach. He stops and treads water, breathing hard, his fingers full of waterlogged paper. His look as he paddles toward shore says he'd like to cut me into a thousand pieces. I back up, away from the waterline. If he pulls me in, I won't survive. But if I run – as I so want to – I'll be running forever. I can't live like that.

I wait until he's on his hands and knees on the bank, hacking water out of his lungs.

"I know what you're doing." I keep a healthy distance between us. "If you ever get near me again, or if I ever hear you're talking about me, I'll tell everyone. You'll lose your boat. That's a promise."

His glare makes me glad he isn't carrying a knife.

"Bastard," he croaks, climbing to his feet.

"Then we both are," I shoot back. "You keep away from me and I'll keep away from you. Or those wine labels will be only the beginning of your problems."

He gives me an evil look. It's ruined when he bends over, hands on his knees, coughing uncontrollably. I leave him then, not quite running, and turning often to make sure he hasn't rallied enough to chase me. Only time will tell if my threat is enough. But I will no longer let someone like Jorge define me.

The last time I look, he's throwing the unsalvageable labels to the ground. I feel a stab of satisfaction. He deserves every misfortune that befalls him.

Back at Sálvio's ship, I tell the first mate that Afonso had an accident and dropped the labels into the water. Swearing loudly, the first mate stomps up the gangway. On the deck, Sálvio winks at me. There's no sign of Jorge. I hope he's making his way, like a half-drowned rat, back to the *barco rabelo*.

It starts raining in earnest as I duck into the passageway leading to the *ilha*. Every house, it seems, has someone in it who is coughing. I run the last few meters and burst through Joaquim's door. He's kneeling in front of the cabinet, one of the glass jars in his hands. He jumps and almost drops it.

"*Merda!* This is my house! You can't barge in like that!"

"It's pouring out there." Beneath the smell of mold and cigarette smoke is a faint chemical odor.

Joaquim glares.

"I'm sorry. Next time, I'll knock." I sniff. "What's that smell?"

"Nothing that concerns you." He replaces the jar on the shelf with barely controlled anger. "You've been here almost a week. How many *next times* are there going to be?"

"I'm …"

"*I'm sorry* isn't enough," he growls. "*I'm trying* isn't enough."

"I'll pay you. I told you I will." I don't dare tell him about the incident with Jorge and the money I threw away. If he berates me for missing an opportunity, I'll say something I'll regret.

"What you'll pay me won't do a whit of good."

"My money's just as good as anyone else's." Or it will be, once I have some.

"I came here to live alone," he grates. "Not to have someone walking in on me all the time."

It sounds like he's getting ready to kick me out. Into the rain and a city overflowing with visitors.

"I'll try to find something else on Monday." I'm desperate to head off what he might say next.

"Yet another thing to thank the royal family and that godforsaken bridge for," he snaps. "An unwanted visitor who won't leave."

"Joaquim, did I do something?" This level of hostility can't stem solely from my failure to knock. "I'm trying to spend as little time here as possible."

He throws himself onto his bed and stares at the ceiling. "Spend less, will you?"

I swallow a sharp retort, not wanting to antagonize him further. "I'll go see Ana Maria and Miguel. Get some rest." I know that's not his problem. As the bridge's inauguration approaches, he's become increasingly short-tempered and on edge. I just hope that things will even out once the celebrations are over and the royal family is gone. Or that by then I'll have found other lodgings and a job.

CHAPTER 47

I WAKE TO a clear blue sky and a town that's vibrating with excitement.

"I'll save you a spot on the Rua de São João," I hear Ana Maria telling Miguel. "There's no better place to see the procession."

Miguel's at their door, practically bouncing in anticipation.

"Get there as early as you can," Ana Maria says. "It'll be crowded."

"As soon as the shoemaker lets me go, I'll come running." Turning, he sees me. "You'll be there too, won't you?"

"I'll try." I wish I could watch it with Inês, but Miguel and his sister are pleasant company too. Even if Ana Maria ignored my veiled suggestion last evening that I move into their tiny attic for a few nights.

"The king and queen are to arrive in Gaia when the bells ring four," Miguel says. "You have to be there before that."

"I'll try," I repeat. I have some unfinished and very important business to attend to first.

"I'm glad to see you haven't been poisoned by Joaquim the killjoy," Ana Maria says, loudly enough that he can surely hear. "He wouldn't raise a glass to the royal family if the king offered it to him himself."

"While you'd fawn and lick his filthy boots." Joaquim's harsh voice comes through the door I left open.

He and I haven't spoken since last night.

"Pfft." Ana Maria brushes his comment away with a flip of her hand. "I doubt the king ever has dirty boots. Besides, we have little enough to celebrate. We may as well enjoy it while we can."

I leave the *ilha* with Miguel, glad to put some distance between

236

myself and Joaquim. Ana Maria wasn't kidding about the crowds. By the time I reach Praça Nova, I'm weaving through clusters of people chattering, laughing, smoking, and shopping. It's as if every town in the north of Portugal has tipped sideways and poured its population onto the streets of Porto. On the Rua das Flores, I push through the press of bodies until I can see Gomes & Filho. Hugo had better be working today. Because the moment he leaves, he's mine.

I wait, shifting back and forth on my feet and always keeping a good sightline to the goldsmith's. Customers enter and exit, but there's no sign of Hugo. Or of Inês.

When the shop's green shutters come down, I curse loudly enough to get shocked looks from the women within earshot. Then the door opens once again and Hugo slips out. Alone. He slouches in my direction, hands in his pockets. Through gaps in the shifting mass of people, I track his progress, then fall in behind him.

When he reaches the open square in front of the São Bento convent, I clamp both hands down on his shoulders and shove him forward, squeezing harder than I need to. He gasps and twists, trying to get away.

"Keep walking." I should feel worse about frightening a child half my size. But there's no excuse for what he did. Wrecking my life for no reason. I just have to get him to admit it.

From behind, I guide him into the street that I took with Miguel and Jorge the day we got to Porto. It rises steeply and turns, becoming narrower, darker, and much less trafficked.

"What do you want?" he squeaks.

I propel him forward and don't answer.

"You're supposed to stay away from us," he tries next.

I still don't react.

"I'll scream."

I jerk him to a stop. "If anyone asks why, I'll say I'm thrashing you because you were caught stealing." I keep a firm grip on his spindly arms and bring my face close to his. "And you know what? It's the Lord's own truth. So I wouldn't if I were you."

His eyes dart from side to side, seeking help. But I've miraculously found what is probably the only lane in Porto where hardly a soul is visible. Besides, he knows people will be more likely to believe me than a hysterical child.

He hunches his shoulders miserably.

"Well?" I ask. "What do you have to say?"

"Nothing."

His defiance makes me want to box his ears. But I need him talking, not crying.

"You remember that man with the missing fingers?"

Hugo regards me, hardly breathing.

"The. One. Who. Gave. You. A. COIN?" With every word, my volume rises.

Hugo flinches.

"He isn't happy you kept that gold bar for yourself rather than give it to him."

"What? He didn't pay me to ..." Hugo stops, stricken. He just gave himself away, and he knows it.

"Where is it?" I hiss.

"I didn't steal it," he says sullenly. "It ... got misplaced."

"What does that mean?"

He looks at his feet and doesn't answer.

I shake him. "You. Idiot child. He's mad at you. What makes you think he won't tell Goldsmith Bento what you did? To get back at you for not giving him the gold?" I don't give Hugo time to question the logic of Jorge telling the goldsmith about a theft that originated with him. "You'll probably end up in prison."

Beneath my hands, I feel him tremble.

"Where is it?"

A tear slides down his cheek. Mother would smack me for treating a child this way. But I have to know.

"It fell into a crack," he says defensively. "In the workshop. It never *went* anywhere."

The goldsmith certainly thought it did, and that's what matters. I want to pound that into his brain, but it wouldn't make any difference. Spite and jealousy made him do what he did. I can't change that. At the same time, I'm rejoicing. If he's telling the truth, the gold bar is still in the workshop.

"Well, maybe you should make it fall out of that crack. Save your hide before anyone goes to the goldsmith and accuses *you* of stealing it."

"He wouldn't believe you," Hugo says flatly.

"You'll take that risk? When I can bring someone who says he heard you talking about taking something from the shop?"

"I never did! That man suggested it!"

I lock eyes with him, my head tilted. "We both know how easy it is to make the goldsmith believe a lie, don't we?"

He looks down, shuffles his feet. "The shop's closed."

My heart skips a beat. I can't let him squirm out of this.

"You're expected back in an hour, are you not?" I hope against hope they're planning to reopen for part of the afternoon, despite the royal visit.

Reluctantly, he nods.

"Well then, you'll have the pleasure of my company until the shop opens. Then you'll go in there and just happen to stumble upon that gold bar, which you will present to the goldsmith. Do you understand?"

"Yes," he says resentfully.

"Good. Because I'll be waiting and watching. And I won't hesitate to find your fingerless friend if you don't."

He casts his eyes along the street. Above us, a woman is hanging laundry from a rope strung between two windows. But he's subdued, no longer thinking of calling for help. I release him.

"Will you come back?" he asks. For the first time, he looks vulnerable. He wants that apprenticeship so much. I say what he wants to hear.

"No."

We wait in silence for the hour to pass. When Porto echoes with the bells of two o'clock, I say, "Off you go."

He sets off without a word. I keep pace, one hand on his shoulder again. I don't squeeze quite as hard as before. Near the shop, I stop and stare in surprise. A familiar, bulky figure is putting a necklace into one of the window displays.

"Mestre Vitor is back?"

Hugo nods. "He came back yesterday."

"Ah." His unwillingness to defend me is a burn that hasn't healed. But if the bar is found, I'm sure his presence will work in my favor. Unless Hugo calls my bluff and this all goes terribly wrong. I lean down to the boy's level.

"Be smart," I tell him. "Find that bar somewhere where it truly could have fallen. Act as surprised as you want. But make sure you say nothing that gives the impression that I hid it where you found it. I will know."

He nods solemnly.

"Then go." I push him forward.

This has to work.

He scampers off and an awful, interminable wait begins. What if he finds it in a place that's too improbable? What if they assign him to work in the garden today? I hadn't thought of that. I will Inês to appear at the upstairs windows. The curtains remain closed. I try to count the number of people who pass between me and the shop. Nothing takes my mind off the drama I imagine happening inside.

All the while, customers file in and out of Gomes & Filho and the other shops. The royal visit has supplied a bumper crop of business for local merchants. In this crowded street, at least half of them tread on my toes. Every time the door opens, I hope it's Hugo coming out. Each time, it's not. What can the boy be doing?

I realize suddenly that if Hugo tells them I'm outside, it'll be clear that I knew what was going to happen and perhaps was the one who hid the bar. Goldsmith Bento will have his gold, but might consider me as guilty as before. I clench my hands and hope Hugo is too nervous to figure that out. They just need to praise him enough that he won't risk ruining it by blurting out something stupid.

By the time Hugo appears, broom in hand, I'm jumping out of my skin with impatience. I beckon him out of sight of the shop windows.

"Well?"

He's trying not to show me how pleased he is with himself. "I found it on the floor. Against the wall, when I moved a box of tools to clean. It must've rolled off Mestre Vitor's worktable."

"They believed you?"

"I yelled and threw such a happy fit that they had to. And I told them I was sorry for calling you a thief."

If he thinks I'll try to reclaim the apprenticeship, he'll change his tune. For the time being, I'll leave him to his gleeful satisfaction.

"Very well." I'm not praising him. He's gotten me out of a hard spot, but it's his fault I was in it to start with. "I will come back later and just happen to run into Mestre Vitor."

His smile disappears.

"Just like you *happened* to find the gold," I reassure the boy. "You stick to your story and I will too. But I need to hear from him that my name is cleared."

He presses his lips together and nods.

I want to ask if Inês is there, but don't. He doesn't need to know about my interest. I can't resist one last warning. "Now your conscience is clear. No need for nightmares about what the man with the missing fingers might do."

He grimaces.

I wave him away. "Go back to work. And be very careful what you say." I hope his self-interest will save us both.

I stick close to the shop for the next hour, not taking the chance that Mestre Vitor will leave when I'm not looking. Every time I imagine us coming face to face, my hands break into a sweat. Will he recognize my innocence? Admit what the goldsmith did was wrong?

By now, I'm one in a multitude of people lining both sides of the street, waiting for the royal procession. Everywhere, children clutching colorful ribbons wriggle and fidget. Maybe Inês will come down and I'll get to see her.

As time passes, upstairs windows along the street open. Ladies, young and old, peer out. From their sitting room, the Gomes household has a privileged viewing place. Inês won't be coming out. But I hope Mestre Vitor will.

At this point, there's no way I can join Miguel and Ana Maria on the Rua de São João. I wait and wait. Finally, rifles fire in a military salute from atop the hill on the other side of the river. Their reports echo through the city, followed by the pop of rockets and firecrackers. The chatter around me pauses, then resumes even louder.

"King Luís and Queen Maria Pia have arrived!"

By now, everyone's staking out a spot with the best view possible. No one's shopping. Conceding defeat, the goldsmith's green shutters close. Soon after, Hugo shoves his way into the crowd and disappears. No one follows him out. I let out an exasperated sigh. Today would be the day Mestre Vitor stays to keep the family company.

I shift my focus to the windows above the shop. They're still closed. Goldsmith Bento wouldn't prevent his family from enjoying the festivities from the relative privacy of their own home, would he? I can imagine how furious Inês and Lisete would be.

Finally the curtains twitch, then part, and Dona Ilda opens the two sitting room windows. Behind her, the girls pull chairs to one of them, giggling. They plop down and rest their arms on the sill, gazing over the crowd with eager delight. An instant later, Lisete straightens, preens, and waves – just her fingers, very discretely – at someone on my left. I crane my neck, but there are too many heads. I can't see Ernesto.

I stare at Inês until I catch her eye. A current of pleasure runs through me. But the look she gives me is apprehensive and the lips I long to touch form the words, "What are you doing here?" My joy evaporates. If the goldsmith and Mestre Vitor have declared me innocent, she'd certainly have heard. Does this mean that Hugo wasn't as convincing as he thought?

I mouth back, "It's all right," although I'm not sure it is. Along with the rest of the noisy throng, we wait, trading glances and trying to figure out what the other is saying silently. I'm pretty sure she confirms our rendezvous for tomorrow morning. My mood lifts slightly.

In the Largo de São Domingos, a marching band starts playing. Hooves ring on cobblestones as the cavalry, the horses as resplendent as their riders, appear at the bottom of the street. The crowd whistles and claps. The noise brings Dona Alcina to the other window. Behind her, the goldsmith and Mestre Vitor are talking, paying little attention to what's happening outside.

The subject must be interesting, because even Lisete and Inês lean back and tilt in their direction, trying to hear better. The girls exchange startled glances, then Inês seeks me out, her face alight with joy. I've never seen anything so lovely.

In front of me, carriages pass carrying ministers, mayors, councilors, and members of the royal household, but Inês is all I want to look at. Because of the emotions she's not trying to hide, and because I know what lies behind them. For an instant, I float, suspended in a world that is perfect.

"They found it?" I mouth.

She nods, radiant, and I bask in her elation.

In front of me, a man is counting the carriages. He's interrupted by wild cheers as a gilded coach that's far grander than any other rumbles past. In it, His Royal Highness Dom Luís is stiff but smiling, imposing in his *generalissimo*'s uniform. Queen Maria Pia shimmers in dark green silk, her hat topped with matching feathers. Dom Afonso and Dom Carlos, the teenage princes, are seated in front of them in dark suits, looking mightily unimpressed by the roaring crowd. I raise my voice too, crying out exultantly in this city I've chosen as mine.

Following the royal coach are more carriages carrying ministers and deputies and foreign dignitaries from England, Germany, Italy, Russia,

Holland, and several other countries. In one, I spot Monsieur Eiffel. The man in front of me counts to one hundred and still they come. More horsemen bring up the rear. Finally the procession is past us, winding its way up toward Praça Nova and the Royal Palace. The crowd trails behind it in high spirits.

I don't. Instead, I point at Mestre Vitor and mouth to Inês, "Tell him I'm here."

She nods nervously. When Mestre Vitor moves away from the window, she does too. Seconds later, she reappears and points downward, at the front door.

"He's coming," she mouths, then reluctantly closes the window. My palms start to sweat again. This moment will define my future. I take a deep breath.

On the street, Mestre Vitor spies me immediately. After a brief smile, his face falls into somber, thoughtful lines.

"Let's walk." He heads downhill, away from the joyous mob. "You chose this place to watch the king's entry into Porto?" he asks after a moment.

I opt for partial truth. "I wanted to see Inês."

His eyebrows travel up his forehead. "I see."

We walk in silence. I'm pretending a calm I don't feel. He has to be the one to talk.

"Hugo found the gold bar today," he says finally.

I stop and let him see the relief on my face. "I'm not surprised."

"You're not, eh? I find it hard to believe it was there all that time."

"Maybe Hugo doesn't clean as well as you think he does." I'll not throw the boy under the wagon unless he breaks our pact, but can't resist a little dig. "It had to be somewhere, didn't it? You know I didn't take it." I try not to sound accusing. It doesn't work.

Mestre Vitor sighs heavily. "I'm so sorry. Truly I am."

Sorry isn't enough for allowing my name to be dragged through the mud.

"I was sick about it. But you've seen how Bento is. I have to think about my family ..." His voice trails off. "When I got back to Porto, I didn't know how to find you. I didn't realize you were in touch with Inês." His smile is understanding. He won't try to stop me from seeing her.

"I'd rather you not tell Goldsmith Bento," I say.

He nods. "He's admitted that it was wrong to accuse you. I'm sure he'll apologize."

"I'd appreciate that."

"You were doing so well. I still need your help." Mestre Vitor regards me questioningly. "Will you consider coming back?"

These are words I've longed to hear. The ones that will make up for the humiliation, for the nights on the cold, damp floor of the *ilha*. Mestre Vitor wants me back. And I've been convinced that it's what I wanted too. That becoming a goldsmith or *filigraneiro* was not only a dream but a possibility, one ripped away from me by others. Now it's once again within my reach.

So where is the leap in my chest, the rejoicing? As soon as they're uttered, Mestre Vitor's words fall lifeless to the ground. I don't trust the goldsmith not to go crazy again in a week or a month, and Mestre Vitor just admitted he can't stop him. I can't put myself under the control of someone like that again. Not knowingly.

"I can't." I choke the words out, hardly believing that I'm saying them. "I can't live like that."

Mestre Vitor's hopeful expression disappears. "I understand. But I'm so sorry."

"Me too."

Around us, people are righting potted plants and removing decorations that were torn or crushed during the procession. Am I making a huge mistake?

"Will you speak well of me? To another employer, I mean?"

"You've found a job?"

"Perhaps." I realize, suddenly, that my dreams have grown far beyond this shop on the Rua das Flores. "I hope so." I want it to be true more than I can express.

He looks suddenly alarmed. "Not with another goldsmith?"

"No."

He breathes out in relief. "Of course I will. It's the least I can do. I'll be glad for you." He gives me an encouraging tap on the back, his eyes regretful but warm. "Don't be a stranger," he says, then walks slowly up the street, hands clasped behind his back. Him, I will miss.

I loiter near the shop for a while, hoping Inês will appear. But the curtains upstairs remain in place and the door doesn't open. The goldsmith, it seems, is going to keep them from the evening's festivities. I'm not about to test his reaction to my newly regained innocence by unexpectedly calling on Inês.

As darkness falls, I crisscross the city with no specific destination in mind. Miguel's certainly somewhere, but I don't come across him or Ana Maria. Around me, boisterous people stream through streets and squares made magical by the light from lampposts and lanterns and candles. The smell of smoked sausages and sweets is everywhere. Under one of the streetlamps, a group of men with guitars line up. As they begin to play, a woman's powerful voice rises in song. In front of the musicians, a dozen couples dance in a circle, the women's clogs clattering on the cobblestones.

For a second, I close my eyes, letting myself be transported back to the saints' day celebrations in the Douro. They're good memories, but I want to make new ones, here in Porto. I move on, enveloped by a city that feels like it's reaching out and grabbing the future with both hands. As now, perhaps, I'll be able to. The desire vibrates deep in my chest, along with the music. A sense of belonging. Of hope.

The evening goes on forever but ends too soon. I wander from square to square, from the riverside in Ribeira to a high, level area near the church of Victoria, where I can see the lights of the entire city flickering below. Only when I'm too foot-weary to enjoy it anymore do I turn my steps to the *ilha*. It's late enough that Joaquim may already be asleep. After this momentous day, I want tonight to end on a good note, not soiled by another angry exchange of words.

Outside Joaquim's door, a small shape is slumped.

"Miguel?" My thoughts somersault to Jorge and what he might have done. It's hard to tell in the dark, but I see no blood or damaged limbs. I shake his shoulder.

"Are you all right?"

He opens eyes that are dazed with sleep.

"Is something wrong? Is it Ana Maria?"

"What? No." He gets to his feet with a groan. "I was waiting for you. You have to find Joaquim."

"Why?" If he's not here tonight, I'm all the happier for it.

"I think he's going to do something to the new bridge."

"What?"

"Before he left, I heard him in his room, muttering to himself. He was saying the bridge wouldn't be safe when the king crosses it."

"That's impossible," I scoff. "Was he drunk?"

"I don't know. He packed a bunch of glass jars into a bundle and left. He looked mad. Not drunk."

Glass jars?

"Move over. I need to get inside."

Joaquim's room is pitch black. I feel my way along the wall. Reaching the cabinet without a door, I run my hand across the shelf. The jars and the clear liquid I had assumed was water are gone. I sit back on my heels. What did he tell me about them? Not to touch or drink them. That's all. I remember that unfamiliar, sharp smell when I came in yesterday. And how alarmed he was when the jar almost slipped out of his hands, even though it was closed with a stopper. So the liquid could be dangerous. Enough to damage an iron bridge? That seems unlikely. But Joaquim studied to be a pharmacist. He might know of a chemical that could. I want to kick myself for my lack of curiosity.

"Did he say anything else?"

Miguel shakes his head. "I didn't want him to see me. He was kind of scary."

Disturbed. That's what it sounds like. He wouldn't take his grudge against the royal family that far, would he? With the scratch of a match, I light the oil lamp. The piles of newspapers are still there, his clothes hanging from hooks on the wall, my bedding rolled up in the corner. Nothing in the small space seems out of place or even personal. As if he's living here as temporarily as I am. The realization unsettles me. What is he planning?

My gaze falls on a crumpled ball of paper at the base of the wall. I smooth it out.

Exmo. Snr. Joaquim Pinto,

I am writing to inform you that the contents of Farmácia Pinto and your father's house in Aveiro have been sold. The proceedings went in their entirety toward late payments, outstanding debts, and the loan your father took out for the unfortunate shipment of cotton that went down on the Felicidade. *I regret to inform you that the funds were not enough to liquidate the entire bank loan. You still owe ...*

The number has too many zeros for me to comprehend. Receiving this would make anyone crazy. But to threaten the king and queen because of it? That I can't fathom.

Miguel watches me worriedly from the doorway. "I was right to tell you, wasn't I?"

I nod. "You did well, Miguel. Now go to bed. I'll get him."

"I'll go with you."

"Oh no, you won't. Ana Maria would have my head." I push past him. As soon as I'm out of the *ilha*, I start running.

CHAPTER 48

THE BRIDGE TOUCHES land in seven places. Where would Joaquim have gone? I jog across the upper part of town until the hills take my breath, slow to a fast walk, then run again as I angle toward the spot where the span meets the cliff. If Joaquim wants to stop the train from crossing, he'll damage the track. As I run, I hear sounds of life – a bottle breaking, a wheezy laugh, coughing – but it's the middle of the night. The streets here are mostly deserted. They give way, gradually, to fields and farms.

I'm panting hard when I finally reach the cliff. Atop it looms a long, ruined building. Below the building is the bridge, barely a shadow against the blacker water. The train tracks continue along the bluff and disappear into a tunnel. I smell smoke and crouch down. Two men are standing on the railroad ties where the bridge meets the land, smoking. Guards. Joaquim couldn't have gotten onto the span here. He must've chosen a pillar.

I turn, seeking a path down to the river that's out of sight of the guards. Behind me, a young boy hovers uncertainly.

"Miguel!" I whisper. "What are you doing?"

"I want to help."

"I told you to stay home!" Joaquim was worry enough. I want to wring Miguel's scrawny neck. I glower at him instead.

He ducks his head, then looks at the bridge. "Did you see him?"

I exhale in exasperation. "No. Are you sure you heard him right?"

I so want Miguel to be wrong.

He nods. "I told you what he said."

I approach the edge of the cliff again, the boy following me. The slope is where materials for the bridge were lowered or pulled up. It's rutted, stripped of greenery, and almost vertical. Going down it would be suicide.

"Go home, Miguel."

"I don't know the way."

Damn. Taking him back to the *ilha* would waste too much time.

"There are stairs cut into this hillside somewhere. Let's see if we can get down them."

We wend our way along the cliff, a slight curve hiding us from the guards, and find the staircase Monsieur Eiffel descended the day I got his approval for the cufflinks. How long ago that seems. In a few hours, he'll be wearing them for the inauguration and Queen Maria Pia will have Mestre Vitor's filigree around her neck. Without thinking, I make the sign of the cross. Joaquim can't really damage the bridge, can he?

There's no one on the stairs.

"Absolute silence," I whisper, and lead the way down. We stop several times, thinking we've seen an unusual shape or movement on or around the pillars. Joaquim couldn't have climbed high. Not with five glass jars slung over his back. The moon slides in and out of clouds, creating movement where there is none. By the time we get to river level, my nerves are jangling. At least the guards on the span above haven't raised the alarm.

We stop in the shadow of the cliff. By the river, one of the tallest pillars and the end of the bridge's huge arch come together on a stone foundation that's rectangular and twice my height. There's still no sign of Joaquim. Miguel leans toward me, as if he's going to speak. I put a warning finger over my lips, straining to see into the darkness. The moments drag by. Where can Joaquim be?

I hear the faintest clink, like glass on stone. Miguel inhales sharply.

"Keep watch," I order him.

When the moon disappears again, I race to the foundation. Along its side, leading to a flat area where the pillar and foundation meet, is an incline. I leap onto it and climb. Joaquim – if he's where I think he is – has surely heard me by now. I just hope he doesn't try to push me off. As I reach the top of the incline, I once again get a whiff of that sharp chemical smell.

"Fool!" Joaquim hisses. He's crouched at the very end of the arch, dressed all in black. "Get out of here!" His voice is muffled by a cloth over his nose and mouth and he's holding one of the jars. It's open.

"Joaquim, put a stopper in that thing," I whisper. "We have to get out of here."

"I'm not done." He tips the jar, pouring the liquid in a thin, slow stream onto a massive metal joint at the base of the arch. The smell makes my nose burn.

"Yes, you are."

He regards me, eyes glittering. Three of the five jars are beside him, still full. The fifth is empty.

"Come on, Joaquim. This is stupid."

"I'm making a point." He stifles a cough into his elbow. "If the people have to suffer, so do the king and queen."

"No one's going to understand that," I say fiercely. "They'll just think you're crazy."

He keeps pouring. "As long as I achieve my objective, it doesn't matter."

The area where he's crouched is barely wider than a man's stride's is long. In front of him is the river. Behind him, the center of the foundation is nothing but a deep, dark hole. I don't want to fall in either direction. I advance cautiously.

"Keep away!"

I spread my palms wide, showing Joaquim I'm not intending to grab anything. Yet. Here, the chemical smell is stronger. I cough, feeling my lungs burn, and take a step back. Where he's been pouring, the surface has bubbled. I don't see any holes.

"You're not going to make the bridge fall with…with whatever that is."

"Muriatic acid. You have no idea what it can do."

He's right. And he sounds surer of himself than I'm comfortable with. I try another tack.

"The king and queen won't be on that train alone, you know. You could kill hundreds of people."

"That's the price of being associated with royalty, I'm afraid." His regretful tone rings false, but he puts down the half-full jar. I feel a surge of hope. Then he pulls out a black rag, stuffs it into the joint, and empties the jar over it.

"That'll stop it from dripping off," he mutters to himself.

"Joaquim, stop! There are better ways to make your point."

He laughs bitterly, then hacks again. "There's no other way to change anything in this country."

"This isn't going to either! You'll just end up in prison, where you can't influence anything," I say desperately.

He regards me defiantly. "It will work. And I'll never let myself be caught."

I'm not getting through to him, and he still has three jars full of acid. They'd be far better off in the river than on the bridge. I lunge for them.

Even more quickly, Joaquim surges to his feet and shoves me away. I stumble backwards, windmilling my arms. Below us, Miguel gives a frightened squawk. I catch myself just before I tip off the foundation and into the river.

"Leave me alone!" Joaquim hisses. "You'll ruin everything."

"That's what I'm trying to do, you stupid ass."

"Henrique!"

Miguel's voice is much too loud. It takes me a moment to realize why.

"The guards!" he calls. "They're coming!"

Sure enough, the two men from the span are racing along the cliff towards the staircase.

I leap down the stone incline. "Joaquim, come on!"

He picks up another jar.

"Leave it!"

"I'm not going anywhere."

"I'm not waiting for you!"

The guards are already bounding down the stairs.

Joaquim yanks out another stopper and dumps the liquid onto the metal joint.

"Henrique!" On the ground, Miguel is hopping back and forth like a frightened rabbit.

I jump off the incline, grab his shoulder, and spin him around. "Run!"

We take off, racing along the path to Porto as fast as we can. Joaquim has made his decision, and I'm not getting accused again of something I haven't done. But Miguel's legs are short, and here we're sandwiched between the river and the cliff. I pray we have enough of a head-start to stay ahead of the guards until we reach Ribeira's maze of streets and stairs.

Behind us, glass breaks. I twist around, almost falling when my foot lands in a rut. The guards are climbing the foundation like goats, yelling.

"Keep going," I order Miguel. "We can't help him now."

Another jar breaks, accompanied by a scream. We turn and see Joaquim struggling with one of the guards. The other is balancing on one leg, still screaming. The first guard slams his shoulder into Joaquim's chest. He flies off the foundation, arms and legs flailing. With a splash, the water closes over him.

"No!" Miguel cries. "Joaquim! Joa …"

I clamp my hand over his mouth. "Shut up! You want everyone to know who he is?" I scan the water helplessly. "Come on, man! Swim!" I have no idea if he can.

On top of the foundation, the first guard is bent over the other. They're paying no attention to us. I race to the river's edge. The water is dense and black, revealing no secrets under its surface. I see no pale face, hear no splash of arms. On the foundation, the first guard straightens and looks our way.

"We have to go," I say. "There's nothing we can do."

Miguel's face is wet with tears. I pull him into a run.

By the time we get to the *ilha,* Miguel is crying openly, gasping for breath. Ana Maria meets us at the door, her stormy expression changing to one of alarm. Miguel burrows into her embrace, shoulders heaving.

"He's not hurt," I reassure her. "But Joaquim …" My voice shakes. "He might have drowned." Saying it out loud makes the horror more real.

Ana Maria looks at me in shock. "What?"

I blink, trying to wash the sting of tears from my own eyes, and recount the events of the evening.

"I can't believe you took Miguel with you," she says sharply.

"It's not his fault." Miguel mumbles. "I followed him."

"I've been frantic." She gives him a shake. He tightens his arms around her, not letting her pry him away.

"I'm sorry, sister."

"I told him not to come," I tell Ana Maria. "But I'm grateful he was there. His warning saved me."

"You're sure there's nothing we can do for Joaquim?"

I close my eyes, shake my head.

"Then we'll continue this tomorrow." The severe lines in her face don't soften. "Right now, we all need to sleep."

Joaquim's room is silent, waiting for its rightful occupant to return. I undo my bedding, feeling more like an intruder now than I did before. Unable to settle down, I prowl in circles, willing him to stalk in, dripping and swearing. Tonight, I'd accept his anger without complaint. Welcome it, even. But I wouldn't apologize for trying to stop him.

Whether the acid would have destroyed the pillar, I'll never know. All I can hope is that they'll verify the soundness of the bridge before anyone crosses it. And that Joaquim will come home. I turn his chair so it faces the door and sit, keeping vigil.

CHAPTER 49

THE *ILHA* WAKES a few short hours later, thrumming with excitement. Outside, children run about, squealing and chasing the chickens. Their mothers yell at them not to get dirty. Pails slosh as people haul water from the fountain.

I raise my head off the table. Joaquim's bed is empty, untouched. I grind my knuckles into my eyes, then stand, every muscle aching. Inês is waiting for me, for a day of celebration. But the nightmare last night – it really happened. At the washbasin, I scrub and change into the cleanest clothes I have.

Ana Maria's door is already open. Miguel greets me, drawn and pale. I expect I don't look much better. I put an arm around his shoulders, giving him a brief hug and a tiny shake at the same time. His eyes are puffy and red-rimmed. I tip his chin up so he has to look at me.

"I'm sorry you were there last night."

"So am I."

"Joaquim might be all right. We don't know. Maybe he got to shore and decided it was safer not to come home." In daylight, that's a little easier to believe than it had been last night. I see a glimmer of hope in Miguel eyes and wish with all my being that I'm not wrong to put it there. "If they arrested him for what he did, he'd probably be executed. I think he'd rather be anywhere except in jail, waiting for that to happen."

"But why did he do it?" Miguel's voice cracks.

"I think it was his way of protesting against injustice. Even if it was the wrong way."

"I didn't want anything bad to happen to him."

"No one did. What's important to remember is that you did all you could to prevent it. By warning us. In the end, it was his decision. Do you understand that?"

"Maybe," he says in a small voice.

Ana Maria comes up behind him. *Thank you,* she mouths to me. "Ready to go?" she asks Miguel.

"Yes," he says without enthusiasm.

"Remember," I say as they leave, "you can't talk about this. At all. If anyone learns we were there, we'll get in as much trouble as Joaquim. No one will believe we weren't helping him."

Ana Maria's gaunt face drains of color. "We won't say a word. Will we, Miguel?"

The boy shakes his head.

"Let's be off then."

Somberly, I watch them go, hoping our friendship is strong enough to withstand this. Then I shake myself. I have to get moving too. Inês expects me. Despite the weight that won't lift, a small smile curves my lips. I can go to the goldsmith's without fear. We can see each other without having to hide it. I still can't believe it.

Although the inauguration isn't for hours, people are already lining the streets where the procession will pass from the Royal Palace to the Pênsil bridge and then up the hill to the train station in Gaia. The first ever crossing of the Douro – except for the tests, of course – will be from Gaia to the Pinheiro station east of Porto.

As I make my way to the Rua das Flores, I hear snatches of conversation.

"Did you hear they changed the bridge's name? At the last minute?" one woman is saying. "My husband heard it from the baker. It'll be called Maria Pia, after the queen. Not Dom Fernando."

"Both of our bridges will be named after women, eh?" the other says dryly. "I approve."

"Not women. Queens," the other corrects.

At Gomes & Filho, I thump on the green door, hoping the goldsmith won't be the one to open it. Despite what Mestre Vitor said, I'd rather not run into him. Especially today. Moments later, Dona Ilda flings it open. Before I can say anything, she wraps me in a quick, unexpected hug, then holds me at arms' length, a smile splitting her face.

"I'm so glad to see you," she says.

A warmth I never expected to feel again at this address floods through me. I squeeze her hands. "So am I. Thank you. For believing in me."

Her eyes are moist. She wipes a hand across them. "You've come for Inês."

I nod. "Is she ready?"

"Almost. You'll wait?"

"I'm not going anywhere." That isn't entirely true. I will move on, away from this place. A decision of my own choosing, this time. But at this moment, there's nowhere else I'd rather be.

There's a flutter of movement and Inês comes flying down the stairs. She's wearing a sleeveless red vest over a white blouse, with a white shawl crossed over her chest and a full, pleated, cream-colored skirt. The gaily colored scarf that covers her hair accents her brown eyes and brings out the blush of her lips. My mouth falls open.

"Henrique, say something."

I try, but nothing comes out.

"You look like you've seen a ghost." She pouts. "Should I be offended?"

Not a ghost. A vision. "You're lovely."

She twirls, arms over her head, her skirt billowing. "Today's a party, isn't it? This is how we celebrate in Póvoa."

"Maybe so." I circle my finger, asking her to whirl again. "I'm just not sure I want to share you with anyone else."

Her laugh rings out. "You have no choice. Let's go." She tucks her hand under my arm. Dona Ilda doesn't even look scandalized.

"Have fun, you two." Somehow, she manages to look like a proud mother and a wistful young girl at the same time.

Inês breaks away from me to kiss her lightly on the cheek. "I won't be late."

Dona Ilda pushes us out the door with a smile. "Don't worry. Go on now."

As we leave, Inês whispers, "I don't know how, but she got me out of serving the midday meal. Can you believe it?"

"I will be eternally grateful," I say in an equally quiet voice.

She pulls back and gives me a confused look. "Why are you whispering?"

"Because it allows me to lean closer to you."

"Silly." She pulls me down the street, then hesitates. "Where are we going?"

"I thought we'd try Fontainhas. It's the best viewing point I've found. But if we want a place, we need to go now. You don't mind missing the procession?"

She barely hesitates. "I saw it yesterday."

We walk, Inês like a bright bird beside me. There's so much going on in my head that I hardly know where to start.

"Did you get the position? With the family on the Rua de Cedofeita?"

She turns sparkling eyes on me. "I did." She gives a dancing step.

I squeeze the hand she has on my sleeve. "I knew you would. Did you tell Dona Ilda?"

She nods. "I talked to her before I accepted. She told me I'd be rash not to."

"When do you start?"

"In a week."

"Already?" I hope her new employer will be easier than the goldsmith's family. And that they won't have a problem with me seeing her. I push those concerns to a corner of my mind.

The streets are clogged with families in their festive best. We push past them, going uphill to the *alameda* where I watched the bridge tests. I'm weaving through groups of people, towing Inês behind me, when I hear my name.

It's Telles Ferreira, the mapmaker.

"How do you do, sir?"

"A grand occasion, isn't it?" He looks as buoyant as the rest of the crowd. "I'll see you tomorrow? First thing in the morning?"

"Yes, sir. I'll be there." I sense Inês's curious look.

"Excellent."

"Good day, sir." My heart is singing as Inês and I make our way around the pavilion where the royal family will watch the fireworks later tonight. All the seating on the wall is taken, but we squeeze into a spot where we have a good view of the bridge.

"What was that about?" Inês asks.

"I'll tell you after tomorrow." I want to present her with a success. Not get her hopes up about something that might not happen.

Inês crosses her arms and gives me a level stare. She's having none of it.

I sigh. "Remember I told you about the man who's going to spend twelve years making a map of Porto? That's him."

"And you're going to talk to him? About …?"

I grin and use her own words against her. "Careful. No jinxing."

"Of course not." She beams at me.

Tomorrow *has* to go well. I can't disappoint her.

Around us, people crush in tighter and tighter. I'm glad we got here when we did. On both sides of the river, wherever it's not too steep to climb, the hills pulsate with people. Far below, boats are so densely packed that a person could walk across the river without getting wet.

For a moment, I sober. I truly hope Joaquim isn't tangled up in some obstacle under this multitude that's celebrating what he decided to hate. It might be unlikely, but I'd rather imagine him making his way to a new life elsewhere. Maybe in a land where there are no kings.

"What's wrong?" Inês asks.

"Nothing." I won't ruin this day. Nor is it a subject to discuss with so many ears around. I squint at the base of the pillar. From this distance, the only difference I can see is that guards are now stationed around the foundation.

A cry goes up and, as one, we turn our attention to the bridge. But it's not the royal train on the tracks. Instead, alone on the Gaia end of the span is the figure of a woman in long skirts. She advances jerkily from one railroad tie to the next. Below her is the abyss, and there are no handrails.

"Who's that?"

No one seems to know.

"She'll fall to her death!"

"A madwoman, for sure!"

The breeze picks up, whipping the woman's skirts. She stops, arms out, fighting for balance, then takes another step. After the initial clamor, everyone goes silent, waiting to see if she'll make it. Bit by bit, she advances. When she makes it past the mid-point, I feel Inês exhale.

"Come on," she breathes. "You can do it."

Around us, people are speculating about who it can be. I'm sure that, in the days to come, we'll find out. Finally, after more starts and stops and gasps from the crowd, the woman leaps onto firm land.

A cracked old voice breaks the amazed silence. "It wasn't the queen, that's for sure. Looks like that bridge just got inaugurated by one of our own!"

Cheers greet her pronouncement. With our hearts and voices, Inês and I join in. The woman made it across, and the royal family will too. I'm sure of it. And, in the smallest of ways, I might've played a part. Perhaps the future of Portugal is a little more secure because I acted. It's crazy to think that way, I know. But today, I want optimism and enthusiasm and progress to win. I want the future to be something I can look forward to.

With a thunder of wheels and a long whistle, the royal train appears. All around us, an infinite number of white handkerchiefs wave, hailing the king and queen. I slip behind Inês and wrap my arms around her. She leans into my embrace and I forget about the train.

"You'll be mine?" I ask, my breath moving the hair by her ear.

She twists and we're face to face, our bodies pressed together.

"How funny," she says. "I was going to ask you the same thing."

And we laugh.

∂ ∂ ∂ ∂ ∂

If you enjoyed this journey into Portugal's past, start reading *Rossio Square N.° 59* to see what happens when Claire, a refugee fleeing war-torn France, is thrown into the tumultuous world of WWII Lisbon.

∂ ∂ ∂ ∂ ∂

And please help other readers find *The Filigree Master's Apprentice* by leaving a review on Goodreads, Amazon, or wherever you bought the book. Thank you!

ACKNOWLEDGMENTS

Innumerable people were generous with their time and expertise when I was researching and writing this book. Master filigree maker António Cardoso and Rosa Cardoso, a talented *enchedeira*, graciously opened their workshop in Gondomar to me, allowing me to witness how they make this intricate and historic jewelry from start to finish. (I should note that they even let me try my hand at the little spirals. The result was exactly like Henrique's first attempt in this novel.)

With Alexandre Lage and Anisia Teixeira Pinto, I discovered Mesão Frio and participated in a wine grape harvest on the hills of the Douro river. José Castelo welcomed me into an ilha in Porto and told me stories of what it was like growing up there. João Neto, Director of the Pharmacy Museums in Porto and Lisbon, answered odd questions such as how one could get hold of hydrochloric (muriatic) acid in the late 19th century. José Manuel Lopes Cordeiro, who co-authored the book *As Pontes do Porto*, walked me through the tests performed on Gustave Eiffel's bridge before the first train carried Portugal's king and queen across. António Dixo de Sousa, who owns the last *barco rabelo* shipyard, helped me understand how these boats navigated. I thank them all.

Porto is blessed with historians and storytellers who are passionate about the city's history. I've been fortunate to have access to them, in part through guided tours organized by the Confraria das Almas do Corpo Santo de Massarelos and the Santa Casa da Misericórdia do Porto. Germano Silva, Helder Pacheco, César Santos Silva, Joel Cleto, José Manuel Tedim, Jorge Ricardo Pinto, José Ferreira e Silva, Manuel António, Pedro Jorge Pereira, and Pedro Barros (among others) have inspired and educated me, and I am immensely grateful.

An extra special thanks goes to Manuel de Sousa, who reviewed my manuscript so that it would be as historically accurate as a book of fiction can be. (That said, if any errors slipped through, they are entirely my own.)

I couldn't have written this novel without assistance from the staff at the Arquivo Municipal do Porto, the library of the Museu Soares dos Reis, the Museu do Douro, the Faculdade das Letras library of the University of Porto, and the Instituto dos Vinhos do Douro e Porto, who helped me find books, photos, newspapers, and other resources that were essential to my research.

I also owe a huge debt to A Mar café, my office away from home, where I spent many pleasant hours writing.

Immense thanks goes to my Portuguese editor Cristina Lourenço and to Susana Lima and Dora Alexandre at Marcador / Editorial Presença, whose hard work led to the publication of the Portuguese version of this novel.

I don't know if all authors sometimes feel like their writing is taking them straight into a black hole, but I do. Thankfully, I have a magnificent group of critique partners, readers, and friends who keep me going. Their constructive feedback made this novel what it is today. Laurie Theuer, Katie Hayoz, Phyllis Hall Haislip, Joy Hansford, Teresa Pole-Baker, Mayra Calvani, Rainee Ambrose, Anne Henrich, and José Mota – words can't express how much I appreciate you.

Finally, to my son Daniel, my wonderful brothers Mark and David, and to my Mom and Dad, who accompanied me on my first trip to Mesão Frio: Your support in writing and in life give me wings. I love you.

ABOUT THE AUTHOR

Before moving to Portugal, Jeannine Johnson Maia worked as a journalist in Belgium and Washington, D.C.; served as a press specialist at the U.S. Mission to the European Union in Brussels; studied in the United States and Italy; taught English in France; and lived in Cape Verde. She has a Bachelor's degree in Foreign Policy from the University of Virginia (U.S.), a Master's degree from the Johns Hopkins School of Advanced International Studies (U.S.), and a Master's degree in Creative Writing from Lancaster University (U.K.). Jeannine is the author of two books of historical fiction that take place in Portugal. *The Filigree Master's Apprentice* was first published in Portuguese translation as *O Rapaz do Douro* by Marcador / Editorial Presença. Her first novel, *Rossio Square N.° 59* – published by Casa das Letras / LeYa in Portuguese under the title *Praça do Rossio, N.° 59* – takes place in Lisbon during WWII. Jeannine lives in Vila Nova de Gaia, near Porto, a city she finds irresistibly photogenic.

Website: https://www.jeanninejohnsonmaia.com

Printed in Great Britain
by Amazon

36466874R00158